LOADED FOR BEAR

ABOUT THE EDITORS

Martin H. Greenberg has more than three hundred eighty books to his credit, of which at least three hundred are anthologies. The books he has co-edited include *A Treasury of American Mystery Stories, Cloak & Dagger: A Treasury of 35 Great Espionage Stories, On the Diamond: A Treasury of Baseball Stories,* and *The One that Got Away: A Treasury of Fishing Stories and Lore.* He is professor of regional analysis and political science at the University of Wisconsin-Green Bay, where he also teaches a course in the history of science fiction.

Charles G. Waugh is a leading authority on science fiction and fantasy and has collaborated on more than a hundred anthologies and single-author collections with Martin H. Greenberg and other colleagues.

LOADED FOR BEAR

A TREASURY OF GREAT HUNTING STORIES

Edited by Martin H. Greenberg
and Charles G. Waugh

BONANZA BOOKS
New York

This 1990 edition is published by Bonanza Books,
distributed by Crown Publishers, Inc.,
225 Park Avenue South, New York, New York 10003

Printed and bound in the United States of America

Library of Congress Cataloging-in-Publication Data

Loaded for bear : a treasury of great hunting stories / edited by
    Martin H. Greenberg and Charles G. Waugh.
        p.   cm.
     ISBN 0-517-01765-2
     1. Hunting stories.   I. Greenberg, Martin Harry.   II. Waugh,
Charles.
PN6120.95.H8L62   1990
808.83′108355—dc20   89-18696
                                                                  CIP

8   7   6   5   4   3   2   1

ACKNOWLEDGMENTS

"The Old People" by William Faulkner. Copyright 1940, 1942 and renewed 1968, 1970 by Estelle Faulkner and Jill Faulkner Summers. Reprinted from *Go Down, Moses,* by William Faulkner, by permission of Random House, Inc.

"The Most Dangerous Game" By Richard Connell. Copyright 1924 by Richard Connell; copyright renewed 1952 by Louise Fox Connell. Reprinted by permission of Brandt & Brandt Literary Agents, Inc.

"The Wolf Tracker" by Zane Grey. Copyright 1924 by Curtis Publishing Co; renewed 1952 by Lina Elise Grey. Reprinted by permission of Dr. Loren Grey.

"King of the Hills" by Jesse Stuart. Originally published in "Esquire". It also appears in the Stuart collections *Save Every Lamp* and *Come Gentle Spring.* Copyright 1937, 1940, 1941, 1942, 1946, 1950, 1952, 1953, 1956 by Jesse Stuart. All Rights Reserved. Reprinted by permission of the Jesse Stuart Foundation, P.O. Box 391, Ashland, KY 41114.

"The Last Day in the Field" by Caroline Gordon. From *The Collected Stories* by Caroline Gordon. Copyright © 1935 by Charles Scribner's Sons. Renewal copyright © 1963 by Caroline Gordon Tate. Reprinted by permission of Farrar, Straus and Giroux, Inc.

"Roping Lions in the Grand Canyon" by Zane Grey. Copyright 1924 by Zane Grey; renewed 1951 by Lina Elise Grey. Reprinted by permission of Dr. Loren Grey.

" 'Gator Bait" By Talmadge Powell. Originally appeared in "Alfred Hitchcock's Mystery Magazine," March 1971. Copyright © 1971 by H.S.D. Publications. Reprinted by arrangement with the author.

"The Eye-teeth of O'Hara" by Talbot Mundy. Copyright 1931 by Talbot Mundy. Copyright renewed 1959 by Talbot Mundy. Reprinted by permission of Brandt & Brandt Literary Agents.

"The Fire Killer" by Steve Frazee. From Nights of Terror, "Argosy," August, 1951, Vol. 333, No. 2, Popular Publications, Inc. Reprinted by permission of the author.

"The Long Night" by Edmund Ware Smith. This story appears by arrangement with James Ware Smith.

"The Road to Tinkhamtown" by Corey Ford. Copyright © 1970 by Holt, Rinehart & Winston, Inc. Reprinted by permission of Harold Ober Associates, Inc.

"Time Safari" by David Drake. Copyright 1981 by David Drake for *Destinies,* V. 3 #2; edited by James Patrick Baen. Reprinted by permission of the author.

CONTENTS

CONTENTS

THE
OLD PEOPLE

WILLIAM FAULKNER

I

AT FIRST there was nothing. There was the faint, cold, steady rain, the gray and constant light of the late November dawn, with the voices of the hounds converging somewhere in it and toward them. Then Sam Fathers, standing just behind the boy as he had been standing when the boy shot his first running rabbit with his first gun and almost with the first load it ever carried, touched his shoulder and he began to shake, not with any cold. Then the buck was there. He did not come into sight; he was just there, looking not like a ghost but as if all of light were condensed in him and he were the source of it, not only moving in it but disseminating it, already running, seen first as you always see the deer, in that split second after he has already seen you, already slanting away in that first soaring bound, the antlers even in that dim light looking like a small rocking-chair balanced on his head.

"Now," Sam Fathers said, "shoot quick, and slow."

The boy did not remember that shot at all. He would live to be eighty, as his father and his father's twin brother and their father in his turn had lived to be, but he would never hear that shot nor remember even the shock of the gun-butt. He didn't even remember what he did with the gun afterward. He was running. Then he was standing over the buck where it lay on the wet earth still in the attitude of speed and not looking at all dead, standing over it shaking and jerking, with Sam Fathers beside him again, extending the knife. "Don't walk up to him in front," Sam said. "If

he ain't dead, he will cut you all to pieces with his feet. Walk up
to him from behind and take him by the horn first, so you can
hold his head down until you can jump away. Then slip your
other hand down and hook your fingers in his nostrils."

The boy did that—drew the head back and the throat taut and
drew Sam Fathers' knife across the throat and Sam stooped and
dipped his hands in the hot smoking blood and wiped them back
and forth across the boy's face. Then Sam's horn rang in the wet
gray woods and again and again; there was a boiling wave of dogs
about them, with Tennie's Jim and Boon Hogganbeck whipping
them back after each had had a taste of the blood, then the men,
the true hunters—Walter Ewell whose rifle never missed, and
Major de Spain and old General Compson and the boy's cousin,
McCaslin Edmonds, grandson of his father's sister, sixteen years
his senior and, since both he and McCaslin were only children
and the boy's father had been nearing seventy when he was born,
more his brother than his cousin and more his father than either
—sitting their horses and looking down at them: at the old man
of seventy who had been a Negro for two generations now but
whose face and bearing were still those of the Chickasaw chief
who had been his father; and the white boy of twelve with the
prints of the bloody hands on his face, who had nothing to do
now but stand straight and not let the trembling show.

"Did he do all right, Sam?" his cousin McCaslin said.

"He done all right," Sam Fathers said.

They were the white boy, marked forever, and the old dark
man sired on both sides by savage kings, who had marked him,
whose bloody hands had merely formally consecrated him to that
which, under the man's tutelage, he had already accepted, humbly and joyfully, with abnegation and with pride too; the hands,
the touch, the first worthy blood which he had been found at last
worthy to draw, joining him and the man forever, so that the
man would continue to live past the boy's seventy years and then
eighty years, long after the man himself had entered the earth as
chiefs and kings entered it;—the child, not yet a man, whose
grandfather had lived in the same country and in almost the same
manner as the boy himself would grow up to live, leaving his
descendants in the land in his turn as his grandfather had done,

and the old man past seventy whose grandfathers had owned the land long before the white men ever saw it and who had vanished from it now with all their kind, what of blood they left behind them running now in another race and for a while even in bondage and now drawing toward the end of its alien and irrevocable course, barren, since Sam Fathers had no children.

His father was Ikkemotubbe himself, who had named himself Doom. Sam told the boy about that—how Ikkemotubbe, old Issetibbeha's sister's son, had run away to New Orleans in his youth and returned seven years later with a French companion calling himself the Chevalier Soeur-Blonde de Vitry, who must have been the Ikkemotubbe of his family too and who was already addressing Ikkemotubbe as *Du Homme;*—returned, came home again, with his foreign Aramis and the quadroon slave woman who was to be Sam's mother, and a gold-laced hat and coat and a wicker wine-hamper containing a litter of month-old puppies and a gold snuffbox filled with a white powder resembling fine sugar. And how he was met at the River landing by three or four companions of his bachelor youth, and while the light of a smoking torch gleamed on the glittering braid of the hat and coat Doom squatted in the mud of the land and took one of the puppies from the hamper and put a pinch of the white powder on its tongue and the puppy died before the one who was holding it could cast it away. And how they returned to the Plantation where Issetibbeha, dead now, had been succeeded by his son, Doom's fat cousin Moketubbe, and the next day Moketubbe's eight-year-old son died suddenly and that afternoon, in the presence of Moketubbe and most of the others (the People, Sam Fathers called them) Doom produced another puppy from the wine-hamper and put a pinch of the white powder on its tongue and Moketubbe abdicated and Doom became in fact The Man which his French friend already called him. And how on the day after that, during the ceremony of accession, Doom pronounced a marriage between the pregnant quadroon and one of the slave men which he had just inherited (that was how Sam Fathers got his name, which in Chickasaw had been Had-Two-Fathers) and two years later sold the man and woman and the child who was his own son to his white neighbor, Carothers McCaslin.

That was seventy years ago. The Sam Fathers whom the boy knew was already sixty—a man not tall, squat rather, almost sedentary, flabby-looking though he actually was not, with hair like a horse's mane which even at seventy showed no trace of white and a face which showed no age until he smiled, whose only visible trace of Negro blood was a slight dullness of the hair and the fingernails, and something else which you did notice about the eyes, which you noticed because it was not always there, only in repose and not always then—something not in their shape nor pigment but in their expression, and the boy's cousin McCaslin told him what that was: not the heritage of Ham, not the mark of servitude but of bondage; the knowledge that for a while that part of his blood had been the blood of slaves. "Like an old lion or a bear in a cage," McCaslin said. "He was born in the cage and has been in it all his life; he knows nothing else. Then he smells something. It might be anything, any breeze blowing past anything and then into his nostrils. But there for a second was the hot sand or the cane-brake that he never even saw himself, might not even know if he did see it and probably does know he couldn't hold his own with it if he got back to it. But that's not what he smells then. It was the cage he smelled. He hadn't smelled the cage until that minute. Then the hot sand or the brake blew into his nostrils and blew away, and all he could smell was the cage. That's what makes his eyes look like that."

"Then let him go!" the boy cried. "Let him go!"

His cousin laughed shortly. Then he stopped laughing, making the sound, that is. It had never been laughing. "His cage aint McCaslins," he said. "He was a wild man. When he was born, all his blood on both sides, except the little white part, knew things that had been tamed out of our blood so long ago that we have not only forgotten them, we have to live together in herds to protect ourselves from our own sources. He was the direct son not only of a warrior but of a chief. Then he grew up and began to learn things, and all of a sudden one day he found out that he had been betrayed, the blood of the warriors and chiefs had been betrayed. Not by his father," he added quickly. "He probably never held it against old Doom for selling him and his mother into slavery, because he probably believed the damage was already done before then and it was the same warriors' and chiefs' blood in him and Doom both that was betrayed through the black blood which his mother gave him. Not betrayed by the black blood and not wilfully betrayed by his mother, but betrayed by her all the same, who had bequeathed him not only the blood of slaves but even a little of the very blood which had enslaved it; himself his own battleground, the scene of his own vanquishment and the mausoleum of his defeat. His cage aint us," McCaslin said. "Did you ever know anybody yet, even your father and Uncle Buddy, that ever told him to do or not do anything that he ever paid any attention to?"

That was true. The boy first remembered him as sitting in the door of the plantation blacksmith shop, where he sharpened plow-points and mended tools and even did rough carpenter-work when he was not in the woods. And sometimes, even when the woods had not drawn him, even with the shop cluttered with work which the farm waited on, Sam would sit there, doing nothing at all for half a day or a whole one, and no man, neither the boy's father and twin uncle in their day nor his cousin McCaslin after he became practical though not yet titular master, ever to say to him, "I want this finished by sundown" or "why wasn't this done yesterday?" And once each year, in the late fall, in November, the boy would watch the wagon, the hooped canvas top erected now, being loaded—the food, hams and sausage from the smokehouse, coffee and flour and molasses from the commissary, a whole beef killed just last night for the dogs until there would be meat in camp, the crate containing the dogs themselves, then the bedding, the guns, the horns and lanterns and axes, and his cousin McCaslin and Sam Fathers in their hunting clothes would mount to the seat and with Tennie's Jim sitting on the dog-crate they would drive away to Jefferson, to join Major de Spain and General Compson and Boon Hogganbeck and Walter Ewell and go on into the big bottom of the Tallahatchie where the deer and bear were, to be gone two weeks. But before the wagon was even loaded the boy would find that he could watch

no longer. He would go away, running almost, to stand behind
the corner where he could not see the wagon and nobody could
see him, not crying, holding himself rigid except for the trembling, whispering to himself: "Soon now. Soon now. Just three
more years" (or two more or one more) "and I will be ten. Then
Cass said I can go."

White man's work, when Sam did work. Because he did nothing else: farmed no allotted acres of his own, as the other ex-
slaves of old Carothers McCaslin did, performed no field-work
for daily wages as the younger and newer Negroes did—and the
boy never knew just how that had been settled between Sam and
old Carothers, or perhaps with old Carothers' twin sons after
him. For, although Sam lived among the Negroes, in a cabin
among the other cabins in the quarters, and consorted with Negroes (what of consorting with anyone Sam did after the boy got
big enough to walk alone from the house to the blacksmith-shop
and then to carry a gun) and dressed like them and talked like
them and even went with them to the Negro church now and
then, he was still the son of that Chickasaw chief and the Negroes knew it. And, it seemed to the boy, not only Negroes. Boon
Hogganbeck's grandmother had been a Chickasaw woman too,
and although the blood had run white since and Boon was a
white man, it was not chief's blood. To the boy at least, the
difference was apparent immediately you saw Boon and Sam together, and even Boon seemed to know it was there—even Boon,
to whom in his tradition it had never occurred that anyone might
be better born than himself. A man might be smarter, he admitted that, or richer (luckier, he called it) but not better born. Boon
was a mastiff, absolutely faithful, dividing his fidelity equally between Major de Spain and the boy's cousin McCaslin, absolutely
dependent for his very bread and dividing that impartially too
between Major de Spain and McCaslin, hardy, generous, courageous enough, a slave to all the appetites and almost unratiocina-
tive. In the boy's eyes at least it was Sam Fathers, the Negro, who
bore himself not only toward his cousin McCaslin and Major de
Spain but toward all white men, with gravity and dignity and
without servility or recourse to that impenetrable wall of ready
and easy mirth which Negroes sustain between themselves and

white men, bearing himself toward his cousin McCaslin not only
as one man to another but as an older man to a younger.

He taught the boy the woods, to hunt, when to shoot and when
not to shoot, when to kill and when not to kill, and better, what
to do with it afterward. Then he would talk to the boy, the two of
them sitting beneath the close fierce stars on a summer hilltop
while they waited for the hounds to bring the fox back within
hearing, or beside a fire in the November or December woods
while the dogs worked out a coon's trail along the creek, or
fireless in the pitch dark and heavy dew of April mornings while
they squatted beneath a turkey roost. The boy would never question him; Sam did not react to questions. The boy would just wait
and then listen and Sam would begin, talking about the old days
and the People whom he had not had time ever to know and so
could not remember (he did not remember ever having seen his
father's face), and in place of whom the other race into which his
blood had run supplied him with no substitute.

And as he talked about those old times and those dead and
vanished men of another race from either that the boy knew,
gradually to the boy those old times would cease to be old times
and would become a part of the boy's present, not only as if they
had happened yesterday but as if they were still happening, the
men who walked through them actually walking in breath and
air and casting an actual shadow on the earth they had not quit-
ted. And more: as if some of them had not happened yet but
would occur tomorrow, until at last it would seem to the boy that
he himself had not come into existence yet, that none of his race
nor the other subject race which his people had brought with
them into the land had come here yet; that although it had been
his grandfather's and then his father's and uncle's and was now
his cousin's and someday would be his own land which he and
Sam hunted over, their hold upon it actually was as trivial and
without reality as the now faded and archaic script in the chan-
cery book in Jefferson which allocated it to them and that it was
he, the boy, who was the guest here and Sam Fathers' voice the
mouthpiece of the host.

Until three years ago there had been two of them, the other a
fullblood Chickasaw, in a sense even more incredibly lost than

Sam Fathers. He called himself Jobaker, as if it were one word.
Nobody knew his history at all. He was a hermit, living in a foul
little shack at the forks of the creek five miles from the plantation
and about that far from any other habitation. He was a market
hunter and fisherman and he consorted with nobody, black or
white; no Negro would even cross his path and no man dared
approach his hut except Sam. And perhaps once a month the boy
would find them in Sam's shop—two old men squatting on their
heels on the dirt floor, talking in a mixture of Negroid English
and flat hill dialect and now and then a phrase of that old tongue
which as time went on and the boy squatted there too listening,
he began to learn. Then Jobaker died. That is, nobody had seen
him in some time. Then one morning Sam was missing, nobody,
not even the boy, knew when nor where, until that night when
some Negroes hunting in the creek bottom saw the sudden burst
of flame and approached. It was Jobaker's hut, but before they
got anywhere near it, someone shot at them from the shadows
beyond it. It was Sam who fired, but nobody ever found Jobaker's
grave.

The next morning, sitting at breakfast with his cousin, the boy
saw Sam pass the dining-room window and he remembered then
that never in his life before had he seen Sam nearer the house
than the blacksmith shop. He stopped eating even; he sat there
and he and his cousin both heard the voices from beyond the
pantry door, then the door opened and Sam entered, carrying his
hat in his hand but without knocking as anyone else on the place
except a house servant would have done, entered just far enough
for the door to close behind him and stood looking at neither of
them—the Indian face above the nigger clothes, looking at something over their heads or at something not even in the room.

"I want to go," he said. "I want to go to the Big Bottom to
live."

"To live?" the boy's cousin said.

"At Major de Spain's and your camp, where you go to hunt,"
Sam said. "I could take care of it for you all while you aint there.
I will build me a little house in the woods, if you rather I didn't
stay in the big one."

"What about Isaac here?" his cousin said. "How will you get

away from him? Are you going to take him with you?" But still Sam looked at neither of them, standing just inside the room with that face which showed nothing, which showed that he was an old man only when it smiled.

"I want to go," he said. "Let me go."

"Yes," the cousin said quietly. "Of course. I'll fix it with Major de Spain. You want to go soon?"

"I'm going now," Sam said. He went out. And that was all. The boy was nine then; it seemed perfectly natural that nobody, not even his cousin McCaslin, should argue with Sam. Also, since he was nine now, he could understand that Sam could leave him and their days and nights in the woods together without any wrench. He believed that he and Sam both knew that this was not only temporary but that the exigencies of his maturing, of that for which Sam had been training him all his life some day to dedicate himself, required it. They had settled that one night last summer while they listened to the hounds bringing a fox back up the creek valley; now the boy discerned in that very talk under the high, fierce August stars a presage, a warning, of this moment today. "I done taught you all there is of this settled country," Sam said. "You can hunt it good as I can now. You are ready for the Big Bottom now, for bear and deer. Hunter's meat," he said. "Next year you will be ten. You will write your age in two numbers and you will be ready to become a man. Your pa" (Sam always referred to the boy's cousin as his father, establishing even before the boy's orphanhood did that relation between them not of the ward to his guardian and kinsman and chief and head of his blood, but of the child to the man who sired his flesh and his thinking too) "promised you can go with us then." So the boy could understand Sam's going. But he couldn't understand why now, in March, six months before the moon for hunting.

"If Jobaker's dead like they say," he said, "and Sam hasn't got anybody but us at all kin to him, why does he want to go to the Big Bottom now, when it will be six months before we get there?"

"Maybe that's what he wants," McCaslin said. "Maybe he wants to get away from you a little while."

But that was all right. McCaslin and other grown people often said things like that and he paid no attention to them, just as he

paid no attention to Sam saying he wanted to go to the Big
Bottom to live. After all, he would have to live there for six
months, because there would be no use in going at all if he was
going to turn right around and come back. And, as Sam himself
had told him, he already knew all about hunting in this settled
country that Sam or anybody else could teach him. So it would
be all right. Summer, then the bright days after the first frost,
then the cold and himself on the wagon with McCaslin this time
and the moment would come and he would draw the blood, the
big blood which would make him a man, a hunter, and Sam
would come back home with them and he too would have out-
grown the child's pursuit of rabbits and 'possums. Then he too
would make one before the winter fire, talking of the old hunts
and the hunts to come as hunters talked.

So Sam departed. He owned so little that he could carry it. He
walked. He would neither let McCaslin send him in the wagon,
nor take a mule to ride. No one saw him go even. He was just
gone one morning, the cabin which had never had very much in
it, vacant and empty, the shop in which there never had been
very much done, standing idle. Then November came at last, and
now the boy made one—himself and his cousin McCaslin and
Tennie's Jim, and Major de Spain and General Compson and
Walter Ewell and Boon and old Uncle Ash to do the cooking,
waiting for them in Jefferson with the other wagon, and the surrey in which he and McCaslin and General Compson and Major
de Spain would ride.

Sam was waiting at the camp to meet them. If he was glad to
see them, he did not show it. And if, when they broke camp two
weeks later to return home, he was sorry to see them go, he did
not show that either. Because he did not come back with them. It
was only the boy who returned, returning solitary and alone to
the settled familiar land, to follow for eleven months the childish
business of rabbits and such while he waited to go back, having
brought with him, even from his brief first sojourn, an unforgettable sense of the big woods—not a quality dangerous or particularly inimical, but profound, sentient, gigantic and brooding,
amid which he had been permitted to go to and fro at will,

unscathed, why he knew not, but dwarfed and, until he had drawn honorably blood worthy of being drawn, alien.

Then November, and they would come back. Each morning Sam would take the boy out to the stand allotted him. It would be one of the poorer stands of course, since he was only ten and eleven and twelve and he had never even seen a deer running yet. But they would stand there, Sam a little behind him and without a gun himself, as he had been standing when the boy shot the running rabbit when he was eight years old. They would stand there in the November dawns, and after a while they would hear the dogs. Sometimes the chase would sweep up and past quite close, belling and invisible; once they heard the two heavy reports of Boon Hogganbeck's old gun with which he had never killed anything larger than a squirrel and that sitting, and twice they heard the flat unreverberant clap of Walter Ewell's rifle, following which you did not even wait to hear his horn.

"I'll never get a shot," the boy said. "I'll never kill one."

"Yes you will," Sam said. "You wait. You'll be a hunter. You'll be a man."

But Sam wouldn't come out. They would leave him there. He would come as far as the road where the surrey waited, to take the riding horses back, and that was all. The men would ride the horses and Uncle Ash and Tennie's Jim and the boy would follow in the wagon with Sam, with the camp equipment and the trophies, the meat, the heads, the antlers, the good ones, the wagon winding on among the tremendous gums and cypresses and oaks where no axe save that of the hunter had ever sounded, between the impenetrable walls of cane and brier—the two changing yet constant walls just beyond which the wilderness whose mark he had brought away forever on his spirit even from that first two weeks seemed to lean, stooping a little, watching them and listening, not quite inimical because they were too small, even those such as Walter and Major de Spain and old General Compson who had killed many deer and bear, their sojourn too brief and too harmless to excite to that, but just brooding, secret, tremendous, almost inattentive.

Then they would emerge, they would be out of it, the line as sharp as the demarcation of a doored wall. Suddenly skeleton cotton- and corn-fields would flow away on either hand, gaunt and motionless beneath the gray rain; there would be a house, barns, fences, where the hand of man had clawed for an instant, holding, the wall of the wilderness behind them now, tremendous and still and seemingly impenetrable in the gray and fading light, the very tiny orifice through which they had emerged apparently swallowed up. The surrey would be waiting, his cousin McCaslin and Major de Spain and General Compson and Walter and Boon dismounted beside it. Then Sam would get down from the wagon and mount one of the horses and, with the others on a rope behind him, he would turn back. The boy would watch him for a while against that tall and secret wall, growing smaller and smaller against it, never looking back. Then he would enter it, returning to what the boy believed, and thought that his cousin McCaslin believed, was his loneliness and solitude.

II

So the instant came. He pulled trigger and Sam Fathers marked his face with the hot blood which he had spilled and he ceased to be a child and became a hunter and a man. It was the last day. They broke camp that afternoon and went out, his cousin and Major de Spain and General Compson and Boon on the horses, Walter Ewell and the Negroes in the wagon with him and Sam and his hide and antlers. There could have been (and were) other trophies in the wagon. But for him they did not exist, just as for all practical purposes he and Sam Fathers were still alone together as they had been that morning. The wagon wound and jolted between the slow and shifting yet constant walls from beyond and above which the wilderness watched them pass, less than inimical now and never to be inimical again since the buck still and forever leaped, the shaking gun-barrels coming constantly and forever steady at last, crashing, and still out of his instant of immortality the buck sprang, forever immortal;—the wagon jolting and bouncing on, the moment of the buck, the shot, Sam Fathers and himself and the blood with which Sam had marked him forever one with the wilderness which had accepted him since Sam said that he had done all right, when suddenly Sam reined back and stopped the wagon and they all heard the unmistakable and unforgettable sound of a deer breaking cover.

Then Boon shouted from beyond the bend of the trail and while they sat motionless in the halted wagon, Walter and the boy already reaching for their guns, Boon came galloping back, flogging his mule with his hat, his face wild and amazed as he shouted down at them. Then the other riders came around the bend, also spurring.

"Get the dogs!" Boon cried. "Get the dogs! If he had a nub on his head, he had fourteen points! Laying right there by the road in that pawpaw thicket! If I'd a knowed he was there, I could have cut his throat with my pocket knife!"

"Maybe that's why he run," Walter said. "He saw you never had your gun." He was already out of the wagon with his rifle. Then the boy was out too with his gun, and the other riders came up and Boon got off his mule somehow and was scrabbling and clawing among the duffel in the wagon, still shouting, "Get the dogs! Get the dogs!" And it seemed to the boy too that it would take them forever to decide what to do—the old men in whom the blood ran cold and slow, in whom during the intervening years between them and himself the blood had become a different and colder substance from that which ran in him and even in Boon and Walter.

"What about it, Sam?" Major de Spain said. "Could the dogs bring him back?"

"We wont need the dogs," Sam said. "If he dont hear the dogs behind him, he will circle back in here about sundown to bed."

"All right," Major de Spain said. "You boys take the horses. We'll go on out to the road in the wagon and wait there." He and General Compson and McCaslin got into the wagon and Boon and Walter and Sam and the boy mounted the horses and turned back and out of the trail. Sam led them for an hour through the gray and unmarked afternoon whose light was little different from what it had been at dawn and which would become darkness without any graduation between. Then Sam stopped them.

"This is far enough," he said. "He'll be coming upwind, and he dont want to smell the mules." They tied the mounts in a thicket. Sam led them on foot now, unpathed through the markless afternoon, the boy pressing close behind him, the two others, or so it seemed to the boy, on his heels. But they were not. Twice Sam turned his head slightly and spoke back to him across his shoulder, still walking: "You got time. We'll get there fore he does."

So he tried to go slower. He tried deliberately to decelerate the dizzy rushing of time in which the buck which he had not even seen was moving, which it seemed to him must be carrying the buck farther and farther and more and more irretrievably away from them even though there were no dogs behind him now to make him run, even though, according to Sam, he must have completed his circle now and was heading back toward them. They went on; it could have been another hour or twice that or less than half, the boy could not have said. Then they were on a ridge. He had never been in here before and he could not see that it was a ridge. He just knew that the earth had risen slightly because the underbrush had thinned a little, the ground sloping invisibly away toward a dense wall of cane. Sam stopped. "This is it," he said. He spoke to Walter and Boon: "Follow this ridge and you will come to two crossings. You will see the tracks. If he crosses, it will be at one of these three."

Walter looked about for a moment. "I know it," he said. "I've even seen your deer. I was in here last Monday. He aint nothing but a yearling."

"A yearling?" Boon said. He was panting from the walking. His face still looked a little wild. "If the one I saw was any yearling, I'm still in kindergarden."

"Then I must have seen a rabbit," Walter said. "I always heard you quit school altogether two years before the first grade."

Boon glared at Walter. "If you dont want to shoot him, get out of the way," he said. "Set down somewhere. By God, I—"

"Aint nobody going to shoot him standing here," Sam said quietly.

"Sam's right," Walter said. He moved, slanting the worn,

silver-colored barrel of his rifle downward to walk with it again. "A little more moving and a little more quiet too. Five miles is still Hogganbeck range, even if he wasn't downwind." They went on. The boy could still hear Boon talking, though presently that ceased too. Then once more he and Sam stood motionless together against a tremendous pin oak in a little thicket, and again there was nothing. There was only the soaring and sombre solitude in the dim light, there was the thin murmur of the faint cold rain which had not ceased all day. Then, as if it had waited for them to find their positions and become still, the wilderness breathed again. It seemed to lean inward above them, above himself and Sam and Walter and Boon in their separate lurking-places, tremendous, attentive, impartial and omniscient, the buck moving in it somewhere, not running yet since he had not been pursued, not frightened yet and never fearsome but just alert also as they were alert, perhaps already circling back, perhaps quite near, perhaps conscious also of the eye of the ancient immortal Umpire. Because he was just twelve then, and that morning something had happened to him: in less than a second he had ceased forever to be the child he was yesterday. Or perhaps that made no difference, perhaps even a city-bred man, let alone a child, could not have understood it; perhaps only a country-bred one could comprehend loving the life he spills. He began to shake again.

"I'm glad it's started now," he whispered. He did not move to speak; only his lips shaped the expiring words: "Then it will be gone when I raise the gun—"

Nor did Sam. "Hush," he said.

"Is he that near?" the boy whispered. "Do you think—"

"Hush," Sam said. So he hushed. But he could not stop the shaking. He did not try, because he knew it would go away when he needed the steadiness—had not Sam Fathers already consecrated and absolved him from weakness and regret too?—not from love and pity for all which lived and ran and then ceased to live in a second in the very midst of splendor and speed, but from weakness and regret. So they stood motionless, breathing deep and quiet and steady. If there had been any sun, it would be near to setting now; there was a condensing, a densifying, of what he had thought was the gray and unchanging light until he realised suddenly that it was his own breathing, his heart, his blood— something, all things, and that Sam Fathers had marked him indeed, not as a mere hunter, but with something Sam had had in his turn of his vanished and forgotten people. He stopped breathing then; there was only his heart, his blood, and in the following silence the wilderness ceased to breathe also, leaning, stooping overhead with its breath held, tremendous and impartial and waiting. Then the shaking stopped too, as he had known it would, and he drew back the two heavy hammers of the gun.

Then it had passed. It was over. The solitude did not breathe again yet; it had merely stopped watching him and was looking somewhere else, even turning its back on him, looking on away up the ridge at another point, and the boy knew as well as if he had seen him that the buck had come to the edge of the cane and had either seen or scented them and faded back into it. But the solitude did not breathe again. It should have suspired again then but it did not. It was still facing, watching, what it had been watching and it was not here, not where he and Sam stood; rigid, not breathing himself, he thought, cried *No! No!,* knowing already that it was too late, thinking with the old despair of two and three years ago: *I'll never get a shot.* Then he heard it—the flat single clap of Walter Ewell's rifle which never missed. Then the mellow sound of the horn came down the ridge and something went out of him and he knew then he had never expected to get the shot at all.

"I reckon that's it," he said. "Walter got him." He had raised the gun slightly without knowing it. He lowered it again and had lowered one of the hammers and was already moving out of the thicket when Sam spoke.

"Wait."

"Wait?" the boy cried. And he would remember that—how he turned upon Sam in the truculence of a boy's grief over the missed opportunity, the missed luck. "What for? Dont you hear that horn?"

And he would remember how Sam was standing. Sam had not moved. He was not tall, squat rather and broad, and the boy had been growing fast for the past year or so and there was not much difference between them in height, yet Sam was looking over the boy's head and up the ridge toward the sound of the horn and the boy knew that Sam did not even see him; that Sam knew he was still there beside him but he did not see the boy. Then the boy saw the buck. It was coming down the ridge, as if it were walking out of the very sound of the horn which related its death. It was not running, it was walking, tremendous, unhurried, slanting and tilting its head to pass the antlers through the undergrowth, and the boy standing with Sam beside him now instead of behind him as Sam always stood, and the gun still partly aimed and one of the hammers still cocked.

Then it saw them. And still it did not begun to run. It just stopped for an instant, taller than any man, looking at them; then its muscles suppled, gathered. It did not even alter its course, not fleeing, not even running, just moving with that winged and effortless ease with which deer move, passing within twenty feet of them, its head high and the eye not proud and not haughty but just full and wild and unafraid, and Sam standing beside the boy now, his right arm raised at full length, palm-outward, speaking in that tongue which the boy had learned from listening to him and Jobaker in the blacksmith shop, while up the ridge Walter Ewell's horn was still blowing them in to a dead buck.

"Oleh, Chief," Sam said. "Grandfather."

When they reached Walter, he was standing with his back toward them, quite still, bemused almost, looking down at his feet. He didn't look up at all.

"Come here, Sam," he said quietly. When they reached him he still did not look up, standing above a little spike buck which had still been a fawn last spring. "He was so little I pretty near let him go," Walter said. "But just look at the track he was making. It's pretty near big as a cow's. If there were any more tracks here besides the ones he is laying in, I would swear there was another buck here that I never even saw."

III

It was dark when they reached the road where the surrey waited. It was turning cold, the rain had stopped, and the sky was beginning to blow clear. His cousin and Major de Spain and General Compson had a fire going. "Did you get him?" Major de Spain said.

"Got a good-sized swamp-rabbit with spike horns," Walter said. He slid the little buck down from his mule. The boy's cousin McCaslin looked at it.

"Nobody saw the big one?" he said.

"I dont even believe Boon saw it," Walter said. "He probably jumped somebody's straw cow in that thicket." Boon started cursing, swearing at Walter and at Sam for not getting the dogs in the first place and at the buck and all.

"Never mind," Major de Spain said. "He'll be here for us next fall. Let's get started home."

It was after midnight when they let Walter out at his gate two miles from Jefferson and later still when they took General Compson to his house and then returned to Major de Spain's, where he and McCaslin would spend the rest of the night, since it was still seventeen miles home. It was cold, the sky was clear now; there would be a heavy frost by sunup and the ground was already frozen beneath the horses' feet and the wheels and beneath their own feet as they crossed Major de Spain's yard and entered the house, the warm dark house, feeling their way up the dark stairs until Major de Spain found a candle and lit it, and into the strange room and the big deep bed, the still cold sheets until they began to warm to their bodies and at last the shaking stopped and suddenly he was telling McCaslin about it while McCaslin listened, quietly until he had finished. "You dont believe it," the boy said. "I know you dont—"

"Why not?" McCaslin said. "Think of all that has happened here, on this earth. All the blood hot and strong for living, pleasuring, that has soaked back into it. For grieving and suffering too, of course, but still getting something out of it for all that, getting a lot out of it, because after all you dont have to continue to bear what you believe is suffering; you can always choose to stop that, put an end to that. And even suffering and grieving is better than nothing; there is only one thing worse than not being alive, and that's shame. But you cant be alive forever, and you always wear out life long before you have exhausted the possibilities of living. And all that must be somewhere; all that could not have been invented and created just to be thrown away. And the earth is shallow; there is not a great deal of it before you come to the rock. And the earth dont want to just keep things, hoard them; it wants to use them again. Look at the seed, the acorns, at what happens even to carrion when you try to bury it: it refuses too, seethes and struggles too until it reaches light and air again, hunting the sun still. And they—" the boy saw his hand in silhouette for a moment against the window beyond which, accustomed to the darkness now, he could see sky where the scoured and icy stars glittered "—they dont want it, need it. Besides, what would it want, itself, knocking around out there, when it never had enough time about the earth as it was, when there is plenty of room about the earth, plenty of places still unchanged from what they were when the blood used and pleasured in them while it was still blood?"

"But we want them," the boy said. "We want them too. There is plenty of room for us and them too."

"That's right," McCaslin said. "Suppose they dont have substance, cant cast a shadow—"

"But I saw it!" the boy cried. "I saw him!"

"Steady," McCaslin said. For an instant his hand touched the boy's flank beneath the covers. "Steady. I know you did. So did I. Sam took me in there once after I killed my first deer."

THE MOST DANGEROUS GAME

RICHARD CONNELL

OFF THERE to the right—somewhere—is a large island," said Whitney. "It's rather a mystery—"

"What island is it?" Rainsford asked.

"The old charts call it 'Ship-Trap Island,' " Whitney replied. "A suggestive name, isn't it? Sailors have a curious dread of the place. I don't know why. Some superstition—"

"Can't see it," remarked Rainsford, trying to peer through the dank tropical night that was palpable as it pressed its thick warm blackness in upon the yacht.

"You've good eyes," said Whitney, with a laugh, "and I've seen you pick off a moose moving in the brown fall bush at four hundred yards, but even you can't see four miles or so through a moonless Caribbean night."

"Nor four yards," admitted Rainsford. "Ugh! It's like moist black velvet."

"It will be light enough in Rio," promised Whitney. "We should make it in a few days. I hope the jaguar guns have come from Purdey's. We should have some good hunting up the Amazon. Great sport, hunting."

"The best sport in the world," agreed Rainsford.

"For the hunter," amended Whitney. "Not for the jaguar."

"Don't talk rot, Whitney," said Rainsford. "You're a big-game hunter, not a philosopher. Who cares how a jaguar feels?"

"Perhaps the jaguar does," observed Whitney.

"Bah! They've no understanding."

"Even so, I rather think they understand one thing—fear. The fear of pain and the fear of death."

"Nonsense," laughed Rainsford. "This hot weather is making you soft, Whitney. Be a realist. The world is made up of two classes—the hunters and the huntees. Luckily, you and I are hunters. Do you think we've passed that island yet?"

"I can't tell in the dark. I hope so."

"Why?" asked Rainsford.

"The place has a reputation—a bad one."

"Cannibals?" suggested Rainsford.

"Hardly. Even cannibals wouldn't live in such a God-forsaken place. But it's gotten into sailor lore, somehow. Didn't you notice that the crew's nerves seemed a bit jumpy today?"

"They were a bit strange, now you mention it. Even Captain Nielsen—"

"Yes, even that tough-minded old Swede, who'd go up to the devil himself and ask him for a light. Those fishy blue eyes held a look I never saw there before. All I could get out of him was: 'This place has an evil name among seafaring men, sir.' Then he said to me, very gravely: 'Don't you feel anything?'—as if the air about us was actually poisonous. Now, you mustn't laugh when I tell you this—I did feel something like a sudden chill.

"There was no breeze. The sea was as flat as a plate-glass window. We were drawing near the island then. What I felt was a —a mental chill; a sort of sudden dread."

"Pure imagination," said Rainsford. "One superstitious sailor can taint the whole ship's company with his fear."

"Maybe. But sometimes I think sailors have an extra sense that tells them when they are in danger. Sometimes I think evil is a tangible thing—with wavelengths, just as sound and light have. An evil place can, so to speak, broadcast vibrations of evil. Anyhow, I'm glad we're getting out of this zone. Well, I think I'll turn in now, Rainsford."

"I'm not sleepy," said Rainsford. "I'm going to smoke another pipe up on the after deck."

"Good night, then, Rainsford. See you at breakfast."

"Right. Good night, Whitney."

There was no sound in the night as Rainsford sat there but

the muffled throb of the engine that drove the yacht swiftly through the darkness, and the swish and ripple of the wash of the propeller.

Rainsford, reclining in a steamer chair, indolently puffed on his favorite brier. The sensuous drowsiness of the night was on him. "It's so dark," he thought, "that I could sleep without closing my eyes; the night would be my eyelids—"

An abrupt sound startled him. Off to the right he heard it, and his ears, expert in such matters, could not be mistaken. Again he heard the sound, and again. Somewhere, off in the blackness, someone had fired a gun three times.

Rainsford sprang up and moved quickly to the rail, mystified. He strained his eyes in the direction from which the reports had come, but it was like trying to see through a blanket. He leaped upon the rail and balanced himself there, to get greater elevation; his pipe, striking a rope, was knocked from his mouth. He lunged for it; a short, hoarse cry came from his lips as he realized he had reached too far and had lost his balance. The cry was pinched off short as the blood-warm waters of the Caribbean Sea closed over his head.

He struggled up to the surface and tried to cry out, but the wash from the speeding yacht slapped him in the face and the salt water in his open mouth made him gag and strangle. Desperately he struck out with strong strokes after the receding lights of the yacht, but he stopped before he had swum fifty feet. A certain cool-headedness had come to him; it was not the first time he had been in a tight place. There was a chance that his cries could be heard by someone aboard the yacht, but that chance was slender, and grew more slender as the yacht raced on. He wrestled himself out of his clothes, and shouted with all his power. The lights of the yacht became faint and ever-vanishing fireflies; then they were blotted out entirely by the night.

Rainsford remembered the shots. They had come from the right, and doggedly he swam in that direction, swimming with slow, deliberate strokes, conserving his strength. For a seemingly endless time he fought the sea. He began to count his strokes; he could do possibly a hundred more and then—

Rainsford heard a sound. It came out of the darkness, a high, screaming sound, the sound of an animal in an extremity of anguish and terror.

He did not recognize the animal that made the sound; he did not try to; with fresh vitality he swam toward the sound. He heard it again; then it was cut short by another noise, crisp, staccato.

"Pistol shot," muttered Rainsford, swimming on.

Ten minutes of determined effort brought another sound to his ears—the most welcome he had ever heard—the muttering and growling of the sea breaking on a rocky shore. He was almost on the rocks before he saw them; on a night less calm he would have been shattered against them. With his remaining strength he dragged himself from the swirling waters. Jagged crags appeared to jut up into the opaqueness; he forced himself upward, hand over hand. Gasping, his hands raw, he reached a flat place at the top. Dense jungle came down to the very edge of the cliffs. What perils that tangle of trees and underbrush might hold for him did not concern Rainsford just then. All he knew was that he was safe from his enemy, the sea, and that utter weariness was on him. He flung himself down at the jungle edge and tumbled headlong into the deepest sleep of his life.

When he opened his eyes he knew from the position of the sun that it was late in the afternoon. Sleep had given him new vigor; a sharp hunger was picking at him. He looked about him, almost cheerfully.

"Where there are pistol shots, there are men. Where there are men, there is food," he thought. But what kind of men, he wondered, in so forbidding a place? An unbroken front of snarled and ragged jungle fringed the shore.

He saw no sign of a trail through the closely knit web of weeds and trees; it was easier to go along the shore, and Rainsford floundered along by the water. Not far from where he had landed, he stopped.

Some wounded thing, by the evidence a large animal, had thrashed about in the underbrush; the jungle weeds were crushed down and the moss was lacerated; one patch of weeds was stained crimson. A small, glittering object not far away caught Rainsford's eye and he picked it up. It was an empty cartridge.

"A twenty-two," he remarked. "That's odd. It must have been a fairly large animal, too. The hunter had his nerve with him to tackle it with a light gun. It's clear that the brute put up a fight. I suppose the first three shots I heard was when the hunter flushed his quarry and wounded it. The last shot was when he trailed it here and finished it."

He examined the ground closely and found what he had hoped to find—the print of hunting boots. They pointed along the cliff in the direction he had been going. Eagerly he hurried along, now slipping on a rotten log or a loose stone, but making headway; night was beginning to settle down on the island.

Bleak darkness was blacking out the sea and jungle when Rainsford sighted the lights. He came upon them as he turned a crook in the coastline, and his first thought was that he had come upon a village, for there were many lights. But as he forged along he saw to his great astonishment that all the lights were in one enormous building—a lofty structure with pointed towers plunging upward into the gloom. His eyes made out the shadowy outlines of a palatial chateau; it was set on a high bluff, and on three sides of it cliffs dived down to where the sea licked greedy lips in the shadows.

"Mirage," thought Rainsford. But it was no mirage, he found, when he opened the tall spiked iron gate. The stone steps were real enough; the massive door with a leering gargoyle for a knocker was real enough; yet about it all hung an air of unreality.

He lifted the knocker, and it creaked up stiffly as if it had never before been used. He let it fall, and it startled him with its booming loudness. He thought he heard steps within; the door remained closed. Again Rainsford lifted the heavy knocker, and let it fall. The door opened then, opened as suddenly as if it were on a spring, and Rainsford stood blinking in the river of glaring gold light that poured out. The first thing Rainsford's eyes discerned was the largest man Rainsford had ever seen—a gigantic creature, solidly made and black-bearded to the waist. In his hand the man held a long-barrelled revolver, and he was pointing it straight at Rainsford's heart.

Out of the snarl of beard two small eyes regarded Rainsford.

"Don't be alarmed," said Rainsford, with a smile which he

hoped was disarming. "I'm no robber. I fell off a yacht. My name is Sanger Rainsford of New York City."

The menacing look in the eyes did not change. The revolver pointed as rigidly as if the giant were a statue. He gave no sign that he understood Rainsford's words, or that he had even heard them. He was dressed in uniform, a black uniform trimmed with gray astrakhan.

"I'm Sanger Rainsford of New York," Rainsford began again. "I fell off a yacht. I am hungry."

The man's only answer was to raise with his thumb the hammer of his revolver. Then Rainsford saw the man's free hand go to his forehead in a military salute, and he saw him click his heels together and stand at attention. Another man was coming down the broad marble steps, an erect, slender man in evening clothes. He advanced to Rainsford and held out his hand.

In a cultivated voice marked by a slight accent that gave it added precision and deliberateness, he said: "It is a very great pleasure and honor to welcome Mr. Sanger Rainsford, the celebrated hunter, to my home."

Automatically Rainsford shook the man's hand.

"I've read your book about hunting snow leopards in Tibet, you see," explained the man. "I am General Zaroff."

Rainsford's first impression was that the man was singularly handsome; his second was that there was an original, almost bizarre quality about the general's face. He was a tall man past middle age, for his hair was a vivid white; but his thick eyebrows and pointed military moustache were as black as the night from which Rainsford had come. His eyes, too, were black and very bright. He had high cheek-bones, a sharp-cut nose, a spare, dark face, the face of a man used to giving orders, the face of an aristocrat. Turning to the giant in uniform, the general made a sign. The giant put away his pistol, saluted, withdrew.

"Ivan is an incredibly strong fellow," remarked the general, "but he has the misfortune to be deaf and dumb. A simple fellow, but, I'm afraid, like all his race, a bit of a savage."

"Is he Russian?"

"He is a Cossack," said the general, and his smile showed red lips and pointed teeth. "So am I.

"Come," he said, "we shouldn't be chatting here. We can talk later. Now you want clothes, food, rest. You shall have them. This is a most restful spot."

Ivan had reappeared, and the general spoke to him with lips that moved but gave forth no sound.

"Follow Ivan, if you please, Mr. Rainsford," said the general. "I was about to have my dinner when you came. I'll wait for you. You'll find that my clothes will fit you, I think."

It was to a huge, beam-ceilinged bedroom with a canopied bed big enough for six men that Rainsford followed the silent giant. Ivan laid out an evening suit, and Rainsford, as he put it on, noticed that it came from a London tailor who ordinarily cut and sewed for none below the rank of duke.

The dining room to which Ivan conducted him was in many ways remarkable. There was a medieval magnificence about it; it suggested a baronial hall of feudal times with its oaken panels, its high ceiling, its vast refectory table where two score men could sit down to eat. About the hall were the mounted heads of many animals—lions, tigers, elephants, moose, bears; larger or more perfect specimens Rainsford had never seen. At the great table the general was sitting, alone.

"You'll have a cocktail, Mr. Rainsford," he suggested. The cocktail was surpassingly good; and, Rainsford noted, the table appointments were of the finest—the linen, the crystal, the silver, the china.

They were eating borsch, the rich red soup with whipped cream so dear to Russian palates. Half apologetically General Zaroff said: "We do our best to preserve the amenities of civilization here. Please forgive any lapses. We are well off the beaten track, you know. Do you think the champagne has suffered from its long ocean trip?"

"Not in the least," declared Rainsford. He was finding the general a most thoughtful and affable host, a true cosmopolite. But there was one small trait of the general's that made Rainsford uncomfortable. Whenever he looked up from his plate he found the general studying him, appraising him narrowly.

"Perhaps," said General Zaroff, "you were surprised that I recognized your name. You see, I read all books on hunting published in English, French, and Russian. I have but one passion in my life, Mr. Rainsford, and it is the hunt."

"You have some wonderful heads here," said Rainsford as he ate a particularly well-cooked filet mignon. "That Cape buffalo is the largest I ever saw."

"Oh, that fellow. Yes, he was a monster."

"Did he charge you?"

"Hurled me against a tree," said the general. "Fractured my skull. But I got the brute."

"I've always thought," said Rainsford, "that the Cape buffalo is the most dangerous of all big game."

For a moment the general did not reply; he was smiling his curious red-lipped smile. Then he said slowly: "No. You are wrong, sir. The Cape buffalo is not the most dangerous big game." He sipped his wine. "Here in my preserve on this island," he said, in the same slow tone, "I hunt more dangerous game."

Rainsford expressed his surprise. "Is there big game on this island?"

The general nodded. "The biggest."

"Really?"

"Oh, it isn't here naturally, of course. I have to stock the island."

"What have you imported, General?" Rainsford asked. "Tigers?"

The general smiled. "No," he said. "Hunting tigers ceased to interest me some years ago. I exhausted their possibilities, you see. No thrill left in tigers, no real danger. I live for danger, Mr. Rainsford."

The general took from his pocket a gold cigarette case and offered his guest a long black cigarette with a silver tip; it was perfumed and gave off a smell like incense.

"We will have some capital hunting, you and I," said the general. "I shall be most glad to have your society."

"But what game—" began Rainsford.

"I'll tell you," said the general. "You will be amused, I know. I think I may say, in all modesty, that I have done a rare thing. I have invented a new sensation. May I pour you another glass of port, Mr. Rainsford?"

"Thank you, General."

The general filled both glasses, and said: "God makes some men poets. Some He makes kings, some beggars. Me He made a hunter. My hand was made for the trigger, my father said. He was a very rich man with a quarter of a million acres in the Crimea, and he was an ardent sportsman. When I was only five years old he gave me a little gun, specially made in Moscow for me, to shoot sparrows with. When I shot some of his prize turkeys with it, he did not punish me; he complimented me on my marksmanship. I killed my first bear in the Caucasus when I was ten. My whole life has been one prolonged hunt. I went into the army—it was expected of noblemen's sons—and for a time commanded a division of Cossack cavalry, but my real interest was always the hunt. I have hunted every kind of game in every land. It would be impossible for me to tell you how many animals I have killed."

The general puffed at his cigarette.

"After the debacle in Russia I left the country, for it was imprudent for an officer of the Czar to stay there. Many noble Russians lost everything. I, luckily, had invested heavily in American securities, so I shall never have to open a tearoom in Monte Carlo or drive a taxi in Paris. Naturally, I continued to hunt—grizzlies in your Rockies, crocodiles in the Ganges, rhinoceroses in East Africa. It was in Africa that the Cape buffalo hit me and laid me up for six months. As soon as I recovered I started for the Amazon to hunt jaguars, for I had heard they were unusually cunning. They weren't." The Cossack sighed. "They were no match at all for a hunter with his wits about him, and a high-powered rifle. I was bitterly disappointed. I was lying in my tent with a splitting headache one night when a terrible thought pushed its way into my mind. Hunting was beginning to bore me! And hunting, remember, had been my life. I have heard that in America businessmen often go to pieces when they give up the business that has been their life."

"Yes, that's so," said Rainsford.

The general smiled. "I had no wish to go to pieces," he said. "I must do something. Now, mine is an analytical mind, Mr. Rainsford. Doubtless that is why I enjoy the problems of the chase."

"No doubt, General Zaroff."

"So," continued the general, "I asked myself why the hunt no longer fascinated me. You are much younger than I am, Mr. Rainsford, and have not hunted as much, but you perhaps can guess the answer."

"What was it?"

"Simply this: hunting had ceased to be what you call 'a sporting proposition.' It had become too easy. I always got my quarry. Always. There is no greater bore than perfection."

The general lit a fresh cigarette.

"No animal had a chance with me any more. That is no boast; it is a mathematical certainty. The animal had nothing but his legs and his instinct. Instinct is no match for reason. When I thought of this it was a tragic moment for me, I can tell you."

Rainsford leaned across the table, absorbed in what his host was saying.

"It came to me as an inspiration what I must do," the general went on.

"And that was?"

The general smiled the quiet smile of one who has faced an obstacle and surmounted it with success. "I had to invent a new animal to hunt," he said.

"A new animal? You're joking."

"Not at all," said the general. "I never joke about hunting. I needed a new animal. I found one. So I bought this island, built this house, and here I do my hunting. The island is perfect for my purposes—there are jungles with a maze of trails in them, hills, swamps—"

"But the animal, General Zaroff?"

"Oh," said the general, "it supplies me with the most exciting hunting in the world. No other hunting compares with it for an instant. Every day I hunt, and I never grow bored now, for I have a quarry with which I can match my wits."

Rainsford's bewilderment showed in his face.

"I wanted the ideal animal to hunt," explained the general. "So I said: 'What are the attributes of an ideal quarry?' And the answer was, of course: 'It must have courage, cunning, and, above all, it must be able to reason.' "

"But no animal can reason," objected Rainsford.

"My dear fellow," said the general, "there is one that can."

"But you can't mean—" gasped Rainsford.

"And why not?"

"I can't believe you are serious, General Zaroff. This is a grisly joke."

"Why should I not be serious? I am speaking of hunting."

"Hunting? Good God, General Zaroff, what you speak of is murder."

The general laughed with entire good nature. He regarded Rainsford quizzically. "I refuse to believe that so modern and civilized a young man as you seem to be harbors romantic ideas about the value of human life. Surely your experiences in the war—"

"Did not make me condone cold-blooded murder," finished Rainsford, stiffly.

Laughter shook the general. "How extraordinarily droll you are!" he said. "One does not expect nowadays to find a young man of the educated class, even in America, with such a naïve, and, if I may say so, mid-Victorian point of view. It's like finding a snuffbox in a limousine. Ah, well, doubtless you had Puritan ancestors. So many Americans appear to have had. I'll wager you'll forget your notions when you go hunting with me. You've a genuine new thrill in store for you, Mr. Rainsford."

"Thank you, I'm a hunter, not a murderer."

"Dear me," said the general, quite unruffled, "again that unpleasant word. But I think I can show you that your scruples are quite ill founded."

"Yes?"

"Life is for the strong, to be lived by the strong, and, if needs be, taken by the strong. The weak of the world were put here to give the strong pleasure. I am strong. Why should I not use my gift? If I wish to hunt, why should I not? I hunt the scum of the earth—sailors from tramp ships—lascars, blacks, Chinese, whites, mongrels—a thoroughbred horse or hound is worth more than a score of them."

"But they are men," said Rainsford, hotly.

"Precisely," said the general. "That is why I use them. It gives me pleasure. They can reason, after a fashion. So they are dangerous."

"But where do you get them?"

The general's left eyelid fluttered down in a wink. "This island is called Ship Trap," he answered. "Sometimes an angry god of the high seas sends them to me. Sometimes, when Providence is not so kind, I help Providence a bit. Come to the window with me."

Rainsford went to the window and looked out toward the sea.

"Watch! Out there!" exclaimed the general, pointing into the night. Rainsford's eyes saw only blackness, and then, as the general pressed a button, far out to sea Rainsford saw the flash of lights.

The general chuckled. "They indicate a channel," he said, "where there's none: giant rocks with razor edges crouch like a sea monster with wide-open jaws. They can crush a ship as easily as I crush this nut." He dropped a walnut on the hardwood floor and brought his heel grinding down on it. "Oh, yes," he said, casually, as if in answer to a question. "I have electricity. We try to be civilized here."

"Civilized? And you shoot down men?"

A trace of anger was in the general's black eyes, but it was there for but a second, and he said, in his most pleasant manner: "Dear me, what a righteous young man you are! I assure you I do not do the thing you suggest. That would be barbarous. I treat these visitors with every consideration. They get plenty of good food and exercise. They get into splendid physical condition. You shall see for yourself tomorrow."

"What do you mean?"

"We'll visit my training school," smiled the general. "It's in the cellar. I have about a dozen pupils down there now. They're from the Spanish bark *Sanlúcar* that had the bad luck to go on the rocks out there. A very inferior lot, I regret to say. Poor specimens and more accustomed to the deck than to the jungle."

He raised his hand, and Ivan, who served as waiter, brought thick Turkish coffee. Rainsford, with an effort, held his tongue in check.

"It's a game, you see," pursued the general, blandly. "I suggest to one of them that we go hunting. I give him a supply of food and an excellent hunting knife. I give him three hours' start. I am to follow, armed only with a pistol of the smallest calibre and range. If my quarry eludes me for three whole days, he wins the game. If I find him"—the general smiled—"he loses."

"Suppose he refuses to be hunted?"

"Oh," said the general, "I give him his option, of course. He need not play that game if he doesn't wish to. If he does not wish to hunt, I turn him over to Ivan. Ivan once had the honor of serving as official knouter to the Great White Czar, and he has his own ideas of sport. Invariably, Mr. Rainsford, invariably they choose the hunt."

"And if they win?"

The smile on the general's face widened. "To date I have not lost," he said.

Then he added, hastily: "I don't wish you to think me a braggart, Mr. Rainsford. Many of them afford only the most elementary sort of problem. Occasionally I strike a tartar. One almost did win. I eventually had to use the dogs."

"The dogs?"

"This way, please. I'll show you."

The general steered Rainsford to a window. The lights from the windows sent a flickering illumination that made grotesque patterns on the courtyard below, and Rainsford could see moving about there a dozen or so huge black shapes; as they turned toward him, their eyes glittered greenly.

"A rather good lot, I think," observed the general. "They are let out at seven every night. If any one should try to get into my house—or out of it—something extremely regrettable would occur to him." He hummed a snatch of song from the Folies Bergère.

"And now," said the general, "I want to show you my new collection of heads. Will you come with me to the library?"

"I hope," said Rainsford, "that you will excuse me tonight, General Zaroff. I'm really not feeling at all well."

"Ah, indeed?" the general inquired, solicitously. "Well, I suppose that's only natural, after your long swim. You need a good, restful night's sleep. Tomorrow you'll feel like a new man,

I'll wager. Then we'll hunt, eh? I've one rather promising prospect—"

Rainsford was hurrying from the room.

"Sorry you can't go with me tonight," called the general. "I expect rather fair sport—a big, strong black. He looks resourceful— Well, good night, Mr. Rainsford; I hope you have a good night's rest."

The bed was good, and the pajamas of the softest silk, and he was tired in every fiber of his being, but nevertheless Rainsford could not quiet his brain with the opiate of sleep. He lay, eyes wide open. Once he thought he heard stealthy steps in the corridor outside his room. He sought to throw open the door; it would not open. He went to the window and looked out. His room was high up in one of the towers. The lights of the chateau were out now, and it was dark and silent, but there was a fragment of sallow moon, and by its wan light he could see, dimly, the courtyard; there, weaving in and out in the pattern of shadow, were black, noiseless forms; the hounds heard him at the window and looked up, expectantly, with their green eyes. Rainsford went back to the bed and lay down. By many methods he tried to put himself to sleep. He had achieved a doze when, just as morning began to come, he heard, far off in the jungle, the faint report of a pistol.

General Zaroff did not appear until luncheon. He was dressed faultlessly in the tweeds of a country squire. He was solicitous about the state of Rainsford's health.

"As for me," sighed the general, "I do not feel so well. I am worried, Mr. Rainsford. Last night I detected traces of my old complaint."

To Rainsford's questioning glance the general said: "Ennui. Boredom."

Then, taking a second helping of crepes suzette, the general explained: "The hunting was not good last night. The fellow lost his head. He made a straight trail that offered no problems at all. That's the trouble with these sailors; they have dull brains to begin with, and they do not know how to get about in the woods. They do excessively stupid and obvious things. It's most annoying. Will you have another glass of Chablis, Mr. Rainsford?"

"General," said Rainsford, firmly, "I wish to leave this island at once."

The general raised his thickets of eyebrows; he seemed hurt. "But, my dear fellow," the general protested, "you've only just come. You've had no hunting—"

"I wish to go today," said Rainsford. He saw the dead black eyes of the general on him, studying him. General Zaroff's face suddenly brightened.

He filled Rainsford's glass with venerable Chablis from a dusty bottle.

"Tonight," said the general, "we will hunt—you and I."

Rainsford shook his head. "No, General," he said. "I will not hunt."

The general shrugged his shoulders and delicately ate a hothouse grape. "As you wish, my friend," he said. "The choice rests entirely with you. But may I not venture to suggest that you will find my idea of sport more diverting than Ivan's?"

He nodded toward the corner to where the giant stood, scowling, his thick arms crossed on his hogshead of chest.

"You don't mean—" cried Rainsford.

"My dear fellow," said the general, "have I not told you I always mean what I say about hunting? This is really an inspiration. I drink to a foeman worthy of my steel—at last."

The general raised his glass, but Rainsford sat staring at him.

"You'll find this game worth playing," the general said, enthusiastically. "Your brain against mine. Your woodcraft against mine. Your strength and stamina against mine. Outdoor chess! And the stake is not without value, eh?"

"And if I win—" began Rainsford, huskily.

"I'll cheerfully acknowledge myself defeated if I do not find you by midnight of the third day," said General Zaroff. "My sloop will place you on the mainland near a town."

The general read what Rainsford was thinking.

"Oh, you can trust me," said the Cossack. "I will give you my word as a gentleman and a sportsman. Of course, you, in turn, must agree to say nothing of your visit here."

"I'll agree to nothing of the kind," said Rainsford.

"Oh," said the general, "in that case— But why discuss that

now? Three days hence we can discuss it over a bottle of Veuve Cliquot, unless—"

The general sipped his wine.

Then a businesslike air animated him. "Ivan," he said to Rainsford, "will supply you with hunting clothes, food, a knife. I suggest you wear moccasins; they leave a poorer trail. I suggest, too, that you avoid the big swamp in the southeast corner of the island. We call it Death Swamp. There's quicksand there. One foolish fellow tried it. The deplorable part of it was that Lazarus followed him. You can imagine my feelings, Mr. Rainsford. I loved Lazarus; he was the finest hound in my pack. Well, I must beg you to excuse me now. I always take a siesta after lunch. You'll hardly have time for a nap, I fear. You'll want to start, no doubt. I shall not follow till dusk. Hunting at night is so much more exciting than by day, don't you think? *Au revoir,* Mr. Rainsford, *au revoir.*"

General Zaroff, with a deep, courtly bow, strolled from the room.

From another door came Ivan. Under one arm he carried khaki hunting clothes, a haversack of food, a leather sheath containing a long-bladed hunting knife; his right hand rested on a cocked revolver thrust in the crimson sash about his waist.

Rainsford had fought his way through the bush for two hours. "I must keep my nerve. I must keep my nerve," he said, through tight teeth.

He had not been entirely clear-headed when the chateau gates snapped shut behind him. His whole idea at first was to put distance between himself and General Zaroff, and, to this end, he had plunged along, spurred on by the sharp rowels of something very like panic. Now he had got a grip on himself, had stopped, and was taking stock of himself and the situation.

He saw that straight flight was futile; inevitably it would bring him face to face with the sea. He was in a picture with a frame of water, and his operations, clearly, must take place within that frame.

"I'll give him a trail to follow," muttered Rainsford, and he struck off from the rude path he had been following into the trackless wilderness. He executed a series of intricate loops; he doubled on his trail again and again, recalling all the lore of the fox hunt, and all the dodges of the fox. Night found him leg-weary, with hands and face lashed by the branches, on a thickly wooded ridge. He knew it would be insane to blunder on through the dark, even if he had the strength. His need for rest was imperative and he thought: "I have played the fox, now I must play the cat of the fable." A big tree with a thick trunk and outspread branches was nearby, and, taking care to leave not the slightest mark, he climbed up into the crotch, and stretching out on one of the broad limbs, after a fashion, rested. Rest brought him new confidence and almost a feeling of security. Even so zealous a hunter as General Zaroff could not trace him there, he told him-self; only the devil himself could follow that complicated trail through the jungle after dark. But perhaps the general was a devil—

An apprehensive night crawled slowly by like a wounded snake, and sleep did not visit Rainsford, although the silence of a dead world was on the jungle. Toward morning, when a dingy gray was varnishing the sky, the cry of some startled bird focused Rainsford's attention in that direction. Something was coming through the bush, coming slowly, carefully, coming by the same winding way Rainsford had come. He flattened himself down on the limb, and through a screen of leaves almost as thick as tapes-try, he watched. The thing that was approaching was a man.

It was General Zaroff. He made his way along with his eyes fixed in utmost concentration on the ground before him. He paused, almost beneath the tree, dropped to his knees, and stud-ied the ground. Rainsford's impulse was to hurl himself down like a panther, but he saw that the general's right hand held something metallic—a small automatic pistol.

The hunter shook his head several times, as if he were puzzled. Then he straightened up and took from his case one of his black cigarettes; its pungent incense-like smoke floated up to Rains-ford's nostrils.

Rainsford held his breath. The general's eyes had left the ground and were travelling inch by inch up the tree. Rainsford froze there, every muscle tensed for a spring. But the sharp eyes of the hunter stopped before they reached the limb where Rainsford lay; a smile spread over his brown face. Very deliberately he blew a smoke ring into the air; then he turned his back on the tree and walked carelessly away, back along the trail he had come. The swish of the underbrush against his hunting boots grew fainter and fainter.

The pent-up air burst hotly from Rainsford's lungs. His first thought made him feel sick and numb. The general could follow a trail through the woods at night; he could follow an extremely difficult trail; he must have uncanny powers; only by the merest chance had the Cossack failed to see his quarry.

Rainsford's second thought was even more terrible. It sent a shudder of cold horror through his whole being. Why had the general smiled? Why had he turned back?

Rainsford did not want to believe what his reason told him was true, but the truth was as evident as the sun that had by now pushed through the morning mists. The general was playing with him! The general was saving him for another day's sport! The Cossack was the cat; he was the mouse. Then it was that Rainsford knew the full meaning of terror.

"I will not lose my nerve. I will not."

He slid down from the tree, and struck off again into the woods. His face was set and he forced the machinery of his mind to function. Three hundred yards from his hiding place he stopped where a huge dead tree leaned precariously on a smaller, living one. Throwing off his sack of food, Rainsford took his knife from its sheath and began to work with all his energy.

The job was finished at last, and he threw himself down behind a fallen log a hundred feet away. He did not have to wait long. The cat was coming again to play with the mouse.

Following the trail with the sureness of a bloodhound came General Zaroff. Nothing escaped those searching black eyes, no crushed blade of grass, no bent twig, no mark, no matter how faint, in the moss. So intent was the Cossack on his stalking that he was upon the thing Rainsford had made before he saw it. His foot touched the protruding bough that was the trigger. Even as he touched it, the general sensed his danger and leaped back with the agility of an ape. But he was not quite quick enough; the dead tree, delicately adjusted to rest on the cut living one, crashed down and struck the general a glancing blow on the shoulder as it fell; but for his alertness, he must have been smashed beneath it. He staggered, but he did not fall; nor did he drop his revolver. He stood there, rubbing his injured shoulder, and Rainsford, with fear again gripping his heart, heard the general's mocking laugh ring through the jungle.

"Rainsford," called the general, "if you are within sound of my voice, as I suppose you are, let me congratulate you. Not many men know how to make a Malay man-catcher. Luckily for me I, too, have hunted in Malacca. You are proving interesting, Mr. Rainsford. I am going now to have my wound dressed; it's only a slight one. But I shall be back. I shall be back."

When the general, nursing his bruised shoulder, had gone, Rainsford took up his flight again. It was flight now, a desperate, hopeless flight, that carried him on for some hours. Dusk came, then darkness, and still he pressed on. The ground grew softer under his moccasins; the vegetation grew ranker, denser; insects bit him savagely. Then, as he stepped forward, his foot sank into the ooze. He tried to wrench it back, but the muck sucked viciously at his foot as if it were a giant leech. With a violent effort he tore his foot loose. He knew where he was now. Death Swamp and its quicksand.

His hands were tight closed as if his nerve were something tangible that someone in the darkness was trying to tear from his grip. The softness of the earth had given him an idea. He stepped back from the quicksand a dozen feet or so and, like some huge prehistoric beaver, he began to dig.

Rainsford had dug himself in in France when a second's delay meant death. That had been a placid pastime compared to his digging now. The pit grew deeper; when it was above his shoulders, he climbed out and from some hard saplings cut stakes and sharpened them to a fine point. These stakes he planted in the bottom of the pit with the points sticking up. With flying fingers he wove a rough carpet of weeds and branches and with it he covered the mouth of the pit. Then, wet with sweat and aching with tiredness, he crouched behind the stump of a lightning-charred tree.

He knew his pursuer was coming; he heard the padding sound of feet on the soft earth, and the night breeze brought him the perfume of the general's cigarette. It seemed to Rainsford that the general was coming with unusual swiftness; he was not feeling his way along, foot by foot. Rainsford, crouching there, could not see the general, nor could he see the pit. He lived a year in a minute. Then he felt an impulse to cry aloud with joy, for he heard the sharp crackle of the breaking branches as the cover of the pit gave way; he heard the sharp scream of pain as the pointed stakes found their mark. He leaped up from his place of concealment. Then he cowered back. Three feet from the pit a man was standing, with an electric torch in his hand.

"You've done well, Rainsford," the voice of the general called. "Your Burmese tiger pit has claimed one of my best dogs. Again you score. I think, Mr. Rainsford, I'll see what you can do against my whole pack. I'm going home for a rest now. Thank you for a most amusing evening."

At daybreak Rainsford, lying near the swamp, was awakened by a sound that made him know that he had new things to learn about fear. It was a distant sound, faint and wavering, but he knew it. It was the baying of a pack of hounds.

Rainsford knew he could do one of two things. He could stay where he was and wait. That was suicide. He could flee. That was postponing the inevitable. For a moment he stood there, thinking. An idea that held a wild chance came to him, and, tightening his belt, he headed away from the swamp.

The baying of the hounds drew nearer, then still nearer, nearer, ever nearer. On a ridge Rainsford climbed a tree. Down a watercourse, not a quarter of a mile away, he could see the bush moving. Straining his eyes, he saw the lean figure of General Zaroff; just ahead of him, Rainsford made out another figure whose wide shoulders surged through the tall jungle weeds; it was the giant Ivan, and he seemed pulled forward by some unseen force; Rainsford knew that Ivan must be holding the pack in leash.

They would be on him any minute now. His mind worked frantically. He thought of a native trick he had learned in Uganda. He slid down the tree. He caught hold of a springy young sapling and to it he fastened his hunting knife, with the blade pointing down the trail; with a bit of wild grapevine he tied back the sapling. Then he ran for his life. The hounds raised their voices as they hit the fresh scent. Rainsford knew now how an animal at bay feels.

He had to stop to get his breath. The baying of the hounds stopped abruptly, and Rainsford's heart stopped, too. They must have reached the knife.

He shinned excitedly up a tree and looked back. His pursuers had stopped. But the hope that was in Rainsford's brain when he climbed died, for he saw in the shallow valley that General Zaroff was still on his feet. But Ivan was not. The knife, driven by the recoil of the springing tree, had not wholly failed.

Rainsford had hardly tumbled to the ground when the pack took up the cry again.

"Nerve, nerve, nerve!" he panted, as he dashed along. A blue gap showed between the trees dead ahead. Ever nearer drew the hounds. Rainsford forced himself on toward that gap. He reached it. It was the shore of the sea. Across a cove he could see the gloomy gray stone of the chateau. Twenty feet below him the sea rumbled and hissed. Rainsford hesitated. He heard the hounds. Then he leaped far out into the sea. . . .

When the general and his pack reached the place by the sea, the Cossack stopped. For some minutes he stood regarding the blue-green expanse of water. He shrugged his shoulders. Then he sat down, took a drink of brandy from a silver flask, lit a perfumed cigarette, and hummed a bit from *Madama Butterfly.*

General Zaroff had an exceedingly good dinner in his great panelled dining hall that evening. With it he had a bottle of Pol Roger and half a bottle of Chambertin. Two slight annoyances kept him from perfect enjoyment. One was the thought that it would be difficult to replace Ivan; the other was that his quarry had escaped him; of course the American hadn't played the game —so thought the general as he tasted his after-dinner liqueur. In his library he read, to soothe himself, from the works of Marcus Aurelius. At ten he went up to his bedroom. He was deliciously tired, he said to himself, as he locked himself in. There was a

little moonlight, so before turning on his light he went to the
window and looked down at the courtyard. He could see the
great hounds, and he called: "Better luck another time," to them.
Then he switched on the light.

A man, who had been hiding in the curtains of the bed, was
standing there.

"Rainsford!" screamed the general. "How in God's name did
you get here?"

"Swam," said Rainsford. "I found it quicker than walking
through the jungle."

The general sucked in his breath and smiled. "I congratulate
you," he said. "You have won the game."

Rainsford did not smile. "I am still a beast at bay," he said, in
a low, hoarse voice. "Get ready, General Zaroff."

The general made one of his deepest bows. "I see," he
said. "Splendid! One of us is to furnish a repast for the hounds.
The other will sleep in this very excellent bed. On guard,
Rainsford. . . ."

He had never slept in a better bed, Rainsford decided.

THE
WOLF TRACKER

ZANE GREY

I

THE HARD-RIDING cowmen of Adam's outfit returned to camp, that last day of the fall roundup, weary and brush-torn, begrimed with dust and sweat, and loud in their acclaims against Old Gray, the loafer wolf, notorious from the Cibeque across the black belt of rugged Arizona upland to Mount Wilson in New Mexico.

"Wal, reckon I allowed the Tonto had seen the last of Old Gray's big tracks," said Benson, the hawk-eyed foreman, as he slipped the bridle off his horse.

"An' for why?" queried Banty Smith, the little arguing rooster of the outfit. "Ain't Old Gray young yet—just in his prime? Didn't we find four carcasses of full-grown steers he'd pulled down last April over on Webber Creek? Shore he allus hit for high country in summer. What for did you think he'd not show up when the frost come?"

"Aw, Banty, cain't you savvy Ben?" drawled a long, lean rider. "He was jest voicin' his hopes."

"Yep, Ben is thet tender-hearted he'd weep over a locoed calf —if it happened to wear his brand," remarked Tim Bender, with a huge grin, as if he well knew he had acquitted himself wittily.

"Haw. Haw," laughed another rider. "Old Gray has shore made some deppredashuns on Ben's stock of twenty head. Most as much as one heifer."

"Wal, kid me all you like, boys," replied Benson, good naturedly. "Reckon I had no call to think Old Gray wouldn't come back. He's done thet for years. But it's not onnatural to live in hopes. An' it's hard luck we had to run acrost his tracks an' his work the last day of the roundup. Only last night the boss was sayin' he hadn't heard anythin' about Old Gray for months."

"Nobody heerd of anyone cashin' on thet five thousand dollars reward for Old Gray's scalp, either," replied Banty, with sarcasm.

Thus after the manner of the range the loquacious cowboys volleyed badinage while they performed the last tasks of the day.

Two streams met below the pine-shaded bench where the camp was situated; and some of the boys strode down with towels and soap to attend to ablutions that one washpan for the outfit made a matter of waiting. It was still clear daylight, though the sun had gone down behind a high timbered hill to the west. The blue haze that hung over the bench was not all campfire smoke. A rude log cabin stood above the fork of the streams, and near by the cook busied himself between his chuck wagon and the campfire. Both the cool, pine-scented air and the red gold patches of brush on the hillside told of the late October. The rich amber light of the woods had its reflection in the pools of the streams.

Adams, the boss of the outfit, had ridden over from his Tonto ranch at Spring Valley. He was a sturdy, well-preserved man of sixty, sharp of eye, bronze of face, with the stamp of self-made and prosperous rancher upon him.

"Ben, the boss is inquirin' about you," called Banty from the bench above the stream.

Whereupon the foreman clambered up the rocky slope, vigorously rubbing his ruddy face with a towel, and made his way to where Adams sat beside the campfire. In all respects, except regarding Old Gray, Benson's report was one he knew would be gratifying. This naturally he reserved until after Adams had expressed his satisfaction. Then he supplemented the news of the wolf.

"That loafer," ejaculated Adams, in dismay. "Why, only the other day I heard from my pardner, Barrett, an' he said the government hunters were trackin' Old Gray up Mount Wilson."

"Wal, boss thet may be true," responded the foreman. "But Old Gray killed a yearlin' last night on the red ridge above

Doubtful Canyon. I know his tracks like I do my hoss's. We found four kills today, an' I reckon all was the work of thet loafer. You don't need to see his tracks. He's shore a clean killer. An' sometimes he kills for the sake of killin'."

"I ain't sayin' I care about the money loss, though that old gray devil has cost me an' Barrett twenty-five hundred," replied Adams, thoughtfully. "But he's such a bloody murderer—the most aggravatin' varmint I ever—"

"Huh. Who's the gazabo comin' down the trail?" interrupted Benson, pointing up the bench.

"Stranger to me," said Adams. "Anybody know him?"

One by one the cowboys disclaimed knowledge of the unusual figure approaching. At that distance he appeared to be a rather old man, slightly bowed. But a second glance showed his shoulders to be broad and his stride the wonderful one of a mountaineer. He carried a pack on his back and a shiny carbine in his hand. His garb was ragged homespun, patched until it resembled a checkerboard.

"A stranger without a hoss," exclaimed Banty, as if that were an amazingly singular thing.

The man approached the campfire, and halted to lean the worn carbine against the woodpile. Then he unbuckled a strap round his breast and lifted a rather heavy pack from his back, to deposit it on the ground. It appeared to be a pack rolled in a rubber-lined blanket, out of which protruded the ends of worn snowshoes. When he stepped to the campfire he disclosed a strange physiognomy—the weather-beaten face of a matured man of the open, mapped by deep lines, strong, hard, a rugged mask, lighted by penetrating, quiet eyes of gray.

"Howdy, stranger. Get down an' come in," welcomed Adams, with the quaint, hearty greeting always resorted to by a Westerner.

"How do. I reckon I will," replied the man, extending big brown hands to the fire. "Are you Adams, the cattleman?"

"You've got me. But I can't just place you, stranger."

"Reckon not. I'm new in these parts. My name's Brink. I'm a tracker."

"Glad to meet you, Brink," replied Adams, curiously. "These

are some of my boys. Set down an' rest. I reckon you're tired an'
hungry. We'll have grub soon. . . . Tracker, you said? Now, I
just don't savvy what you mean."

"I've been prospector, trapper, hunter, most everythin'," replied Brink as he took the seat offered. "But I reckon my callin' is
to find tracks. Tracker of men, hosses, cattle, wild animals—
'specially sheep-killen' silvertips an' stock-killen' wolves."

"Aha. You don't say?" ejaculated Adams, suddenly shifting
from genial curiosity to keen interest. "An' you're after that five
thousand dollars we cattlemen offered for Old Gray's scalp?"

"Nope. I hadn't thought of the reward. I heard of it, up in
Colorado, same time I heard of this wolf that's run amuck so
long on these ranges. An' I've come down here to kill him."

Adams showed astonishment along with his interest, but his
silence and expression did not approach the incredulity manifested by the men of his outfit. Banty winked a roguish eye at his
comrades; Benson leaned forward with staring eyes and dropping
jaw; Tim Bender made covert and significant signs to indicate the
stranger had wheels in his head; the other riders were amiably
nonplussed as to the man's sanity. Nothing more than the response of these men was needed to establish the reputation of Old
Gray, the loafer wolf. But Brink did not see these indications; he
was peering into the fire.

"So—ho. You have?" exclaimed Adams, breaking the silence.
"Wal, now, Brink, that's good of you. We sure appreciate your
intent. Would you mind tellin' us how you mean to set about
killin' Old Gray?"

"Reckon I told you I was a tracker," rejoined Brink, curtly.

"Hell, man. We've had every pack of hounds in two states on
the track of that wolf."

"Is he on the range now?" queried Brink, totally ignoring Adam's strong protestation.

Adams motioned to his foreman to reply to this question. Benson made evident effort to be serious.

"I seen his tracks less'n two hours ago. He killed a yearlin' last
night."

At these words Brink turned his gaze from the fire to the
speaker. What a remarkable fleeting flash crossed his rugged face.

It seemed one of passion. It passed, and only a gleam of eye attested to strange emotion under that seamed and lined mask of bronze. His gaze returned to the fire, and the big hands, that he held palms open to the heat, now clasped each other, in strong and tense action. Only Adams took the man seriously, and his attitude restrained the merriment his riders certainly felt.

"Adams, would you mind tellin' me all you know about this wolf?" asked the stranger, presently.

"Say, man," expostulated Adams, still with good nature, "it wouldn't be polite to keep you from eatin' an' sleepin'. We don't treat strangers that way in this country."

"Old Gray has a history, then?" inquired Brink, as intent as if he had been concerned with the case of a human being.

"Humph. Reckon I couldn't tell you all about him in a week," said the cattleman, emphatically.

"It wouldn't matter to me how long you'd take," returned Brink, thoughtfully.

At that Adams laughed outright. This queer individual had not in the least considered waste of time to a busy rancher. Manifestly he thought only of the notorious wolf. Adams eyed the man a long speculative moment, divided between amusement and doubt. Brink interested him. Having had to deal with many and various kinds of men, Adams was not quite prepared to take this stranger as the young riders took him. Adams showed the shrewdness of appreciation of the many-sidedness of human nature. Brink's face and garb and pack were all extraordinarily different from what was usually met with on these ranges. He had arrived on foot, but he was not a tramp. Adams took keener note of the quiet face, the deep chest, the muscular hands, the wiry body, and the powerful legs. No cowboy, for all his riding, ever had wonderful legs like these. The man was a walker.

These deductions, slight and unconvincing as they were, united with an amiability that was characteristic of Adams, persuaded him to satisfy the man's desire to hear about the wolf.

"All right, Brink, I'll tell you somethin' of Old Gray—at least-ways till the cook calls us to come an' get it. . . . There used to be a good many loafers—timber wolves, we called them—in this country. But they're gettin' scarce. Accordin' to the hunters

there's a small bunch of loafers rangin' from Black Butte to Clear
Creek Canyon. That's a deer country, an' we cattlemen don't run
much stock over there. Now an' then a cowboy will see a wolf
track, or hear one bay. But outside of Old Gray we haven't had
much loss from loafers of late years.

"Naturally there are lots of stories in circulation about this
particular wolf. Some of them are true. I can't vouch for his
parentage, or whether he has mixed blood. Seven or eight, maybe
ten years ago, some trapper lost a husky—one of them regular
Alaskan snow-sled dogs—over in the Mazatzels. Never found
him. Some natives here claim Old Gray is a son of this husky, his
mother bein' one of the range loafers. Another story is about a
wolf escapin' from a circus over heah in a railroad wreck years
ago. I remember well the report told at Winslow. A young gray
wolf got away. This escaped wolf might be Old Gray. No one can
ever tell that. But both stories are interestin' enough to think
about.

"The name Old Gray doesn't seem to fit this particular wolf,
because it's misleadin'. He's gray, yes, almost white, but he's not
old. Bill Everett, a range hand, saw this wolf first. Tellin' about it
he called him an old gray Jasper. The name stuck, though now
you seldom hear the Jasper tacked on.

"From that time stories began to drift into camp an' town
about the doin's of Old Gray. He was a killer. Cowboys an'
hunters took to his trail with cow dogs an' bear hounds. But
though they routed him out of his lairs an' chased him all over,
they never caught him. Trappers camped all the way from the
Cibeque to Mount Wilson, tryin' to trap him. I never heard of
Old Gray touchin' a trap.

"In summer Old Gray lit out for the mountains. In winter he
took to the foothills an' ranges. I've heard cattlemen over in New
Mexico say he had killed twenty-five thousand dollars' worth of
stock. But that was years ago. It would be impossible now to
estimate the loss to ranchers. Old Gray played at the game. He'd
run through a bunch of stock, hamstringin' right an' left, until he
had enough of his fun, then he'd pull down a yearlin', eat what he
wanted, an' travel on.

"He didn't always work alone. Sometimes he'd have several

loafers with him. Two years ago I saw his tracks with at least four other wolves. That was on my pardner's ranch at Vermajo Park, New Mexico. But Old Gray always was an' is a lone wolf. He didn't trust company. Accordin' to report he'd led off more than one she dog, always shepherds. They never came back. It's a good bet he led them away, for his tracks were seen, an' perhaps he killed them.

"The government hunters have been tryin' to get him, these several years. They don't tell about this hunt any more. But the forest rangers sometimes make fun at the expense of these predatory game hunters of the government. Anyway, so far as I know, Old Gray has never been scratched. My personal opinion is this. He's a magnificent wild brute, smarter than any dog. An' you know how intelligent dogs can be. Well, Old Gray is too savage, too wild, too keen to be caught by the ordinary means employed so far. . . . There, Brink, is the plain blunt facts from a blunt man. If you listened to a lot of the gossip about Old Gray you'd be sure locoed."

"Much obliged," replied Brink, with a break in his rapt intensity. "Have you ever seen this loafer?"

"No, I never had the good luck," replied Adams. "Nor have many men. But Benson, here, has seen him."

"What's he look like?" queried Brink, turning eagerly to the foreman.

"Wal, Old Gray is about the purtiest wild varmint I ever clapped my eyes on," drawled Benson, slow and cool, as if to tantalize this wolf hunter. "He's big—a heap bigger'n any loafer I ever saw before—an' he's gray all right, a light gray, with a black ring part round his neck, almost like a ruff. He's a bold cus, too. He stood watchin' me, knowin' darn well he was out of gunshot."

"Now what kind of a track does he make?"

"Wal, jest a wolf track bigger's you ever seen before. Almost as big as a hoss track. When you see it once, you'll never forget."

"Where did you run across that track last?"

Benson squatted down before the fire, and with his hand smoothed a flat clear place in the dust, on which he began to trace lines.

"Heah, foller up this creek till you come to a high falls. Climb up the slope on the right. You'll head out on a cedar an' pinon ridge. It's red dirt, most all soft. Halfway up this ridge from there you'll strike a trail. It runs this heah way. Foller it round under the bluff till you strike Old Gray's tracks. I seen them this mawnin', fresh as could be. Sharp an' clean in the dust. He was makin' for the Rim, I reckon soon after he had killed the heifer."

By this time all the cowboys were grouped round the central figures. Banty appeared to be the only one not seriously impressed. As to the others, something about Brink and the way he had moved Adams to talk, had inhibited for the moment their characteristic humor.

Brink slowly rose from his scrutiny of the map that Benson had drawn in the dust. His penetrating gaze fixed on Adams.

"I'll kill your old gray wolf," he said.

His tone, his manner, seemed infinitely more than his simple words. They all combined to make an effect that seemed indefinable, except in the case of Banty, who grew red in the face. Manifestly Banty took this man's statement as astounding and ridiculous. The little cowboy enjoyed considerable reputation as a hunter—a reputation that he cherished, and which, to his humiliation, had not been lived up to by his several futile hunts after Old Gray.

"Aw, now—so you'll kill thet loafer," he ejaculated, in the most elaborate satire possible for a cowboy. "Wal, Mr. Brink, would you mind tellin' us jest when you'll perpetuate this execushun? Shore all the outfits in the Tonto will want to see Old Gray's scalp. We'll give a dance to celebrate. . . . Say when you'll fetch his skin down—tomorrow around sunup, or mebbe next day, seein' you have to travel on shank's mare—or possible the day after."

Banty's drawling scorn might never have been spoken, for all the intended effect it had on the wolf hunter. Brink was beyond the levity of a cowboy.

"Reckon I can't say just when I'll kill Old Gray," he replied, with something sonorous in his voice. "It might be any day, accordin' to luck. But if he's the wolf you all say he is, it'll take long."

"You don't say," spoke up Banty. "Wal, by gosh, my walkin'

gent, I figgered you had some Injun medicine that you could put on Old Gray's tail."

The cowboy's roared. Adams showed constraint in his broad grin. Brink suffered no offense, no sign of appreciating the ridicule. Thoughtfully he bent again to the fire, and did not hear the cook's lusty call to supper.

"Never mind the boys," said Adams, kindly, putting a hand on the bowed shoulder. "Come an' eat with us."

II

The morning sun had not yet melted the hoarfrost from the brush when Brink halted in the trail before huge wolf tracks in the red dust.

"Same as any wolf tracks, only big," he soliloquized. "Biggest I ever saw—even in Alaska."

Whereupon he leaned his shiny carbine against a pine sapling, and lifted his pack from his shoulders, all the time with gaze riveted on the trail. Then, with head bent, he walked slowly along until he came to a place where all four tracks of the wolf showed plainly. Here he got to his knees, scrutinizing the imprints, photographing them on his inward eye, taking intent and grave stock of them, as if these preliminaries in the stalking of a wolf were a ritual. For moments he remained motionless, like one transfixed. Presently he relaxed, and seating himself beside the trail, seemed to revel in a strange, tranquil joy.

Brink's state of mind was a composite of a lifetime's feelings, thoughts, actions, never comprehensible to him. As a boy of three he had captured his first wild creature—a squirrel that he tamed and loved, and at last freed. All his early boyhood he had been a haunter of the woods and hills, driven to the silent places and the abode of the wild. At sixteen he had run away from school and home; at fifty he knew the west from the cold borders of the Yukon to the desert-walled Yaqui. Through those many and eventful years the occupations of men had held him, but never for long. Caravans, mining camps, freighting posts, towns and settlements, ranches and camps had known him, though never for any length of time. Women had never drawn him, much less men.

Again the solitude and loneliness of the wilderness claimed him; and his eyes feasted on the tracks of a beast commonly supposed to be stronger, keener than any human. Around these two facts clung the fibers of the spell that possessed Brink's soul.

The October morning seemed purple in the shade, golden in the sun. A profound and unbroken stillness held this vast cedar slope in thrall. A spicy tang, cold to the nostrils, permeated the air. The sheath-barked cedars and the junipers with their lavender-hued berries stretched a patchwork of light and shadow across the trail. Far down, the ridged sweep of timbered country fell. Beyond the black vague depths of the Basin rose the sharp, ragged mountains to the south. Above him towered bold promontories of rock, fringed by green, clearly etched against the blue. Nothing of mankind tainted this loneliness for Brink— nothing save the old, seldom-trodden trail, and that bore the tracks of an enormous wolf, wildest of all American animals.

Brink's serenity had returned—the familiar state that had ceased at the end of his last pursuit. This huge track was a challenge. But this strange egotism did not appear to be directed toward the hunters and cowboys who had failed on Old Gray's trail. Rather toward the wolf. The issue was between him and the great loafer. Here began the stalk that for Brink had but one conclusion. The wonderful tracks showed sharply in the dust. Old Gray had passed along there yesterday. He was somewhere up or down those ragged slopes. Cunning as he was, he had to hold contact with earth and rock. He had to slay and eat. He must leave traces of his nature, his life, his habit, and his action. To these Brink would address himself, with all the sagacity of an old hunter, but with something infinitely more—a passion which he did not understand.

"Wal, Old Gray, I'm on your track," muttered Brink, grimly; and strapping the heavy pack on his broad shoulders, he took up the carbine and strode along the trail.

It pleased Brink to find that his first surmise was as correct as if he had cognizance of Old Gray's instincts. The wolf tracks soon sheered off the trail. Old Gray was not now a hunting or a prowling wolf. He was a traveling wolf, but he did not keep to the easygoing, direct trail.

On soft ground like this, bare except for patches of brush and brown mats under the cedar and pinon trees, Brink could discern the wolf tracks far ahead. Old Gray was light-footed, but he had weight, and his trail along here was as easy for the keen eyes of the tracker as if he had been traveling on wet ground or snow. Where he did not leave tracks there was a pressed tuft of grass or a disturbed leaf or broken twig or dislodged bit of stone, or an unnatural displacement of the needles under the pinons.

The trail led down over the uneven ridges and gullies of the slope, down into timbered thickets, and on through an increasingly rugged and wild country, to the dark shade of a deep gorge, where the melodious murmur of a stream mingled with the mourn of a rising wind in the lofty pines and spruces. The wolf had drunk his fill, leaving two huge tracks in the wet sand along the brookside. Brink could not find tracks on gravel and boulders, so he crossed the wide bottom of the gorge, and after a while found Old Gray's trail on the opposite slope. Before he struck it he had believed the wolf was heading for high country.

Brink tracked him over a forested ridge and down into an intersecting canyon, where on the rocks of a dry stream bed the trail failed. This did not occasion the wolf tracker any concern. Old Gray would most likely choose that rugged lonely stream bed and follow it to where the canyon headed out above. Brink, in such cases as this, trusted to his instincts. Many times he had been wrong, but more often he had been right. To this end he slowly toiled up the rough ascent, halting now and then to rest a moment, eyes roving from side to side. It was a steep ascent, and grew rougher, narrower, and more shaded as he climbed. At length he came to pools of water in rocky recesses, where the sand and gravel bars showed the tracks of cattle, bear, and deer. But if Old Gray had passed on up that narrowing canyon he had avoided the water holes.

Patches of maple and thickets of oak covered the steep slopes, leading up to the base of cracked and seamed cliffs, and they in turn sheered up to where the level rim shone black-fringed against the blue. Here the stream bed was covered with the red and gold and purple of fallen autumn leaves. High up the thickets had begun to look shaggy. The sun, now at the zenith, fell hot upon Brink's head. He labored on to climb out a narrow defile that led to the level forest above.

Here the wind blew cool. Brink rested a moment, gazing down into the colorful void, and across the black rolling leagues to the mountains. Then he strode east along the precipice, very carefully searching for the wolf trail he had set out upon. In a mile of slow travel he did not discover a sign of Old Gray. Retracing his steps, he traveled west for a like distance, without success. Whereupon he returned to the head of the canyon out of which he had climbed, and there, divesting himself of his pack, he set about a more elaborate scrutiny of ground, grass, moss, and rock. He searched from the rim down into an aspen swale that deepened into a canyon, heading away from the rim. He had no reason to believe Old Gray would travel this way, except that long experience had taught him where to search first for tracks. And quite abruptly he came upon the huge footprints of the loafer, made in soft black mud beside elk tracks that led into a hole where water had recently stood.

"Hah," ejaculated Brink. "You're interested in that yearlin' elk. . . . Wal, Old Gray, I'll let this do for today."

Brink returned to get his pack, and carried it down into the ravine, to a point where he found clear water. Here he left the pack in the fork of a tree, and climbed out to the level forest, to hunt for meat.

The afternoon was far spent and the warmth of the westering sun soon declined. Brink found deer and wild turkey signs in abundance, and inside of the hour he had shot a two-year-old spike-horn buck. He cut out the haunches and packed them back to where he had decided to camp.

With a short-handled ax he carried in his belt he trimmed off the lower branches of a thick-foliaged spruce and, cutting them into small pieces, he laid them crosswise to serve as a bed. Then he unrolled his pack. The snowshoes he hung on the stub of a branch; the heavy, rubber-covered blanket he spread on the spruce boughs, and folded it so that the woolen side would be under him and over him while he slept. Next he started a large fire of dead sticks.

Brink's pack of supplies weighed about fifty pounds. He had three sheet-iron utensils, which telescoped together, a tin cup, a spoon, matches, towel, and soap. His food was carried in canvas sacks of varying sizes, all tightly tied. He had coffee, sugar, salt, and the sugar sack was almost disproportionately large. No flour, no butter, no canned milk. The biggest sack contained pemmican, a composite food of small bulk and great nourishing power. The chief ingredients were meat and nuts. This prepared food Brink had learned to rely upon during long marches in Alaska. His next largest sack contained dried apples. By utilizing, when possible, the game meat of the forest Brink expected this supply to last a long time, possibly until he had run down the wolf.

Like those of an Indian on the march, Brink's needs were few. He prepared his frugal meal, ate it with the relish and gratefulness of a man used to the wilderness. Then before darkness overtook him he cut the fresh deer meat into strips so that it would dry readily.

Twilight found his tasks ended for the day. The melancholy autumn night darkened and stole down upon him, cold and sharp, with threads of cloud across the starry sky. The wind moaned in the black pines above, and seemed to warn of the end of autumn. There was no other sound except the sputter of the campfire.

Brink's enjoyment lay in spreading his horny palms to the genial heat of the red coals. His attitude was one of repose and serenity. If there was sadness about his lonely figure, it was something of which he had no conscious thought. Brink had only dim remembrance of home and family, vague things far back in the past. He had never loved a woman. He had lived apart from men, aloof even when the accident of life and travel had thrown him into camps or settlements. Once he had loved a dog. Seldom did his mind dwell on the past, and then only in relation to some pursuit or knowledge that came to him from the contiguity of the present task.

He liked the loneliness, the wildness, the solitude. He seemed
to be part of them. When a very young boy he had been forced by
a stepmother to hate a house. As a child he had been punished at
the table, and never in his life afterward could he outgrow hate of
a dining room and the fear that had been instilled into his
consciousness.

Night settled down black, with but few stars showing through
the gathering clouds. Listening and watching and feeling were
sensorial habits with Brink. Rain or snow breathed on the chill
wind. He hailed the possibility of either with satisfaction. It was
through the snow that he meant to track Old Gray to his last lair.
When the heat of the fire died out Brink went to his bed, rolled in
the blanket, and at once fell asleep.

The cold, raw dawn found him stirring. A blanket of cloud had
prevented a white frost on the grass, but there glistened a film of
ice on the brook. As the sun came up it brightened a blue sky,
mostly clear. The drift of the thin clouds was from the southwest,
and they were traveling fast.

Before the sun had warmed out the shade of the canyon,
Brink, with pack on his back and rifle in hand, had taken up Old
Gray's trail. It was easy to follow. The wolf showed a preference
for the open canyon, and in many places left plain imprints in the
sand. The canyon, running away from the rim, deepened and
widened; and its disconnected pools of water at last became a
running stream. Elk and deer and turkeys filed before Brink;
likewise scattered bands of cattle and an occasional bunch of wild
horses.

Evidently the great wolf was not losing time to place distance
between him and his last kill. Brink found no more sign of his
evincing interest in any tracks. About noon, by which time Brink
had trailed the animal fully ten miles down the canyon, seldom
losing the tracks for long, Old Gray took to an intersecting canyon, rough-walled and brushy, and soon he went up into the
rocks. It took Brink all afternoon to find where the wolf had lain,
but Brink would gladly have spent days for such a triumph.

"Aha, you old gray devil," he soliloquized, as he bent his gaze
on a snug retreat under shelving rocks, where showed the be-
traying impress of feet and body of the wolf. "So you have to

sleep an' rest, huh? Wal, I reckon you can't get along without killin' an' eatin' too. Old Gray, you're bound to leave tracks, an' I'll find them."

Brink camped that night under the cliff where Old Gray had slept the day before. Next day he spent much time finding tracks along the water course in this narrow canyon, and succeeding ones that led off to the west. This canyon soon opened out into grassy ovals that appeared to be parks for elks. Brink surprised a herd of eleven, two bulls with enormous spread of antlers, a young bull, several cow elks, and four calves. They trooped up the canyon, trampling the trails and sandy spots. Brink kept on, feeling sure that he had the general direction Old Gray had adopted. This held to the west and slightly northward, which course led toward the wildest country in that section, deep canyon, rough buttes, and matted jungles of pine saplings. Here, according to information Brink had obtained from the cowboys, ranged the last of the timber wolves known to exist in Arizona. It was Brink's conviction that Old Gray knew the country well.

The band of elks soon climbed out of the canyon. Beyond that point the bare spots showed only old tracks of game. At length Brink came to a beaver dam; and on the very edge of it, deep in the wet mud, showed the unmistakable tracks of the giant wolf. Brink had another of those strange thrills, an inward leaping of blood, somehow savage. From that point Old Gray's tracks showed in the wet places up and down the banks of the narrow ponds of water. He had been vastly curious about these dams and mounds erected by the beaver. Everywhere he left tracks. But Brink could not find any sign of the wolf's catching a beaver unawares. The beaver of this colony had been at work that night cutting the aspen trees and dragging boughs and sections of trunks under the water.

Sunset came before Brink had found a track of the wolf leading away from that park. Still, he made camp satisfied with the day. Any day in which he found a single fresh track of this wolf was indeed time well spent. Unless he were extremely lucky, he must lose the trail for days. His hope was that he might keep the general direction Old Gray had taken until the snow began to fall. So far his hope had been more than fulfilled.

The night was clearer and colder than the preceding ones, yet there were thin, ragged clouds sweeping up out of the southwest, and a moaning wind that whined of storm. Late October without rain or snow was most unusual for that latitude. Brink camped near the beaver dam, and the cold windy darkness found him snug in his blanket. During the night he was awakened by a yelp of coyotes, and later by a pattering of sleet on the dry brush. A black cloud was scudding across the sky. It passed with the threatening storm. Morning broke brighter than ever. He began to fear wet weather had been sidetracked indefinitely. But after all there was no good in his being impatient. If he lost Old Gray's trail on dry ground, sooner or later he would find it again. This three-hundred-mile strip of comparatively low country was the winter range of the great wolf. He had a taste for young cattle. It was unlikely that he would go back into the high altitude of his summer range in the New Mexico mountains.

Brink's good luck persisted. He discovered Old Gray's tracks leading up out of the canyon. The direction then was all he could hope for at present, because, naturally, he expected to lose the trail on the hard and dry ridge tops. He did lose it. All signs of the wolf vanished. But Brink had ascertained that Old Gray had traveled almost straight toward the rough country to the northwest. Therefore Brink zig-zagged the ridges and canyons for three days without a sign of his quarry's movements. He wondered if the wolf had made a kill during this period. He traveled into a cut-up country of deep canyons and rock ridges, overgrown with heavy forest. He saw no more elk or bear signs, but deer tracks became as plentiful as cattle tracks in a corral.

Late on the afternoon of that third day, as Brink was hunting for a suitable camp, he came to an open glade in the pine forest. In the center of it was a pond of surface water about an acre in size. Deer tracks both old and fresh were numerous. Brink, after deciding the water was safe to drink, deposited his pack in a likely camp spot amid a thicket of pine saplings, and started to walk round the pond. Before he had gone halfway he encountered wolf tracks, made the night before. They were loafer marks, but not Old Gray's.

"Wal, wolf tracks cross each other on any range," decided

Brink. "Reckon I'll take to these. . . . Ahuh. There's been a couple of loafers here, an' one of them has a bad foot. Been in a trap, mebbe."

Brink made camp leisurely. He was getting into wolf country. The sunset shone ominously overcast and threatening. The temperature had moderated and the feeling of frost gave way to dampness. Brink cleared a space in the pine thicket, and erected a shelving lean-to on the windward side. Under this he made his bed. His next move was to gather a goodly store of dry firewood and to pile it under the shelter. After that he cooked his meal, and this time, to his satisfaction, he broiled a young turkey he had shot the day before.

Night settled down like a black blanket, starless and gloomy. The wind moaned louder than usual. Brink soliloquized that the wind was warning Old Gray to leave the country before the fatal snow fell. Brink enjoyed this meal more than any heretofore on this hunt. The wild scene, the somber tarn, the menacing solitude were all to his liking. He was settling into his routine. Contrary to his custom on the preceding nights, he sat up a long time, and whether he had his face to the fire or his back, his palms were always spread to the comforting heat. Brink looked and listened with more than usual attention during this vigil beside the campfire. It appeared that the wind grew more raw, damper.

"Rain or snow sure," he muttered, and the note boded ill to certain wild denizens of that forestland.

At length drowsiness made his eyelids heavy and he sought his bed under the shelter of pine boughs. Sleep claimed him. He awakened with a feeling that only a moment had elapsed, but he could tell by the dead campfire how misleading this was. Something had roused him.

Suddenly from the dark forest on the cold wind came the deep, wild bay of a hunting wolf. With a start Brink sat up. A quiver ran over him. How intensely he listened. No other wild sound in nature had such power over him. It seemed as if this bay came from a vague dim past. Again it peeled out, but with a sharper note, not greatly different from that of a hunting hound.

"Loafers trailin' a deer," said Brink. "Two of them, mebbe more."

Again he heard the bays, growing farther away, and another time, quite indistinct. After that the weird moaning solitude of the forest remained undisturbed.

Brink lay back in his blanket, but not to sleep. He would lie awake now for a long while. How that wolf bay brought back memories of the frozen northland. All wolves were of the same species. They loved hot blood. It was their savage instinct to feed ravenously off a still-living victim.

Brink imagined he heard deep low bays back in the forest. Always the wind made the sound for which the eager ears were attuned. And even when he was not listening for any particular sound, the wind deceived with its wild cry of beast, its wail of lost humans, its mourning for the dead, its distant approach to a trampling army.

All the same, Brink again suddenly sat up. "Say, have I got a nightmare?" He turned his ear away from the cold wind, and holding his breath, he listened. Did he hear a bay or a moan in the forest? Long he remained stiff, intent.

The wolves had resorted to a trick Brink knew well. The pack had split into several parts, one of which relayed the deer for a time, driving it round while the others rested. In Brink's experience the trick was common for a pack that had a great leader.

Once again in the succeeding hour Old Gray passed near Brink's camp, ringing out that hoarse cry of hunger for blood. Long after the sound had rolled through the forest to die away, it lingered on his ears. But it did not come again.

Instead, something happened to Brink which sent a tight cold prickle to his skin. It was the touch of soft misty snow on his face. A tiny seeping rustle, almost indistinguishable, fell about him on the brush. Snow. Cloud and wind and atmosphere had combined in the interest of the wolftracker.

III

A lowering gray dawn disclosed the forest mantled in a wet snow, deep enough to cover the ground and burden the trees. The wind had eased somewhat and was colder, which facts augured for clearing weather. Thin broken clouds moved close to the tops of the loftiest pines.

"Wal, reckon it's only a skift," remarked Brink, as his gaze swept the white-carpeted glade, with its round pond of dark water in the center. "But it's snow, an' right here my trackin' begins. If it melts, it'll leave the ground soft. If it doesn't, well an' good."

Brink was singularly happy. The raw dawn with its changed forest-world would have alienated most men, but he was not that kind of a hunter. The Indian summer days were past. The white banner of winter had been unrolled. Moreover, Old Gray had passed in the night, ringing his wild and unearthly voice down the aisles of the forest. Somehow Brink had no doubt that the hoarse hound-like bay belonged to the wolf he was stalking.

"I know his tracks," said Brink, "an' I've heard him yelp. Sooner or later I'll see him. Wal now, that'll be a sight. . . . But I reckon I'm over reachin' this good luck."

A pale light behind the gray clouds in the east marked the rise of the sun. Only a few inches of snow had fallen. As Brink trudged away from his camp, out into the white glade, he was victim to an eagerness and joy extraordinary in a man. But the most driving instinct of his life had been the hunting of animals by the tracks they left. As a boy it had been play; in manhood it had become a means of livelihood; now it was a passion. Therefore he hailed the pure white covering of snow with pleasure and affection.

His educated eyes sought the ground. Here were the tiny footprints of a chipmunk; next the ragged tracks of a squirrel, showing where his tail had dragged; coyote and fox had also visited the pond since the fall of snow. Brink crossed the open glade to enter the forest. A blue jay screeched at him from an oak tree and a red squirrel chattered angrily. Brink passed under a spruce where the little squirrel had already dug for the seed cones he had stored for winter food.

Brink espied the wolf and buck tracks fully fifty yards ahead of him. Soon he stood over them. The tracks had been made before the snow had ceased to fall, yet they were clear enough to be read by the hunter. The buck had been running. Two wolves had been chasing him, but neither was Old Gray. After a long scrutiny of the tracks Brink left them and stalked on deeper into the forest. He crossed the trail of a lynx. What a betrayer of wild beasts was the white snow they loved so well. Brink seemed to read the very thoughts of that prowling hunting cat.

Toward noon the sun came out, lighting up the forest, until it appeared to be an enchanted place of gleaming aisles, of brown-barked trunks and white-burdened branches. Everywhere snow was sliding, slipping, falling from the trees. Rainbows showed through the mist. The aspens with their golden leaves and the oaks with their bronze belied the wintry forest scene. On the snow lay leaves of yellow and red and brown, fallen since the storm. Pine needles were floating down from the lofty pines, and aspen leaves, like butterflies, fluttered in the air. Through the green-and-white canopy overhead showed rifts in the clouds and sky of deep blue. Though the forest was white and cold, autumn yielded reluctantly to winter, squirrels and jays and woodpeckers acclaimed a welcome to the sun.

Brink missed none of the beauty, though his grim task absorbed him. All of the moods of nature were seriously accepted by him. He was a man of the open.

He arrived at last where the buck had reached the end of his tragic race, and by some strange paradox of nature the woodland scene was one of marvelous color and beauty. Over a low swale the pine monarchs towered and the silver spruces sent their exquisite spiral crests aloft. On one side a sheltered aspen thicket still clung tenaciously to its golden fluttering foliage. Maples burned in cerise and magenta and scarlet hues.

Underfoot, however, the beauty of this spot had been marred.

Here the buck had been overtaken, pulled down, torn to pieces, and devoured, even to the cracking of its bones. The antlers, the skull, part of the ragged hide were left, ghastly evidences of the ferocity of that carnage. The snow had been crushed, dragged, wiped, and tracked out, yet there were left vestiges soaked by blood. Coyotes had visited the scene, and these scavengers had quarreled over the bones.

As Brink had seen the beauty of the colorful forest, so now he viewed the record of the tragic balance of nature. The one to him was the same as the other. He did not hate Old Gray for being the leader in this butchery of a gentle forest creature.

"Wal now, I wonder how long he'll trail with this pack of loafers," he soliloquized. "If I was guessin' I'd say not long."

How different from those running wolf tracks he had been following were these leisurely trotting paces that led up to the rough bluffs. Brink calculated they had been made just before dawn. The wolves had gorged. They were heavy and sluggish. At this moment they would be sleeping off that orgy of blood and meat. Brink reached the foot of a very rugged butte, not so high as the adjoining one, Black Butte, which dominated the landscape, but of a nature which rendered it almost insurmountable for man. Manzanita and live oak choked all the interstices between the rugged broken fragments of cliff. Obstacles, however, never daunted Brink.

Brink strode on, keen to find the second trail of wolves, and to settle absolutely the question as to Old Gray's presence with this marauding band of loafers. There might be two great-voiced wolves on the range. But the track would decide. When at length he encountered the trail he was seeking, abruptly at the top of a low ridge, he stood motionless, gazing with rapt, hard eyes. Two loafers besides Old Gray had chased the buck along here. So there were at least five in the pack.

"I was right," said Brink, with a deep breath. Old Gray's tracks in the snow were identical with those he left in the dust. Yet how vastly more potent to Brink. For snow was the medium by which he had doomed the great timber wolf. Without snow to betray him Old Gray would have been as safe as the eagles in their trackless air. This, then, was the moment of exceeding significance to Brink. Here again the test of endurance. All the hunters who had failed on Old Gray's trail had matched their intelligence with his cunning instinct. The hounds that had chased the wolf had failed because the fleet and powerful animal had outdistanced them and run out of the country. But Brink did not work like other hunters. His idea was the result of long stalking of wild game. And this moment when he gazed down into the huge tracks in the snow was one in which he felt all the tremendous advantage in his favor. Somewhere in a rocky recess or cave Old Gray was now sleeping after the chase and the gorge, unaware of his relentless and inevitable human foe. But Brink was in possession of facts beyond the ken of any wild creature. Perhaps his passion was to prove the superiority of man over beast.

Without a word he set off on the trail so plain in the snow, and as he stalked along he sought to read through those telltale tracks the speed and strength of the buck, the cunning and endurance of the wolves, and all the wild nature suggested therein. Through level open forest, down ridge and over swale, into thickets of maple and aspen, across parks where bleached grass glistened out of the snow, he strode on with the swing of a mountaineer. He did not tire. His interest had mounted until the hours seemed moments.

Cougar tracks, deer tracks, turkey tracks crossed the trail he was following. It swung in a ragged circle, keeping clear of rocks, canyons, and the windfalls where running would be difficult. Brink passed three relay stations where resting and running wolves had met; and at the last of these all five wolves took the trail of the doomed buck. They had chased him all night. Their baying had kept all of them within hearing of each other. The resting relay had cunningly cut in or across at times, thus to drive the buck out of a straightaway race.

Laying aside pack and snowshoes, with rifle in hand he essayed the ascent. Part of the time over rock and the rest through the brush he made his way, wholly abandoning the direction of the wolf trail.

After an hour of prodigious labor Brink reached the base of a low bulging wall of rock, marked by cracks and fissures. The snow was somewhat deeper at this altitude and afforded a perfect medium in which to track animals. Bobcat, lynx, their lairs. And then, around on the windward cougar, fox, and coyote had climbed the bluff. There Brink found the trail of the loafers. The difference between their sagacity and that of the other wild beasts was indicated by their selection of the windy side of the bluff. Brink tracked them toward the dark hole of a den. Upon reaching the aperture he was not in the least surprised to see Old Gray's tracks leading out. The other loafers were still in the cave. But Old Gray had gotten a scent on the wind, perhaps even in his sleep, and he had departed alone.

"Wal, you bloody loafers can sleep, for all we care," soliloquized Brink. "Old Gray an' me have work."

Somehow Brink took exceeding pleasure in the fact that the great wolf had been too cunning to be holed up by a hunter. This was just what Brink had anticipated. Old Gray was beginning to show the earmarks of a worthy antagonist. Brink thought he was going to have respect and admiration for the loafer.

Brink knelt to study the tracks, and did not soon come to a conclusion.

"Reckon he scented me," he said finally. "But I wonder if he suspects he's bein' tracked. . . . Wal now, when he learns that."

The wolf tracker clambered around over the slabs of rock and under the cliffs until he found where Old Gray had started to descend the bluff. Then Brink retraced his steps, finding the return as easy as the climb had been hard. Once more donning his pack, he set out, keeping to the forest where it edged on the rising ground. Before he had gone a mile he encountered Old Gray's big tracks.

Here Brink sustained a genuine surprise. He had made sure the wolf would head straight for the northwest, instinctively making for the wildest country. But instead the tracks struck into the woods straight as a beeline, and no more were they leisurely.

"Huh. The son-of-a-gun. If he circles I'll sure take off my hat to him," said Brink.

With his mountaineer's stride Brink set off through open forest, downhill, over a few inches of snow, making four miles an hour. Brink did not circle. Vastly curious did the hunter become. It looked as if the wolf was making a shortcut for somewhere. If

he kept up this course he would soon cross his back trail. Perhaps
that was just what Old Gray had in mind. Still, if he suspected he
was being pursued, why had he not circled long ago to find what
was following his tracks? Brink reflected that there was no absolute telling what a wild animal might do. He had trailed grizzly
bears in the snow, and found they had abruptly turned uphill a
little way, then had gone back, closer and closer to the lower
trail, at last to lie and wait for him in ambush.

A wolf, especially a great loafer like Old Gray, rather enjoyed
such a short chase as men and dogs gave him. He could run right
away from them. His chief resource was his speed. But Old Gray
had not heard the bay of hounds or yell of men or crack of iron-
shod hoof on stone. He was very probably suspicious that something new hung in the wind.

Brink warmed to the pursuit, both physically and in his spirit.
By and by the thing would narrow down to the supreme test
between man and beast. This for Brink was just getting underway; for the wolf it was the beginning of a period of uncertainty.

Toward the middle of the afternoon the sun came out fitfully,
warming the glades with color, if not with heat. The snow soft-
ened to the extent that at the bottom of Old Gray's deep tracks it
grew dark and wet. The wind lulled, too. Brink did not want a
warm spell, even for a day. Still, come what might, he believed,
even if the snow did melt, the ground would stay soft until another storm. November had arrived, and at that height of land
winter had come.

Old Gray kept to his straight course until halted by the trail he
and his loafer allies and Brink and the buck had left in the snow.
Here Old Gray had stood in his tracks. Brink imagined he could
see the great gray brute, awakening to the scent and trail of man,
and their relation to him. Old Gray had crossed and recrossed
the trail, trotted forward and back, and then he had left it to
continue the straight course at precisely the same gait.

This nonplussed the hunter, who had calculated that the wolf
would deliberately set out to find what was tracking him. But
there seemed nothing sure here, except that the beast had tarried
at this crossing to smell the man tracks.

Brink took comfort in the assurance that the future trail would prove everything. He trudged on as before. A cold drab twilight halted him in dense forest, mostly spruce. He selected one so thick of foliage that the snow had not even whitened the brown mat of needles and cones under it. And here he camped. Making fire, melting snow, and roasting strips of deer meat occupied him till dark, and then he sought his fragrant bed under the spruce.

Next day it snowed intermittently, drizzly and mistily, in some places half filling Old Gray's tracks. The wolf, soon after leaving the spot where he had crossed the old tracks, had taken to a running lope and had sheered to the east. The hunter had signalized this change by a grim, "Ahuh."

Brink was seven days in covering the hundred or so miles that Old Gray had run during the day and the night after he had left the den on the bluff. He had run close to the New Mexico line, almost to the foothills of the White Mountains. It beat any performance Brink could recall in his experience. He must have covered the distance in eighteen hours or less; and in his wolf mind, Brink was absolutely certain, he believed he had traveled far beyond pursuit. For then he had abandoned the straight running course for one of a prowling, meandering hunt. But deer tracks were scarce and he had to go down into the range country for a kill.

Three days more of travel for Brink brought him to the spot where Old Gray had pulled down a yearling and had eaten his fill. Coyotes had left the carcass in such condition that Brink could not tell anything from it, except the mere presence and its meaning.

"Nine days behind," soliloquized Brink. "But it has showed some, an' I reckon I'm playin' on velvet."

Even the lowland cattle ranges were covered with a thin mantle of snow. Toward the foothills it deepened. Mount Ord and Old Baldy showed pure white in the distance.

Brink strode on, wed to those wolf tracks. Old Gray left a gruesome record of his night marauds. How bold he was. Yet wide apart indeed were his kills. He would travel miles away from the scene of his last attack, up into the high country, where deep snow made it impossible for hounds to follow. Brink found tracks of both dogs and hunters that had taken his trail, only to abandon it. Old Gray had the spirit of a demon. He wrote his size, ferocity, cunning, age, strength, speed, character, and history in his tracks. He was a lone wolf in all the tremendous significance of that name. For him there was no safety in numbers. He ran alone, bold, defiant, vicious. It seemed to Brink that he killed out of wild love for shedding blood. He chased stock to the very corral gates of some rancher, and in one instance he killed a calf in a pasture. His tracks showed that he played at the game of killing. Like a playful dog he cavorted beside his intended victim.

It was impossible for Brink to believe otherwise than that this wolf ran at large with an instinct only second in wildness to the one of killing to eat. Not self-preservation in a sense of aloofness to ranches. He risked his life many times out of sheer wild confidence in his mastery of the ranges. He was lord of that region from mountain to desert. Many years he had been hunted. How infinitely more he must have known of hunters than they knew of him. Man was his enemy. The heritage of hatred, descended from the primal days of mastodon, saber-toothed tiger, and giant wolf, in their antagonism to the arboreal ape that was the parent of man, must have throbbed strong and fierce in Old Gray's heart. In no other way could Brink read the signs of the wolf tracks. He flaunted his wolfness in the faces of mankind. There was a terrible egotism in his assurance of his superiority. Fear of man he had never yet known. Apparently he was as secure as a swift-winged eagle that kept to the peaks.

Brink bided his time and kept to his methodical trailing. So far all the favorable breaks of fortune had been his. The gradual fall of snow, layer by layer, instead of a sudden heavy blizzard, was especially good for Brink and bad for Old Gray. Winter had come, and snow lay everywhere, even to the slopes of the low country. The deer and turkey had moved down out of the high forests.

Some time late in December the hunter struck Old Gray's trail in fresh snow that had fallen the day before. The wolf was headed down-country and the tracks had been made in the night.

"So I've ketched up with you," ejaculated the hunter. "An'

that without follerin' you hard. Wal, I reckon you'll soon know I'm trackin' you."

Brink left the trail, and journeyed half a day down into the range country, and halted at a little hamlet called Pine. Here he replenished his store of provisions. His sack of pemmican he had not yet touched. That he had reserved for the strenuous last lap of this strange race. The kindly and inquisitive Mormons of the village took Brink for a trapper, and assured him there were not many fur bearing animals left.

"Wal, if you tracked round much as I do you'd be surprised how many animals are left," replied Brink dryly, and went his way.

What Brink was ready for now was to strike the trail Old Gray would break after a kill, when he was making for a high lair to rest and sleep during the day. Brink tracked himself back to the point where he had left the trail of the loafer, and here he camped. During the succeeding week he traveled perhaps fifty miles to and fro across country, striking Old Gray's tracks several times, heading both ways. The morning came then, as much by reason of Brink's good judgment as the luck that favored him, when he fell upon a fresh trail, only a few hours old.

The snow lay six inches in depth. By the time Brink had climbed out of the cedars into the pines the snow was three times as deep. Old Gray had navigated it as easily as if it had been grass. Brink trudged slowly, but did not take recourse to his snowshoes.

The winter day was bright, cold and keen, though not biting, and the forest was a solemn, austere world of white and brown and green. Not a bird or a living creature crossed Brink's vision, and tracks of animals were few and far between. It so happened that there was no wind, an absolutely dead calm, something rather unusual for high altitude at this season. The section of the country contained almost as much park area as forest. It was easy going despite a gradual ascent.

Old Gray traveled at least eighteen miles up and down, mostly up, before he took to a rocky brushy recess. Brink considered the distance at least that far, because he had walked six hours since he struck the trail.

Taking the general direction of Old Gray's tracks, Brink left them and making a wide detour he approached on the opposite side of this fastness. He encountered no tracks leading out on that side. The wolf was there, or had been there when Brink arrived. Naturally he wanted the wolf to see him. There was no sense in trying to surprise the loafer. After a careful survey of the thicketed ridge he chose the quickest way up and scaled it.

As Brink swept sharp sight down over the jumble of boulders and vine-matted thickets, to the saddle of the ridge where it joined another, he espied a gray trotting wolf shape.

It was a quarter of a mile distant. Yet did his eyes deceive him? Not that he might not see a wolf, but that its size was incredible.

Brink let out a stentorian yell, which pealed on the cold air like a blast. The wolf leaped as if he had been shot at. But he did not run. He looked back and up. Then he trotted, nervously and hurriedly, it seemed, peering all around and especially behind, until he attained a bare rise of ridge.

There he stood motionless, gazing up at Brink. But for the background of snow the wolf would have appeared white. He was gray, with a black slash on his neck. Even at that distance Brink clearly made out the magnificence of him, the unparalleled wildness, the something that could be defined only as an imperious and contemptuous curiosity.

Brink uttered another yell, more stentorian than the first, concatenated and mounting, somewhat similar to the Comanche war whoop, which he had heard in all its appalling significance. Brink meant this yell to serve a purpose, so that Old Gray would recognize it again; yet all the same it was an expression of his own passion, a challenge, a man's incomprehensible menace to a hereditary foe.

Old Gray raised his front feet, an action of grace that lifted his great gray shape into moving relief against the background of snow, and then, dropping back on all fours, he trotted up the ridge, looking backward.

IV

Brink had long fortified himself to meet the grueling test of this chase—the most doubtful time—the weeks of cold tracking—the ever-increasing distance between him and the great wolf. For when Old Gray espied him that morning he took to real flight. Suspicious of this strange pursuer without horse or dog, he left the country. But as range and mountain, valley and dale, canyon and ridge were all snow covered, he left a record of his movements. His daily and nightly tracks were open pages for Brink to read.

Five weeks, six, seven—then Brink lost count of time. The days passed, and likewise the miles under his snowshoes. Spruce and cedar and pinon, thicket of pine and shelving ledge of rock, afforded him shelter at night. Sunshine or snowstorm were all the same to him. When the fresh snow covered Old Gray's tracks, which sometimes happened, Brink with uncanny sagacity and unerring instinct eventually found them again. Old Gray could not spend the winter in a cave, as did the hibernating bears. The wolf had to eat; his nature demanded the kill—hot blood and flesh. Thus his very beastliness, his ferocity, and his tremendous activity doomed him in this contest for life with a man creature of a higher species.

His tracks led back to the Cibeque, down into the Tonto Basin, across Hell-Gate, and east clear to the Sierra Ancas, then up the bare snow-patched ridges of the Basin, into the chaparral of juniper and manzanita and mescal, on up the rugged Mazatal range; over it and west to the Red Rock country, then across the pine-timbered upland to the San Francisco Peaks, around them to the north and down the gray bleak reaches of the desert to the Little Colorado, and so back to the wild fastnesses where that winding river had its source in the White Mountains.

What a bloody record Old Gray left. It seemed pursuit had redoubled his thirst for slaughter, his diabolical defiance of the

ranches, his magnificent boldness. Perhaps he was not yet sure
that there was a tireless step on his trail. But Brink believed the
wolf had sensed his enemy, even though he could not scent him.
This conviction emanated from Brink's strange egotism. Yet the
wolf had roused to no less than a frenzy of killing, over a wider
territory than ever before. Far and wide as he wandered he yet
kept within night raid of the cattle range. He must have known
the vast country as well as the thicket where he had been
whelped.

The time came when the ceaseless activity of the loafer began
to tell on even his extraordinary endurance. He slowed up; he
killed less frequently; he traveled shorter distances; he kept more
to the south slopes and nearer the rangeland. All of which might
have attested to the gradual lulling of his suspicions. The greatest
of wild animals could not help forget, or at least grow less cautious, when safety day by day wore fear into oblivion. Nevertheless, Brink could never satisfy himself that Old Gray did not
think his tracks were haunted.

Thus tracker and fugitive drew closer together. The man,
driven by an unquenchable spirit, seemed to gather strength from
toil and loneliness and the gradual overtaking of his quarry. The
wolf, limited to instinct and the physical power endowed by nature, showed in his tracks an almost imperceptible, yet inevitable
decline of strength. Any wolf would wear slower and lighter
through a hard winter.

The sun worked higher in the heavens and the days grew
longer. The thin crust of snow in exposed places slowly dis-
integrated until it no longer supported the weight of a wild cat or
coyote, deer or wolf. This was the crowning treachery of the
snow.

Why did Old Gray stand sometimes in the early morning, leaving telltale tracks on ridges and high points? Why did he circle
back and cross his old trail? Brink knew, and the long trail was
no more monotonous. The dawn came, too, when he knew the
wolf had spied him. That day changed life for Old Gray. He
proceeded on what Brink called a serious even track. No burst of
speed. No racing out of the country. No running amuck among
the cattle, leaving a red tinge on his trail.

Brink halted at sunset under a brushy foothill, dark and shaggy against the cold rose sky. The air was still, and tight with frost. Brink led out his stentorian yell that pealed like a blast of thunder out over the snow-locked scene. The echo clapped back from the hill and rolled away, from cliff to forest wall, and died hollowly in the distance. If Old Gray hid within two miles of where Brink stood, that ominous knell must have reached his ears. Brink, in his mind's eye, saw the great beast start, and raise his sharp, wild head to listen, and tremble with instinct which had come down to him from the ages. No day since the advent of man on earth had ever seen the supremacy of beast.

The king of the gray wolves became a hunted creature. He shunned the rangelands where the cattle nipped the bleached grass out of the thinning snow. At night, on the cedar slopes, he stalked deer, and his kills grew infrequent. At dawn he climbed to the deep snows of the uplands, and his periods of sleep waxed shorter. Brink's snowshoes were as seven-league boots. The snow was nothing to him. But Old Gray labored through the drifts. The instinct of the wild animal prompts it to react to a perilous situation in a way that most always is right. Safety for the intelligent wolf did lie away from the settlements, the ranches, and the lowlands, far up in the snowy ridges. Many a pack of hounds and band of horsemen Old Gray had eluded in the deep snows. In this case, however, he had something to reckon with far beyond his ken.

Hunger at length drove Old Gray farther down the south slopes, where he stalked deer and failed to kill as often as he killed. Time passed, and the night came when the wolf missed twice on chances that, not long ago, would have been play for him. He never attempted to trail another deer. Instead he tracked turkeys to their roosts and skulked in the brush until at dawn they alighted. Not often was his cunning rewarded. Lower still he was forced to go, into the canyons, and on the edge of the lowlands, where like any common coyote he chased rabbits. And then his kills became few and far between. Last and crowning proof of his hunger and desperation he took to eating porcupines. How the mighty had fallen. Brink read this tragedy in the tracks in the snow.

For weeks Brink had expected to overtake Old Gray and drive
him from his day's lair. This long-hoped for event at length took
place at noon on a cold, bright day, when Brink suddenly espied
the wolf on the summit of a high ridge, silhouetted against the
pale sky. Old Gray stood motionless, watching him. Brink burst
out with his savage yell. The wolf might have been a statue, for
all the reaction he showed.

"Huh. Reckon my eyes are tired of this snow glare," muttered
Brink, "but I ain't blind yet. That's sure Old Gray."

The black slash at the neck identified the notorious loafer;
otherwise Brink could not have made certain. Old Gray appeared
ragged and gaunt. The hunter shaded his eyes with his hand and
looked long at his coveted quarry. Man and beast gazed at each
other across the wide space. For Brink it was a moment of most
extraordinary exultation. He drew a great breath and expelled it
in a yell that seemed to pierce the very rocks. Old Gray dropped
his head and slunk down out of sight behind the ridge.

On each succeeding day, sooner or later, Brink's approach
would rout the wolf out of covert in rocks or brush, always high
up in places that commanded a view of the back trail. The pursuit would continue then, desperate on the part of the wolf,
steady and relentless on that of the man, until nightfall. Then
Brink would halt in the best place which offered, and, cutting
green wood, he would lay pieces close together on the snow and
build his little fire of dead sticks or bark upon them. Here he
would cook his meager meal. His supplies were low, but he knew
they would hold out. And Old Gray would have to spend the
night hunting. Not one night in four would he kill meat.

It was early one morning, crisp and clear, cracking with frost,
when the sunlight glinted on innumerable floating particles of ice
in the air. The snow was soft and deep. Only in shady places on
the north side of rocks, ridges, or hills did the crust hold. Blue
jays screeched and red squirrels chattered. The sun felt warm on
Brink's cheek. Somehow he knew that spring had come. But
here, on the solemn, forested heights, winter held undisputed
away. Old Gray had traveled for days along the south slopes of
the Blue Range; with the strange instinct of the wild he had

climbed through a pass, and now he was working down on the north side.

Far below Brink saw the black belt of forest, brightened by the open white senecas, little bare parks peculiar to the region. He would see and hear the tumbling streams, now released from their ice-locked fastnesses. Lower still stretched the rangeland, a patchwork of white and black. The air held a hint of spring. Brink smelled it, distinguished it from the cold tang of spruce and pine, and the faint fragrance of wood smoke.

Old Gray was not far ahead. His dragging tracks were fresh. Long had it been since he had stepped lightly and quickly over thin crust. And in the soft snow he waded. He did not leave four-foot tracks, but ragged furrows, sometimes as deep as his flanks.

The spruce and fir were dwarfed in size and few in number, growing isolated from one another. Below these straggling trees stood out patches and clumps of forest. Brink plodded on wearily, every step a torture. Only the iron of his will, somehow projected into his worn muscles and bones, kept him nailed to that trail. His eyes had begun to trouble him. He feared snow-blindness, that bane of the mountaineer. His mind seemed to have grown old, steeped in monotonous thoughts of wolf and track.

Upon rounding a thicket of spear-pointed spruce Brink came to a level white bench, glistening like a wavy floor of diamonds in the sunlight.

Halfway across this barren mantle of snow a gray beast moved slowly. Old Gray. He was looking back over his shoulder, wild of aspect, sharp in outline. The distance was scarce three hundred yards, a short range for Brink's unerring aim. This time he did not yell. Up swept his rifle and froze to his shoulder. His keen eye caught the little circular sight and filled it with gray.

But Brink could not pull the trigger. A tremendous shock passed over him. It left him unstrung. The rifle wavered out of alignment with the dragging wolf. Brink lowered the weapon.

"What's come—over me?" he rasped out, in strange amaze. Weakness? Exhaustion? Excitement? Despite a tumult in his breast, and a sudden numbness of his extremities, he repudiated each of these queries. The truth held aloof until Old Gray halted out there on the rim of the bench and gazed back at his human foe.

"I'll kill you with my bare hands," yelled Brink, in terrible earnestness.

Not until the ultimatum burst from his lips did the might of passion awake in him. Then for a moment he was a man possessed with demons. He paid in emotion for the months of strain on body and mind. That spell passed. It left him rejuvenated.

"Old Gray, if I shot you it'd prove nothin," he called, grimly, as if the wolf could understand. "It's man ag'in wolf."

And he threw his rifle aside in the snow, where it sank out of sight. As Brink again strode forward, with something majestic and implacable in his mien, Old Gray slunk out of sight over the rim of the snow bench. When the tracker reached the edge of this declivity the wolf had doubled the distance between them. Downhill he made faster time. Brink stood a moment to watch him. Old Gray had manifestly worn beyond the power to run, but on places where the snow crust upheld his weight he managed a weary trot. Often he looked back over his shoulder. These acts were performed spasmodically, at variance with his other movements, and betrayed him victim to terror. Uncertainty had ceased. There was a monster on his trail. Man. His hereditary foe.

Brink had to zigzag down snowy slopes, because it was awkward and sometimes hazardous to attempt abrupt descents on snowshoes. Again the loafer drew out of sight. Brink crossed and recrossed the descending tracks. Toward the middle of the afternoon the mountain slope merged into a level and more thickly timbered country. Yet the altitude was too great for dense forest. It was a wilderness of white and black, snowy ridges, valleys, swales, and senecas interspersed among strips of forest, patches and thickets of spruce, deep belts of timber.

By the strange perversity of instinct Old Gray chose the roughest travel, the darkest thicket, the piece of wood most thickly obstructed by windfalls. Brink avoided many of these sections of the trail; sometimes he made shortcuts. He did not see the wolf again that day, though he gained upon him. Night intervened.

In the cold, gray dawn, when the ghostly spruces were but shadows, Brink strode out on the trail. There was now a difference in his stride. For months he had tramped along, reserving his strength, slowly, steadily, easily without hurry or impatience. That restraint constituted part of his greatness as a tracker. But now he had the spring of a deer-stalker in his step. The weariness and pang of muscle and bone had strangely fled.

Old Gray's tracks now told only one story. Flight. He did not seek to hunt meat. He never paused to scent at trail of deer or cat. His tracks seemed to tell of his wild yet sure hope of soon eluding his pursuer.

Before noon Brink again came in sight of the wolf, and did not lose it except when declivities or obstruction came between them. Old Gray passed the zone of snow crust. He walked and waded and wallowed through the deep white drifts. How significant that he gazed backward more than forward. Whenever he espied Brink he forced a harder gait that kept the hunter from gaining.

All afternoon the distance between them varied from four to five hundred yards. At intervals Brink let out his stentorian yell, that now rang with a note of victory. Always it made Old Gray jerk as if he had been stung from behind. It forced him into an action that would have terminated in a leap forward had his strength answered to his wild spirit. Then soon again his strained efforts would sink back to the weary drag through the snow.

When the chill mountain dusk fell Brink abandoned the pursuit for the day and made camp under a thick-branched, tent-like spruce, his favorite kind of place. Here he had to cut the first drooping branches, so that he could obtain head room under the canopy. A rousing fire soon melted the snow down to the ground. It was significant that he broke his rule of eating sparingly. This meal was almost a hearty one. Likewise he returned to his old habit of sitting and standing before the fire, watching the blaze, the red embers, the growing opal ashes. He had no thought aside from the wolf and the surroundings that insulated them. The moon shone brightly down on a cold, solemn mountain world. No wind, no cry of bird or beast, no sound except the crackling of the dying fire. He seemed a part of the wilderness. When he rolled in his blanket he heaved a deep breath, almost a sigh, and muttered, "Tomorrow, mebbe—or sure the day after."

The next morning was not half gone before Brink caught up with Old Gray. The wolf had not eaten or slept or rested, yet he had traveled scarcely ten miles. But he had lagged along. At sight of the hunter he exhibited the panic of a craven dog. The action of his accelerated pace was like the sinking of his body forward. Then he went on, and for long kept even with his pursuer.

The time came, however, when Brink began almost impercep-tibly to gain. Brink's practiced eye saw it long before the wolf. But at length Old Gray looked back so often that he bumped into brush and trees. Then he seemed hurried into a frenzy which did not in the least augment his speed. He knew his pursuer was gaining, yet even that could not spur his jaded body to greater effort.

The sun set; twilight fell gray and black; dusk mantled the wintry scene; then night followed imperceptibly. But this night the wolf tracker did not abandon the tracks.

Above the cold white peaks a brightness illumined the dark blue sky. It had strange power over the shadows below. They changed, retreated, lightened. The moon rose above the moun-tain and flooded that lonely solitude with radiance.

The black spear-pointed spruces stood motionless, weird and spectral on the moon-blanched snow. The cliffs loomed gray and obscure. Dead bleached trees shone ghastly in the moonlight. Night, moon, snow, winter, solitude, nature seemed to grip all in a lifeless vice.

But two objects wound slowly across the white spaces. How infinitesimal against that background. An animal pursued by a human. Two atoms endowed with strange spirit down upon which the moon shone in seeming pity.

The hours wore on. The moon soared. The scene changed. A wind mourned out of the north. The spectral spruces swayed against the blue sky. A muffled roar of slipping avalanche rose from a long distance and died away. On the level reaches of snow that bright eye above could see the slow diminishing of space between man and wolf. Five hundred yards—four hundred—three hundred.

The shadows of peaks and cliffs and trees gradually turned to the other side. The moon slanted through the hours, paled and waned, and slanted behind the range. Through the gray gloom and obscurity, pursued and pursuer wended a deviating way, indifferent to Nature and elements and darkness or light.

Dawn was at hand, gray, mysterious, strange, beautiful, as it had broken millions of times in the past. The earth was turning on its axis. The sun was on the rise. In that mountain solitude there brooded the same life and death as had always been there. Five hundred thousand years before this hour the same drama of man and beast might have been enacted.

Yet hardly the same. The cave man fought the cave bear and saber-toothed tiger and giant wolf only to survive. Self-preservation was the primal law. Now only the instinct of the wolf remained the same.

Before man lived in caves he was arboreal; he descended from his abode in trees to walk on his feet and work with his hands, and fight. Through the dim dark ages forward, his instinct, reason, intelligence developed. In his four-footed foes these qualities remained static.

The meaning of that revolved vaguely in Brink's somber thoughts. But this wolf tracker had no clear conception of the great passion which possessed his soul. When daylight came and he saw Old Gray dragging his gaunt body through the snow, now only a hundred paces distant, he awoke the cold mocking echoes with his terrible yell. And the shock of it appeared to send the wolf staggering off his feet. When the sun tipped the snow-rimmed mountain far above, to bathe the valley in morning glory, Brink was gaining inch by inch.

The end of the long chase was not far off. Old Gray's heart had broken. It showed in every step he made. Sagging and lame, he struggled through the snow; he wove along and fell and got up to drive his worn-out body to yet another agony. Seldom he gazed back now. When he did turn he showed to Brink a wolf face that seemed extraordinarily to express the unalterable untameableness of the wild. That spirit was fear. If in that instant Old Gray could have suddenly become endowed with all his former strength, he would never have turned to kill his age-long enemy.

Brink's endurance was almost spent. Yet he knew he would last, and his stride did not materially lessen. Sometimes a haze overspread his eyes and black spots danced in his sight. The pangs of his body were innumerable and almost unbearable. Yet he went on.

What was in his mind? What had driven him to these super-human exertions? The remote past was with him surely, though he had no consciousness of that. The very marrow of his bones seemed to gather and swell and throb in readiness to burst into a mighty thrill when he had proved that he was stronger than this beast. Often he scooped up a handful of snow to put into his dry mouth. His heart labored heavily with sharp pains, and there was a drumming in his ears. Inch by inch he gained. But he stifled his strange exultation.

The battle must go to the strong—to prove the survival of the fittest. Nature had developed this wolf to the acme of perfection. But more merciless than nature was life, for life had weakness. Man shared this weakness with all animals, but man possessed some strange, sustaining, unutterable, ineradicable power. Brink relied upon it. Old Gray was yielding to it.

The last hour grew appalling. Brink felt on the verge of col-lapse. Old Gray's movements were those of a dying creature. The hunter did not gain any more. Over white benches, through spruce thickets, under the windfalls man and beast remained only a few paces apart. Brink could have knocked the wolf over with a club. But he only stretched out a great clutching hand, as if the next moment he could close it round that black-slashed neck.

The solemn day advanced. And from the last slope of moun-tain in the rangeland below spread out gray and green in the habiliments of spring. The long winter was over. Cattle dotted the pasture lands.

Under Brink's snowshoes the snow grew wet and soft. Soon he must take them off. But there would be drifts in the black belt of pine forest below. He smelled the tang of the pines, warm, sweet, woody.

The irregular furrow which he trod out with his snowshoes led down over slope and bench to level forest. Under the stately spreading pines the snow swelled into wavy mounds.

Old Gray sank the length of his legs, fell on his side, and lay still.

Soon the wolf tracker stood over him, gaping down.

"Ahuh—Old Gray—you're done," he panted huskily.

All that appeared left of magnificence about this wolf was his beautiful gray coat of fur, slashed at the neck with a glossy mark of black. Old Gray was lean and thin. His wild head lay on the snow, with mouth open, tongue protruding. How white and sharp the glistening fangs.

It was nothing new for Brink to see the coward in a beaten wolf. The legend of the ferocity of a trapped wolf was something he knew to be untrue. This notorious loafer, so long a menace to the range, showed in his wonderful gray eyes his surrender to man. The broken heart, the broken spirit, the acceptance of death. Brink saw no fear now—only resignation. And for a moment it halted his propelling rush to violence.

Man and wolf, age-long hereditary foes, alone there in the wilderness. Man the conqueror—man obsessed with the idea that man was born in the image of God. No wolf—no beast had ever been or could ever be man's equal. Brink's life had been an unconscious expression of this religion. This last and supreme test to which he had so terribly addressed himself had been the climax of his passion to prove man's mastery over all the beasts of the field.

Yet, with brawny hand extended, Brink suffered a singular and dismaying transformation of thought. What else did he read in those wild gray eyes? It was beyond him, yet from it he received a chilling of his blood, a sickening sense of futility even in possession of his travail-earned truth. Could he feel pity for Old Gray, blood-drinker of the cattle ranges?

"Ahuh. . . . Reckon if I held back longer—" he muttered, darkly, wonderingly. Then stepping out of his snowshoes he knelt and laid hold of Old Gray's throat with that great clutching hand.

Brink watched the wild eyes fade and glaze over and set. The long tremble of the wolf in the throes of death was strangely similar to the intense vibrating thrill of the man in his response to the heritage of a primitive day.

V

It was springtime down at Barrett's ranch. The cows were lowing and the calves were bawling. Birds and wet ground and budding orchard trees were proof of April even if there had not been the sure sign of the rollicking cowboys preparing for the spring roundup.

"I'm a-rarin' to go. Oh, boy!" shouted Sandy McLean.

"Wal, I'm the damndest best cowman that ever forked a hoss," replied the lean and rangy Juniper Edd, star rider for Barrett.

The shaggy, vicious mustangs cavorted in the corral, and whistled, squealed, snorted, and kicked defiance at their masters.

"Reckon I gotta stop smokin' them coffin nails. I jest cain't see," complained Thad Hickenthorp.

"Aw, it ain't cigarettes, Hick," drawled the redheaded Matty Lane. "Your eyes had plumb wore out on Sally Barrett."

"She's shore dazzlin', but thet's far enough for you to shoot off your chin," replied Thad.

"Cheese it, you fellars. Hyar comes the boss," added another cowboy.

Barrett strode from the ranch house. Once he had been a cowboy as lithe and wild as any one of his outfit. But now he was a heavy, jovial, weather-beaten cattleman.

"Boys' heah's word from my pardner, Adams," he said, with satisfaction. "All's fine an' dandy over on the Cibeque. You got to rustle an' shake dust or that outfit will show us up. Best news of all is about Old Gray. They haven't seen hide nor hair nor track of that wolf for months. Neither have we. I wonder now. . . . Wouldn't it be dod-blasted good luck if we was rid of that loafer?"

On that moment a man appeared turning into the lane, and his appearance was so unusual that it commanded silence on the part of Barrett and his cowboys. This visitor was on foot. He limped. He sagged under a pack on his shoulder. His head was bowed somewhat, so that the observers could not see his face. His motley garb was so tattered that it appeared to be about to fall from him in bits of rags.

He reached the group of men and, depositing his pack on the ground, he looked up to disclose a placid, grizzled face, as seamed and brown as a mass of pine needles.

"Howdy, stranger. An' who might you be?" queried Barrett, gruffly.

"My name's Brink. I'm new in these parts. Are you Barrett, pardner to Adams over on the Cibeque?" he replied.

"Yes, I'm Barrett. Do you want anythin' of me?"

"I've got something to show you," returned Brink, and kneeling stiff-legged he laboriously began to untie his pack. It was bulky and securely roped. Out of one end of the bundle protruded the frayed points of snowshoes. The cowboys surrounded him and Barrett, curiously silent, somehow sensing the dramatic.

When Brink drew out a gray furry package and unfolded it to show the magnificent pelt of a great loafer wolf the cowboys burst into gasps and exclamations of amaze.

"Ever seen that hide?" demanded Brink, with something subtle and strong under his mild exterior.

"Old Gray," boomed Barrett.

"I'm a locoed son-of-a-gun if it ain't," said Juniper Edd.

"Wal. I never seen Old Gray, but thet's him," ejaculated Thad.

"Damn me. It's shore thet grey devil with the black ruff. Old Gray wot I seen alive more'n any man on the ranges," added Matty Lane, in an incredulity full of regret.

"Stranger, how'n hell did you ketch this heah wolf?" demanded Sandy McLean.

Brink stood up. Something tame and deceiving fell away from the man. His face worked, his eyes gleamed.

"I walked him to death in the snow," he replied.

Barrett swore a lusty oath. It gave full expression to his acceptance of Brink's remarkable statement, yet held equal awe and admiration.

"When? How long?" he queried, hoarsely.

"Well, I started in early last October, an' I saw the end of his tracks yesterday."

"It's April tenth," exclaimed Barrett. "Tracked—walked Old

Gray to death. . . . My God, man, but you look it. . . . An'
you've come for the reward?"

"Reckon I'd forgot that," replied Brink, simply. "I just wanted
you to know the loafer was dead."

"Ah-hum. So that's why?" returned the rancher, ponderingly,
with a hand stroking his chin. His keen blue eyes studied the wolf
tracker gravely, curiously. His cowboys, likewise, appeared at the
end of their wits. For once their loquaciousness had sustained a
check. One by one, silent as owls and as wide-eyed, they walked
to and fro around Brink, staring from his sad, lined face to the
magnificent wolf pelt. But least of all did their faces and actions
express doubt. They were men of the open range. They saw at a
glance the manifestations of tremendous toil, of endurance, pri-
vation, and time that had reduced this wolf tracker to a semblance of a scarecrow in the cornfield. Of all things, these hardy
cowboys respected indomitableness of spirit and endurance of
body. They wondered at something queer about Brink, but they
could not grasp it. Their need of silent conviction, their reverent
curiosity, proclaimed that to them he began to loom incompre-
hensibly great.

"Never felt so happy in my life," burst out Barrett. "Come in
an' eat an' rest. I'll write you a check for that five thousand. . . .
An' fetch Old Gray's hide to show my womenfolks. I'll sure have
that hide made into a rug."

Brink gave a slight start and his serenity seemed to shade into
a somber detachment. Without a glance at Barrett he knelt, and
folded up the wolf skin and tied it in his pack. But when he arose,
lifting the pack to his shoulder, he said:

"Keep your money. Old Gray is mine."

Then he strode away from the bewildered ranchman and his
cowboys.

"Hey. What d'ye mean, rarin' off that way?" called Barrett,
growing red in the face. It was as if his sincerity or generosity
had been doubted. "Fetch the wolf hide back hyar an' take your
money."

Brink appeared not to hear. His stride lengthened, showing
now no trace of the limp which had characterized it upon his

arrival. The cattleman yelled angrily for him to stop. One of the cowboys let out a kindlier call. But Brink, swinging into swifter strides, remarkable even at that moment to his watchers, passed into the cedars out of sight.

KING
OF THE HILLS

JESSE STUART

"POOR BLACK BOY," Finn said as he stood beneath the pine tree in our front yard and watched Black Boy wallowing on the pine needles. "His short hair is not black as a crow's wing like it used to be. Black Boy is gettin old. He's gettin too old to hunt."

The October harvest moon like a big wagon wheel rolled above the autumn-colored hills. It was one of the prettiest nights I had ever seen for the moonlight on the hills and fields was bright as day.

"Most dogs are in their graves when they get as old as Black Boy," I said. "He'll be nineteen years old tomorrow. Black Boy is older than you are."

"I know it," Finn said. "That's why I hate to see him get so old he can't get up when he lays down."

"That dog taught me to hunt," I said. "I didn't teach him."

"He taught me to hunt too," Finn said. "We ought to try somethin to make him live longer. Try somethin that will put pep in him and make him happy."

"You're right, Finn," I said as I watched Black Boy make several tries before he was able to get up from the pine needle bed and stand on his feet.

"After he gets on his feet, he's all right," Finn said. "It's just hard for him to get back on his feet after he lays down."

Now Black Boy came up to us and smelled of our pants legs. He put his nose against my hand. The soft tip of his nose rubbed against my arm as he sniffled the familiar scent of me—a scent that he had tracked in the huntin woods—a scent that he had known all his life. I rubbed Black Boy's head and petted him. After I had petted him, he walked lazily over to Finn and sniffled the scent of his hand—sniffled another old familiar scent that he had known most of his lifetime. Finn patted his head and rubbed his nose. Black Boy was so pleased that he barked to Finn.

"Watch Black Boy strut after he gets up on his feet," Finn said. "You couldn't tell that he was an old dog only by the gray hair around his mouth and on his head. And he's lost all his teeth."

There Black Boy stood between us. He was kickin the pine needles high in the air with his hind feet. As he kicked the pine needles he growled as if he were still master of the place. He looked like a small black lion except for his gray toothless mouth and his gray head. Black Boy had a big mouth, big neck and his barrel chest rested on strong forelegs that were set wide apart. His hips were narrow like a lion's hips; his tail was long but he shortened it by carryin it over his back in two bristlin curls. Black Boy had been for many years, and was still, the king of the hills. But now age was showin its marks upon him; still he had never been whipped by any dog.

Now Black Boy stopped kickin the pine needles high into the air. He just stood and growled. There wasn't anythin near for him to growl at. Maybe he wanted to hear the importance of his own growl—maybe he growled at the wind.

"You're still king of the hills, Black Boy," Finn said. "But you won't be long. Too stiff to get up after you lay down. You can't last much longer. But you need pep today. You need to have one more glorious huntin night, Black Boy."

"He needs a spring-herb tonic," I said.

"Say, that makes me think," Finn said. "Pa's got a pint of Honorable Herbs that he keeps in the barnloft for his 'cold remedy.' That ought to be good for Black Boy."

"I'm not givin Black Boy that moonshine," I said.

"It will be good for him," Finn said. "A hangover won't bother Black Boy."

Finn hurried to the barn fast as his long legs could step. He climbed up the wall of barn logs, placin his feet and hands in the cracks until he reached the place where hard-pressed hay bulged through a wide crack between the logs. There was a little hole in the hay where Finn ran his hand back and pulled out a bottle. He scurried back down the low-walk and hurried back where Black Boy stood growlin at the wind hissin through the pine needles.

"This is the tonic that will make him young again," Finn said.

"It might kill him," I said.

"Wonder if he'll drink it raw," Finn said.

"Finn, let's don't give Black Boy that whiskey," I said.

"Why not?" Finn asked.

"It will be mean of us to give him whiskey."

"Ah, hell," Finn said as he poured the pint of whiskey in a trough where we watered the chickens.

"Here Black Boy," he coaxed.

Black Boy walked up to the trough, smelled of the moonshine, kicked his feet and growled. But he wouldn't drink it.

"He's almost in a notion," Finn said. "And I know what will put him in a notion."

Finn ran to the cellar and came back with a crock of sweet milk. He poured the gallon of sweet milk in the trough to mix with the moonshine. And Black Boy went to the trough growlin and kickin the pine needles with his hind feet. He started drinkin the milk-and-moonshine. Black Boy gorged himself to hold the gallon of sweet milk and the pint of moonshine whiskey. He licked the trough clean as a pawpaw whistle.

"We're goin to see somethin happen," Finn said. "I don't know what it will be. But somethin will happen!"

Black Boy got down on the pine needles and rolled. He opened his big mouth as he looked at us with eyes that sparkled with livin fire. Black Boy growled as he wallowed on the ground. Then Black Boy jumped to his feet like he was a young pup. He ran circles around us with his tongue out.

"That tonic is workin on 'im," Finn said. "He's a happy dog. It's doin 'im good."

Then Black Boy made a beeline toward the barn. He leaped over the gate like a red fox. He took down the path that leads from our barn to the big pasture field. He was out of sight under the trees whose pine needles looked good in the moonlight.

"Where's that dog goin?" I asked Finn.

"He's goin to hunt," Finn laughed.

"He's got so he can't smell a track when the ground is damp," I said. "I know he can't carry a track dry as it is now."

We hadn't stood there talkin five minutes until we heard Black Boy bark treed.

"What did I tell you," Finn said. "Black Boy's got somethin. Listen to that music won't you!"

"He's barkin to a bunch of poplar leaves," I said. "That dog's drunk. He doesn't know what he's doin."

Finn started runnin toward the sound. I followed Finn out the path by the barn and under the oaks and pines to the far pasture field. We saw Black Boy jumpin up on a small sourwood at the edge of the pasture field, barkin every breath.

"Sure he's got somethin treed," Finn said.

"I believe he has," I said. "I believe he can see it. Probably a house cat."

We ran across the field.

"House cat," Finn laughed as he got to the tree first. "It's the biggest groundhog I've ever seen."

Tall, bean-pole, freckled-faced Finn reached high on the small tree and with his big hand he gave the tree a shake. The ground-hog tumbled to the ground. He hadn't more than hit the ground until Black Boy had him. He gummed the groundhog to death with a throat hold.

"Let's take it to the house," I said.

"Hell no," Finn said. "You go to the house and get a mattock and two coffee sacks. Black Boy is runnin in high gear tonight. Let's stay with him. It may be his last great hunt!"

Before I got back with the mattock and the two sacks I heard Black Boy bark treed. When I reached the pasture field, I saw Finn with the groundhog in his hand, lookin up the black gum where Black Boy was barkin. I hurried across the field to the tree.

"He just walked up here and started barkin," Finn said. "May be somethin down in the hollow of that tree. I don't know. Can't see anything from the outside."

"Probably nothin there," I said. "That dog is drunk and you can't trust him."

"Trust hell," Finn said. "I believe there's somethin in that tree."

Finn pulled off his shoes and climbed the big black gum. He grunted as he climbed for it was a hard tree to climb. When Finn got to the top, he looked down in the tree where the top was broken off.

"Have a surprise for you, Shan," he said. "I'll show you something."

"What is it, Finn?" I asked, for I could hardly wait to see.

Now Finn had braced his foot against a black gum limb. He reached down in the hollow top of the black gum carefully. And he pulled a big possum up by the tail.

"Has the drunk dog lied?" Finn asked.

He threw the possum to the ground. Black Boy grabbed it soon as it hit the ground. But I took Black Boy off the possum and put it in a sack.

"That possum had the prettiest bed up in that tree," Finn said soon as he reached the ground. "He was layin up there asleep."

After Black Boy saw me put the possum in the sack, he went off over the hill like a blowin wind. He was goin with his nose high in the air, snifflin as he went.

"He's after somethin' right now," Finn said. "He's windin somethin."

Black Boy hadn't been gone long enough for us to get our sacks and mattock and walk down the hollow when we heard him bark deep in a hollow on the other side of the low ridge.

"He's barkin in a hole," Finn said as he stopped and listened, holdin his breath with his hand cupped over his ear to catch the low sound.

I followed Finn as he made his way through the brier thickets over the low ridge and down into the next hollow. Before we reached Black Boy, we heard him kickin the dirt with his feet. We heard it sprinklin over the dry leaves below 'im. Then we heard him growlin as he jerked on a root with his toothless mouth. When we reached him, he had a hole dug big enough to bury himself in by the end of a blackberry brier thicket. The hole was in the soft loamy dirt and he was diggin fast; he was barkin like he was close to somethin. We made our way through the thicket to him. Finn held Black Boy while I struck a few licks with the mattock. Then Finn let Black Boy loose to clean the hole out with his paws. He rammed his head back in the hole and pulled out a polecat that was black as a moonless midnight. I jumped back. I didn't want its scent to settle on me.

"He can't kill it," Finn said. "He doesn't have the teeth."

But he did kill it. He crushed its head with his powerful jaws.

"What a powerful dog he is today," I said. "How can a dog old as he is crush a polecat's head when he doesn't have a tooth in his head?"

We put the skunk in one end of the sack where we had the possum.

"That's the prettiest polecat hide I've ever seen," Finn said. "That will bring a good price."

"Seven or eight dollars," I said.

Now Black Boy was sick. He wallowed on the leaves. He rooted his nose under the dry leaves on top of the ground down to the wet, half-rotten leaves against the ground. He ran his nose down in the fresh dirt that he had dug from the hole.

"The hunt's over," I said. "He's really sick."

"After a dog gets that polecat scent on him he's through," Finn said. "This may end our hunt."

Soon as we had reached the little hollow below us we saw Black Boy standin to his knees in a hole of clean spring water. Then he left the water and took up the hill as if nothin had ever happened. He was soon out of sight over the hill where there was a beech grove between our farm and Uncle Mel's farm. And soon as we reached the hilltop, he barked in another hole. Wet with sweat, and tired of keepin after Black Boy, we hurried down the hill. Black Boy was barkin in the end of a hollow beech log.

"There's somethin there, Finn," I said as I took the ax-end of my mattock and started pryin away rottin slabs from the log.

"We'll soon know," Finn said as he held the dog back so I wouldn't hit his head with the ax-end of my mattock. "I'll bet it's another possum."

"You're right," I said. "Look!"

I pulled off a slab from over the possum's bed of leaves. He stuck his head out to see what was goin on. Black Boy broke the

collar that Finn was holdin him by and leaped three times his
length to the possum. I had to choke him loose before I could
free the possum to put in the sack with the other possum.

"What a possum," Finn said as I put it in the sack. "Did you
ever see this dog do any better in your life?"

"Never saw him work this fast," I said.

Black Boy wagged his tail at us. But he didn't hang around for
us to pat his head and rub his nose. He was off like a black flash
over the brown leaves to the bluff beyond us. We saw him with
his head held high in the night wind, go straight to a little rock.
We saw him put his head under the rock; we heard him sniffle.
Then he barked. Then he started diggin fast as he could. His hind
feet threw sprinkles of loam and wet leaves twenty feet behind
him down the steep bluff.

"He's got somethin," I said, grabbin the mattock and one of
the sacks.

"You damn right he has," Finn said, grabbin the other sack
and followin me.

Soon as we started up the bluff he brought somethin from the
hole.

"Phew," Finn screamed. "It's a damned polecat sure as the
world."

They came rollin end over end down the steep bluff toward us.
And soon as they reached the bottom of the bluff, the polecat's
legs stretched out limber. It was dead. Black Boy had crushed its
skull with his jaws.

"It's a broad-striped polecat," Finn said, tense with excitement.

Finn put the polecat in the sack while Black Boy rooted his
nose down under the dry leaves to the wet half-rotten half-loam
leaves. Then Black Boy made for the little fresh spring water
creek that flowed from the steep bluffs to drink water. He wallowed in one of the little deep holes against a fern-covered bank.

"Two livin possums in one end of this sack," Finn laughed.
"Two dead polecats in the other. It's gettin heavy."

"Wonder when the herbs will die in Black Boy," I said.

"When they die in Black Boy," Finn said, "his huntin will be
done for tonight."

"Maybe forever," I said.

"But this is wonderful," Finn said. "I've never seen anythin like it."

Now Black Boy left us. He went down the creek toward Rag-weed Hollow. And we followed the cattle path down to the fence. We didn't hear from Black Boy. He didn't return to us nor did he bark. Tired of runnin after him and carryin the game, we sat down on a beech log to rest. But we didn't rest long. We heard Black Boy bark in a hole on the hill across the hollow. We started runnin toward him. When we climbed the hill, sweaty, tired and out-of-breath, we found Black Boy in a dirt hole in a little drain.

Finn poked a long stick back in the hole and told me where to dig down to strike the hole. I soon put a hole down for it was shallow down to the hole. Then Finn put the stick back again and told me where to dig. I put down another hole and then another. When Finn put the stick back, he felt a bed of leaves.

"It's a groundhog or a possum," Finn said. "I feel it."

He twisted with his stick; then he pulled it out.

"Red hairs," Finn said, examinin the hairs on the end of the stick in the moonlight.

"Let Black Boy loose before somethin jumps out," I said.

Soon as Black Boy put his nose in the hole to sniffle, he yelled. Then he started fightin.

"Somethin bit 'im," I said.

"A young red fox," Finn roared as Black Boy and the fox tangled.

"What do you know about that," I said. "Who ever dreamed of a fox bein in a dirt hole?"

"He's found him a rabbit in that hole," Finn said. "He was havin a good meal when Black Boy found him."

"He's finished the fox," I said.

"We'll just carry it outside the sack," Finn said. "It would take too much room in a sack."

"This will about end our hunt," I said. "Black Boy is gettin tired. Look at his tongue. It's dropped down like a shoe-tongue."

Finn carried the sack of possums and polecats and the mat-tock; I carried the fox and the groundhog. It was like carryin a full-grown hound-dog pup to carry the fox. Now we made our way off the hill. Black Boy walked in front of us. But soon he disappeared.

When we reached the foot of the hill, we started up the Ragweed Hollow jolt-wagon road for home. We were tired now; we were wet with sweat—our clothes looked like we had jumped in the river. And the load of game was gettin heavier every step we took.

"I hope he won't find anythin more," I said.

"Listen," Finn said turnin his head sideways for his ear to catch the sound. "I hear 'im! He's got somethin!"

We hurried toward the sound. By a log pile at the upper side of the field where Doore's had had tobacco, Black Boy had found another polecat under the log pile. He had it killed when we got there and he was wallowin on the tobacco-patch dirt. He was rootin his nose in the ground like a hog.

"It's a narrow-stripe," Finn said. "He's crushed its skull."

"Another damned polecat," I said. "You can put it in the sack or we'll leave it. I don't aim to put my hands on it."

"It's got wonderful fur," Finn said. "Sure, I'll put it in the sack."

Finn opened the sack and put his dead polecat with the other two. He tied the sack and grunted as he swung the sack across his shoulder with one big heave.

"Some load," Finn said. "But there's money in these hides."

"Thank God this hunt's over," I said. "Look at Black Boy. He's sick enough to eat grass."

Black Boy was eatin stems of dead crab-grass that he found in the tobacco balks.

"You can't tell about Black Boy," Finn said.

And Finn was right. As we were slowly trudgin toward home, weary under our heavy loads, Black Boy let out a blast of barks that came hard and fast.

"He's treed," Finn screamed. "He can see it! He's close to it!"

Even with our heavy loads, we broke out in a slow run. He was barkin on Doore's bluff just above the road. We had a good road to get to him.

"Look up there at that groundhog," Finn laughed.

The groundhog was up a little sassafras saplin. It was bigger than the first groundhog that we had caught. We hurried up the bank to the tree. Black Boy was backin off and runnin toward the tree, then leapin up and barely missin the groundhog.

"He's got plenty of pep left," Finn said.

Then Black Boy tried to climb the tree but his toenails wouldn't hold in the sassafras bark. Finn shook the sassafras. When the groundhog hit the ground, it hit the ground runnin. But before it had got many steps Black Boy grabbed it by the throat and choked it to death. It made my load heavier. Two big groundhogs and a fox for me. Three polecats and two possums for Finn. And he carried the mattock. Now we called Black Boy and started home. The October wagon-wheel moon beamed on us; the night wind rustled leaves on the trees dry as oakchips. But now we were goin home to show Pa the game we had caught with Black Boy before eleven o'clock.

Before we reached home Black Boy barked at somethin in the bottom.

"You go to him, Finn," I said. "Leave your sack here and I'll watch the game. We can't carry all of this and follow that dog."

Finn walked across the bottom where Black Boy was barkin on the creek bank. Soon as Finn reached him, I heard him laughin. He came back across the bottom carryin a big black bug that had pincers.

"Back to his old age," Finn said. "The herbs have died in 'im."

And just as we reached the hog-lot bluff, Black Boy barked treed somewhere upon the bluff. I went to him this time and Finn watched the game. Finn heard me laugh when I saw that he was barkin at a cluster of leaves lodged in the forks of a shell-barked hickory. The herbs had really died; Black Boy had been livin in his old world. Now Black Boy was livin in another world where he was an old dog.

"My God! Black Boy is going back to his prime," Pa said as he looked at the pile of game. "That's the way he used to hunt when he's a young dog."

"Thirty dollars worth of hides," Finn said. "And enough groundhog hide shoestrings to lace our boots for a couple of years."

Black Boy laid down that night soon as we had skinned the

game and stretched the hides. Next mornin at sunrise when we went to feed him he couldn't get up. But he ate a little layin down. His eyes were not like embers glowin in the night; his eyes were glassy.

"It's probably a tough hangover," Finn whispered in my ear so Pa wouldn't hear him.

But Black Boy's breath grew shorter; his great panels of ribs didn't heave when he breathed like they always had. And today was his nineteenth birthday. Before the sun had set, Black Boy had gone to the Great Huntin Ground where there was plenty of game. Pa was up on the barn logs with his hand back in the hay huntin for his medicine to break his October cold when we told him that Black Boy had finally breathed his last.

KRAG,
THE KOOTENAY
RAM

ERNEST SETON-THOMPSON

Part One

A GREAT BROAD WEB of satin, shining white, and strewn across, long clumps and trailing wreaths of lilac—almost white—wistaria bloom—pendant, shining, and so delicately wrought in palest silk that still the web was white; and in and out and trailed across, now lost, now plain, two slender twining intertwining chains of golden thread.

I see a broken upland in the far Northwest. Its gray and purple rocks are interpatched with colors rich and warm, the newborn colors of the upland spring, the greatest springtime in the world; for where there is no winter there can be no spring. The gloom is measure of the light. So, in this land of long, long winter night, where nature stints her joys for six hard months, then owns her debt and pays it all at once, the spring is glorious compensation for the past. Six months' arrears of joy are paid in one great lavish outpour. And latest May is made the date of payment. Then spring, great, gorgeous, sixfold spring holds carnival on every ridge.

Even the sullen Gunder Peak, that pierces the north end of the ridge, unsombers just a whit. The upland beams with all the flowers it might have grown in six lost months; yet we see only one. Here, by our feet and farther on, and right and left and onward far away, in great, broad acre beds, the purple lupin blooming. Irregular, broken, straggling patches near, but broader, denser farther on; till on the distant slopes they lie, long, devious belts, like purple clouds at rest.

But late May though it be, the wind is cold; the pools tell yet of frost at night. The white wind blows. Broad clouds come up, and down comes driving snow. Over the peaks, over the upland and over the upland flowers. Hoary, gray, and white the landscape grows in turn; and one by one the flowers are painted out. But the lupins on their taller, stiffer stems, can fight the snow for long, they bow their whitened heads beneath its load, then, thanks no little to the wind itself, shake free and stand up defiantly straight, and as fits their royal purple. And when the snow-fall ends as suddenly as it began, the clouds roll by and the blue sky sees an upland shining white, but streaked and patched with blots and belts of lovely purple bloom.

And wound across, and in and out, are two long trails of track.

Late snow is good trailing, and Scotty Macdougall took down his rifle and climbed the open hills behind his shanty on Tobacco Creek toward the well-known Mountain Sheep range. The broad white upland, with its lupin bands and patches, had no claim on Scotty's notice, nor was his interest aroused until he came on the double trail in the new snow. At a glance he read it—two full-grown female mountain sheep, wandering here and there across the country, with their noses to the wind. Scotty followed the prints for a short time and learned that the sheep were uneasy, but not alarmed, and less than an hour ahead. They had wandered from one sheltered place to another. Once or twice they had lain down for a minute, only to rise and move on, apparently not hungry, as the abundant food was untouched.

Scotty pushed forward cautiously, scanning the distance and keeping watch on the trail without following it, when, all at once, he swung round a rocky point into view of a little lupin-crowded hollow and from the middle of it leaped the two sheep.

Up went his rifle, and in a moment one or both would have fallen, had not Scotty's eye, before he pulled, rested on two tiny newborn lambs that got up on their long wobbly legs, in doubt, for a moment, whether to go to the newcomer, or to follow their mothers.

The old sheep bleated a shrill alarm to their young and circled back. The lambs' moment of indecision was over, they felt that their duties lay with the creatures that looked and smelled like themselves, and coolly turned their uncertain steps to follow their mothers.

Of course Scotty could have shot any or all of the sheep, as he was within twenty yards of the farthest, but there is in man an unreasoning impulse, a wild hankering to catch alive; and without thinking of what he could do with them afterward, Scotty, seeing them so easily in his power, leaned his gun in a safe place and ran after the lambs. But the distressed mothers had by now communicated a good deal of their alarm to their young, the little things were no longer in doubt that they should avoid the stranger, and when he rushed forward, his onset added the necessary final touch and for the first time in their brief lives they knew danger and instinctively sought to escape it. They were not yet an hour old, but nature had equipped them with a set of valuable instincts. And though the lambs were slow of foot compared with the man, they showed at once a singular aptitude at dodging, and Scotty failed to secure them at once as he had expected.

Meanwhile the mothers circled about, bleating piteously and urging the little ones to escape. Scotty, plunging around in his attempt, alarmed them more and more, and they put forth all the strength of their feeble limbs in the effort to go to their mothers. The man slipping and scrambling after them was unable to catch either, although more than once he touched one with his hand. But very soon this serious game of tag was adroitly steered by the timid mothers away from the lupin bed, and once on the smooth, firmer ground, the lambs got an advantage that quite offset the weariness they began to feel, and Scotty, dashing and chasing first this way and then that, did not realize that the whole thing was being managed by the old ones, till they reached the lowest spur of the Gunder Peak, a ragged, broken, rocky cliff, up which the mothers bounded. Then the little ones felt a new sense, just as a young duck must when first he drops in the water. Their little black rubber hoofs gripped the slippery rocks as no man's foot

can do it, and they soared on their newfound mountain wings, up
and away, till led by their mothers out of sight.

It was well for them that Scotty had lain aside his rifle, for a
sheep at a hundred yards was as good as dead when he pulled on
it. He now rushed back for his weapon, but before he could harm
them, a bank of fog from the peak came rolling between. The
same white wind that brought the treacherous trailing snow that
had betrayed them to their deadliest foe, now brought the fog
that screened them from his view.

So Scotty could only stare up the cliff and, half in admiration,
mutter "the little divils, the little divils, too smart for me, and
them less'n an hour old."

For now he fully knew the meaning of the restless wandering
of the old ones, and the sudden appearance of two new tiny trails.

He spent the rest of the day in bootless hunting and at night
went home hungry, to dine off a lump of fat bacon.

The rugged peaks are not the chosen home but rather the safe
and final refuge of the sheep. Once there the mothers felt no fear,
and thenceforth, in the weeks that followed, they took care that
in feeding, they should never wander far on the open away from
their haven on the crags.

The lambs were of a sturdy stock and grew so fast that within
a week they were strong enough to keep up with their mothers
when the sudden appearance of a mountain lion forced them all
to run for their lives.

The snow of the lambs' birthday had gone again within a few
hours and all the hills were now carpeted with grass and flowers,
the abundant food for the mothers meant plenty of the best for
the little ones and they waggled their tails in satisfaction as they
helped themselves.

One of the little fellows, whose distinguishing mark was a very
white nose, was stockily built, while his playmate, slightly taller
and more graceful, was peculiar in having little nubbins of horns
within a few days of his birth.

They were fairly matched and frisked and raced alongside
their mothers or fought together the live-long day. One would
dash away and the other behind him try to butt him; or if they

came on an inviting hillock they began at once the world-old, worldwide game of king of the castle. One would mount and hold his friend at bay. Stamping and shaking his little round head, he would give the other to understand that *he* was "king of the castle"—and then back would go their pretty pink ears, the round woolly heads would press together and the innocent brown eyes roll as they tried to look terribly fierce and push and strive till one, forced to his knees, would wheel and kick up his heels as though to say: "I didn't want your old castle, anyway," but would straightway give himself the lie by seeking out a hillock for himself and, posing on its top with his fiercest look, would stamp and shake his head, after the way that in their language stands for the rhyming challenge in ours, and the combat scene would be repeated.

In these encounters Whitenose generally had the best of it because of his greater weight, but in the races, Nubbins was easily first. His activity was tireless. From morning till evening he seemed able to caper and jump.

At night they usually slept close against their mothers in some sheltered nook, where they could see the sunrise, or rather where they could feel it, for that was more important, and Nubbins, always active, was sure to be up first of the lambs. Whitenose was inclined to be lazy, and would stay curled up, the last of the family to begin the day of activity. His snowy nose was matched by a white patch behind, as in all bighorn sheep, only larger and whiter than usual, and this patch afforded so tempting a mark that Nubbins never could resist a good chance to charge at it. He was delighted if, in the morning, he could waken his little friend by what he considered a tremendous butt on his beautiful patch of white.

Mountain sheep usually go in bands; the more in the band the more eyes for danger. But the hunter had been very active in the Kootenay country, Scotty in particular had been relentless in the hunting. His shanty roof was littered over with horns of choice rams, and inside it was half filled with a great pile of sheepskins awaiting a market. So the droves of bighorn were reduced to a few scattering bands, the largest of which was less than thirty, and many, like that of which I speak, had but three or four in it.

Once or twice during the first fortnight of June old Scotty had crossed the sheeprange with his rifle ready, for game was always in season for him, but each time one or the other of the alert mothers saw him afar, and either led quickly away, or by giving a short, peculiar sniff, had warned the others not to move; then all stood still as stones, and so escaped, when a single move might easily have brought sure death. When the enemy was out of sight they quickly changed to some distant part of the range.

One day they had wandered downward toward the piney valley, tempted by the rich grasses. As they reached the edge of the woods, Nubbins' mother held back; she had a deep-laid distrust of the lower levels, especially where wooded. But Whitenose's mother, cropping eagerly at the mountain clover that was here in profusion, was led farther on till she passed under some rocks among the pines. A peculiar smell caused her to start, she looked around, then wheeled to quit the woods, but a moment later a great wolverine sprang from the bank on to her back and laid her low in an instant.

Nubbins and his mother got a glimpse of the great brown enemy and fled up the rocks, but little Whitenose was stupefied with terror. He stood by staring and feebly bleating till the wolverine, with merciful mercilessness, struck him down as he had done the mother.

Nubbins' mother was a medium-sized, well-knit creature. She had horns longer and sharper than usual for a ewe, and they were of the kind called spikehorns or spikers; she also had plenty of good sheep sense. The region above Tobacco Creek had been growing more dangerous each month, thanks chiefly to Scotty, but the mother sheep's intention to move out was decided for her by the morning's tragedy.

She careered along the slope of the Gunder Peak at full speed, but before going over each rising ground she stopped and looked over it, ahead and back, remaining still as a lichen-patched rock for a minute or more in each place while she scanned the range around.

Once as she did this she saw a dark, moving figure on a range behind her. It was old Scotty. She was in plain view, but she held as still as could be and so escaped notice, and when the man was lost behind the rocks she bounded away faster than before, with little Nubbins scampering after. At each ridge she looked out carefully, but seeing no more either of her enemy or her friends, she pushed on quietly all that day, traveling more slowly as the danger field was left behind.

Toward evening, as she mounted the Yak-in-i-kak watershed, she caught a glimpse of moving forms on a ridge ahead; after a long watch she made out that they were in the uniform of sheep —gray, with white striped stockings and white patches on face and stern. They were going up wind. Keeping out of view she made so as to cross their back trail, which she soon found, and thus learned that her guess was right. There were the tracks of two large bighorn, but the trail also said that they were rams. According to mountain sheep etiquette the rams form one community and the ewes and lambs another. They must not mix or seek each other's society, except during the early winter, the festal months, the time of love and mating.

Nubbins' mother, the spikerdoe, left the trail and went over the watershed, glad to know that this was a sheep region. She rested for the night in a hollow, and next morning she journeyed on, feeding as she went. Presently the mother caught a scent that made her pause. She followed it a little. Others joined on or crisscrossed, and she knew now that she had found the trail of a band of ewes and lambs. She followed steadily, and Nubbins skipped alongside, missing his playmate, but making up as far as possible by doing double work.

Within a very few minutes she sighted the band, over a dozen in all—her own people. The top of her head was just over a rock, so that she saw them first, but when Nubbins poked up his round head to see, the slight movement caught the eye of a watchful mother in the flock. She gave the signal that turned all the band to statues, with heads their way. It was now the spiker's turn. She walked forth in plain view. The band dashed over the hill, but circled behind it to the left, while Nubbins and his mother went to the right.

In this way their positions in the wind were reversed. Formerly she could smell them; now they could smell her, and, having

already seen her uniform from afar, they were sure her creden-
tials were right. She came cautiously up to them. A leading ewe
walked out to meet her. They sniffed and gazed. The leader
stamped her feet, and the spikerdoe got ready to fight. They
advanced, their heads met with a "whack," then, as they pushed,
the spikerdoe twisted so that one of her sharp points rested on
the other ewe's ear. The pressure became very unpleasant. The
enemy felt she was getting the worst of it, so she sniffed, turned,
and, shaking her head, rejoined her friends. The spikerdoe
walked after her, while little Nubbins, utterly puzzled, stuck
close to her side. The flock wheeled and ran, but circled back,
and as the spiker stood her ground, they crowded around her,
and she was admitted one of their number. This was the ceremony, so far as she was concerned. But Nubbins had to establish
his own footing. There were some seven or eight lambs in the
flock. Most of them were older and bigger than he, and, in common with some other animals, they were ready to persecute the
stranger simply because he was strange.

The first taste of this that Nubbins had was an unexpected
"bang" behind. It had always seemed very funny to him when he
used to give Whitenose a surprise of this kind, but now there
seemed nothing funny about it. It was simply annoying, and
when he turned to face the enemy, another one charged from
another direction, and whichever way he turned, there was a
lamb ready to butt at him, till poor Nubbins was driven to take
refuge under his mother. Of course she could protect him, but he
could not stay there always, and the rest of the day with the herd
was an unhappy one for poor Nubbins, but a very amusing one
for the others. He was so awed by their numbers, the suddenness
of it all, that he did not know what to do. His activity helped but
little. Next morning it was clear that the others intended to have
some more fun at his expense. One of these, the largest, was a
stocky little ram. He had no horns yet, but when they did come
they were just like himself, thickset and crooked and rough, so
that, reading ahead, we may style him Krinklehorn. He came
over and, just as Nubbins rose, hind legs first, as is sheep fashion,
the other hit him square and hard. Nubbins went sprawling, but
jumped up again, and in something like a little temper went for

the bully. Their small heads came together with about as much noise as two balls of yarn, but they both meant to win. Nubbins was aroused now, and he dashed for that other fellow. Their heads slipped past, and now it was head to shoulder, both pounding away. At first Nubbins was being forced back, but soon his unusual sprouts of horns did good service, and, after getting one or two punches in his ribs from them, the bully turned and ran. The others, standing round, realized that the newcomer was fit. They received him as one of their number, and the hazing of Nubbins was ended.

The spikerdoe soon became known as a very wise sheep, wiser than any other in the flock except one, the chosen leader, and that leader was no other than the mother of Krinklehorn, the little bully. (Sheep do not give each other names—but they have the idea which in time resulted in names with us. They always think of their leaders as the Wise One, who is safe to follow, and I shall speak of her as such.)

Within a few weeks she was killed by a mountain lion. The herd scattered as the terrible animal sprang, and the spikerdoe led for the cliffs, followed by the rest. When she reached a safe place high up, she turned to wait for the stragglers, who came up quickly. Then they heard from far below a faint baah of a lamb. All cocked their ears and waited. It is not wise to answer too quickly, it may be the trick of some enemy. But it came again, the familiar baah of one of their own flock, and Spikerdoe answered it.

A rattling of stones, a scrambling up banks, another baah for guidance and there appeared among them little Krinklehorn—an orphan now.

Of course he did not know this yet, any more than the others did. But as the day wore on and no mother came in response to his plaintive calls, and as his little stomach began also to cry out for something more than grass or water, he realized his desolation and baahed more and more plaintively. When night came he was cold as well as hungry—he must snuggle up to someone or freeze. No one took much notice of him, but Spikerdoe, seemingly the new leader, called once or twice in answer to his call, and almost by accident he drifted near her when she lay down and warmed himself against her beside his ancient enemy, young Nubbins.

In the morning he seemed to Mother Spikerdoe to be her own, in a limited sense. Rubbing against Nubbins made him smell like her own, and when Nubbins set about helping himself to a breakfast of warm milk, poor hungry Krinklehorn took the liberty of joining in on the other side. Thus Nubbins found himself nose to nose and dividing his birthright with his old-time enemy. But neither he nor his mother made any objection, and thus it was that Krinklehorn was adopted by his mother's rival.

There was no one of the others that could equal Spikerdoe in sagacity. She knew all the range now, and it was soon understood that she was to lead. It was also understood that Krinklehorn, as well as Nubbins, was her lamb. The two were like brothers in many things. But Krinklehorn had no sense of gratitude to his foster-mother and he always nursed his old grudge against Nubbins, and now that they drank daily of the same drink, he viewed Nubbins as his rival and soon showed his feeling by a fresh attempt to master him. But Nubbins was better able to take care of himself now than ever. Krinklehorn got nothing but a few good prods for his pains, and their relative status was settled.

During the rest of the season they grew up side by side. Krinklehorn, thickset and sulky, with horns fast growing, but thick and crinkly. And Nubbins—well! it is not fair to call him Nubbins any longer, as his horns were growing fast and long, so that we may henceforth speak of him as Krag, a name that he got years afterward in the country around Gunder Peak, and the name by which he went down to history.

During the summer Krag and Krinklehorn grew in wit as well as in size. They learned all the ordinary rules of life among bighorn. They knew how to give the warning "sniff" when they saw something, and the danger "Snoo-of" when they were sure it was dangerous. They were acquainted with all the pathways and could have gone alone to any of the near saltlicks when they felt the need of it.

They could do the zigzag bounding that baffles the rush of an

enemy, as well as the stiff-legged jumping which carries them safely up glassy slippery slopes. Krag even excelled his mother in these accomplishments. They were well-equipped to get their own living, they could eat grass, and so it was time they were weaned, for Spikerdoe had to lay on her fat to keep warm in the coming winter. The youngsters themselves would have been in no hurry to give up their comforting breakfast, but the supply began to run short, and the growing horns of the lambs began to interfere with the mother's comfort so much that she proceeded firmly and finally with their weaning, and long before the earliest snow flurry grizzled the upland, she had them quite independent of her for their daily food.

When the earliest snows of winter came, all the lambs were weaned and doing for themselves, and the ewes were fat and flourishing, but, being free from domestic cares, had thoughts for other matters.

With the early frosts and the bracing air came the mating season and, determined to find their mates, the sheep traveled about the likeliest parts of the hills.

Several times during the summer they had seen one or two great rams in the distance, but an exchange of signals had made clear to each what the other was, and they had avoided each other's company.

But now, when a pair of large sheep were sighted, and the usual signals exchanged, there seemed no sign of a wish to avoid each other. As the two tall strangers came on, their great size, majestic forms, and vast curling horns, left no doubt as to their sex, and, proud of their horns and powers, they pranced forward. But the forwardness of Spikerdoe and her band now gave place to a decided bashfulness. They turned, as though to avoid the newcomers. This led to pursuit and to much maneuvering before the two rams were permitted to join the herd. Then came the inevitable quarrel. The rams had so far been good friends, were evidently chums, but chumship and love rivalry cannot dwell together. It was the old story—the jealous pang, the seeking for cause, the challenge, and the duel. But these are not always duels to the death. The rams charged at each other, their horns

whacked together till the chips flew from them, but after a few rounds one of them, the lighter, of course, was thrown backward, and, leaping up, he tried to escape. The other followed for a quarter of a mile, and, as he declined a further fight, the victor came proudly back, and claimed and was allowed the position and joys of sultan of the band.

Krag and Krinklehorn were ignored. They were in awe of the great ram who now took charge, and they felt that their safest plan was to keep as far as possible away from the present social activities of the flock, as they were not very sure of their own standing.

During the first part of that winter they were under guidance of the ram. He was a big, handsome fellow, not without a streak of masculine selfishness that made him take care to have the best of the food and to keep a sharp lookout for danger. Food was plentiful, for the ram knew enough to lead them not into the sheltered ravines where the snow was deep, but up on the bleakest ridges of the upland, where the frigid wind lays bare the last year's grass and, furthermore, where no enemy can approach unseen; so all went well.

The springtime came, with its thrilling sounds and feelings. Obedient to their ancient law, the ram and the band of ewes had parted company in midwinter. The feeling had been growing for days. They were less disposed to follow him, and sometimes he lingered far away for hours. One day he did not rejoin them, and thenceforth to the end of the winter they followed the spikerdoe as of old.

The little ones came about the first of June. Many of the mothers had two each, but Spikerdoe, now the Wise One, had but one, as the year before, and this little one displaced Krag for good and engrossed all the mother's attention. He even hindered her in her duties as a leader, and one day, as she was feeding him and watching the happy wagging of his tail, another sheep gave an alarm. All froze except a certain nervous, fidgety, young ewe, who never could keep still. She crossed before the Wise One. There was a faraway "crack." Fidgets dropped dead, and the spikerdoe fell with a stifled "baah!" But she sprang to her feet,

forgetting her own pain, and, looking wildly about her for her lamb, she leaped on the ridge to follow the others. "Bang!" went the rifle again, and the old sheep got a first glimpse of the enemy. It was the man who had once so nearly caught the lambs. He was a long way off, but the ball whistled before the sheep's nose. She sprang back and changed her course, thereby leaving the rest, then leaped over the ridge bleating to her little one to follow— bleating, too, from pain, for she was hard hit. But she leaped headlong down a rocky place, and the high ground came between. Down the gully she bounded, and out along the further ridge, keeping out of sight so well that, though Scotty ran as fast as he could to the edge, he never saw her again. He chuckled as he noted the clots of blood, but these soon ceased, and after a long attempt to keep the trail, he gave it up, cursed his luck, and went back to the victim he had secured.

Away went Spikerdoe and her lamb, the mother guiding, but the little one ahead. Her instinct told her that upward was the way to safety. Up the Gunder Peak she must go, but keep from being seen. So she went on, in spite of a burning wound, always keeping a ridge between, till round the nearest rocks she paused to look. She saw no sign of either her friends or her foe. She felt she had a deadly wound. She must escape lest her strength give out. She set off again at a run, forging ahead, and the little one following or running ahead as he pleased. Up they went till the timber line was reached, and upward still, her instinct urged her on.

Another lofty bench was scaled, and then she sighted a long white streak, a snow-drift lingering in a deep ravine. She eagerly made for that. There was a burning pain through her loins, and on each side was a dark stain on her coat. She craved a cooling touch, and on reaching the white patch sank on her side, her wound against the snow.

There could be only one end to such a wound—two hours, three hours at farthest, and then—well, never mind.

And the little one? He stood dumbly gazing at her. He did not understand. He only knew that he was cold and hungry now, and that his mother, to whom he had looked for everything, food, warmth, guidance, and sympathy, was so cold and still.

He did not understand it. He did not know what next. But we do, and the raven on the rock knew. Better for him, far better, quicker and more merciful, had the rifle served him as it did his mother.

Krag was a fine young ram now, taller than any of the ewes, and with long scimitars of horns. Krinklehorn also was well-grown, as heavy as Krag, but not so tall, and with horns that looked diseased, they were so short, thick, and bumpy.

The autumn came again, with the grand reunion of the families, the readvent of the ram, and also with a readjustment that Krag did not look for. He was just beginning to realize his importance in the flock, when the great ram came, with his curling horns and thick bull neck, and the first thing he did was to bundle Krag out of the flock. Krag, Krinklehorn, and three or four more of their age, were packed off by themselves, for such is etiquette among sheep. As soon as the young males reach or nearly reach maturity they must go off to study life for themselves. And during the four years that followed Krag led a roving bachelor life with a half dozen companions. He became the leader, for he inherited his mother's wit, and they traveled into far countries, learning new pastures, new ways, and new wisdom, and fitted themselves to become fathers of large and successful families.

It was not choice that left Krag unmated, but a combination of events against which he vainly chafed still left him with his bachelor crew. It was really better so. It seemed hard at the time, but it proved his making, for he was thus enabled to develop to the full his wonderful powers before being hampered and weakened by the responsibilities and mingled joys of a family. Each year the bachelor rams grew handsomer. Even sulky Krinklehorn became a tall and strong, if not a fine-looking, ram. He had never gotten over his old dislike of Krag. Once or twice he put forth his strength to worst him, and even tried to put him over a cliff, but he got so severely punished for it that thenceforth he kept away from his foster brother. But Krag was a joy to behold. As he bounded up the jagged cliffs, barely touching each successive point with his clawed and padded hoofs, floating up like a bird, deriding all foes that thought of following afoot, and the sunbeams changing and flashing from his back as the supple muscles working changed the surface form—he was more like a spirit thing that had no weight and knew no fear of falling than a great three-hundred-pound ram with five year-rings on his horns.

And such horns! The bachelors that owned his guidance had various horns reflecting each the owner's life and gifts. Some rough half moons, some thick, some thin, but Krag's curled in one great sweep, three-quarters of a circle, and the five year-marks told, first beginning at the point, of the year when he was a lamb, and grew the straight long spikes that had helped him so well in his early fight. Next year the growth thicker and much longer. The next two years told of yet more robust growth with lesser length, but the last was a record of a year of good food, of perfect health, and unexampled growth, for the span grown then was longer, wider, and cleaner horns than any of the others.

Tucked away under the protecting shadow of each rugged base, like things too precious to expose, were his beautiful eyes. Dark brown when he was a lamb, yellowish brown when a yearling, they were now, in his early prime, great orbs of shining gold, or splendid amber jewels, with a long, dark, misty depth in each, through which the whole bright world was born and mirrored on his brain.

There is no greater joy to the truly living thing than the joy of being alive, of feeling alive in every part and power. It was a joy to Krag now to stretch his perfect limbs in a shock of playful battle with his friends. It was a joy to press his toes on some thin ledge then sail an impossible distance across some fearful chasm to another ledge, whose size and distance he gauged with absolute precision. It was a joy to him to set the mountain lions at naught by a supple ricochet from rock to rock, or to turn and drive the bounding Blacktail band down pell-mell backward to their own, the lower, levels.

There was a subtle pleasure in every move, and a glorying in his glorious strength, which, after all, is beauty. And when to such a being the early winter brought also the fire of love and set him all aglow, he was indeed a noble thing to see. In very wantonness of strength and power he bounded, ball-like, up or down long rugged slopes, leaping six feet high where one would have fully answered every end, except the pleasure of doing it. But so he went. Seeking, searching—for what? He could not have told. But he would know when he found it. Away he went at the head of his band, careering until they crossed the trail of another band and, instinct guided, he followed after. In a mile or two the other band was sighted, a group of ewes. They fled, of course, but being cornered on a rugged bench, they stood, and after due punctilio they allowed the rams to approach.

The bighorn is no monogamist. The finest ram claims all of the ewes in the flock, and any question of his claims must be settled on the spot in mortal fight. Hitherto there had been a spirit of good fellowship among the rams, but now that was changed, and when great Krag bounded forward, snorting out a challenge to all the rest to disprove his right of might, there was none to face him; and, strange to tell, with many claimants, there was no fight. There was nothing now for the rest to do but to wheel at his command and leave him to the devotion and admiration of his conquest.

If, as they say, beauty and prowess are winning cards in all walks of animal life, then Krag must have been the idol of his band. For matched with rams he had seemed a wonder, and among the ewes his strength, his size, and the curling horns must have made of him a demi-god, and the winged heart and the brimming cup were his.

But on the second day of joy two rams appeared, and after maneuvering came near. One was a fine big animal, as heavy in the body as Krag, but with smaller horns, and the other was Krinklehorn. The new ram snuffed a challenge as he came near, then struck the ground with his foot, meaning "I am a better ram than you and mean to oust you from your present happy position."

Krag's eyes blazed. He curled his massive neck. He threw his chin up and down like a champing horse. Shook his great horns as though they were twigs, laid back his ears and charged, and forward sprang the foe. They came together, but the stranger had an advantage of ground, which left the first onset a draw.

The rams backed off, each measuring the other and the dis-

tance and seeking for firm footing, kept on the edge of the great
bench, then they came on again. The splinters flew, for they both
were prime. But this time Krag clearly had the best of it. He
followed up his advantage at once with a second "whack" at
short range, and twisting around, his left horn hooked under the
right of his foe, when to his utter dismay he received a terrific
blow on his flank from an unknown enemy. He was whirled
around and would have been dashed over the cliff, but his horn
was locked in that of his first foeman and so he was saved; for no
ram has weight enough in his hind quarter to oppose the headlong charge of another. Krag scrambled to his feet again, just in
time to see the new enemy irresistibly carried by the violence of
his own charge over the ledge and down.

It was a long time before a faraway crash told those on the
ledge that Krinklehorn had found the very end he plotted for his
foster brother. Ram fights are supposed to be fair duels. Krinklehorn, failing in fair fight, had tried foul, and had worked his
own destruction; for not even a bighorn can drop two hundred
feet on rock and live.

Krag now turned on his other foe with double fury. One more
shock and the stranger was thrown, defeated. He leaped to his
feet and bounded off. For a time Krag urged him to further flight
by the same means that Krinklehorn once used to persecute him,
then returned in triumph to live unmolested with his family.

Scotty had gone from his Tobacco Creek location in 1887. The
game was pretty well hunted out. Sheep had become very scarce;
news of new gold strikes in Colorado had attracted him southward, and the old shanty was deserted. Five years went by with
Krag as the leading ram. It was five years under a good genius,
with an evil genius removed. Five years of prosperity then, for
the bighorn.

Krag carried farther the old ideas that were known to his
mother. He taught his band to abjure the lowlands entirely. The
forest coverts were full of evil, and the only land of safety was the
open windswept peaks where neither lions nor riflemen could
approach unseen. He found more than one upland saltlick where
their natural need could be supplied without the dangerous low-

land journeys that they once had thought necessary. He taught his band never to walk along the top of a ridge, but always along one side so as to look down both ways without being conspicuous. And he added one famous invention of his own. This was the "hide." If a hunter happens close to a band of sheep before they see him, the old plan was to make a dash for safety. A good enough plan in the days of bows and arrows or even of muzzle-loading rifles, but the repeating rifle is a different arm. Krag himself learned and then taught his tribe to crouch and lie perfectly still when thus surprised. In nine cases out of ten this will baffle a human hunter, as Krag found time and time again.

It is always good for a race, when a great one arises in it. Krag marked a higher level for the bighorns. His children multiplied on the Yak-i-ni-kak around the Gunder Peak, and eastward as far as Kintla Lake at least. They were healthier and much wiser than had been the bighorn of other days, and being so their numbers steadily increased.

Five years had made some changes in Krag's appearance, but his body was square and round and muscular as ever; his perfect legs seemed unchanged in form or in force; his head was as before, with the heart-shaped white patch on his nose; and his jewel eyes blazed as of old; but his horns, how they had changed! Before they were uncommon; now they were unique. The massive sweeps—the graven records of his life—were now a circle and a quarter, and they told of years of joy and years of strife, and one year, tallied in a narrow band of dark and wrinkled horn, told of the year when all the mountains were scourged by the epidemic of grip; when many lambs and their mothers died; when many strong rams succumbed; when Krag himself had been smitten but recovered, thanks to his stalwart growth and native force, and after a time of misery had shown no traces of those wretched months, except in the yearly growth of horn. For that year, 1889, it was barely an inch in width, plain for those who read such things—a record of a time of want.

At length old Scotty came back. Like all mountaineers he was a wanderer, and he once more returned alone to his shanty on Tobacco Creek. The sod roof had fallen in, and he hesitated to

repair it. Anyhow he would prospect awhile first. He took his
rifle, and sought the familiar upland. Before he returned, he had
sighted two large bands of mountain sheep. That decided him.
He spent a couple of days repairing the shanty, and the curse of
the Yak-i-ni-kak returned.

Scotty was now a middleaged man. His hand was strong and
steady, but his eyes had lost some of their power. As a youth he
scorned all aids to sight. But now he carried a fieldglass. In the
weeks that followed he scanned a thousand benches through the
glass, and many a time his eye rested on the form of the Gunder
ram. The first time he saw him, he exclaimed, "Heavens, what
horns!" Then added, prophetically, "Them's mine!" and he set
out to make them his. But the bighorn of his early days were
fools to these, and month after month passed without his ever
getting a nearer view of the great ram. The ram had more than
once seen him at short range, but Scotty never knew it.

Several times through the glass he marked old Krag from afar
on a bench. Then after a labor of hours stalked round to the place
only to find him gone. Sometimes he really was gone, but on
more than one occasion, the ram was close at hand and hidden,
watching his foe.

Then came a visitor to Scotty's shanty, a cattleman named
Lee, a sportsman by instinct and a lover of dogs and horses. His
horses were of little use in mountain hunting, but his wolfhounds
—three beautiful Russian barzois—were his constant companions, and he suggested to Scotty that it would be a good plan to
try the dogs on the bighorn.

Scotty grinned, "Guess you're from the plains, pard. Wait till
you see the kind of place whar ole Krag hangs around."

Where the Yak-i-ni-kak River leaves its parent mountains, south
of Gunder Peak, it comes from a tremendous gorge called Skinkler's Gulch. This is a mere crack in the vast granite hill, but is at
least five hundred feet in depth. Southward from the back of
Gunder Peak is a broken upland that runs to a point at this
canyon, and ends in a long promontory over the raging walled-in
stream.

This upland is good sheep range and by a strange chance

Scotty, coming up there with Lee and the three wolfhounds, got a glimpse of the Gunder ram. The men kept out of sight and hurried along by the hollows toward the spot. But it was the old story. No sign of their quarry. They found his great hoof mark just where they had seen him, so it was no illusion, but the hard rocks about refused further information, and no doubt Scotty would have had another mysterious disappearance to add to his list, but that the dogs, nosing about in all of the near hollows and thickets of dwarf birch, broke out suddenly into a loud clamor, and as they did so, up jumped a huge, gray, white-sterned animal —the ram, the wonderful Gunder ram. Over the low bushes, over the broken rocks—bounding, soaring, floating; supple, certain, splendid—he bore the great curling wonders on his head as lightly as a lady might her earrings, and then, from various other coverts, sprang up his band and joined him.

Up flew the rifles, but in a moment the three great dogs closing in, gave unwitting screen to the one victim on which every thought was fixed, and not a shot was heard. Away they went, the ram forging quickly to the lead and the others stringing along after. Over the upland, flying, sailing, leaping, and swerving they went. Over the level plains the dogs would soon have caught the hindmost, or perhaps their noblest prey, but on the rugged rocks, it was clear that the sheep were gaining. The men ran, one to the right, the other to the left, the better to keep sight, and Krag, cut off from the peak, dashed southward, over the benchland.

Now it was a straight race. On it went—on, southward. The dogs gained and were near catching the hindmost sheep—then it seemed that the ram dropped back and now ran the rearmost. A rugged stretch was reached and there the sheep gained steadily, though little. One, two, three miles and the chase was sweeping along the rocky ridge that ends in the sudden gash of Skinkler's Gulch. A minute more and the crowd of sheep were rounded up and cornered on the final rock. They huddled together in terror, five hundred feet of dizzy canyon all around, three fierce dogs, and two fiercer men behind. Then, a few seconds later, old Krag dashed up. Cornered at last, he wheeled to fight, for the wild thing never yields.

He was now so far from the bounding dogs, that two rifle balls whistled near. Of the dogs he had no fears; them he could fight, but the rifles were sure death. There was one chance left. The granite walls of the Yak-i-ni-kak could prove no harder than the human foe, the dogs were within forty yards, now, fine courageous animals, keen for fight, fearless of death, and behind, the hunters, remorseless and already triumphant. Sure death from them or doubtful life in the gulch. There was no time to hesitate, he, the leader, must act. He wheeled to the edge and—leaped down—down, not to the bottom, not blindly—thirty feet downward, across the dizzy chasm, was a little jut of rock, no bigger than his nose. The only one in sight, all the rest smooth, sheer, or overhanging. But Krag landed fairly, poised just a heartbeat, in a flash his blazing eyes took in another point, his only hope, on the other side, hidden under the overhanging rocks he had leaped from. His supple loins and corded limbs, bent, pulsed, and floated him across, there got fresh guidance to his flight, then back and sometimes to a mere roughness of the rock on which his hoofs gripped for an instant, took fresh ricochet to another point. Then, sidewise fifteen feet and down, down with modulated impact from point to point, until, with a final drop of twenty feet, he reached a ledge of safety far below.

And the others inspired by his example followed fast, a long cascade of sheep. Had he failed at one point all must have failed. But now they came down headlong. It was splendid, it was inspiring, hop, skip, down they came, one after the other, now ten, now twenty feet, first to last, leaping, sailing, bounding, from point to ledge, from ledge to point, with masterly command of thew and hoof, with marvelous poise and absolute success.

But just as the last had reached the second slender specklike foothold for its life—three white and yellow creatures whirled past her in the air with gurgled gasps of horror, to perish far below. The hounds, impetuous and brave, never hesitated to follow a foe and never knew how far more gifted was that foe than themselves, until it was too late. Down below almost at the water's edge Krag paused at length. Far above he heard the yells and whistles of the hunters; below in the boiling Yak-i-ni-kak he saw a battered white and yellow form being hurried to the sea.

Lee and Scotty stood blankly at the edge. Sheep and dogs had vanished: no possibility of escape for any. Scotty uttered words that had no bearing on the case, only they were harsh blasphemous words and seemed to be necessary. Lee had a choking feeling in his throat, and he felt as no man can comprehend who has not lost a noble dog by a sudden, tragic, and untimely end.

"Bran! Rollo! Ida!" he called in lingering hope, but the only response was from wind that whistled as it swept down Skinkler's Gulch.

Part Two

Lee was a young, warm-hearted, impulsive cattleman. For a day or two he hung about the shanty. The loss of his three friends was a sad blow: he had no heart for more mountaineering. But a few days later, a spell of bracing weather helped his spirits, and he agreed, when Scotty suggested a hunt.

They reached the upper level when Scotty, who had from time to time been scanning the hills with his glass, suddenly exclaimed, "Hell! If thar ain't the old Gunder ram; thought he was smashed in Skinkler's Gulch," and he sat down in amazement. Lee took the glass and he recognized the wonderful ram by his superb horns; the color rushed to the young man's face. Now was his chance for glory and revenge at once! "Poor old Bran, good Rollo, and Ida!"

But few animals have cunning enough to meet the combined drive and ambush. Scotty knew the lay of the land as well as the habits of the ram.

"He ain't agoin' to run down the wind and he ain't agoin' to quit the rocks. That means he'll pass up by the Gunder Peak, if he moves at all, an' he must take one side or the other. He won't go the west side. I show meself once that ar way. So you take the east, I'll give you two hours to get placed. I've a notion he'll cross that spur by that ledge."

Lee set out for his post, Scotty waited two hours, then moved

on to a high ridge and clear against the sky he waved his arms
and walked up and down a few times. The ram was not in sight,
but Scotty knew he would see.

Then the old mountaineer circled back by hidden ways to the
south and began to walk and cut over the ridges toward the place
where the ram had been. He did not expect to see old Krag, but
he did expect the ram to see him.

Lee was at his post and, after a brief spell, he sighted the great
ram himself bounding lightly down a ridge a mile away, and
close behind him were three ewes. They disappeared down a
pineclad hollow, and when they reappeared on the next ridge
they were running as though in great alarm, their ears laid back
and from the hollow behind came, not as Lee expected, the crack
of Scotty's rifle, or the sound of his yell, but the hunting chorus
of timber wolves.

Among the rocks the sheep could easily escape, but among the
timber or on the level such as now lay ahead, the advantage was
with the wolves and a minute later these swept up in sight, five
shaggy furry monsters. The level open was crossed at whirling
speed. The sheep, racing for their lives, soon lengthened out into
a procession in order of speed. Far ahead the great ram, behind
him, with ten-yard gaps between each, the three ewes, and forty
yards behind the last the five grim wolves—closing, gaining at
every leap. The benchland narrowed eastward to pass a rocky
shoulder.

Long years and countless perils had taught the sheep that in
the rocks was safety, and that way led the ram. But in the tangled
upland birch the last of the ewes was losing ground, she gasped a
short "baah," as thrown by a curling root she lost a few more
precious yards. The wolves were almost within leaping distance
when Krag reached the shoulder ledge. But a shoulder above
means a ravine below. In a moment, at that call of distress, Krag
wheeled on the narrow ledge and faced the foe. He stood to one
side and the three ewes leaped past him and on to safety. Then on
came the wolves with a howl of triumph. Many a sheep had they
pulled down and now they knew they soon would feast. Without
a pause they closed, but in such a narrow pass it was one at a
time. The leader sprang, but those death-dealing fangs closed

only on a solid mass of horn and back of that was a force that crushed his head against himself and dashed him at his friend behind with such a fearful vim that both were hurled over the cliff to perish on the rocks.

On came the rest. The ram had no time to back up for a charge, but a sweep of that great head was enough, the points, forefronting now, as they did when he was a lamb, speared and hurled the next wolf and the next, and then Krag found a chance to back up and gather his force. None but a mad wolf could have failed to take warning, but on he came and Krag, in savage glory of the fight, met the last of the furry monsters with a shock that crushed him flat against the rock, then picked him up on his horns as he might a rag and hurled him farthest yet, and standing on the edge he watched him whirl and gasp until he was swallowed in the chasm.

The great ram raised his splendid head, blew a long blast from his nostrils like a warhorse and gazed a moment to see if more were coming, then turned and lightly bounded after the ewes he had so ably guarded.

From his hiding place young Lee took in the whole scene with eager, blazing eyes. Only fifty yards away from him it had passed.

He was an easy mark, fifty yards standing—he was a splendid mark, all far beyond old Scotty's wildest talk; but Lee had seen a deed that day that stirred his blood. He felt no wish to end that life, but sat with brightened eyes and said, with fervor, "You grand old warrior! I don't care if you did kill my dogs. You did it fair. I'll never harm you. For me you may go in safety."

But the ram never knew; and Scotty never understood.

There was once a wretch who, despairing of other claims to notice, thought to achieve a name by destroying the most beautiful building on earth. This is the mind of the head-hunting sportsman. The nobler the thing that he destroys, the greater the deed, the greater his pleasure, and the greater he considers his claim to fame.

During the years that followed more than one hunter saw the great ram, and feasted his covetous eyes on his unparalleled horns. His fame even reached the cities. Dealers offered fabulous prices for the head that bore them—set blood money on the life that grew them, and many came to try their luck, and failed. Then Scotty, always needy, was fired by an even larger money offer, and setting out with his partner they found the ram, with his harem about him. But in three days of hard following they never got a second glimpse, and the partner "reckoned thar was easier money to git" and returned home.

But back of Scotty's sinister gray eyes was a dogged persistency. He returned to the shanty, but only to prepare for a long and obstinate hunt. His rifle, his blanket, his pipe, with matches, tobacco, a pot, a bundle of jerked venison, and three or four pounds of chocolate were all he carried. He returned alone next day to the place where he had left the track of the ram and followed it fast in the snow; winding about in and out and obscured by those of his band, but always distinguishable by its size. Once or twice Scotty came on the spots where the band had been lying down and from time to time he scanned the distance with his glass. But he saw nothing of them. At night he camped on their trail, next day he took it up again; after following for hours, he came on the place where evidently the ram had stopped to watch him afar, and so knew of his pursuer. Thenceforth the trail of the band for a long time was a single line as they headed for distant pastures.

Scotty followed doggedly behind, all day he followed, and at night, in a little hollow, crouched like a wild beast in his lair, with difference only that he had a fire and he smoked a pipe in very human fashion. In the morning he went on as before—once or twice in the far distance he saw the band of sheep traveling steadily southward. Next day passed and the sheep were driven to the south end of the Yak-i-ni-kak range, just north of White-fish Lake.

South of this was the Half-moon Prairie, east the broken land that stretched toward the north fork of the Flathead, and north of them their pertinacious and deadly foe. The sheep were in doubt now, and as old Krag sought to sneak back by the lower benches of the east slope, he heard a crack and a stinging something touched one horn and tore the hair from his shoulder.

The touch of a rifleball on the horn of a ram has a more or less

stunning effect, and Krag, dazed for a moment, gave the signal
which in our speech is "Everyone for himself now," and so the
band was scattered.

Some went this way and some that, running more or less
openly. But Scotty's one thought was old Krag. He heeded no
other, and when the ram made straight away eastward down the
hill, Scotty again took up his trail and cursed and gasped as he
followed.

The Flathead River was only a few miles away. The ram
crossed on the ice and keeping the roughest ground, turning
when the wind turned, he traveled all day northeastward, with
Scotty steadily behind. On the fifth day they passed near Terry's
Lake. Scotty knew the ground. The ram was going east and
would soon run into a lot of lumber camps; then turn he must,
for the region was a box canyon; there was only one way out.
Scotty quit the trail and crossing northward to this one defile,
down which the ram must go, he waited. The West, the Chinook
wind had been rising for an hour or more, the one damp wind of
the Rockies, the snow wind of the hills, and as it rose the flakes
began to fly. In half an hour more it was a blinding snowstorm.
Things twenty yards away were lost to view. But it did not last,
the heaviest of it was over in a few minutes and in two hours the
skies were clear again. Scotty waited another hour, but seeing
nothing he left his post and searched about for sign; and found it,
too, a dimpling row of tracks much hidden by the recent snow,
but clear in one place under a ledge. The ram had passed unseen,
had given him the slip, saved by the storm wind and the snow.

Now, Scotty thought, there must be an object in the ram's bold
dash for the east side of the Flathead, and that object must be to
reach the hills around Kintla Lake, on which he was well known
and had many times been seen. He might keep west all day today,
while the Chinook blew, but if the wind changed in the night he
would surely turn eastward. So Scotty made no further attempt
to keep the trail, or to make the west point of the Kintla Range,
but cut straight northward over the divide toward the lake.

The wind did change in the night. And next day, as Scotty
scanned the vast expanse between him and the lake, he saw a

moving speck below. He quickly got out of sight, then ran to intercept the traveler. But when he got to the spot he aimed at, and cautiously peered, there, five hundred yards away, on the next ridge, he stood—the famous ram. Each in plain view of the other.

Scotty stood for a minute and gazed in silence. Then, "Wal, old Krag, ye kin see the skull and crossbones on my gun; I'm death on yer track; ye can't shake me off; at any price, I mean to have them horns. And here's for luck." Then he raised the rifle and fired, but the distance was great. The ram stood until he saw the puff of smoke, then moved quickly to one side, and the snow was tossed by the ball not far from his former stand.

The ram turned and made eastward, skirting the rugged southern shore of the lake, making for the main divide, and Scotty, left far behind for a time, trudged steadily, surely, behind him. For, added to his tireless strength, was the understreak of brutish grit, of senseless, pig-dogged pertinacity. The inflexible determination that still sticks to its purpose long after sense, reason, and honor have abandoned the attempt; that blinds its owner to his own defeat and makes him, even when he is downed, still feebly strike —to spend his final mite of strength in madly girding at his conqueror, whose quick response he knows will be to wipe him out.

It was on, on, all day. Then camp for the night and up again in the morning. Sometimes the trail was easy to follow, sometimes blotted out by new-fallen snow. But day after day they went; sometimes Scotty was in sight of the prize that he pertinaciously was hunting, but never very near. The ram seemed to have learned that five hundred yards was the farthest range of the rifle, and allowed the man to come up to that, the safety limit. After a time it seemed as though he much preferred to have him there, for then he knew where he was. One time Scotty stole a march, and would have had a close shot had not the fateful west wind borne the taint, and Krag was warned in time, but this was in the first month of that dogged, fearful following. After awhile the ram was never out of sight.

Why did he not fly far away and baffle the hunter by his speed? Because he must feed. The man had his dried venison and chocolate, enough for many days, and when they were gone he could shoot a hare or a grouse, hastily cook it, and travel all day on that, but the ram required hours to seek the scanty grass under the snow. The long pursuit was telling on him. His eye was blazing bright as ever, his shapely corded limbs as certain in their stride, but his belly was pinching up and hunger—weakening hunger—was joining with his other foe.

For five long weeks the chase went on, and the only respite to the Gunder ram was when some snowstorm from the west would interpose its veil.

Then came two weeks when they were daily in sight of each other. In the morning Scotty, rising wolflike from his frosty lair, would call out, "Come, Krag, time we wuz a-movin'," and the ram on the distant ridge would stamp defiantly, then setting his nose to the wind move on, now fast, now slow, but keeping ever the safe five hundred yards or more ahead. When Scotty sat down to rest the ram would graze. If Scotty hid the ram would run in alarm to some place where near approach unseen would be impossible. If Scotty remained still for some time the ram would watch him intently and as still as himself. Thus they went on, day after day, until ten eventless weeks dragged slowly by. A singular feeling had grown between the two. The ram became so used to the sleuth on his track that he accepted him as an inevitable, almost a necessary evil, and one day, when Scotty rose and scanned the northern distance for the ram, he heard the long snort far behind, and turning, he saw old Krag impatiently waiting. The wind had changed and Krag had changed his route to suit. One day after their morning's start Scotty had a difficult two hours in crossing a stream over which old Krag had leaped. When he did reach the other side he heard a snort, and looked around to find that the ram had come back to see what was keeping him.

Thus in the winter all the Chief Mountain was traversed. The Kootenay Rockies, spur by spur, right up to the Crow's Nest Pass, then westward in the face of the white wind, the indomitable pair turned their steps, west and south, to the MacDonald Range. And onward still, until the Galtom Range was reached.

Day by day the same old mechanical following, two dark moving specks on the great expanse of snow. Many a time their trail was crossed by that of other sheep and other game. Once they met a party of miners who knew of Scotty and his hunt, and chaffed him now, but he stared blankly, heeded them not and went on. Many a time the ram sought to hide his fateful footprints in the wake of some passing herd. But Scotty was not to be balked, his purpose had become his nature; all puzzles he worked out, and now there were fewer interruptions of the chase, for the snow-storms seemed to cease, the white wind held aloof, and Nature offered no rebuke.

On and on, still the same scant half-mile apart and on them both the hands of time and death seemed laid. Both were growing hollow-eyed and were gaunter every day. The man's hair had bleached since he set out on this insane pursuit, and the head and shoulders of the ram were grizzling; only his jewel eyes and his splendid sweeping horns were the same, and borne as proudly as when first the chase began.

Each morning the man would rise stiff, half-frozen, and gaunt, but dogged as a very hound infernal, and shout across and Krag would respond, and springing into view from his own couch, the chase went on. Until in the third month, they crossed again from Galtom to Tobacco Range, then eastward back to Gunder Peak —the ram and the sleuth inexorable, upon his trail behind him. Here, on the birthplace of the ram, they sat one morning, at rest. The ram on one ridge; Scotty six hundred yards away on the next. For twelve long weeks the ram had led him through the snow, through ten long mountain ranges—five hundred rugged miles.

And now they were back to their starting point. Each with his lifetime wasted by one-half in that brief span. Scotty sat down and lit his pipe. The ram made haste to graze. As long as the man stayed there in view the ram would keep that ridge. Scotty knew this well; a hundred times he had proved it. Then as he sat and smoked, some evil spirit entered in and sketched a cunning plot. He emptied his pipe deliberately, put it away, then cut some rods of the low creeping birch behind him; he gathered some stones, and the great ram watched afar. The man moved to the edge of

the ridge and with sticks, some stones, and what clothing he
could spare, he made a dummy of himself. Then keeping exactly
behind it, he crawled backward over the ledge and disappeared.
After an hour of crawling and stalking he came up on a ridge
behind the ram.

There he stood, majestic as a bull, graceful as a deer, with
horns that rolled around his brow like thunder clouds about a
peak. He was gazing intently on the dummy, wondering why his
follower was so long still. Scotty was nearly three hundred yards
away. Behind the ram were some low rocks, but between was
open snow. Scotty lay down and threw snow on his own back
until he was all whitened, then set out to crawl two hundred
yards, watching the great ram's head and coming on as fast as he
dared. Still old Krag stared at the dummy; sometimes impatiently stamping. Once he looked about sharply, and once he
would have seen that deadly crawler in the snow, but that his
horn itself, his great right horn, must interpose its breadth between his eye and his foe, and so his last small chance of escape
was gone.

Nearer, nearer to the sheltering rocks crawled Scotty. Then,
safely reaching them at last, he rested, a scant half-hundred yards
away. For the first time in his life he saw the famous horns quite
close. He saw the great, broad shoulders, the curving neck, still
massive, though the mark of famine was on all. He saw this
splendid fellow creature blow the hot breath of life from his nostrils, vibrant in the sun; and he even got a glimpse of the life light
in those glowing amber eyes, but he slowly raised the gun.

The Gunder ram was spellbound, watching that enemy, im-
movable across the dip.

Up went the gun that never failed—directed by the eye that
never erred. But the hand that had never trembled taking twenty
human lives, now shook as though in fear.

Then the hand grew steady. The hunter's face was calm and
hard. The rifle rang, and Scotty hid his head. For the familiar
crack! had sounded as it never did before. He heard a rattling on
the distant stones, then a long-drawn "snoof!" But he neither
looked nor moved. Two minutes later all was still, and he timidly
raised his head. Was he gone?

There on the snow lay a great gray-brown form, and at one end, like a twin-necked hydra coiling, were the horns, the wonderful horns, the sculptured record of the splendid life of a splendid creature, his fifteen years of life made visible at once. There were the points, much worn now, that once had won his lamb-days' fight. There were the years of robust growth, each long in measure of that growth; here was that year of sickness; there the splinter on the fifth year's ring, which notched his first love fight. The points had now come round, and on them were the lives of many gray wolves that had sought his life. And so the rings read on, the living record of a life whose very preciousness had brought it to a sudden end.

The golden chain across the web of white was broken for its gold.

Scotty walked slowly over, and gazed in sullen silence, not at the dear-bought horns, but at the calm yellow eyes, unclosed and yet undimmed by death. Stone cold was he. He did not understand himself. He did not know that this was the sudden drop after the long, long slope up which he had been forcing himself for months. He sat down twenty yards away, with his back to the horns. He put a quid of tobacco in his mouth. But his mouth was dry. He spat it out again. He did not know what he felt. Words played but little part in his life, and his lips uttered only a torrent of horrid blasphemies, his only emotional outburst.

A long silence, then, "I'd give it back to him if I could."

He stared at the distance. His eyes fell on the coat he had left, and, realizing that he was cold, he walked across and gathered up his things. Then he returned to the horns, and over him came the wild, inhuman lusting for his victim's body, that he had heard his comrades speak of, but had never before understood. The reactionary lust that makes the panther fondle and caress the deer he has stricken down. He made a fire. Then feeling more like himself, he skinned the ram's neck and cut off the head. This was familiar work and he followed it up mechanically, cutting meat enough to satisfy his hunger. Then bowing his shoulders beneath the weight of his massive trophy—a weight he would scarcely have noticed three months ago, he turned from the chase—old, emaciated, grizzled, and haggard—and toiled slowly down to the shanty he had left twelve weeks before.

"No! money couldn't buy it," and Scotty turned sullenly away to end discussion. He waited a week until the taxidermist had done his best, then he retraversed three hundred miles of mountain to his lonely home. He removed the cover, and hung the head where it got the best light. The work was well done, the horns were unchanged, the wonderful golden eyes were there, and when a glint of light gave to them a semblance of regard, the mountaineer felt once more some of the feelings of that day on the ridge. He covered up the head again.

Those who knew him best say he kept it covered and never spoke about it. But one man said, "Yes, I saw him uncover it once and look kind o' queer." The only remark he ever made about it was, "Them's my horns, but he'll get even with me yet."

Four years went by. Scotty, now known as Old Man Scotty, had never hunted since. He had broken himself down in that long madness. He lived now entirely by his gold pan, was quite alone and was believed to have something on his mind. One day late in the winter an old partner stopped at his shanty. Their hours of conversation did not amount to as many paragraphs.

"I heerd about ye killin' the Gunder ram."

Scotty nodded.

"Let's see him, Scotty."

"Suit yourself," and the old man jerked his head toward the draped thing on the wall. The stranger pulled off the cloth and then followed the usual commonplace exclamations. Scotty received them in silence. But he turned to look. The firelight reflected in the glassy eyes lent a red and angry glare.

"Kivver him up when you're through," said Scotty, and turned to his smoking.

"Say, Scotty, why don't ye sell him if he bothers ye that a way? That there New Yorker told me to tell ye that he'd give—"

"To hell with yer New Yorker. I'll niver sell him, I'll niver part with him. I stayed by him till I done him up, and he'll stay by me till he gits even. He's been a-gittin' back at me these four years. He broke me down on that trip. He's made an old man o' me.

He's left me half luny. He's sucking my life out now, but he ain't through with me yet. There's more o' him round than that head. I tell ye when that old Chinook comes a-blowing up the Tobacco Creek, I've heerd noises that the wind don't make. I've heerd him just the same as I done that day when he blowed his life out through his nose, and me a-lyin' on my face afore him. I'm up agin it, and I'm a-goin' to face it out—right—here—on—Tobacco Creek."

The white wind rose high that night, and hissed and wailed about Scotty's shanty. Ordinarily, the stranger might not have noticed it. But once or twice there came in over the door a long "Snoof" that jarred the latch and rustled violently the drapery of the head. Scotty glanced at his friend with a wild, scared look. No need for a word, the stranger's face was white.

In the morning it was snowing, but the stranger went his way. All that day the white wind blew, and the snow came down harder and harder. Deeper and deeper it piled on everything. All the smaller peaks were rounded off with snow, and all the hollows of the higher ridges leveled. Still it came down, not drifting but piling up, heavy, soft, adhesive. All day long, deeper, heavier, rounder. As night came on, the Chinook blew yet harder. It skipped from peak to peak like a living thing. It came like a mighty goddess, like an angry angel with a bugle horn, with a dreadful message from the far-off western sea.

And here and there there were mighty doings among the peaks. Here new effects were carven with a stroke. Here lakes were made or unmade. An avalanche from Purcell's Peak went down to gash the sides, and show long veins of gold; another hurried, by the white wind sent, to block a stream and turn its wasted waters to a thirsty land—a messenger of mercy. But down the Gunder Peak there whirled a monstrous mass, charged with a mission of revenge. Down, down, down, loud "snoofing" as it went, sliding from shoulder, ledge, and long incline, now wiping out a forest that would bar its path, then crashing, leaping, rolling, smashing over cliff and steep descent, still gaining as it sped. Down, down, faster, fiercer in one fell and fearful rush, and Scotty's shanty, in its track, with all that it contained, was crushed and swiftly blotted out. The hunter had forefelt his doom.

Over the rocky upland came the spring, over the level plain of Tobacco Creek. Gently the rains from the westward washed the great white pile of the snowslide. Slowly the broken shanty came to light, and there in the middle, quite unharmed, was the head of the Gunder ram. His amber eyes were gleaming bright as of old, under cover of those wonderful horns; and below him were some broken bones, with rags and grizzled human hair.

Old Scotty is forgotten, but the ram's head hangs enshrined on a palace wall today, a treasure among kingly treasures; and men, when they gaze on those marvelous horns, still talk of the glorious Gunder ram who grew them far away on the heights of the Kootenay.

LONG ODDS

H. RIDER HAGGARD

THE STORY which is narrated in the following pages came to me from the lips of my old friend Allan Quatermain, or Hunter Quatermain, as we used to call him in South Africa. He told it to me one evening when I was stopping with him at the place he bought in Yorkshire. Shortly after that, the death of his only son so unsettled him that he immediately left England, accompanied by two companions who were old fellow-voyagers of his, Sir Henry Curtis and Captain Good, and has now utterly vanished into the dark heart of Africa. He is persuaded that a white people, of which he has heard rumors all his life, exists somewhere on the highlands in the vast, still unexplored interior, and his great ambition is to find them before he dies. This is the wild quest upon which he and his companions have departed, and from which I shrewdly suspect they never will return. One letter only have I received from the old gentleman, dated from a mission station high up the Tana, a river on the east coast, about three hundred miles north of Zanzibar; in it he says they have gone through many hardships and adventures, but are alive and well, and have found traces which go far toward making him hope that the results of their wild quest may be a "magnificent and unexampled discovery." I greatly fear, however, that all he has discovered is death; for this letter came a long while ago, and nobody has heard a single word of the party since. They have totally vanished.

It was on the last evening of my stay at his house that he told

the ensuing story to me and Captain Good, who was dining with
him. He had eaten his dinner and drunk two or three glasses of
old port, just to help Good and myself to the end of the second
bottle. It was an unusual thing for him to do, for he was a most
abstemious man, having conceived, as he used to say, a great
horror of drink from observing its effects upon the class of men—
hunters, transport-riders, and others—among whom he had
passed so many years of his life. Consequently the good wine
took more effect on him than it would have done on most men,
sending a little flush into his wrinkled cheeks, and making him
talk more freely than usual.

Dear old man! I can see him now, as he went limping up and
down the vestibule, with his gray hair sticking up in scrubbing-
brush fashion, his shriveled yellow face, and his large dark eyes,
that were as keen as any hawk's and yet soft as a buck's. The
whole room was hung with trophies of his numerous hunting
expeditions, and he had some story about every one of them, if
only you could get him to tell them. Generally he would not, for
he was not very fond of narrating his own adventures, but tonight
the port wine made him more communicative.

"Ah, you brute!" he said, stopping beneath an unusually large
skull of a lion, which was fixed just over the mantelpiece, beneath
a long row of guns, its jaws distended to their utmost width. "Ah,
you brute! You have given me a lot of trouble for the last dozen
years, and will, I suppose, to my dying day."

"Tell us the yarn, Quatermain," said Good. "You have often
promised to tell me, and you never have."

"You had better not ask me to," he answered, "for it is a
longish one."

"All right," I said, "the evening is young and there is some
more port."

Thus adjured, he filled his pipe from a jar of coarse-cut Boer
tobacco that was always standing on the mantelpiece, and, still
walking up and down the room began:

"It was, I think, in the March of '69 that I was up in
Sikukuni's country. It was just after old Sequati's time, and
Sikukuni had got into power—I forget how. Anyway, I was
there. I had heard that the Bapedi people had got down an enor-

mous quantity of ivory from the interior, and so I started with a wagon-load of goods, and came straight away from Middelburg to try and trade some of it. It was a risky thing to go into the country so early, on account of the fever; but I knew that there were one or two others after that lot of ivory, so I determined to have a try for it, and take my chance of fever. I had got so tough from continual knocking about that I did not set it down at much. Well, I got on all right for a while. It is a wonderfully beautiful piece of bush veldt, with great ranges of mountains running through it, and round granite koppies starting up here and there, looking out like sentinels over the rolling waste of bush. But it is very hot—hot as a stew-pan—and when I was there that March, which, of course, is autumn in that part of Africa, the whole place reeked of fever. Every morning, as I trekked along down by the Oliphant River, I used to creep out of the wagon at dawn and look out. But there was no river to be seen—only a long line of billows of what looked like the finest cotton wool tossed up lightly with a pitchfork. It was the fever mist. Out from among the scrub, too, came little spirals of vapor, as though there were hundreds of tiny fires alight in it—reek rising from thousands of tons of rotting vegetation. It was a beautiful place, but the beauty was the beauty of death; and all those lines and blots of vapor wrote one great word across the surface of the country, and that word was 'fever.'

"It was a dreadful year of illness that. I came, I remember, to one little kraal of knobnoses, and went up to it to see if I could get some *maas* (curdled buttermilk) and a few mealies. As I got near I was struck with the silence of the place. No children began to chatter, and no dogs barked. Nor could I see any native sheep or cattle. The place, though it had evidently been recently inhabited, was as still as the bush round it, and some guinea fowl got up out of the prickly-pear bushes right at the kraal gate. I remember that I hesitated a little before going in, there was such an air of desolation about the spot. Nature never looks desolate when man has not yet laid his hand upon her breast; she is only lovely. But when man has been, and has passed away, then she looks desolate.

"Well, I passed into the kraal, and went up to the principal hut. In front of the hut was something with an old sheepskin *kaross* (rug) thrown over it. I stooped down and drew off the rug, and then shrank back amazed, for under it was the body of a young woman recently dead. For a moment I thought of turning back, but my curiosity overcame me; so, going past the woman, I went down on my hands and knees and crept into the hut. It was so dark that I could not see anything, though I could smell a great deal; so I lit a match. It was a 'tandstickor' match and burned slowly and dimly, and as the light gradually increased I made out what I thought was a lot of people, men, women, and children, fast asleep. Presently it burned up brightly, and I saw that they too, five of them altogether, were quite dead. One was a baby. I dropped the match in a hurry, and was making my way out of the hut as hard as I could go, when I caught sight of two bright eyes staring out of a corner. Thinking it was a wildcat, or some such animal, I redoubled my haste, when suddenly a voice near the eyes began first to mutter, and then to send up a succession of awful yells. Hastily I lit another match, and perceived that the eyes belonged to an old woman, wrapped up in a greasy leather garment. Taking her by the arm, I dragged her out, for she could not, or would not, come by herself, and the stench was overpowering me. Such a sight as she was—a bag of bones, covered over with black, shriveled parchment. The only white thing about her was her hair, and she seemed to be pretty well dead except for her eyes and her voice. She thought that I was a devil come to take her, and that was why she yelled so. Well, I got her down to the wagon, and gave her a tot of Cape smoke, and then, as soon as it was ready, poured about a pint of beef tea down her throat, made from the flesh of a blue vilder-beeste I had killed the day before, and after that she brightened up wonderfully. She could talk Zulu—indeed, it turned out that she had run away from Zululand in T'Chaka's time—and she told me that all the people that I had seen had died of fever. When they had died, the other inhabitants of the kraal had taken the cattle and gone away, leaving the poor old woman, who was helpless from age and infirmity, to perish of starvation or disease, as the case might be. She had been sitting there for three days among the bodies when I found her. I took her on to the next kraal, and gave the head man a blanket to look after her, promising him another if I found her well when I came back. I remember that he was much astonished at my parting with two blankets for the sake of such a worthless old creature. Why did I not leave her in the bush? he asked. Those people carry the doctrine of the survival of the fittest to its extreme, you see.

"It was the night after I had got rid of the old woman that I made my first acquaintance with my friend yonder," and he nodded toward the skull that seemed to be grinning down at us in the shadow of the wide mantel shelf. "I had trekked from dawn till eleven o'clock—a long trek—but I wanted to get on; and then had the oxen turned out to graze, sending the voorlooper to look after them, meaning to inspan again about six o'clock, and trek with the moon till ten. Then I got into the wagon and had a good sleep till half-past two or so in the afternoon, when I got up and cooked some meat, and had my dinner, washing it down with a pannikin of black coffee; for it was difficult to get preserved milk in those days. Just as I had finished, and the driver, a man called Tom, was washing up the things, in comes the young scoundrel of a voorlooper, driving one ox before him.

" 'Where are the other oxen?' I asked.

" 'Koos!' he said, 'koos! [chief] the other oxen have gone away. I turned my back for a minute, and when I looked round again they were all gone except Kaptein, here, who was rubbing his back against a tree.'

" 'You mean that you have been asleep, and let them stray, you villain. I will rub your back against a stick,' I answered, feeling very angry, for it was not a pleasant prospect to be stuck up in that fever-trap for a week or so while we were hunting for the oxen. 'Off you go, and you too, Tom, and mind you don't come back till you have found them. They have trekked back along the Middelburg road, and are a dozen miles off by now, I'll be bound. Now, no words; go, both of you.'

"Tom, the driver, swore and caught the lad a hearty kick, which he richly deserved, and then, having tied old Kaptein up to the dissel-boom with a riem, they got their assegais and sticks, and started. I would have gone too, only I knew that somebody must look after the wagon, and I did not like to leave either of the boys with it at night. I was in a very bad temper, indeed, although I was pretty well used to these sort of occurrences, and soothed myself by taking a rifle and going to kill something. For a couple of hours I poked about without seeing anything that I could get a shot at, but at last, just as I was again within seventy yards of the wagon, I put up an old Impala ram from behind a mimosa-thorn. He ran straight for the wagon, and it was not till he was passing within a few feet of it that I could get a decent shot at him. Then I pulled, and caught him halfway down the spine; over he went, dead as a doornail, and a pretty shot it was, though I ought not to say it. This little incident put me into rather a better temper, especially as the buck had rolled over right against the after part of the wagon, so I had only to gut him, fix a riem round his legs, and haul him up. By the time I had done this the sun was down, and the full moon was up, and a beautiful moon it was. And then there came down that wonderful hush that sometimes falls over the African bush in the early hours of the night. No beast was moving, and no bird called. Not a breath of air stirred the quiet trees, and the shadows did not even quiver; they only grew. It was very oppressive and very lonely, for there was not a sign of the cattle or the boys. I was quite thankful for the society of old Kaptein, who was lying down contentedly against the disselboom, chewing the cud with a good conscience.

"Presently, however, Kaptein began to get restless. First he snorted, then he got up and snorted again. I could not make it out, so, like a fool, I got down off the wagon-box to have a look round, thinking it might be the lost oxen coming.

"Next instant I regretted it, for all of a sudden I heard an awful roar and saw something yellow flash past me and light on poor Kaptein. Then came a bellow of agony from the ox, and a crunch as the lion put his teeth through the poor brute's neck, and I began to realize what had happened. My rifle was in the wagon, and my first thought was to get hold of it, and I turned and made a bolt for it. I got my foot on the wheel and flung my body forward on to the wagon, and there I stopped as if I were frozen, and no wonder, for as I was about to spring up I heard the lion behind me, and next second I felt the brute, ay, as plainly as I can feel this table. I felt him, I say, sniffing at my left leg that was hanging down.

"My word! I did feel queer; I don't think that I ever felt so queer before. I dared not move for the life of me, and the odd thing was that I seemed to lose power over my leg, which had an insane sort of inclination to kick out of its own mere motion— just as hysterical people want to laugh when they ought to be particularly solemn. Well, the lion sniffed and sniffed, beginning at my ankle and slowly nosing away up to my thigh. I thought that he was going to get hold then, but he did not. He only growled softly, and went back to the ox. Shifting my head a little I got a full view of him. He was the biggest lion I ever saw—and I have seen a great many—and he had a most tremendous black mane. What his teeth were like you can see—look there, pretty big ones, ain't they? Altogether he was a magnificent animal, and, as I lay there sprawling on the fore tongue of the wagon, it occurred to me that he would look uncommonly well in a cage. He stood there by the carcass of poor Kaptein, and deliberately disembowelled him as neatly as a butcher could have done. All this while I dared not move, for he kept lifting his head and keeping an eye on me as he licked his bloody chops. When he had cleaned Kaptein out, he opened his mouth and roared, and I am not exaggerating when I say that the sound shook the wagon. Instantly there came back an answering roar.

"Heavens! I thought, there is his mate.

"Hardly was the thought out of my head when I caught sight in the moonlight of the lioness bounding along through the long grass, and after her a couple of cubs about the size of mastiffs. She stopped within a few feet of my head, and stood, and waved her tail, and fixed me with her glowing yellow eyes; but just as I thought that it was all over she turned, and began to feed on Kaptein, and so did the cubs. There were the four of them within eight feet of me, growling and quarreling, rending and tearing and crunching poor Kaptein's bones; and there I lay shaking with terror, and the cold perspiration pouring out of me, feeling like another Daniel come to judgment in a new sense of the phrase. Presently the cubs had eaten their fill, and began to get restless. One went round to the back of the wagon and pulled at the Impala buck that hung there, and the other came round my way and began the sniffing game at my leg. Indeed, he did more than that, for, my trouser being hitched up a little, he began to lick the bare skin with his rough tongue. The more he licked the more he liked it, to judge from his increased vigor and the loud purring noise he made. Then I knew that the end had come, for in another second his filelike tongue would have rasped through the skin of my leg—which was luckily pretty tough—and have got to the blood, and then there would be no chance for me. So I just lay there and thought of my sins, and prayed to the Almighty, and thought that, after all, life was a very enjoyable thing.

"And then all of a sudden I heard a crashing of bushes and the shouting and whistling of men, and there were the two boys coming back with the cattle, which they had found trekking along all together. The lions lifted their heads and listened, and then without a sound bounded off—and I fainted.

"The lions came back no more that night, and by the next morning my nerves had got pretty straight again; but I was full of wrath when I thought of all that I had gone through at the hands, or rather noses, of those four lions, and of the fate of my after-ox Kaptein. He was a splendid ox, and I was very fond of him. So wroth was I that, like a fool, I determined to go for the whole family of them. It was worthy of a greenhorn out on his first hunting trip; but I did it nevertheless. Accordingly after breakfast, having rubbed some oil upon my leg, which was very sore from the cub's tongue, I took the driver, Tom, who did not half like the job, and having armed myself with an ordinary double No. 12 smooth-bore, the first breech-loader I ever had, I started. I took the smooth-bore because it shot a bullet very well; and my experience has been that a round ball from a smooth-bore is quite as effective against a lion as an express bullet. The lion is soft and not a difficult animal to finish if you hit him anywhere in the body. A buck takes far more killing.

"Well, I started, and the first thing I set to work to do was to try to make out whereabouts the brutes lay up for the day. About three hundred yards from the wagon was the crest of a rise covered with single mimosa trees, dotted about in a parklike fashion, and beyond this was a stretch of open plain running down to a dry pan, or waterhole, which covered about an acre of ground, and was densely clothed with reeds, now in the sear and yellow leaf. From the farther edge of this pan the ground sloped up again to the great cleft, or nullah, which had been cut out by the action of water, and was pretty thickly sprinkled with bush, among which grew some large trees, I forget of what sort.

"It at once struck me that the dry pan would be a likely place to find my friends in, as there is nothing a lion is fonder of than lying up in reeds, through which he can see things without being seen himself. Accordingly thither I went and prospected. Before I had got halfway round the pan I found the remains of a blue vilder-beeste that had evidently been killed within the last three or four days and partially devoured by lions; and from other indications about I was soon assured that if the family were not in the pan that day, they spent a good deal of their spare time there. But if there, the question was how to get them out; for it was clearly impossible to think of going in after them unless one was quite determined to commit suicide. Now there was a strong wind blowing from the direction of the wagon, across the reedy pan, toward the bush-clad kloof or donga, and this first gave me the idea of firing the reeds, which, as I think I told you, were pretty dry. Accordingly, Tom took some matches and began starting little fires to the left, and I did the same to the right. But the reeds were still green at the bottom, and we should never have got them well alight had it not been for the wind, which got stronger and stronger as the sun got higher, and forced the fire into them. At last, after half an hour's trouble, the flames got a hold, and began to spread out like a fan, whereupon I got round to the farther side of the pan to wait for the lions, standing well out in the open, as we stood at the copse today where you shot the woodcock. It was a rather risky thing to do, but I used to be so sure of my shooting in those days that I did not so much mind the risk. Scarcely had I got round when I heard the reeds parting before the onward rush of some animal. 'Now for it,' said I. On it came. I could see that it was yellow, and prepared for action, when instead of a lion out bounded a beautiful rietbok which had been lying in the shelter of the pan. It must, by the way, have

been a rietbok of a peculiarly confiding nature to lay itself down
with the lion like the lamb of prophecy, but I suppose that the
reeds were thick, and that it kept a long way off.

"Well, I let the rietbok go, and it went like the wind, and kept
my eyes fixed upon the reeds. The fire was burning like a furnace
now; the flames crackling and roaring as they bit into the reeds,
sending spouts of fire twenty feet and more into the air, and
making the hot air dance above it in a way that was perfectly
dazzling. But the reeds were still half green, and created an enormous quantity of smoke, which came rolling toward me like a
curtain, lying very low on account of the wind. Presently, above
the crackling of the fire, I heard a startled roar, and then another
and another. So the lions were at home.

"I was beginning to get excited now, for, as you fellows know,
there is nothing in experience to warm up your nerves like a lion
at close quarters, unless it is a wounded buffalo; and I got still
more so when I made out through the smoke that the lions were
all moving about on the extreme edge of the reeds. Occasionally
they would pop their heads out like rabbits from a burrow, and
then, catching sight of me standing about fifty yards out, draw
them back again. I knew that it must be getting pretty warm
behind them, and that they could not keep the game up for long;
and I was not mistaken, for suddenly all four of them broke cover
together, the old black-maned lion leading by a few yards. I never
saw a more splendid sight in all my hunting experience than
those four lions bounding across the veldt, overshadowed by the
dense pall of smoke and backed by the fiery furnace of the burning reeds.

"I reckoned that they would pass, on their road to the bushy
kloof, within about five and twenty yards of me; so, taking a long
breath, I got my gun well on to the lion's shoulder—the black-
maned one—so as to allow for an inch or two of motion, and
catch him through the heart. I was on, dead on, and my finger
was just beginning to tighten on the trigger, when suddenly I
went blind—a bit of reed-ash had drifted into my right eye. I
danced and rubbed, and got it more or less clear just in time to
see the tail of the last lion vanishing round the bushes up the
kloof.

"If ever a man was mad I was that man. It was too bad; and such a shot in the open, too! However, I was not going to be beaten, so I just turned and marched for the kloof. Tom, the driver, begged and implored me not to go; but though as a general rule I never pretended to be very brave (which I am not), I was determined that I would either kill those lions or they should kill me. So I told Tom that he need not come unless he liked, but I was going; and being a plucky fellow, a Swazi by birth, he shrugged his shoulders, muttered that I was mad or bewitched, and followed doggedly in my tracks.

"We soon got to the kloof, which was about three hundred yards in length and but sparsely wooded, and then the real fun began. There might be a lion behind every bush—there certainly were four lions somewhere; the delicate question was, where. I peeped and poked and looked in every possible direction, with my heart in my mouth, and was at last rewarded by catching a glimpse of something yellow moving behind a bush. At the same moment, from another bush opposite me, out burst one of the cubs and galloped back toward the burned-out pan. I whipped round and let drive a snap-shot that tipped him head over heels, breaking his back within two inches of the root of the tail, and there he lay helpless but glaring. Tom afterward killed him with his assegai. I opened the breech of the gun and hurriedly pulled out the old case, which, to judge from what ensued, must, I suppose, have burst and left a portion of its fabric sticking to the barrel. At any rate, when I tried to get in the new case it would only enter halfway; and—would you believe it?—this was the moment that the lioness, attracted no doubt by the outcry of her cub, chose to put in an appearance. There she stood, twenty paces or so from me, lashing her tail and looking just as wicked as it is possible to conceive. Slowly I stepped backward, trying to push in the new case, and as I did so she moved on in little runs, dropping down after each run. The danger was imminent, and the case would not go in. At the moment I oddly enough thought of the cartridge-maker, whose name I will not mention, and earnestly hoped that if the lion got me some condign punishment would overtake him. It would not go in, so I tried to pull it out. It would not come out, either, and my gun was useless if I could not shut it to use the other barrel. I might as well have had no gun. Meanwhile I was walking backward, keeping my eye on the lioness, who was creeping forward on her belly without a sound, but lashing her tail and keeping her eye on me; and in it I saw that she was coming in a few seconds more. I dashed my wrist and the palm of my hand against the brass rim of the cartridge till the blood poured from them—look, there are the scars of it to this day!"

Here Quatermain held up his right hand to the light and showed us seven or eight white cicatrices just where the wrist is set into the hand.

"But it was not of the slightest use," he went on; "the cartridge would not move. I only hope that no other man will ever be put in such an awful position. The lioness gathered herself together, and I gave myself up for lost, when suddenly Tom shouted out from somewhere in my rear: 'You are walking on to the wounded cub; turn to the right.'

"I had the sense, dazed as I was, to take the hint, and slewing round at right angles, but still keeping my eyes on the lioness, I continued my backward walk.

"To my intense relief, with a low growl she straightened herself, turned, and bounded off farther up the kloof.

" 'Come on, inkoos,' said Tom; 'let's get back to the wagon.'

" 'All right, Tom,' I answered. 'I will when I have killed those three other lions,' for by this time I was bent on shooting them as I never remember being bent on anything before or since. 'You can go if you like, or you can get up a tree.'

"He considered the position a little, and then he very wisely got up a tree. I wish that I had done the same.

"Meanwhile I had got out my knife, which had an extractor in it, and succeeded after some difficulty in hauling out the case which had so nearly been the cause of my death, and removing the obstruction in the barrel. It was very little thicker than a postage stamp; certainly not thicker than a piece of writing paper. This done I loaded the gun, bound my handkerchief round my wrist and hand to stanch the flowing of the blood, and started on again.

"I had noticed that the lioness went into a thick green bush, or rather cluster of bushes, growing near the water; for there was a little stream running down the kloof, about fifty yards higher up, and for this I made. When I got there, however, I could see nothing, so I took up a big stone and threw it into the bushes. I believe that it hit the other cub, for out it came with a rush, giving me a broadside shot of which I promptly availed myself, knocking it over dead. Out, too, came the lioness like a flash of light, but quick as she went I managed to put the other bullet into her ribs, so that she rolled right over three times like a shot rabbit. I instantly got two more cartridges into the gun, and as I did so the lioness got up again and came crawling toward me on her fore paws, roaring and groaning, and with such an expression of diabolical fury on her countenance as I have not often seen. I shot her again through the chest, and she fell over on her side quite dead.

"That was the first and last time that I ever killed a brace of lions right and left, and, what is more, I never heard of anybody else doing it. Naturally I was considerably pleased with myself, and, having again loaded up, went on to look for the black-maned beauty who had killed Kaptein. Slowly and with the greatest care I proceeded up the kloof, searching every bush and tuft of grass as I went. It was wonderfully exciting work, for I never was sure from one moment to another but that he would be on me. I took comfort, however, from the reflection that a lion rarely attacks a man—rarely, I say; sometimes he does, as you will see—unless he is cornered or wounded. I must have been nearly an hour hunting after the lion. Once I thought I saw something move in a clump of tambouki grass, but I could not be sure, and when I trod out the grass I could not find him.

"At last I got up to the head of the kloof, which made a cul-de-sac. It was formed of a wall of rock about fifty feet high. Down this rock trickled a little waterfall, and in front of it, some seventy feet from its face, was a great piled-up mass of boulders, in the crevices and on the top of which grew ferns and grass and stunted bushes. This mass was about twenty-five feet high. The sides of the kloof here were also very steep. Well, I got up to the top of the nullah and looked all round. No signs of the lion. Evidently I had either overlooked him farther down, or he had escaped right away. It was very vexatious; but still three lions were not a bad bag for one gun before dinner, and I was fain to be content. Accordingly, I departed back again, making my way round the isolated pillar of boulders, and beginning to feel that I was pretty well done up with excitement and fatigue, and should be more so before I had skinned those three lions. When I had got, as nearly as I could judge, about eighteen yards past the pillar or mass of boulders, I turned to have another look round. I have a pretty sharp eye, but I could see nothing at all.

"Then, on a sudden, I saw something sufficiently alarming. On the top of the mass of boulders, opposite to me, standing out clear against the rock beyond, was the huge black-maned lion. He had been crouching there, and now arose as though by magic. There he stood lashing his tail, just like a statue of the animal on the gateway of Northumberland House that I have seen a picture of. But he did not stand long. Before I could fire—before I could do more than get the gun to my shoulder—he sprang straight up and out from the rock, and, driven by the impetus of that one mighty bound, came hurtling through the air toward me.

"Heavens! how grand he looked, and how awful! High into the air he flew, describing a great arch. Just as he touched the highest point of his spring I fired. I did not dare to wait, for I saw that he would clear the whole space and land right upon me. Without a sight, almost without aim, I fired, as one would fire a snap-shot at a snipe. The bullet told, for I distinctly heard its thud above the rushing sound caused by the passage of the lion through the air. Next second I was swept to the ground (luckily I fell into a low, creeper-clad bush, which broke the shock), and the lion was on top of me, and the next those great white teeth of his had met in my thigh—I heard them grate against the bone. I yelled out in agony, for I did not feel in the least benumbed and happy, like Dr. Livingstone—whom, by the way, I knew very well—and gave myself up for dead. But suddenly, as I did so, the lion's grip on my thigh loosened, and he stood over me, swaying to and fro, his huge mouth, from which the blood was gushing, wide opened. Then he roared, and the sound shook the rocks.

"To and fro he swung, and suddenly the great head dropped on me, knocking all the breath from my body, and he was dead.

My bullet had entered in the center of his chest and passed out on the right side of the spine about halfway down the back.

"The pain of my wound kept me from fainting, and as soon as I got my breath I managed to drag myself from under him. Thank heavens, his great teeth had not crushed my thigh bone; but I was losing a great deal of blood, and had it not been for the timely arrival of Tom, with whose aid I got the handkerchief off my wrist and tied it round my leg, twisting it tight with a stick, I think I should have bled to death.

"Well, it was a just reward for my folly in trying to tackle a family of lions singlehanded. The odds were too long. I have been lame ever since, and shall be to my dying day; in the month of March the wound always troubles me a great deal, and every three years it breaks out raw. I need scarcely add that I never traded the lot of ivory at Sikukuni's. Another man got it—a German—and made five hundred pounds out of it after paying expenses. I spent the next month on the broad of my back, and was a cripple for six months after that. And now I've told you the yarn, so I will have a drop of hollands and go to bed."

THE LAST DAY
IN THE FIELD

CAROLINE GORDON

THAT WAS THE FALL when the leaves stayed green so long. We had a drought in August and the ponds everywhere were dry and the watercourses shrunken. Then in September heavy rains came. Things greened up. It looked like winter was never coming.

"You aren't going to hunt this year, Aleck?" Molly said. "Remember how you stayed awake nights last fall with that pain in your leg."

In October light frosts came. In the afternoons when I sat on the back porch going over my fishing tackle I marked their progress on the elderberry bushes that were left standing against the stable fence. The lower, spreading branches had turned yellow and were already sinking to the ground but the leaves in the top clusters still stood up stiff and straight.

"Ah-ha, it'll get you yet!" I said, thinking how frost creeps higher and higher out of the ground each night of fall.

The dogs next door felt it and would thrust their noses through the wire fence scenting the wind from the north. When I walked in the backyard they would bound twice their height and whine, for meat scraps Molly said, but it was because they smelled blood on my old hunting coat.

They were almost matched liver-and-white pointers. The big dog had a beautiful, square muzzle and was deep-chested and rangy. The bitch, Judy, had a smaller head and not so good a muzzle but she was springy-loined too and had one of the merriest tails I've ever watched.

When Joe Thomas, the boy that owned them, came home from the hardware store he would change his clothes and then come down the back way and we would stand there watching the dogs and wondering how they would work. They had just been with a trainer up in Kentucky for three months. Joe said they were keen as mustard. He was going to take them out the first good Saturday and he wanted me to come along.

"I can't make it," I said. "My leg's worse this fall than it was last."

The fifteenth of November was clear and so warm that we sat out on the porch till nine o'clock. It was still warm when we went to bed toward eleven. The change must have come in the middle of the night. I woke once, hearing the clock strike two, and felt the air cold on my face and thought before I went back to sleep that the weather had broken at last. When I woke again toward dawn the cold air slapped my face hard. I came wide awake, turned over in bed, and looked out of the window. The sun was just coming up behind a wall of purple clouds streaked with amber. As I watched, it burned through and the light everywhere got bright.

There was a scaly bark hickory tree growing on the east side of the house. You could see its upper branches from the bedroom window. The leaves had turned yellow a week ago. But yesterday evening when I walked out there in the yard they had still been flat, with green streaks showing in them. Now they were curled up tight and a lot of leaves had fallen to the ground.

I got out of bed quietly so as not to wake Molly, dressed, and went down the back way over to the Thomas house. There was no one stirring but I knew which room Joe's was. The window was open and I could hear him snoring. I went up and stuck my head in.

"Hey," I said, "killing frost!"

He opened his eyes and looked at me and then his eyes went shut. I reached my arm through the window and shook him. "Get up," I said. "We got to start right away."

He was awake now and out on the floor stretching. I told him to dress and be over at the house as quick as he could. I'd have breakfast ready for us both.

Aunt Martha had a way of leaving fire in the kitchen stove at night. There were red embers there now. I poked the ashes out and piled kindling on top of them. When the flame came up I put some heavier wood on, filled the coffeepot, and put some grease on in a skillet. By the time Joe got there I had coffee ready and had stirred up some hoecakes to go with our fried eggs. Joe had brought a thermos bottle. We put the rest of the coffee in it and I found a ham in the pantry and made some sandwiches.

While I was fixing the lunch Joe went down to the lot to hitch up. He was just driving the buggy out of the stable when I came down the back steps. The dogs knew what was up, all right. They were whining and surging against the fence and Bob, the big dog, thrust his paw through and into the pocket of my hunting coat as I passed. While Joe was snapping on the leashes I got a few handfuls of straw from the rack and put it in the foot of the buggy. It was twelve miles where we were going; the dogs would need to ride warm coming back.

Joe said he would drive. We got in the buggy and started out, up Seventh Street, on over to College, and out through Scufftown. When we got into the nigger section we could see what a killing frost it had been. A light shimmer over all the ground still and the weeds around all the cabins dark and matted the way they are when the frost hits them hard and twists them.

We drove on over the Red River bridge and out into the open country. At Jim Gill's place the cows had come up and were standing there waiting to be milked but nobody was stirring yet from the house. I looked back from the top of the hill and saw that the frost mists still hung heavy in the bottom and thought it was a good sign. A day like this when the earth is warmer than the air currents is good for the hunter. Scent particles are borne on the warm air; and birds will forage far on such a day.

It took us over an hour to get from Gloversville to Spring Creek. Joe wanted to get out as soon as we hit the big bottom there but I held him down and we drove on through and up Rollow's hill to the top of the ridge. We got out there, unhitched Old Dick and turned him into one of Rob Fayerlee's pastures—I thought how surprised Rob would be when he looked out and saw him grazing there—put our guns together, and started out, with the dogs still on leash.

It was rough, broken ground, scrub oak with a few gum trees and lots of buckberry bushes. One place a patch of corn ran clear up to the top of the ridge. As we passed along between the rows, I could see the frost glistening on the north side of every stalk. I knew it was going to be a good day.

I walked over to the brow of the hill. From there you could see off over the whole valley—I've hunted over every foot of it in my time—tobacco land, mostly. One or two patches of cowpeas there on the side of the ridge. I thought we might start there and then I knew that wouldn't do. Quail will linger on the roost a cold day and feed in shelter during the morning. It is only in the afternoon that they will work out well into the open.

The dogs' whining made me turn around. Joe had bent down and was about to slip the leashes. "Hey, boy," I said, "wait a minute."

I turned around and looked down the other side of the hill. It looked better that way. The corn land of the bottoms ran high up onto the ridge in several places there and where the corn stopped there were big patches of ironweed and buckberry. I stooped and knocked my pipe out on a stump.

"Let's go that way," I said.

Joe was looking at my old buckhorn whistle that I had slung around my neck. "I forgot to bring mine," he said.

"All right," I said, "I'll handle 'em."

He unfastened their collars and cast off. They broke away, racing for the first hundred yards and barking, then suddenly swerved. The big dog took off to the right along the hillside. The bitch, Judy, skirted a belt of corn along the upper bottomlands. I kept my eye on the big dog. A dog that has bird sense knows cover when he sees it. This big Bob was an independent hunter. I could see him moving fast through the scrub oaks, working his way down toward a patch of ironweed. He caught the first scent traces just on the edge of the weed patch and froze. Judy, meanwhile, had been following the line of the cornfield. A hundred yards away she caught sight of Bob's point and backed him.

We went up and flushed the birds. They got up in two bunches.

I heard Joe's shot while I was in the act of raising my gun and I saw his bird fall not thirty paces from where I stood. I had covered a middle bird of the larger bunch—that's the one led by the boss cock—the way I usually do. He fell, whirling head over heels, driven a little forward by the impact. A well-centered shot. I could tell by the way the feathers fluffed as he tumbled.

The dogs were off through the grass. They had retrieved both birds. Joe stuck his in his pocket. He laughed. "I thought there for a minute you were going to let him get away."

I looked at him but I didn't say anything. It's a wonderful thing to be twenty years old.

The majority of the singles had flown straight ahead to settle in the rank grass that jutted out from the bottomland. Judy got down to work at once but the big dog broke off to the left, wanting to get footloose to find another covey. I thought of how Gyges, the best dog I ever had—the best dog any man ever had—used always to want to do the same thing, and I laughed.

"Naw, you won't," I said. "Come back here, you scoundrel, and hunt these singles."

He stopped on the edge of a briar patch, looked at me, and heeled up promptly. I clucked him out again. He gave me another look. I thought we were beginning to understand each other better. We got some nice points among those singles and I found him reasonably steady to both wing and shot, needing only a little control.

We followed that valley along the creek bed through two or three more cornfields without finding another covey. Joe was disappointed but I wasn't worrying yet; you always make your bag in the afternoon.

It was twelve o'clock by this time. We turned up the ravine toward Buck Springs. They had cleared out some of the big trees on the sides of the ravine but the spring itself was just the same: the tall sycamore tree and the water pouring in a thin stream over the slick rocks. I unwrapped the sandwiches and the pieces of cake and laid them on a stump. Joe had got the thermos bottle out of his pocket. Something had gone wrong with it and the coffee was stone cold. We were about to drink it that way when

Joe saw a good tin can flung down beside the spring. He made a trash fire and we put the coffee in the can and heated it to boiling.

Joe finished his last sandwich and reached for the cake. "Good ham," he said.

"It's John Ferguson's," I said. I was watching the dogs. They were tired, all right. Judy had scooped out a soft place between the roots of a sycamore but the big dog, Bob, lay there with his forepaws stretched out before him, never taking his eyes off our faces. I looked at him and thought how different he was from his mate and like some dogs I had known—and men, too—who lived only for hunting and could never get enough no matter how long the day was. There was something about his head and his markings that reminded me of another dog I used to hunt with a long time ago and I asked the boy who had trained him. He said the old fellow he bought the dogs from had been killed last spring, over in Trigg: Charley Morrison.

Charley Morrison. I remembered how he died. Out hunting by himself and the gun had gone off, accidentally, they said. Charley had called the dog to him, got blood all over him, and sent him home. The dog went, all right, but when they got there Charley was dead. Two years ago that was and now I was hunting the last dogs he'd ever trained . . .

Joe lifted the thermos bottle. "Another cup?"

I held my cup out and he filled it. The coffee was still good and hot. I lit my pipe and ran my eye over the country in front of us. I always enjoy figuring out which way they'll go. This afternoon with the hot coffee in me and the ache gone from my leg I felt like I could do it. It's not as hard as it looks. A well-organized covey has a range, like chickens. I knew what they'd be doing this time of day: in a thicket, dusting—sometimes they'll get up in grapevine swings. Then after they've fed and rested they'll start out again, working always toward the open.

Joe was stamping out his cigarette. "Let's go."

The dogs were already out of sight but I could see the sedge grass ahead moving and I knew they'd be making for the same thing that took my eye: a spearhead of thicket that ran far out into this open field. We came up over a little rise. There they were. Bob on a point and Judy, the staunch little devil, backing him, not fifty feet from the thicket. I saw it was going to be tough shooting. No way to tell whether the birds were between the dog and the thicket or in the thicket itself. Then I saw that the cover was more open along the side of the thicket and I thought that that was the way they'd go if they were in the thicket. But Joe had already broken away to the left. He got too far to the side. The birds flushed to the right and left him standing, flat-footed, without a shot.

He looked sort of foolish and grinned.

I thought I wouldn't say anything and then found myself speaking:

"Trouble with you, you try to outthink the dog."

There was nothing to do about it now, though, and the chances were that the singles had pitched through the trees below. We went down there. It was hard hunting. The woods were open, the ground heavily carpeted everywhere with leaves. Dead leaves make a tremendous rustle when the dogs surge through them; it takes a good nose to cut scent keenly in such dry, noisy cover. I kept my eye on Bob. He never faltered, getting over the ground in big, springy strides but combing every inch of it. We came to an open place in the woods. Nothing but big hickory trees and bramble thickets overhung with trailing vines. Bob passed the first thicket and came to a beautiful point. We went up. He stood perfectly steady but the bird flushed out fifteen or twenty steps ahead of him. I saw it swing to the right, gaining altitude very quickly, and it came to me how it would be.

I called to Joe: "Don't shoot yet."

He nodded and raised his gun, following the bird with the barrel. It was directly over the treetops when I gave the word and he shot, scoring a clean kill.

He laughed excitedly as he stuck the bird in his pocket. *"Man! I didn't know you could take that much time!"*

We went on through the open woods. I was thinking about a day I'd had years ago, in the woods at Grassdale, with my uncle James Morris and his son Julian. Uncle James had given Julian and me hell for missing just such a shot. I can see him now, standing up against a big pine tree, his face red from liquor and his gray hair ruffling in the wind: *"Let him alone. Let him alone!* And establish your lead as he *climbs!"*

Joe was still talking about the shot he'd made. "Lord, I wish I could get another one like that."

"You won't," I said. "We're getting out of the woods now."

We struck a path that led through the woods. My leg was stiff from the hip down and every time I brought it over the pain would start in my knee, zing, and travel up and settle in the small of my back. I walked with my head down, watching the light catch on the ridges of Joe's brown corduroy trousers and then shift and catch again as he moved forward. Sometimes he would get on ahead and then there would be nothing but the black tree trunks coming up out of the dead leaves that were all over the ground.

Joe was talking about that wild land up on the Cumberland. We could get up there some Saturday on an early train. Have a good day. Might even spend the night. When I didn't answer he turned around. "Man, you're sweating!"

I pulled my handkerchief out and wiped my face. "Hot work," I said.

He had stopped and was looking about him. "Used to be a spring somewhere around here."

He had found the path and was off. I sat down on a stump and mopped my face some more. The sun was halfway down through the trees, the whole west woods ablaze with light. I sat there and thought that in another hour it would be good dark and I wished that the day could go on and not end so soon and yet I didn't see how I could make it much farther with my leg the way it was.

Joe was coming up the path with his folding cup full of water. I hadn't thought I was thirsty but the cold water tasted good. We sat there awhile and smoked. It was Joe said we ought to be starting back, that we must be a good piece from the rig by this time.

We set out, working north through the edge of the woods. It was rough going and I was thinking that it would be all I could do to make it back to the rig when we climbed a fence and came out at one end of a long field. It sloped down to a wooded ravine, broken ground badly gullied and covered with sedge everywhere except where sumac thickets had sprung up—as birdy a place as ever I saw. I looked it over and I knew I'd have to hunt it, leg or no leg, but it would be close work, for me and the dogs too.

I blew them in a bit and we stood there watching them cut up the cover. The sun was down now; there was just enough light left to see the dogs work. The big dog circled the far wall of the basin and came upwind just off the drain, then stiffened to a point. We walked down to it. The birds had obviously run a bit, into the scraggly sumac stalks that bordered the ditch. My mind was so much on the dogs that I forgot Joe. He took one step too many and the fullest-blown bevy of the day roared up through the tangle. It had to be fast work. I raised my gun and scored with the only barrel I had time to peg. Joe shouted: I knew he had got one too.

We stood awhile trying to figure out which way the singles had gone. But they had fanned out too quick for us and after beating around the thicket for fifteen minutes or so we gave up and went on.

We came to the rim of the swale, eased over it, crossed the dry creek bed that was drifted thick with leaves, and started up the other side. I had blown in the dogs, thinking there was no use for them to run their heads off now we'd started home, but they didn't come. I walked a little way, then I looked back and saw Bob's white shoulders through a tangle of cinnamon vines.

Joe had turned around too. "Look a yonder! They've pinned a single out of that last covey."

"Your shot," I told him.

He shook his head. "No, you take it."

I went back and flushed the bird. It went skimming along the buckberry bushes that covered that side of the swale. In the fading light I could hardly make it out and I shot too quick. It swerved over the thicket and I let go with the second barrel. It staggered, then zoomed up. Up, up, up, over the rim of the hill and above the tallest hickories. I saw it there for a second, its wings black against the gold light, before, wings still spread, it came whirling down, like an autumn leaf, like the leaves that were everywhere about us, all over the ground.

ROPING LIONS
IN THE
GRAND CANYON

ZANE GREY

I

THE GRAND CANYON of Arizona is over two hundred miles long, thirteen wide, and a mile and a half deep; a titanic gorge in which mountains, tablelands, chasms, and cliffs lie half veiled in purple haze. It is wild and sublime, a thing of wonder, of mystery; beyond all else a place to grip the heart of a man, to unleash his daring spirit.

On April 20, 1908, after days on the hot desert, my weary party and pack train reached the summit of Powell's Plateau, the most isolated, inaccessible, and remarkable mesa of any size in all the canyon country. Cut off from the mainland, it appeared insurmountable; standing aloof from the towers and escarpments, rugged and bold in outline, its forest covering like a strip of black velvet, its giant granite walls gold in the sun, it seemed apart from the world, haunting with its beauty, isolation, and wild promise.

The members of my party harmoniously fitted the scene. Buffalo Jones, burly-shouldered, bronze-faced, and grim, proved in his appearance what a lifetime on the plains could make of a man. Emett was a Mormon, a massively built gray-bearded son of the desert; he had lived his life on it; he had conquered it and in his falcon eyes shone all its fire and freedom. Ranger Jim Owens had the wiry, supple body and careless, tidy garb of the cowboy, and the watchful gaze, quiet face and locked lips of the frontiersman. The fourth member was a Navajo Indian, a copper-skinned, raven-haired, beady-eyed desert savage.

I had told Emett to hire someone who could put the horses on grass in the evening and then find them the next morning. In Northern Arizona this required more than genius. Emett secured the best trailer of the desert Navajos. Jones hated an Indian; and Jim, who carried an ounce of lead somewhere in his person, associated this painful addition to his weight with an unfriendly Apache, and swore all Indians should be dead. So between the two, Emett and I had trouble in keeping our Navajo from illustrating the plainsman idea of a really good Indian—a dead one.

While we were pitching camp among magnificent pine trees, and above a hollow where a heavy bank of snow still lay, a sodden pounding in the turf attracted our attention.

"Hold the horses!" yelled Emett.

As we all made a dive among our snorting and plunging horses the sound seemed to be coming right into camp. In a moment I saw a string of wild horses thundering by. A noble black stallion led them, and as he ran with beautiful stride he curved his fine head backward to look at us, and whistled his wild challenge.

Later a herd of large white-tailed deer trooped up the hollow. The Navajo grew much excited and wanted me to shoot, and when Emett told him we had not come out to kill, he looked dumbfounded. Even the Indian felt it a strange departure from the usual mode of hunting to travel and climb hundreds of miles over hot desert and rock-ribbed canyons, to camp at last in a spot so wild that deer were tame as cattle, and then not kill.

Nothing could have pleased me better, incident to the settling into permanent camp. The wild horses and tame deer added the all-satisfying touch to the background of forest, flowers, and mighty pines and sunlit patches of grass; the white tents and red blankets, the sleeping hounds and blazing fire logs, all making a picture like that of a hunter's dream.

"Come, saddle up," called the never restful Jones. "Leave the Indian in camp with the hounds, and we'll get the lay of the land." All afternoon we spent riding the plateau. What a wonderful place! We were completely bewildered with its physical properties, and surprised at the abundance of wild horses and mustangs, deer, coyotes, foxes, grouse and other birds, and overjoyed to find innumerable lion trails. When we returned to

camp I drew a rough map, which Jones laid flat on the ground as
he called us around him.

"Now, boys, let's get our heads together."

In shape the plateau resembled the ace of clubs. The center
and side wings were high and well-wooded with heavy pines; the
middle wing was longest, sloped west, had no pine, but a dense
growth of cedar. Numerous ridges and canyons cut up this central wing. Middle Canyon, the longest and deepest, bisected the
plateau, headed near camp, and ran parallel with two smaller
ones, which we named Right and Left Canyons. These three were
lion runways and hundreds of deer carcasses lined the thickets.
North Hollow was the only depression, as well as runway, on the
northwest rim. West Point formed the extreme western cape of
the plateau. To the left of West Point was a deep cut-in of the rim
wall, called the Bay. The three important canyons opened into it.
From the Bay, the south rim was regular and impassable all the
way round to the narrow Saddle, which connected it to the mainland.

"Now, then," said Jones, when we assured him that we were
pretty well informed as to the important features, "you can
readily see our advantage. The plateau is about nine or ten miles
long, and six wide at its widest. We can't get lost, at least for
long. We know where lions can go over the rim and we'll head
them off, make short-cut chases, something new in lion hunting.
We are positive the lions cannot get over the second wall, except
where we came up, at the Saddle. In regard to lion signs, I'm
doubtful of the evidence of my own eyes. This is virgin ground.
No white man or Indian has ever hunted lions here. We have
stumbled on a lion home, the breeding place of hundreds of lions
that infest the north rim of the canyon."

The old plainsman struck a big fist into the palm of his hand, a
rare action with him. Jim lifted his broad hat and ran his fingers
through his white hair. In Emett's clear desert-eagle eyes shone a
furtive, anxious look, which yet could not overshadow the
smouldering fire.

"If only we don't kill the horses!" he said.

More than anything else that remark from such a man thrilled
me with its subtle suggestion. He loved those beautiful horses.

What wild rides he saw in his mind's eye! In cold calculation we perceived the wonderful possibilities never before experienced by hunters, and as the wild spell clutched us my last bar of restraint let down.

During supper we talked incessantly, and afterward around the campfire. Twilight fell with the dark shadows sweeping under the silent pines; the night wind rose and began its moan.

"Shore there's some scent on the wind," said Jim, lighting his pipe with a red ember. "See how uneasy Don is."

The hound raised his fine, dark head and repeatedly sniffed the air, then walked to and fro as if on guard for his pack. Moze ground his teeth on a bone and growled at one of the pups. Sounder was sleepy, but he watched Don with suspicious eyes. The other hounds, mature and somber, lay stretched before the fire.

"Tie them up, Jim," said Jones, "and let's turn in."

II

When I awakened next morning the sound of Emett's axe rang out sharply. Little streaks of light from the campfire played between the flaps of the tent. I saw old Moze get up and stretch himself. A jangle of cowbells from the forest told me we would not have to wait for the horses that morning.

"The Injun's all right," Jones remarked to Emett.

"All rustle for breakfast," called Jim.

We ate in the semidarkness with the gray shadow ever brightening. Dawn broke as we saddled our horses. The pups were limber, and ran to and fro on their chains, scenting the air; the older hounds stood quietly waiting.

"Come, Navvy—come chase cougie," said Emett.

"Dam'! No!" replied the Indian.

"Let him keep camp," suggested Jim.

"All right; but he'll eat us out," Emett declared.

"Climb up, you fellows," said Jones impatiently. "Have I got everything—rope, chains, collars, wire, nippers? Yes, all right. Hyar, you lazy dogs—out of this!"

We rode abreast down the ridge. The demeanor of the hounds contrasted sharply with what it had been at the start of the hunt the year before. Then they had been eager, uncertain, violent; they did not know what was in the air; now they filed after Don in an orderly trot.

We struck out of the pines at half-past five. Floating mist hid the lower end of the plateau. The morning had a cool touch but there was no frost. Crossing Middle Canyon about halfway down, we jogged on. Cedar trees began to show bright green against the soft gray sage. We were nearing the dark line of the cedar forest when Jim, who led, held up his hand in a warning check. We closed in around him.

"Watch Don," he said.

The hound stood stiff, head well up, nose working, and the hair on his back bristling. All the other hounds whined and kept close to him.

"Don scents a lion," whispered Jim. "I've never known him to do that unless there was the scent of a lion on the wind."

"Hunt 'em up, Don, old boy," called Jones.

The pack commenced to work back and forth along the ridge. We neared a hollow when Don barked eagerly. Sounder answered and likewise Jude. Moze's short angry "bow-wow" showed the old gladiator to be in line.

"Ranger's gone," cried Jim. "He was farthest ahead. I'll bet he's struck it. We'll know in a minute, for we're close."

The hounds were tearing through the sage, working harder and harder, calling and answering one another, all the time getting down into the hollow.

Don suddenly let out a string of yelps. I saw him running head up, pass into the cedars like a yellow dart. Sounder howled his deep, full bay, and led the rest of the pack up the slope in angry clamor.

"They're off!" yelled Jim, and so were we.

In less than a minute we had lost one another. Crashings among the dry cedars, thud of hoofs, and yells kept me going in one direction. The fiery burst of the hounds had surprised me. I remembered that Jim had said Emett and his charger might keep the pack in sight, but that none of the rest of us could.

It did not take me long to realize what my mustang was made of. His name was Foxie, which suited him well. He carried me at a fast pace on the trail of some one; and he seemed to know that by keeping in this trail part of the work of breaking through the brush was already done for him. Nevertheless, the sharp dead branches, more numerous in a cedar forest than elsewhere, struck and stung us as we passed. We climbed a ridge, and found the cedars thinning out into open patches. Then we faced a bare slope of sage and I saw Emett below on his big horse.

Foxie bolted down this slope, hurdling the bunches of sage, and showing the speed of which Emett had boasted. The open ground, with its brush, rock, and gullies, was easygoing for the little mustang. I heard nothing save the wind singing in my ears. Emett's trail, plain in the yellow ground, showed me the way. On entering the cedars again I pulled Foxie in and stopped twice to yell "Waa-hoo!" I heard the baying of the hounds, but no answer to my signal. Then I attended to the stern business of catching up. For what seemed a long time I threaded the maze of cedar, galloped the open sage flats, always on Emett's track.

A signal cry, sharp to the right, turned me. I answered, and with the exchange of signal cries found my way into an open glade where Jones and Jim awaited me.

"Here's one," said Jim. "Emett must be with the hounds. Listen."

With the labored breathing of the horses filling our ears we could hear no other sound. Dismounting, I went aside and turned my ear to the breeze.

"I hear Don," I cried instantly.

"Which way?" both men asked.

"West."

"Strange," said Jones. "The hound wouldn't split, would he, Jim?"

"Don leave that hot trail? Shore he wouldn't," replied Jim. "But his runnin' do seem queer this morning."

"The breeze is freshening," I said. "There! Now listen! Don, and Sounder, too."

The baying came closer and closer. Our horses threw up long ears. It was hard to sit still and wait. At a quick cry from Jim we saw Don cross the lower end of the flat.

No need to spur our mounts! The lifting of bridles served, and away we raced. Foxie passed the others in short order. Don had long disappeared, but with blended bays, Jude, Moze, and Sounder broke out of the cedars hot on the trail. They, too, were out of sight in a moment.

The crash of breaking brush and thunder of hoofs from where the hounds had come out of the forest, attracted and even frightened me. I saw the green of a low cedar tree shake, and split, to let out a huge, gaunt horse with a big man doubled over his saddle. The onslaught of Emett and his desert charger stirred a fear in me that checked admiration.

"Hounds running wild," he yelled, and the dark shadows of the cedars claimed him again.

A hundred yards within the forest we came again upon Emett, dismounted, searching the ground. Moze and Sounder were with him, apparently at fault. Suddenly Moze left the little glade and venting his sullen quick bark, disappeared under the trees. Sounder sat on his haunches and yelped.

"Now what the hell is wrong?" growled Jones, tumbling off his saddle.

"Shore something is," said Jim, also dismounting.

"Here's a lion track," interposed Emett.

"Ha! and here's another," cried Jones, in great satisfaction. "That's the trail we were on, and here's another crossing it at right angles. Both are fresh; one isn't fifteen minutes old. Don and Jude have split one way and Moze another. By George! that's great of Sounder to hang fire!"

"Put him on the fresh trail," said Jim, vaulting into his saddle.

Jones complied, with the result that we saw Sounder start off on the trail Moze had taken. All of us got in some pretty hard riding, and managed to stay within earshot of Sounder. We crossed a canyon, and presently reached another which, from its depth, must have been Middle Canyon. Sounder did not climb the opposite slope, so we followed the rim. From a bare ridge we distinguished the line of pines above us, and decided that our location was in about the center of the plateau.

Very little time elapsed before we heard Moze. Sounder had caught up with him. We came to a halt where the canyon widened and was not so deep, with cliffs and cedars opposite us, and an easy slope leading down. Sounder bayed incessantly; Moze emitted harsh, eager howls, and both hounds, in plain sight, began working in circles.

"The lion has gone up somewhere," cried Jim. "Look sharp!"

Repeatedly Moze worked to the edge of a low wall of stone and looked over; then he barked and ran back to the slope, only to return. When I saw him slide down a steep place, make for the bottom of the stone wall, and jump into the low branches of a cedar I knew where to look. Then I descried the lion, a round yellow ball, cunningly curled up in a mass of dark branches. He had leaped into the tree from the wall.

"There he is! Treed! Treed!" I yelled. "Moze has found him."

"Down, boys, down into the canyon," shouted Jones, in sharp voice. "Make a racket; we don't want him to jump."

How he and Jim and Emett rolled and cracked the stone! For a moment I could not get off my horse; I was chained to my saddle by a strange vacillation that could have been no other thing than fear.

"Are you afraid?" called Jones from below.

"Yes, but I am coming," I replied, and dismounted to plunge down the hill. It may have been shame or anger that dominated me then; whatever it was I made directly for the cedar, and did not halt until I was under the snarling lion.

"Not too close!" warned Jones. "He might jump. It's a Tom, a two-year-old, and full of fight."

It did not matter to me then whether he jumped or not. I knew I had to be cured of my dread, and the sooner it was done the better.

Old Moze had already climbed a third of the distance up to the lion.

"Hyar, Moze! Out of there, you rascal coon chaser!" Jones

yelled as he threw stones and sticks at the hound. Moze, however, replied with his snarly bark and climbed on steadily.

"I've got to pull him out. Watch close, boys, and tell me if the lion starts down."

When Jones climbed the first few branches of the tree, Tom let out an ominous growl.

"Make ready to jump. Shore he's comin'," called Jim.

The lion, snarling viciously, started to descend. It was a ticklish moment for all of us, particularly Jones. Warily he backed down.

"Boys, maybe he's bluffing," said Jones. "Try him out. Grab sticks and run at the tree and yell, as if you were going to kill him."

Not improbably the demonstration we executed under the tree would have frightened even an African lion. Tom hesitated, showed his white fangs, returned to his first perch, and from there climbed as far as he could. The forked branch on which he stood swayed alarmingly.

"Here, punch Moze out," said Jim handing up a long pole.

The old hound hung like a leech to the tree, making it difficult to dislodge him. At length he fell heavily, and, venting his thick battle cry, attempted to climb again.

Jim seized him, made him fast to the rope with which Sounder had already been tied.

"Say, Emett, I've no chance here," called Jones. "You try to throw at him from the rock."

Emett ran up the rock, coiled his lasso, and cast the noose. It sailed perfectly in between the branches and circled Tom's head. Before it could be slipped tight he had thrown it off. Then he hid behind the branches.

"I'm going farther up," said Jones.

"Be quick," yelled Jim.

Jones evidently had that in mind. When he reached the middle fork of the cedar, he stood erect and extended the noose of his lasso on the point of his pole. Tom, with a hiss and snap, struck at it savagely. The second trial tempted the lion to saw the rope with his teeth. In a flash Jones withdrew the pole, and lifted a loop of the slack rope over the lion's ears.

"Pull!" he yelled.

Emett, at the other end of the lasso, threw his great strength into action, pulling the lion out with a crash, and giving the cedar such a tremendous shaking that Jones lost his footing and fell heavily.

Thrilling as the moment was, I had to laugh, for Jones came up out of a cloud of dust, as angry as a wet hornet, and made prodigious leaps to get out of the reach of the whirling lion.

"Look out——!" he bawled.

Tom, certainly none the worse for his tumble, made three leaps, two at Jones, one at Jim, which was checked by the short length of the rope in Emett's hands. Then for a moment a thick cloud of dust enveloped the wrestling lion, during which the quick-witted Jones tied the free end of the lasso to a sapling.

"Dod gast the luck!" yelled Jones, reaching for another lasso. "I didn't mean for you to pull him out of the tree. Now he'll get loose or kill himself."

When the dust cleared away, we discovered our prize stretched out at full length and frothing at the mouth. As Jones approached, the lion began a series of evolutions so rapid as to be almost indiscernible to the eye. I saw a wheel of dust and yellow fur. Then came a thud and the lion lay inert.

Jones pounced upon him and loosed the lasso around his neck.

"I think he's done for, but maybe not. He's breathing yet. Here, help me tie his paws together. Look out! He's coming to!"

The lion stirred and raised his head. Jones ran the loop of the second lasso around the two hind paws and stretched the lion out. While in this helpless position and with no strength and hardly any breath left in him the lion was easy to handle. With Emett's help Jones quickly clipped the sharp claws, tied the four paws together, took off the neck lasso and substituted a collar and chain.

"There, that's one. He'll come to, all right," said Jones. "But we are lucky. Emett, never pull another lion clear out of a tree. Pull him over a limb and hang him there while some one below ropes his hind paws. That's the only way, and if we don't stick to it, somebody is going to get done for. Come, now, we'll leave this fellow here and hunt up Don and Jude. They've treed another lion by this time."

Remarkable to me was to see how, as soon as the lion lay helpless, Sounder lost his interest. Moze growled, yet readily left the spot. Before we reached the level, both hounds had disappeared.

"Hear that?" yelled Jones, digging spurs into his horse. "Hi! Hi! Hi!"

From the cedars rang the thrilling, blending chorus of bays that told of a treed lion. The forest was almost impenetrable. We had to pick our way. Emett forged ahead; we heard him smashing the deadwood; and soon a yell proclaimed the truth of Jones's assertion.

First I saw the men looking upward; then Moze climbing the cedar, and the other hounds with noses skyward; and last, in the dead top of the tree, a dark blot against the blue, a big tawny lion.

"Whoop!" The yell leaped past my lips. Quiet Jim was yelling; and Emett, silent man of the desert, let from his wide cavernous chest a booming roar that drowned ours.

Jones's next decisive action turned us from exultation to the grim business of the thing. He pulled Moze out of the cedar, and while he climbed up, Emett ran his rope under the collars of all of the hounds. Quick as the idea flashed over me I leaped into the cedar adjoining the one Jones was in, and went up hand over hand. A few pulls brought me to the top, and then my blood ran hot and quick, for I was level with the lion, too close for comfort, but in excellent position for taking pictures.

The lion, not heeding me, peered down at Jones, between widespread paws. I could hear nothing except the hounds. Jones's gray hat came pushing up between the dead snags; then his burly shoulders. The quivering muscles of the lion gathered tense, and his lithe body crouched low on the branches. He was about to jump. His open dripping jaws, his wild eyes, roving in terror for some means of escape, his tufted tail, swinging against the twigs and breaking them, manifested his extremity. The eager hounds waited below, howling, leaping.

It bothered me considerably to keep my balance, regulate my

camera, and watch the proceedings. Jones climbed on with his
rope between his teeth, and a long stick. The very next instant, it
seemed to me, I heard the cracking of branches and saw the lion
biting hard at the noose which circled his neck.

Here I swung down, branch to branch, and dropped to the
ground, for I wanted to see what went on below. Above the
howls and yelps, I distinguished Jones's yell. Emett ran directly
under the lion with a spread noose in his hands. Jones pulled and
pulled, but the lion held on firmly. Throwing the end of the lasso
down to Jim, Jones yelled again, and then they both pulled. The
lion was too strong. Suddenly, however, the branch broke, letting
the lion fall, kicking frantically with all four paws. Emett grasped
one of the four whipping paws, and even as the powerful animal
sent him staggering he dexterously left the noose fast on the paw.
Jim and Jones in unison let go of their lasso, which streaked up
through the branches as the lion fell, and then it dropped to the
ground, where Jim made a flying grab for it. Jones, plunging out
of the tree, fell upon the rope at the same instant.

If the action up to then had been fast, it was slow to what
followed. It seemed impossible for two strong men with one
lasso, and a giant with another, to straighten out that lion. He
was all over the little space under the trees at once. The dust flew,
the sticks snapped, the gravel pattered like shot against the cedars. Jones plowed the ground flat on his stomach, holding on
with one hand, with the other trying to fasten the rope to something; Jim went to his knees; and on the other side of the lion,
Emett's huge bulk tipped a sharp angle, and then fell.

I shouted and ran forward, having no idea what to do, but
Emett rolled backward at the same instant the other men got a
strong haul on the lion. Short as that moment was in which the
lasso slackened, it sufficed for Jones to make the rope fast to a
tree. Whereupon with the three men pulling on the other side of
the leaping lion, somehow I had flashed into my mind the game
that children play, called skipping the rope, for the lion and lasso
shot up and down.

This lasted for only a few seconds. They stretched the beast
from tree to tree, and Jones, running with the third lasso, made
fast the front paws.

"It's a female," said Jones, as the lion lay helpless, her sides swelling; "a good-sized female. She's nearly eight feet from tip to tip, but not very heavy. Hand me another rope."

When all four lassos had been stretched, the lioness could not move. Jones strapped a collar around her neck and clipped the sharp yellow claws.

"Now to muzzle her," he continued.

Jones's method of performing this most hazardous part of the work was characteristic of him. He thrust a stick between her open jaws, and when she crushed it to splinters he tried another, and yet another, until he found one that she could not break. Then while she bit on it, he placed a wire loop over her nose, slowly tightening it, leaving the stick back of her big canines.

The hounds ceased their yelping and, when untied, Sounder wagged his tail as if to say, "Well done," and then lay down; Don walked within three feet of the lion, as if she were now beneath his dignity; Jude began to nurse and lick her sore paw; only Moze the incorrigible retained antipathy for the captive, and he growled, as always, low and deep. And on the moment, Ranger, dusty and lame from travel, trotted wearily into the glade and, looking at the lioness, gave one disgusted bark and flopped down.

III

Transporting our captives to camp bade fair to make us work. When Jones, who had gone after the packhorses, hove in sight on the sage flat, it was plain to us that we were in for trouble. The bay stallion was on the rampage.

"Why didn't you fetch the Indian?" growled Emett, who lost his temper when matters concerning his horses went wrong. "Spread out, boys, and head him off."

We contrived to surround the stallion, and Emett succeeded in getting a halter on him.

"I didn't want the bay," explained Jones, "but I couldn't drive the others without him. When I told that redskin that we had two lions, he ran off into the woods, so I had to come alone."

"I'm going to scalp the Navajo," said Jim complacently.

These remarks were exchanged on the open ridge at the entrance to the thick cedar forest. The two lions lay just within its shady precincts. Emett and I, using a long pole in lieu of a horse, had carried Tom up from the canyon to where we had captured the lioness.

Jones had brought a packsaddle and two panniers. When Emett essayed to lead the horse which carried these, the animal stood straight up and began to show some of his primal desert instincts. It certainly was good luck that we unbuckled the packsaddle straps before he left the vicinity. In about three jumps he had separated himself from the panniers, which were then placed upon the back of another horse. This one, a fine-looking beast, and amiable under surroundings where his life and health were considered even a little, immediately disclaimed any intention of entering the forest.

"They scent the lions," said Jones. "I was afraid of it; never had but one nag that would pack lions."

"Maybe we can't pack them at all," replied Emett dubiously. "It's certainly new to me."

"We've got to," Jones asserted; "try the sorrel."

For the first time in a serviceable and honorable life, according to Emett, the sorrel broke his halter and kicked like a plantation mule.

"It's a matter of fright. Try the stallion. He doesn't look afraid," said Jones, who never knew when he was beaten.

Emett gazed at Jones as if he had not heard right.

"Go ahead, try the stallion. I like the way he looks."

No wonder! The big stallion looked a king of horses—just what he would have been if Emett had not taken him, when a colt, from his wild desert brothers. He scented the lions, and he held his proud head up, his ears erect, and his large, dark eyes shone fiery and expressive.

"I'll try to lead him in and let him see the lions. We can't fool him," said Emett.

Marc showed no hesitation, nor anything we expected. He stood stiff-legged, and looked as if he wanted to fight.

"He's all right; he'll pack them," declared Jones.

The packsaddle being strapped on and the panniers hooked to the horns, Jones and Jim lifted Tom and shoved him down into the left pannier while Emett held the horse. A madder lion than Tom never lived. It was cruel enough to be lassoed and disgrace enough to be "hog-tied," as Jim called it, but to be thrust down into a bag and packed on a horse was adding insult to injury. Tom frothed at the mouth and seemed like a fizzing torpedo about to explode. The lioness, being considerably longer and larger, was with difficulty gotten into the other pannier, and her head and paws hung out. Both lions kept growling and snarling.

"I look to see Marc bolt over the rim," said Emett resignedly, as Jones took up the end of the rope halter.

"No, siree!" sang out that worthy. "He's helping us out; he's proud to show up the other nags."

Jones was always asserting strange traits in animals, and giving them intelligence and reason. As to that, many incidents coming under my observation while with him, and seen with his eyes, made me incline to his claims, the fruit of a lifetime with animals.

Marc packed the lions to camp in short order, and, quoting Jones, "without turning a hair." We saw the Navajo's head protruding from a tree. Emett yelled for him, and Jones and Jim "ha-haed" derisively; whereupon the black head vanished and did not reappear. Then they unhooked one of the panniers and dumped out the lioness. Jones fastened her chain to a small pine tree, and as she lay powerless he pulled out the stick back of her canines. This allowed the wire muzzle to fall off. She signalled this freedom with a roar that showed her health to be still unimpaired. The last action in releasing her from her painful bonds Jones performed with sleight-of-hand dexterity. He slipped the loop fastening one paw, which loosened the rope, and in a twinkling let her work all of her other paws free. Up she sprang, ears flat, eyes ablaze, mouth wide, once more capable of defense, true to her instinct and her name.

Before the men lowered Tom from Marc's back I stepped closer and put my face within six inches of the lion's. He promptly spat on me. I had to steel my nerve to keep so close. But I wanted to see a wild lion's eyes at close range. They were exquisitely beautiful, their physical properties as wonderful as their expression. Great half-globes of tawny amber, streaked with delicate wavy lines of black, surrounding pupils of intense purple fire. Pictures shone and faded in the amber light—the shaggy tipped plateau, the dark pines, and smoky canyons, the great dotted downward slopes, the yellow cliffs and crags. Deep in those live pupils, changing, quickening with a thousand vibrations, quivered the soul of this savage beast, the wildest of all wild Nature, unquenchable love of life and freedom, flame of defiance and hate.

Jones disposed of Tom in the same manner as he had the lioness, chaining him to an adjoining small pine, where he leaped and wrestled.

Presently I saw Emett coming through the woods leading and dragging the Indian. I felt sorry for the Navvy, for I felt that his fear was not so much physical as spiritual. And it seemed no wonder to me that the Navvy should hang back from this sacrilegious treatment of his god. A natural wisdom, which I had in common with all human beings who consider self-preservation the first law of life, deterred me from acquainting my august companions with my belief. At least I did not want to break up the camp.

In the remorseless grasp of Emett, forced along, the Navajo dragged his feet and held his face sidewise, though his dark eyes gleamed at the lions. Terror predominated among the expressions of his countenance. Emett drew him within fifteen feet and held him there, and with voice, and gesticulating of his free hand, tried to show the poor fellow that the lions would not hurt him.

Navvy stared and muttered to himself. Here Jim had some deviltry in mind, for he edged up closer; but what it was never transpired, for Emett suddenly pointed to the horses and said to the Indian:

"Chineago (feed)."

It appeared when Navvy swung himself over Marc's broad back, that our great stallion had laid aside his transiently noble disposition and was himself again. Marc proceeded to show us how truly Jim had spoken: "Shore he ain't no use for the red-skin." Before the Indian had fairly gotten astride, Marc dropped his head, humped his shoulders, brought his feet together and began to buck. Now the Navajo was a famous breaker of wild mustangs, but Marc was a tougher proposition than the wildest mustang that ever romped the desert. Not only was he unusually vigorous; he was robust and heavy, yet exceedingly active. I had seen him roll over in the dust three times each way, and do it easily—a feat Emett declared he had never seen performed by another horse.

Navvy began to bounce. He showed his teeth and twisted his sinewy hands in the horse's mane. Marc began to act like a de-mon; he plowed the ground; apparently he bucked five feet straight up. As the Indian had bounced he now began to shoot into the air. He rose the last time with his heels over his head, to the full extent of his arms; and on plunging down his hold broke. He spun around the horse, then went hurtling to the ground some twenty feet away. He sat up, and seeing Emett and Jones laughing, and Jim prostrated with joy, he showed his white teeth in a smile and said, "No bueno dam'."

I think all of us respected Navvy for his good humor, and especially when he walked up to Marc and, with no show of the mean Indian, patted the glossy neck and then nimbly remounted. Marc, not being so difficult to please as Jim in the way of discom-fiting the Navajo, appeared satisfied for the present, and trotted off down the hollow, with the string of horses ahead, their bells jingling.

Campfire tasks were a necessary wage in order to earn the full enjoyment and benefit of the hunting trip; and looking for some task to which to turn my hand, I helped Jim feed the hounds. To feed ordinary dogs is a matter of throwing them a bone; however, our dogs were not ordinary. It took time to feed them, and a prodigious amount of meat. We had packed between three and four hundred pounds of wild-horse meat, which had been cut into small pieces and strung on the branches of a scrub oak near camp.

Don, as befitted a gentleman and the leader of the greatest pack in the West, had to be fed by hand. I believe he would rather

have starved than have demeaned himself by fighting. Starved he
certainly would have, if Jim had thrown meat indiscriminately to
the ground. Sounder asserted his rights and preferred large portions at a time. Jude begged with great solemn eyes, but was no
slouch at eating, for all her gentleness. Ranger, because of imper-
fectly developed teeth rendering mastication difficult, had to have
his share cut into very small pieces. As for Moze—well, great
dogs have their faults, as do great men—he never got enough
meat; he would fight even poor crippled Jude, and steal even
from the pups; when he had gotten all Jim would give him, and
all he could snatch, he would growl away with bulging sides.

"How about feeding the lions?" asked Emett.

"They'll drink tonight," replied Jones, "but won't eat for days;
then we'll tempt them with fresh rabbits."

We made a hearty meal, succeeding which Jones and I walked
through the woods toward the rim. A yellow promontory, huge
and glistening, invited us westward, and after a detour of half a
mile we reached it. The points of the rim, striking out into the
immense void, always drew me irresistibly. We found the view
from this rock one of startling splendor. The corrugated rim wall
of the middle wing extended to the west, at this moment apparently running into the setting sun. The gold glare touching up the
millions of facets of chiseled stone, created color and brilliance
too glorious and intense for the gaze of men. And looking downward was like looking into the placid, blue, bottomless depths of
the Pacific.

With that a puff of air seemed to rise, and on it the most awful
bellow of thunderous roar. It rolled up and widened, deadened to
burst out and roll louder, then slowly, like mountains on wheels,
rumbled under the rim walls, passing on and on, to roar back in
echo from the cliffs of the mesas. Roar and rumble—roar and
rumble! For two long moments the dull and hollow echoes rolled
at us, to die away slowly in the far-distant canyons.

"That's a darned deep hole," commented Jones.

Twilight stole down on us idling there, silent, content to watch
the red glow pass away from the buttes and peaks, the color
deepening downward to meet the ebon shades of night creeping
up like a dark tide.

On turning toward the camp we essayed a short cut, which brought us to a deep hollow with stony walls, which seemed better to go around. The hollow, however, was quite long and we decided presently to cross it. We descended a little way when Jones suddenly barred my progress with his big arm.

"Listen," he whispered.

It was quiet in the woods; only a faint breeze stirred the pine needles; and the weird, gray darkness seemed to be approaching under the trees.

I heard the patter of light, hard hoofs on the scaly sides of the hollow.

"Deer?" I asked my companion in a low voice.

"Yes; see," he replied, pointing ahead, "just right under that broken wall of rock; right there on this side; they're going down."

I descried gray objects the color of the rocks, moving down like shadows.

"Have they scented us?"

"Hardly; the breeze is against us. Maybe they heard us break a twig. They've stopped, but they are not looking our way. Now I wonder—"

Rattling of stones set into movement by some quick, sharp action, an indistinct crash, but sudden, as of the impact of soft, heavy bodies, a strange wild sound preceded in rapid succession violent brushings and thumpings in the scrub of the hollow.

"Lion jumped a deer," yelled Jones. "Right under our eyes! Come on! Hi! Hi! Hi!"

He ran down the incline yelling all of the way, and I kept close to him, adding my yells to his, and gripping my revolver. Toward the bottom the thicket barred our progress so that we had to slash through and I came out a little ahead of Jones. And farther up the hollow I saw a gray swiftly bounding object too long and too low for a deer, and I hurriedly shot six times at it.

"By George! Come here," called my companion. "How's this for quick work? It's a yearling doe."

In another moment I leaned over a gray mass huddled at Jones's feet. It was a deer, gasping and choking. I plainly heard the wheeze of blood in its throat, and the sound, like a death rattle, affected me powerfully. Bending closer, I saw where one side of the neck, low down, had been terribly lacerated.

"Waa-hoo!" pealed down the slope.

"That's Emett," cried Jones, answering the signal. "If you have another shot put this doe out of agony."

But I had not a shot left, nor did either of us have a clasp knife. We stood there while the doe gasped and quivered. The peculiar sound, probably made by the intake of air through the laceration of the throat, on the spur of the moment seemed pitifully human.

I felt that the struggle for life and death in any living thing was a horrible spectacle. With great interest I had studied natural selection, the variability of animals under different conditions of struggling existence, the law whereby one animal struck down and devoured another. But I had never seen and heard that law enacted on such a scale; and suddenly I abhorred it.

Emett strode to us through the gathering darkness.

"What's up?" he asked quickly.

He carried my Remington in one hand and his Winchester in the other; and he moved so assuredly and loomed up so big in the dusk that I experienced a sudden little rush of feeling as to what his advent might mean at a time of real peril.

"Emett, I've lived to see many things," replied Jones, "but this is the first time I ever saw a lion jump a deer right under my nose!"

As Emett bent over to seize the long ears of the deer, I noticed the gasping had ceased.

"Neck broken," he said, lifting the head. "Well, I'm danged. Must have been an all-fired strong lion. He'll come back, you may be sure of that. Let's skin out the quarters and hang the carcass up in a tree!"

We returned to camp in half an hour, the richer for our walk by a quantity of fresh venison. Upon being acquainted with our adventure, Jim expressed himself rather more fairly than was his customary way.

"Shore that beats hell! I knowed there was a lion somewheres, because Don wouldn't lie down. I'd like to get a pop at the brute."

I believe Jim's wish found an echo in all our hearts. At any rate to hear Emett and Jones express regret over the death of the doe justified in some degree my own feelings, and I thought it was not so much the death, but the lingering and terrible manner of it, and especially how vividly it connoted the wildlife drama of the plateau. The tragedy we had all but interrupted occurred every night, perhaps often in the day and likely at different points at the same time. Emett told how he had found fourteen piles of bleached bones and dried hair in the thickets of less than a mile of the hollow on which we were encamped.

"We'll rope the danged cats, boys, or we'll kill them."

"It's blowing cold. Hey, Navvy, *coco! coco!*" called Emett.

The Indian, carefully laying aside his cigarette, kicked up the fire and threw on more wood.

"Dicass! (cold)," he said to me. *"Coco, bueno* (fire good)."

I replied, "Me savvy—yes."

"Sleep-ie?" he asked.

"Mucha," I returned.

While we carried on a sort of novel conversation full of Navajo, English, and gestures, darkness settled down black. I saw the stars disappear; the wind, changing to the north, grew colder and carried a breath of snow. I like north wind best—from under the warm blankets—because of the roar and lull and lull and roar in the pines. Crawling into the bed presently, I lay there and listened to the rising storm wind for a long time. Sometimes it swelled and crashed like the sound of a breaker on the beach, but mostly, from a low incessant moan, it rose and filled to a mighty rush, then suddenly lulled. This lull, despite a wakeful, thronging mind, was conducive to sleep.

'GATOR BAIT

TALMAGE POWELL

CROUCHED ON THE PROW of the drifting water sled under a brazen Louisiana sky, Chat felt the old dread pouring through him in sickening waves. It was an icy prickling in his clammy, sun-leathered skin. It blurred his vision so that Fornier's Bayou seemed to swirl about him, the canebrakes, the hummocks of greasy green palmetto and saw grass, the towering fingers of heat-blasted gray cypress with their festoons of Spanish moss.

A thin, stringy-muscled, undersized thirteen, Chat clutched the scabrous, weathered gunwales and wallowed his tongue inside his mouth, wishing he could spit out the dry, cottony feeling.

He shivered, listening to the watery whisper as Lefevre, his stepfather, stood in the stern, poling the craft. They had inched into the bayou under power fifteen minutes ago. Lefevre had cut the throttle, kicking the air propeller to a stop in its wire-mesh cage. The slow, careful search for an alligator den had begun.

Within five minutes, Chat had spotted the wet hump, the protrusion of tangled twigs that meant 'gator. As if in supplication, a nearly naked young figure clad in tattered jeans and dingy sneakers, he'd crouched with his lips forming a silent plea for Lefevre to miss the 'gator sign. More than anything, he'd wanted to go home today empty-handed, without a wetting.

The sled lurched from a hard jab of the pole. Chat slipped a glance over his shoulder. A big, strapping, Cajun figure in the stern, bending his dark, hairy weight against the pole, Lefevre split his tangle of black, wiry beard with a snag-toothed grin.

"We got us a skin, boy! Get ready. That 'gator is going to shed his hide!"

Lefevre's words seemed to hang in the muggy, primeval stillness. Chat closed his eyes, the dread in him sharpening until it felt like fishhooks in his stomach.

"Boy," Lefevre rumbled, "what's the matter with you? Get a move on! We got to wake that old 'gator up and get him mad enough to come roaring out of his den."

"I don't feel so good, Pa."

"Belly hurting again?"

"Yeah, Pa."

"Now, boy," Lefevre growled, "you just cut that sissy stuff out. Hear me? Ain't you ashamed? What's the matter with you, anyhow? Ain't you normal? Toutain's boy, and those twins of De Vaux, they take to 'gator baiting like it was candy. You going to be the only yellow-belly boy in the swamp?"

Chat clutched his stomach. "I can't help it, Pa."

Lefevre cleared his throat, making it a heavy sound of disgust and disparagement. "Boy, you lived on your ma's apron strings too long, just you and a woman. It's time you quit acting like a girl. Why, when I was your age, I couldn't wait to go 'gator baiting. I used to beg my pa. I used to prod them out for the pure hell fun of it. You need to change your attitude, boy. It's the greatest excitement in the world. Running a fox or treeing a coon don't hold a candle to it!"

"Yes, Pa." Somehow Chat managed to rise. His knees were weak with an inner trembling, but they supported him. Sparks of panic misted behind his eyes as he saw how close the sled had moved in.

"That's better," Lefevre said. He steadied the peeled-sapling pole with his left hand, bent down and pitched the coil of slender hemp rope that had lain at his feet.

Chat caught the line instinctively. He felt his hands forming the noose, slipping it about his shoulders, securing it under his armpits.

Then he was powerless to move further. "Pa, I swear I can't—"

"Enough!" Lefevre's voice was a cruel, muted roar, thick with contempt for cowardice. "I've heard all the mealy-mouthing I'm going to! Now you get the hell in the water and roust that 'gator out or I'll whale the tar out of you."

Shivering, Chat slipped into the water. It was about shoulder deep, a turgid swath hampering his movements. He slipped the long wooden rod from its homemade wire brackets on the port side of the sled. He forced himself to move, taking slow steps on the soft bottom while Lefevre played out the hemp line and steadied the sled, elbow crooked about the pole.

The first rancid mustiness of the alligator's den came to Chat, choking his thin nostrils. Hesitantly, he lifted the hard wooden rod and poked in the direction of the den.

"In closer, boy!" Lefevre snarled. "You ain't playing pat-a-cake!"

The merciless sun seemed to hide as Chat edged forward. Holding the long rod with both hands just below water level, he snaked the tip into the barely visible mouth of the den. His heart was a motionless lump of ice as the rod searched and probed. He felt it strike scaly hide. Then a piece of it snapped as saw-toothed jaws clicked.

The water suddenly thrashed and boiled.

"Pa!" Chat screamed. He leaped backward. He felt the noose under his armpits pinch tight as Lefevre hauled in the line, hand over hand. Chat lost his footing, gagging on water pouring across his sun-bleached thatch and into his nose as Lefevre retrieved him like a wriggling minnow.

The man's strength swooped him into the air, dumped him onto the deck. Supporting himself half-prone and blowing water from his lungs, Chat saw Lefevre out of the corner of his eyes. The towering figure was leveling a thirty-aught-six rifle at the charging alligator. The brute came like a half-submerged log fired from a catapult, leaving an angry wake.

Grinning broadly, Lefevre squeezed the trigger. The rifle-crack jolted through Chat. He turned his face away from the sight of the rolling convulsions, the sudden redness in the black-surfaced swamp water, as the 'gator died.

Lefevre slapped his thigh and his happy guffaw rang like a delayed echo of the rifle shot. "Boy, I got me a skin! It'll fetch some fine black-market dollars so's a citified gent can wear hisself a hundred-buck pair of alligator shoes!"

Lefevre usually drank to success, and this night was no exception. In his small room, Chat lay sleepless on his pallet, watching the reflections of a kerosene lamp dance about the doorway as Lefevre sat alone, drinking at the rough plank table in the next room. The man was already talking to himself and singing snatches of old Cajun songs in a broken French patois. Chat could predict the next hours accurately. His stepfather would drink himself into a stupor and brief peace would come to the unpainted, clapboard shanty set high on its stilts beneath a hoary old willow tree.

Chat wanted to sleep, but each time he closed his eyes that moment returned, that harrowing instant when he was sure the 'gator would get him. He'd never heard of a 'gator-baiting kid being eaten up. Their daddies, or uncles, or whoever they were poaching with always snaked them out, but the knowledge didn't stop Chat's imagination from working. He could see the unwinking 'gator eyes, the cottonlike interior of the jaws, the cruel teeth.

He clenched his fists and gritted his teeth. "I swear," he sobbed to himself, "I can't do it again."

If Ma were still here, he wouldn't have to; or Pa. His real pa had died so long ago from cottonmouth bite that Chat could hardly remember him, but he could recall his father's contempt for the poachers, the black marketeers, the easy-dollar men who were killing off the alligators. Pa had been content to fish and hunt and go off for a few days at a time to work in the distant sawmill when he needed a hard dollar for sugar or gingham or coffee.

After Pa's death, there'd just been Chat and Ma. Life had been very hard. There were few people so far back up in Big Shandy Swamp, and little a boy and his mother could do for a hard dollar. Ma's sister, Aunt Mavis, had sent them a little money now and then, and they'd made out.

Then Lefevre had come courting in his secondhand suit and wrinkled necktie in the collar of his blue denim shirt. Chat suspected that Ma had married him because she felt her boy needed a father, a man about the place.

That hadn't worked out very well, either. Ma had got a terrible pain in her side and before they could pack her out to the half-dozen sunbaked, slab-and-tin buildings of Rickel's Crossing, much less a hospital, Ma had died from a ruptured appendix.

Aunt Mavis had come to the funeral, hugging Chat long and hard after it was over. She'd told Chat about the strange world far off yonder beyond the swamp, about Houston, Texas, where she made good money working as a waitress in a nice, clean restaurant, where she figured on marrying a fellow named Jim who drove a big trailer truck.

"He would've come," Aunt Mavis had said, "but he was on a cross-country haul when word reached me about Sis. You'd like Jim, little Chat, and he would think the world of you. So you try and get your stepdaddy to let you come and stay with us a while. Even live with us. You've always got a home with us, Chat."

Lefevre had squelched the idea before it could take root. "No dice, boy. I need you here, helping on the trap lines and fish nets and running of the house. You forget it, boy, quick and for good. This is your home. This is where you stay."

A short time after that, Lefevre had taken to poaching, an activity that made Chat far more valuable than a prime, blooded, redbone hound dog.

The day after his drinking bout, Lefevre stayed in bed, sick, calling out to Chat now and then to bring him endless quantities of drinking water. He was red-eyed and gray-faced beneath his wild bush of black beard. It was no time to cross him, and Chat spent the hours weeding the garden patch where yams, corn, squash, and gourds grew.

The next morning, Lefevre was up and away early. Chat went fishing, content to be by himself, thankful he didn't run into the Toutain or De Vaux boys. They were always up to something, and when their paths crossed Chat's he was always in for some rough teasing.

He much preferred to think about Aunt Mavis, how kind and sweet she'd been, how nice she smelled when she'd hugged his neck. He wondered what her Jim looked like. He must be a fine fellow to rate a woman like Aunt Mavis. Chat suspected that they'd written him, perhaps even sent him a little money, but he

had no way of knowing for sure. It was always Lefevre who went
into Rickel's Crossing, end of the line for mail.

The following morning, Chat was awakened by the grip of
Lefevre's heavy hand on his shoulder. The instant he opened his
eyes, Lefevre's face, glowing with greed and excitement, filled his
vision.

"Get a move on, boy! We got us a big one today." On one knee
beside the pallet, Lefevre rubbed his palms and grinned in high
glee. The morning light seemed to make every jet-black, curling
hair about his ears, thick neck and heavy-boned face stand out
individually. "Cut his sign working the trap lines yesterday. Almost under our noses, boy. Right over there in Berdine's Lagoon.
Claw marks and belly drag say he's a whopper, twenty-five feet if
he's an inch!"

"Pa, I don't feel so good," Chat managed.

Lefevre's grin faded. His face darkened. "Boy, how come you
want to kill the real fine feeling of the day?"

"I can't help the way I feel, Pa."

"The devil you can't!" He grabbed Chat by the shoulder and
flung him to his feet. "I've heard the last of this I'm going to, boy!
It's time you got over it. You got a job of 'gator baiting to do, and
you're going to do it! I'm going to bust the yellow streak—or
break you. You understand that?"

"Yes, Pa." Teeth chattering, Chat snubbed the cord that belted
his jeans.

"And don't you forget it," Lefevre warned. "Now you get in
there and get ready. I've already cooked side meat and grits while
you pampered your lazy head. You got exactly five minutes to eat
your breakfast."

With pasty grits and greasy sow-belly wadded in his throat,
Chat moved through a morning that didn't seem quite real. De-
tails all stood out with a strangely sharp clarity as the sled moved
through the trackless, watery wastes. Low-hanging vines swayed,
threatening. A curtain of gray Spanish moss clutched like cob-
webs as Chat reached out to part them for the sled's passage.
Cypress snags reared from the swirling water like sharp, hungry
teeth. A five-foot cottonmouth slithered from a mangrove tangle
and eeled beneath and past the water sled, a fearsome omen.

Flocks of birds and a long-legged white heron fluttered from jungle growth as the whirring air propeller shoved the sled along over grassy marsh, drawing no more draft than a surfboard.

The early sun was a torment, a glare filling the whole of the cloudless sky and stepping up the tempo of the mallets beating inside Chat's skull.

The lagoon opened before his gritty-eyed gaze, a long stretch of water with a surface like black glass, hemmed by palmetto, wild cabbage palms, high grass, and a few gnarled pines.

Lefevre cut the engine and the sled slipped forward silently as he began poling.

Crouched on the prow, Chat thought desperately: *Maybe we'll miss the den this time. Maybe the big bull won't be in it,* but he knew he was wrong. From the way Lefevre was tracking the water sled, Chat knew that his stepfather had located the den yesterday, when he'd cut the 'gator's sign, and he knew the bull would be here. He was emptily certain of it.

"All right, boy, over the side." Lefevre kept his voice down, but it quivered with eagerness.

Chat stood up, facing the man slowly. Lefevre had picked up the line, was tossing it to him.

Chat caught the thin rope. "Pa, are you sure this is the way it's got to be?"

Lefevre's mustache and beard shifted with the angry twisting of his mouth. "Don't start that again, boy! Fair warning, for the last time!"

"All right, Pa." Chat wriggled the lasso under his armpits, picked up his long prodding pole, and slipped into the water. It was deeper than he'd thought, claiming him to his chin. Pole upraised like a long, thin spear, he worked his way forward, buoyancy pulling the mucky bottom away from him at each step.

The den was straight ahead, just a few yards now. He could see the mouth of the huge nest just under the surface.

He stopped moving, settled, his sneakered feet firmly on the bottom. Glancing behind, he saw Lefevre, solid and spread-legged, playing out the line until it dipped into the water.

"Come on, boy!" Lefevre bit out. "Get moving. Take up the slack. You're just about there."

"I can't, Pa." Chat spoke with head lifted, keeping his chin clear.

Lefevre worked the line in his hands. "Boy," he said in a low, deadly tone, "If you ain't moving before I can count to three . . . ."

"You big overgrown fool," Chat said with a heat he'd never before displayed. "There's snags in here. You blind? Can't you see them sticking up here and yonder?"

"Snags in every swamp," Lefevre said. "You just get your foot loose and be quick about it."

Chat ducked, then reappeared with water spilling from his head. He twisted his face once more in Lefevre's direction. "Can't make it. You want your 'gator, you come in and free my ankle."

Lefevre measured the distance to the den with a glance. He hesitated. He cursed the delay. He threw the line down savagely. Then he slipped over the side and labored with slogging steps toward Chat, his eyes despising the boy for his awkwardness. He came to rest beside Chat. Again his small, black eyes flicked in the direction of the den.

"Just free my foot," Chat said, water lapping to his lips, "and then get back and take hold of the line. Please, Pa. Please hurry!"

With a final glower at Chat, Lefevre lowered his bulk beneath the surface. Chat saw his sinking shadow, felt the touch of Lefevre's hands on his leg.

Then, with a release of his hard, stringy muscles, Chat fired himself off the bottom. He stepped on Lefevre, bearing him down, the surprise of the action addling the man for a moment.

The long prod in Chat's hands shot into the den. It lashed the water. He felt it strike the lurking 'gator—once, twice, three times—with all the strength Chat could put behind it.

Lefevre spluttered up to the surface in the same instant the maddened bull charged from his lair with a bellow that jarred trees at the far end of the lagoon.

"Now, big man," Chat screamed, "let's see who's the best man in the swamp . . . ." He gurgled the final word, surface diving with the agility of a young otter.

Lefevre stared into the enormity of cotton-lined jaws. He endured a fear-paralysis for one second before he broke and thrashed toward the water sled. He was one second too late.

Early the following Monday morning, Chat walked into Rickel's Crossing. His jeans and red flannel shirt were washed clean. His freckled, snub-nosed face was scrubbed. His sun-bleached thatch was combed.

The village hunkered in its usual air of desertion, a couple of muddy pickup trucks parked on the narrow, dusty road that petered out here on the swamp's edge.

Chat spotted Mr. Fargo sitting in a cane-bottomed chair on the porch of his weathered general store. Mr. Fargo was dozing in the heat, a big, fat, bald-headed fellow whose short-sleeved shirt looked like an extra skin pasted on with sweat.

Chat halted at the porch rail, where whittlers had carved initials, notches, and little primitive resemblances to human faces.

Chat cleared his throat and Mr. Fargo opened his big, bulbous, blue eyes. "Well, hello there, Chat."

"How are you, Mr. Fargo?" Chat said politely, looking up from his stance in the dust.

"I'm just fine, boy, but I hear you been in a terrible experience. By the time you run and fetched the Toutains, wasn't much of your stepdaddy left to bury."

"No, sir." Chat cleared his throat. "But we give him a right fitten funeral. Now I reckon to go to Houston, Texas, and see my Aunt Mavis."

"That's a far piece, boy. You got any money for bus fare, grub, and such like?"

"I figure I can make it." With plenty to spare, Chat added to himself, feeling the three hundred dollars of poacher's money pinned beneath his shirt. Lefevre had kept his treasure trove in a fruit jar buried beneath the old willow tree.

"If you can't hitch a ride, boy," Mr. Fargo said, "you got a ten-mile walk down our back road to the highway where you can flag a bus. And it's a mighty hot day for walking."

"Not to me," Chat said. "I figure it's a real fine day for walking. Good-bye, Mr. Fargo."

"Good-bye, boy, and luck to you."

Chat nodded, turned, and set off down the road. He began whistling as he rounded the first bend in the road, and it was the note of a bird set free.

THE
WHITE STAG

WILLIAM J. LONG

OLD NOEL the Indian told me this story, one winter night, as we sat beside our fire in the open woods. Here is how it came about.

For two weeks I had been hunting a white caribou—not the ordinary grizzly gray bull of the winter barrens, but a pure albino with magnificent antlers. Noël refused absolutely to have anything to do with such a hunt, saying it brought bad luck; so I left him to trap and hunt as he pleased while I followed the white stag alone.

One afternoon, as we returned together from some of his otter traps, we crossed the fresh trail of a dozen caribou and were following it swiftly when the air darkened and snowflakes began to whirl about us. Noël wanted to turn back to camp at once, but I had seen one great track in the snow that I knew very well, and so followed the trail until it led me to the edge of the barrens. There in plain sight were the caribou, a herd of splendid animals, and near them but alone stood the great white stag. Mine at last, I thought as I covered his shoulder, for he was scarcely sixty yards away and a miss seemed impossible.

A snow squall was roaring in the woods and swept over me in a blinding cloud as I pressed the trigger. Perhaps that is why I missed; but Noël thinks otherwise. Anyway the next instant the whole herd, not knowing where the shot came from, were rushing straight past me. A strong hand threw up the muzzle of my rifle as it covered the white side again, and I turned to find the

Indian staring with frightened eyes at the quivering spruce boughs where the stag had disappeared.

"Come," he said sharply, "time to stop huntin' here. I goin' home tomorrow." And I have been in the woods with an Indian long enough to know that it is best to be silent under such circumstances.

We went deep into the woods, dug a hole with our snowshoe, built a fire and a little commoosie of boughs and snow, and ate our simple hunter's meal. Not a word was spoken; but when the pipes were lighted, Noël, who thinks I am part Indian myself and who remembers, even when he is cross and hungry, that I once saved his life, drew near and sat down on the log beside me.

"You goin' hunt um dat white caribou?"

"Not if it troubles you, Noël."

"Does trouble me. Trouble you too, if you don't stop. What happen dat first time you hunt um?"

"I went through an air hole in the lake," I said, shivering at the recollection; "but that had nothing to do with the caribou."

"Mebbe not; mebbe yes," said Noël. "What happened dat second time?"

"Followed him too far, and got lost in a storm, and had to sleep out overnight," I confessed meekly.

"An' what happened just now? Why you miss um easy shot? Why we stay here in snow 'stead of warm camp?" demanded the Indian.

"O, I don't know. Cartridges no good," I ventured.

"Cartridge no good, huh? I see you hit um rabbit twice as far as you miss um caribou, dem same cartridges. You want know why you miss um? why you most dead in air hole? why you have bad luck huntin'?" he asked earnestly. And when I nodded he drew closer to the fire and told me the story, which he had heard from his own father, Baptiste.

One autumn, many years ago, old Tomah and young Baptiste, two Indian hunters, pushed up to a lake and the headwaters of the St. John, which they had chosen for the place of their winter trapping. All the way up the river they had spoken in low tones of their plans, growing more eager as they approached the wild headwaters and the game signs increased; but when their canoe glided around the last bend of the stream and the unnamed lake lay spread before them, not a word was spoken. Some mystery hung over the still water and the dark green hillsides; some subtle influence that both felt, but that neither could define, kept them silent. Three years before a solitary old Indian had gone to the lake trapping, but never came back. The search party that followed in the spring had found his camp and some of his traps, but no sign to tell his story; and they came away and left him in the woods. But until he should be found, and his death explained, the lake was not like other lakes.

For the first month Tomah and Baptiste trapped with remarkable success, although fur-bearing animals had not yet settled into their winter homes. Game too was plentiful, and their table was well-supplied. Only deer were scarce and very wild, undoubtedly on account of the wolves, whose howls often echoed at midnight through the startled woods.

It was late in October when the first unusual thing happened. The lake was still open, though occasional snow squalls told them that winter was nigh. For two weeks now they had tasted no fresh venison, so one day when Baptiste found the place where a deer came down nightly to drink and feed, he determined to watch for the animal. The path made by the buck doubled round a great boulder, and came out upon an open point on the east side of the lake, and there Baptiste stood astonished. Never before had he seen such big hoofmarks left by a deer.

That night, just after sunset, a canoe was lying motionless in the shadow of the evergreens just below the point. Baptiste was watching, his ears growing more and more sensitive as he listened in the tense stillness of the autumn night. The wind moaned in the spruces, came down and rustled among the leaves and, sinking still, went whispering out of hearing among the grasses on the point. Now a whirring rush rolled over him as some startled wild fowl sheered away from the canoe; now the shivering wail of a loon floated over the lake, like the cry of a lost spirit, and again the hillside echoes wakened to a sharp cry of abject terror as the life of some weak, hunted thing went out in the grip of cruel claws and teeth—the last cry of the weak one to the Great Spirit, as Baptiste believed, when no other help was near.

Soon the pines on the eastern ridge began to show clear and sharp above the dark woods; then the moon wheeled slowly above the hills, flooding the lake and point with silver light. Baptiste's paddle dipped silently, the canoe drew slowly away into deeper shadow, and, crouching lower still, he resumed his lonely watch.

Two hours passed with no sight nor sound of game; only the long-drawn howl of a timber wolf came echoing down from the mountain side. Then there was a slight rustle in the woods that was not the wind, and Baptiste, drawing his gun to his shoulder, fixed his eyes on the edge of the gray boulder. A moment later a head with branching antlers appeared dimly in sight; a great stag stepped out from behind the rock and stood with raised head looking off across the lake.

Beside the rock grew an immense hemlock whose shadow was thrown across the deer; yet even in the shadow Baptiste wondered at his strange appearance. The mists of the lake seemed to gather and sway about him. For a moment Baptiste hesitated. Something told him not to shoot; but he was young and eager, and not yet learned to obey instantly the secret influences that often guide an Indian. So he threw the muzzle of his gun against the side of the animal and touched the trigger.

The roar of his gun was appalling in the dead stillness. At the report the stag bounded forward into the moonlight, and Baptiste saw with a thrill of horror that he was snow-white. A moment he stood there, trembling, listening; then, deceived by the echo, turned and bounded back into the forest.

Baptiste understood now his unusual success at trapping. Not for worlds would he willingly have harmed an animal that every Indian regards with a kind of reverence, that brings good luck or dire misfortune wherever it comes. As a boy he had heard the old men tell stories of strange things that happened in winter camps when a white deer appeared. They crowded upon him now and filled him with vague uneasiness. He knew that the stag was not harmed; he had heard the *ping* of his bullet telling of a miss, yet he knew also that any common deer standing in the same place would even now be lying dead on the point. Then he thought of the dead Indian and of the mystery that hung over the lake, and very doubtful, and with a strange thrill creeping over him, he paddled back to camp and told Tomah.

The very next day, halfway home, Tomah came upon the traces of a struggle near one of the traps, and following them up, found the body of a gray wolf which had been torn and trampled by sharp hoofs. At any other time the dead wolf and the deer tracks would have told the Indian's eyes an incredible story, for a single gray wolf drives a whole herd of deer like so many sheep, and kills a buck as easily as a rabbit. But now it needed not the tuft of white hair clinging to the rough bark of a spruce to tell old Tomah that this was the white stag's work, and that some mystery brooded here which was past his hunter's cunning to explain.

One night, nearly a month later, the two hunters stood outside the little camp, listening to the tense stillness that rests eternally over the wilderness. An hour passed, and still they waited silently. Then from far away to the southeast, over beyond the point where Baptiste had first seen the white stag, the hunting cry of a timber wolf came echoing across the lake. Another wolf answered, then another, as the pack gathered for the hunt. Soon the howl changed to a sharp yelp; and there burst out the savage, tremulous cry of the pack in full chase.

The cry grew louder as the chase drew near the lake, and went sweeping along the eastern ridges opposite the camp. Old hunters as they were, uncanny chills coursed over the Indians as they stood listening, while the savage cries cut the stillness and went floating over the hills in fierce confused echoes. The chase turned suddenly from the lake; for miles they could trace its course toward the north and west; then the cry changed abruptly to wild yelping, ceased, broke out again in a frightful uproar; then ceased altogether; and the two silent listeners turned shivering into their camp again.

For two weeks now they had heard that same chase almost nightly, always following the same course, and ending apparently at the same point. They had talked about it over their night fire; each had thought about it on the long lonely round of the marten traps; but no explanation ever came to satisfy them. It might be the white stag; but how did he escape? and why did he return? Then the thought of the lost Indian came over them again; and they knew that these things were not for men to know.

That night the lake froze over; and three nights later the first snowstorm spread over all the woods a pure white chart, on which every animal from moose to woodmouse left a plain trace of his doings.

The next afternoon Tomah had nearly reached the river when he came upon a trap out of which a marten had just been dug and eaten. From the trap the fresh trail of a gray wolf led up toward the lake. Tomah stole rapidly forward on the wolf's trail.

He had gone but a few rods when he stopped suddenly, staring down at the trail with as much astonishment as an Indian's face is ever capable of expressing. He could hardly believe the story the snow was telling him. Directly in front was the trail of a deer, which crossed—no, not crossed, but turned and followed the wolf swiftly, as Tomah was doing.

Again an uncanny chill crept over Tomah; and he hesitated, uncertain whether to go on or turn back. That he was now trailing a spirit of some kind he never doubted—a spirit that left the hoof marks of a deer. Clearly some strange enmity was here; it might not be safe nor right to pry into such things. But he was in the winter woods; the plain trail was before him, and the strong hunter's instinct urged him on. With only a moment's delay therefore, he looked to his gun and hurried on more carefully than before. But there was little need for caution. He had followed the trail scarcely a half mile when the howl of a wolf rang sharply out of the woods in front, and mingled with the echoes came the angry snort of a buck and confused sounds of a terrible battle.

Swiftly but silently Tomah made his way to the outlet and looked out from the fringe of evergreens upon the open shore. There in a circle of bloodstained snow lay a struggling wolf, howling piteously and making futile efforts to crawl away, while over him in wild excitement the white stag was striking him with hoof and antler. In the midst of the stag's fury Tomah saw the underbrush sway violently; and silently, as wolves fight, a huge brute broke through the fringe of bushes and hurled himself out upon the point. In a flash the buck had wheeled to face his enemy; but his fury would not let him wait to be attacked. Even as the wolf leaped the stag lunged forward with lowered head; and Tomah, with all his fighting blood boiling within him, could hardly repress a fierce shout as he saw the wolf raised clear for an instant and dashed down with entrails streaming from a fearful wound opened by the gallant stag's antlers.

It was dusk when Tomah and Baptiste reached their little cabin. As darkness increased the howl of a wolf came up from the lake—a prolonged howl, in which grief and fierce anger seemed struggling for expression. The pack was gathering, and for an hour the hunters listened to the wild dirge wailing about the dead wolves. A loud yelp sounded quick and sharp above the din, which ceased instantly. A moment of silence followed, then the trail cry broke out, and the same mysterious chase went sweeping along the ridges above the lake shore.

Standing without the camp the Indians listened until the cry ceased as before; then turned in to sleep. They had longed for the snow, and it was here; and the chase was run over its tell-tale surface. Spirit or no spirit, tomorrow they would find out more about it.

With the first light they crossed the lake and entered the heavy timber. There, in the summit of the first low ridge, lay the trail they were seeking; and it needed no second glance at the big hoof marks to tell them, what they have long known instinctively, that it was the white stag which led the nightly hunt. The tracks went leaping along, clearing every obstacle with mighty bounds; and running parallel to the trail, but never crossing it, confused footprints showed where a score of wolves had followed on the gallop.

Swiftly the Indians followed, up the ridge and across the inlet and miles away to the northwest, where the chase had ended nightly for a month past. Here the forest opened. A wild ravine cut by the swift mountain torrent stretched straight across their path. On the slope that led down to the edge of it stood an immense pine, towering head and shoulders over all the forest. Straight under this pine at a terrific pace rushed the stag, clearing the thirty-foot ravine at a bound, and standing at the edge the hunters could see his tracks on the other side, where he had turned and waited for his pursuers. But what puzzled them was that not a wolf had approached the edge, nor attempted to follow. A short distance above or below they could easily have gained the other side, but instead of attempting it, the tracks showed that they had formed a half-circle about the tree, wavered back and forth a few minutes in confusion and then slunk away on the back trail, as if something had frightened them.

For a long time Tomah and Baptiste stood there on the edge of the torrent, casting wistful glances across, as if to read some explanation there in the shadowy thickets. But no explanation came; the mystery only deepened. Reluctantly they turned away and went back to the circle of wolf tracks, but no explanation was there either. Beyond a well-defined line not a wolf had set his foot, and following some of the tracks they found that the pack had disbanded, and hurried away to their scattered dens far back among the ridges. Again the Indians turned back and stood silent, baffled, mystified, beneath the pine.

Lying close beside the pine was a small mound of snow, which seemed to force itself gradually upon Tomah's attention as he stood leaning upon his gun. He had noticed it before, but thought it only a rounded boulder. Now in a sudden spirit of curiosity, which was half obedience, he went and thrust his moccasin into it. Some object yielded beneath his foot, and with a quick twist he threw it upon the snow, then recoiled with a startled exclamation as the whole meaning of it flashed over him, in one of those marvelous mind movements which reveal a history as the lightning's flash illumines a landscape at midnight. It was a human skull. They had found the lost Indian.

Carefully they scraped the snow aside and gathered the skeleton together. The half-gowned bones, still showing the marks of wolf fangs, told all too plainly how he met his death. Near the tree they found a rusted knife and rifle, and in the underbrush the bones of three wolves, one with a bullet hole in the skull.

The story was clear as if written for them. Indeed it was written, in the characters an Indian best understands. The poor hunter, coming home late from some lonely visit to his traps, had been chased by the starving wolves and had fled toward the river, hoping to throw them off the scent. They had overtaken him at the ravine before he could clamber down, had rushed out upon him, no doubt, while he yet thought them far away. With his back against the pine he had fought for his life, had killed three, perhaps more, of the wolves, and then was pulled down and eaten.

With the axe that Tomah always carried at his belt they sharpened some stakes and hollowed out a shallow grave beneath the pine. The wind eddied about them and whispered its secrets in the spruces, but the pine's great arms were motionless the while; only a soft, clear note sounded far up among its leaves like the echo of distant music. The Indians were silent; they listened as they worked. Into the grave they gathered the scattered bones, with the old knife and rifle, and covered them with loose earth, upon which they rolled heavy stones to guard them forever from prowling beasts. Deep into the rough trunk of the old pine they carved a rude cross.

That night, just as the moon rose, the uncanny chase began again. Standing by the little cabin the two men listened with breathless interest as the cry swept round toward the river and the lonely grave where it had been wont to end. Again, as before, they heard the trail-cry break into wild howls, and cease abruptly when the wolves reached the pine. Five minutes passed in dead silence. Still they stood waiting, with ears strained to catch the slightest sound. Then a prolonged howl, fierce and exultant, again set the echoes flying, and a moment later the full cry came ringing down the western ridges. The wolves had crossed the ravine. The white stag was running his last race.

The cry passed rapidly along the hillside above the camp and went out of hearing toward the south. Four or five hours passed; the hunters were sleeping. Then strange, faint sounds came creeping through the dark woods to the little camp. Baptiste stirred uneasily in his sleep; Tomah raised himself suddenly from his bed of boughs; the next moment they were both outside the camp. Far away in the southeast they heard the cry of the pack growing louder. It told them that the stag had turned, and seizing their guns they hurried down to an open point that commanded a view of the whole lake, lying white and still under the moonlight.

The minutes dragged on with the cry drawing nearer, but very slowly. Then the alders swayed suddenly on the south shore and the stag broke out upon the lake. A thrill of pity stole over the watchers as they saw him struggling over the ice, still slippery under the light snow. His head, instead of being thrown up and back, as deer run, drooped forward until the protruding tongue almost swept the snow, and he staggered as he ran toward the point where Baptiste had first seen him. His spirit was broken— nay, it had left him, said Tomah—and he ran as if unconscious.

Fifty yards behind him the wolves broke out of the woods with redoubled howls, the sight of their game inspiring them suddenly with new strength and fierceness. Part of the pack at once separated from the rest and disappeared silently into the shadow that bordered the lake below the point. The rest eased up on the chase, giving their leaders a chance to head the quarry.

The stag reached the point and the watchers saw the antlered head go up as he bounded forward. Then from behind the great boulder dark forms leaped squarely athwart his path. An instant the hunted beast seemed to hesitate, frozen with sudden terror, then the antlered head went down again and he lunged straight forward to meet them.

A short, terrible struggle followed. For a few moments they could see him battle with desperate courage, plunging, striking among the leaping forms with the strength and spirit they had seen before. Twice the death howl of a wolf rose above the tense silence of the fighting brutes. Suddenly they saw him rear high above the pack. An instant he stood poised, a gray silhouette against the dark woods, with the writhing brutes below. Then a big wolf leaped up and fastened to his throat and he fell, as the pine falls when the steel has bitten through to its heart.

Tomah and Baptiste left them howling about the body of the stag and stole away to their camp. In the morning they found him just as he had fallen; not a wolf had touched the flesh. No mysterious chase ever again disturbed them, but they hunted and trapped and poisoned the wolves until a howl seldom echoed about the lake.

Noël finished his story, and only the roar of the storm and the singing of the birch logs on the fire broke the silence for several minutes. Then I said, "Noël, you think the old Indian's spirit is in that white stag?"

"Sartin," said Noël.

"Suppose Tomah and Baptiste don't find the old Indian and bury him, how long would his spirit stay in the stag and fight wolves?"

But Noël just believes things and interprets only what he sees. He leaves speculation to the white man, and so he never answers such questions.

THE
TIGER CHARM

ALICE PERRIN

THE SUN, the sky, the burning, dusty atmosphere, the waving sea of tall yellow grass seemed molten into one blinding blaze of pitiless heat to the aching vision of little Mrs. Wingate. In spite of blue goggles, pith sunhat, and enormous umbrella, she felt as if she were being slowly roasted alive; for the month was May, and she and her husband were perched on the back of an elephant, traversing a large tract of jungle at the foot of the Himalayas.

Colonel Wingate was one of the keenest sportsmen in India, and every day for the past week he and his wife and their friend, Captain Bastable, had sallied forth from the camp with a line of elephants to beat through the forests of grass that reached to the animals' ears; to squelch over swamps, disturbing herds of antelope and wild pig; to pierce thick tangles of jungle, from which rose pea fowl, black partridge, and birds of gorgeous plumage; to cross stony beds of dry rivers—ever on the watch for the tigers that had hitherto baffled all their efforts.

As each "likely" spot was drawn a blank, Netta Wingate heaved a sigh of relief; for she hated sport, was afraid of the elephants, and lived in hourly terror of seeing a tiger. She longed for the fortnight in camp to be over, and secretly hoped that the latter week of it might prove as unsuccessful as the first. Her skin was burned to the hue of a berry; her head ached perpetually from the heat and glare; the motion of the elephant made her feel sick; and if she ventured to speak, her husband only impatiently bade her be quiet.

This afternoon, as they plowed and rocked over the hard, un-even ground, she could scarcely keep awake, dazzled as she was by the vista of scorched yellow country and the gleam of her husband's rifle barrels in the melting sunshine. She swayed drowsily from side to side in the howdah, her head drooped, her eyelids closed.

She was roused by a torrent of angry exclamations. Her um-brella had hitched itself obstinately into the collar of Colonel Wingate's coat, and he was making infuriated efforts to free him-self. Jim Bastable, approaching on his elephant, caught a mixed vision of the refractory umbrella and two agitated sun hats, the red face and fierce blue eyes of the Colonel, and the anxious, apologetic, sleepy countenance of Mrs. Wingate as she hurriedly strove to release her irate lord and master. The whole party came to an involuntary halt, the natives listening with interest as the sahib stormed at the memsahib and the umbrella in the same breath.

"That howdah is not big enough for two people," shouted Captain Bastable, coming to the rescue. "Let Mrs. Wingate change to mine. It's bigger, and my elephant has easier paces."

Hot, irritated, angry, Colonel Wingate commanded his wife to betake herself to Bastable's elephant, and to keep her infernal umbrella closed for the rest of the day, adding that women had no business out tiger shooting, and why the devil had she come at all?—ignoring the fact that Mrs. Wingate had begged to be al-lowed to stay in the station, and that he himself had insisted on her coming.

She well knew that argument or contradiction would only make matters worse, for he had swallowed three stiff whisky-and-sodas at luncheon in the broiling sun, and, since the severe sun-stroke that had so nearly killed him two years ago, the smallest quantity of spirits was enough to change him from an exceed-ingly bad-tempered man into something little short of a maniac. She had heedlessly married him when she was barely nineteen, turning a deaf ear to warnings of his violence, and now, at twenty-three, her existence was one long fear. He never allowed her out of his sight; he never believed a word she said; he watched her, suspected her, bullied her unmercifully, and was insanely jealous. Unfortunately, she was one of those nervous, timid women who often rather provoke ill-treatment.

This afternoon she marveled at being permitted to change to Captain Bastable's howdah, and with a feeling of relief scrambled off the elephant, though trembling, as she always did, lest the great beast should seize her with his trunk or lash her with his tail, which was like a jointed iron rod. Then, once safely perched up behind Captain Bastable, she settled herself with a delightful sense of security. He understood her nervousness; he did not laugh or grumble at her little involuntary cries of fear; he was not impatient when she was convinced that the elephant was running away or sinking in a quicksand, or that the howdah was slipping off. He also understood the Colonel, and had several times helped her through a trying situation; and now the sympathy in his kind eyes made her tender heart throb with gratitude.

"All right?" he asked.

She nodded, smiling, and they started again, plowing and lurching through the coarse grass, great wisps of which the elephant uprooted with his trunk and beat against his chest, to get rid of the soil before putting them in his mouth. Half an hour later, as they drew near the edge of the forest, one of the elephants suddenly stopped short, with a jerky, backward movement, and trumpeted shrilly. There was an expectant halt all along the line, and a cry from a native of "Tiger! Tiger!" Then an enormous striped beast bounded out of the grass and stood for a moment in a small open space, lashing its tail and snarling defiance. Colonel Wingate fired. The tiger, badly wounded, charged, and sprang at the head of Captain Bastable's elephant. There was a confusion of noise—savage roars from the tiger, shrieks from the excited elephants, shouts from the natives, banging of rifles. Mrs. Wingate covered her face with her hands. She heard a thud as of a heavy body falling to the ground, and then she found herself being flung from side to side of the howdah, as the elephant bolted madly toward the forest, one huge ear torn to ribbons by the tiger's claws.

She heard Captain Bastable telling her to hold on tight, and shouting desperate warnings to the mahout to keep the elephant as clear of the forest as possible. Like many nervous people, in the face of real danger she suddenly became absolutely calm, and uttered no sound as the pace increased and they tore along the forest edge, escaping overhanging boughs by a miracle. To her it seemed that the ponderous flight lasted for hours. She was bruised, shaken, giddy, and the crash that came at last was a relief rather than otherwise. A huge branch combed the howdah off the elephant's back, sweeping the mahout with it, while the still terrified animal sped on, trumpeting and crashing through the forest.

Mrs. Wingate was thrown clear off the howdah. Captain Bastable had saved himself by jumping, and only the old mahout lay doubled up and unconscious among the debris of shattered wood, torn leather, and broken ropes. Netta could hardly believe she was not hurt. She and Captain Bastable stared at each other with dazed faces for some moments before they could collect their senses. Far away in the distance they could hear the elephant still running. Between them they extricated the mahout, and, seating herself on the ground, Netta took the old man's unconscious head on her lap, while Captain Bastable anxiously examined the wizened, shrunken body.

"Is he dead?" she asked.

"I can't be sure. I'm afraid he is. I wonder if I could find some water? I haven't an idea where we are, for I lost all count of time and distance. I hope Wingate is following us. Should you be afraid to stay here while I have a look round and see if we are anywhere near a village?"

"Oh, no; I shan't be frightened," she said steadily. Her delicate, clear-cut face looked up at him fearlessly from the tangled background of mighty trees and dense creepers; and her companion could scarcely believe that she was the same trembling, nervous little coward of an hour before.

He left her, and the stillness of the jungle was very oppressive when the sound of his footsteps died away. She was alone with a dead or dying man, on the threshold of the vast, mysterious forest, with its possible horrors of wild elephants, tigers, leopards, snakes. She tried to turn her thoughts from such things, but the scream of a peacock made her start as it rent the silence, and then the undergrowth began to rustle ominously. It was only a porcupine that came out, rattling its quills. On seeing her, it ran into further shelter out of sight.

It seemed to be growing darker, and she fancied the evening must be drawing on. She wondered if her husband would overtake them. If not, how were she and Jim Bastable to get back to the camp? Then she heard voices and footsteps, and presently a little party of natives came in sight, led by Jim, and bearing a charpoy, a bedframe strung with rope.

"I found a village not far off," he explained, "and thought we'd better take the poor old chap there. Then, if the Colonel doesn't turn up by the time we've seen him comfortably settled, we must find our way back to the camp as best we can."

The natives chattered and exclaimed as they lifted the unconscious body on to the charpoy, and then the little procession started. Netta was so bruised and stiff she could hardly walk; but, with the help of Bastable's arm, she hobbled along until they reached the village. The headman conducted them to his house, which was a mud hut, shared by himself and his family with several relations, besides a cow and a goat with two kids. He gave Netta a wicker stool to sit on and some smoky buffalo's milk to drink. The village doctor was summoned, and at last succeeded in restoring the mahout to consciousness and pouring a potion down his throat.

"I die," whispered the patient feebly.

Netta went to his side, and he recognized her.

"A—ree! Memsahib!" he quavered. "So Allah has guarded thee. But the anger of the Colonel sahib will be great against me for permitting the elephant to run away, and it is better that I die. Where is that daughter of a pig? She was a rascal from her youth up; but today was the first time she ever really disobeyed my voice."

He tried to raise himself, but fell back groaning, for his injuries were internal and past hope.

"It is growing dark." He put forth his trembling hand blindly. "Where is the little white lady who so feared the sahib, and the elephants, and the jungle? Do not be afraid, Memsahib. Those who fear should never go into the jungle. So if thou seest a tiger, be bold, be bold; call him 'uncle' and show him the tiger charm.

Then will he turn away and harm thee not—" He wandered on incoherently, his fingers fumbling with something at his throat, and presently he drew out a small silver amulet attached to a piece of cord. As he held it toward Netta, it flashed in the light of the oil lamp that someone had just brought in and placed on the floor.

"Take it, Memsahib, and feel no fear while thou hast it, for no tiger would touch thee. It was my father's, and his father's before him, and there is that written on it which has ever protected us from the tiger's tooth. I myself shall need it no longer, for I am going, whereat my nephew will rejoice; for he has long coveted my seat. Thou shalt have the charm, Memsahib, for thou hast stayed by an old man, and not left him to die alone in a Hindu village and a strange place. Some day in the hour of danger thy little fingers may touch the charm, and then thou wilt recall old Mahomed Bux, mahout, with gratitude."

He groped for Netta's hand, and pushed the amulet into her palm. She took it, and laid her cool fingers on the old man's burning forehead.

"Salaam, Mahomed Bux," she said softly. "Bahut, bahut, sa-laam. Thank you."

But he did not hear her. He was wandering again, and for half an hour he babbled of elephants, of tigers, of camps and jungles, until his voice became faint and died away in hoarse gasps.

Then he sighed heavily and lay still. Jim Bastable took Mrs. Wingate out into the air and told her that the old mahout was dead. She gave way and sobbed, for she was aching all over and tired to death, and she dreaded the return to the camp.

"Oh, my dear girl, please don't cry!" said Jim distressfully. "Though really I can't wonder at it, after all you've gone through today; and you've been so awfully plucky, too."

Netta gulped down her tears. It was delicious to be praised for courage, when she was accustomed only to abuse for cowardice.

"How are we to get back to the camp?" she asked dolefully. "It's so late."

And, indeed, darkness had come swiftly on, and the light of the village fires was all that enabled them to see each other.

"The moon will be up presently; we must wait for that. They

say the village near our camp lies about six miles off, and that there is a cart track of sorts toward it. I told them they must let us have a bullock cart, and we shall have to make the best of that."

They sat down side by side on a couple of large stones, and listened in silence to the lowing of the tethered cattle, the ceaseless, irritating cry of the brain-fever bird, and the subdued conversation of a group of children and villagers, who had assembled at a respectful distance to watch them with inquisitive interest. Once a shrill trumpeting in the distance told of a herd of wild elephants out for a night's raid on the crops, and at intervals packs of jackals swept howling across the fields, while the moon rose gradually over the huts and flooded the vast country with a light that made the forest black and fearful.

Then a clumsy little cart, drawn by two small, frightened white bullocks, rattled into view. Jim and Netta climbed into the vehicle, and were politely escorted off the premises by the headman, interested villagers and excited women and children.

They bumped and shook over the rough, uneven track. The bullocks raced or crawled alternately, while the driver twisted their tails and abused them hoarsely. The moonlight grew brighter and more glorious. The air, now soft and cool, was filled with strong scents and the hum of insects released from the heat of the day.

At last they caught the gleam of white tents against the dark background of a mango grove.

"The camp," said Captain Bastable shortly.

Netta made a nervous exclamation.

"Do you think there will be a row?" he asked with some hesitation. They had never discussed Mrs. Wingate's domestic troubles.

"Perhaps he is still out looking for us," she said evasively.

"If he had followed us at all, he would have found us. I believe he went on shooting, or came back to the camp." There was an angry impatience in his voice. "Don't be nervous," he added hastily. "Try not to mind anything he may say. Don't listen. He can't always help it, you know. I wish you could persuade him to retire; the sun out here makes him half off his head."

"I wish I could," she sighed. "But he will never do anything I ask him, and the big game shooting keeps him in India."

Jim nodded, and there was a comprehending silence between them until they reached the edge of the camp, got out of the cart, and made their way to the principal tent. There they discovered Colonel Wingate, still in his shooting clothes, sitting by the table, on which stood an almost empty bottle of whisky. He rose as they entered, and delivered himself of a torrent of bad language. He accused the pair of going off together on purpose, declaring he would divorce his wife and kill Bastable. He stormed, raved, and threatened, giving them no opportunity to speak, until at last Jim broke in and insisted on being heard.

"For heaven's sake, be quiet," he said firmly, "or you'll have a fit. You saw the elephant run away, and apparently you made no effort to follow us and come to our help. We were swept off by a tree, and the mahout was mortally hurt. It was a perfect miracle that neither your wife nor I was killed. The mahout died in a village, and we had to get here in a bullock cart." Then, seeing Wingate preparing for another onslaught, Bastable took him by the shoulders. "My dear chap, you're not yourself. Go to bed, and we'll talk it over tomorrow, if you still wish to."

Colonel Wingate laughed harshly. His mood had changed suddenly.

"Go to bed?" he shouted boisterously. "Why, I was just going out when you arrived. There was a kill last night only a mile off, and I'm going to get the tiger." He stared wildly at Jim, who saw that he was not responsible for his words and actions. His brain, already touched by sunstroke, had given way at last under the power of whisky. Jim's first impulse was to prevent his carrying out his intention of going after the tiger. Then he reflected that it was not safe for Netta to be alone with the man, and that, if Wingate were allowed his own way, it would at least take him out of the camp.

"Very well," said Jim quietly; "and I will come with you."

"Do," answered the Colonel pleasantly, and then, as Bastable turned for a moment, Mrs. Wingate saw her husband make a diabolical grimace at the other's unconscious back. Her heart beat rapidly with fear. Did he mean to murder Jim? She felt convinced he contemplated mischief; but the question was how to warn Captain Bastable without her husband's knowledge. The opportunity came more easily than she had expected, for presently the Colonel went outside to call for his rifle and give some orders. She flew to Bastable's side.

"Be careful," she panted. "He wants to kill you—I know he does. He's mad! Oh, don't go with him—don't go—"

"It will be all right," he said reassuringly. "I'll look out for myself, but I can't let him go alone in this state. We shall only sit up in a tree for an hour or two, for the tiger must have come and gone long ago. Don't be frightened. Go to bed and rest."

She drew from her pocket the little polished amulet the mahout had given her.

"At any rate, take this," she said hysterically. "It may save you from a tiger, if it doesn't from my husband. I know I am silly, but do take it. There may be luck in it—you can never tell; and old Mahomed Bux said it had saved him and his father and his grandfather—and that you ought to call a tiger 'uncle'—" She broke off, half laughing, half crying, utterly unstrung.

To please her he put the little charm into his pocket, and after a hasty drink went out and joined Wingate, who insisted that they should proceed on foot and by themselves. Bastable knew it would be useless to make any opposition, and they started, their rifles in their hands; but when they had gone some distance, and the tainted air told them they were nearing their destination, Jim discovered he had no cartridges.

"Never mind," whispered the Colonel. "I have plenty, and our rifles have the same bore. We can't go back now; we've no time to lose."

Jim submitted, and he and Wingate tiptoed to the foot of a tree, the low branches and thick leaves of which afforded an excellent hiding place, downwind from the half-eaten carcass of the cow. They climbed carefully up, making scarcely any noise, and then Jim held out his hand to the other for some cartridges. The Colonel nodded.

"Presently," he whispered, and Jim waited, thinking it extremely unlikely that cartridges would be wanted at all.

The moonlight came feebly through the foliage of the surrounding trees into the little glade before them, in which lay the remains of the carcass, pulled under a bush to shield it from the carrion birds. A deer pattered by toward the river, casting startled glances on every side; insects beat against the faces of the two men; and a jackal ran out, his brush hanging down, looked round, and retired again with a melancholy howl. Then there arose a commotion in the branches of the neighboring trees, and a troop of monkeys fought and crashed and chattered as they leaped from bough to bough. Jim knew that this often portended the approach of a tiger, and a moment afterward a long, hoarse call from the river told him that the warning was correct. He made a silent sign for the cartridges; but Wingate took no notice: his face was hard and set, and the whites of his eyes gleamed.

A few seconds later a large tiger crept slowly out of the grass, his stomach on the ground, his huge head held low. Jim remembered the native superstition that the head of a maneating tiger is weighed down by the souls of its victims. With a run and a spring, the creature attacked its meal, and began growling and munching contentedly, purring like a cat, and stopping every now and then to tear up the earth with its claws.

A report rang out. Wingate had fired at and hit the tiger. The great beast gave a terrific roar and sprang at the tree. Jim lifted his rifle, only to remember that it was unloaded.

"Shoot again!" he cried excitedly, as the tiger fell back and prepared for another spring. To his horror, Wingate deliberately fired the second barrel into the air, and, throwing away the rifle, grasped him by the arms. The man's teeth were bared, his face was distorted and hideous, his purpose unmistakable—he was trying to throw Bastable to the tiger. Wingate was strong with the diabolical strength of madness, and they swayed until the branches of the tree cracked ominously. Again the tiger roared and sprang, and again fell back, only to gather itself together for another effort. The two men rocked and panted, the branches cracked louder, with a dry, splitting sound, then broke off altogether, and, locked in each other's arms, they fell heavily to the ground.

Jim Bastable went undermost, and was half stunned by the shock. He heard a snarl in his ear, followed by a dreadful cry. He felt the weight of Wingate's body lifted from him with a jerk, and he scrambled blindly to his feet. As in a nightmare, he saw the tiger bounding away, carrying something that hung limply from the great jaws, just as a cat carries a dead mouse.

He seized the Colonel's rifle that lay near him; but he knew it was empty, and that the cartridges were in the Colonel's pocket. He ran after the tiger, shouting, yelling, brandishing the rifle, in the hope of frightening the brute into dropping its prey; but, after one swift glance back, it bounded into the thick jungle with the speed of a deer, and Bastable was left standing alone.

Faint and sick, he began running madly toward the camp for help, though he knew well that nothing in this world could ever help Wingate again. His forehead was bleeding profusely, either hurt in the fall or touched by the tiger's claw, and the blood trickling into his eyes nearly blinded him. He pulled his handkerchief from his pocket as he ran, and something came with it that glittered in the moonlight and fell to the ground with a metallic ring.

It was the little silver amulet: the tiger charm.

THE
BEAR HUNT

LEO TOLSTOY

WE WERE OUT on a bear-hunting expedition. My comrade had shot at a bear, but only gave him a flesh wound. There were traces of blood on the snow, but the bear had got away.

We all collected in a group in the forest, to decide whether we ought to go after the bear at once, or wait two or three days till he should settle down again. We asked the peasant bear-drivers whether it would be possible to get round the bear that day.

"No. It's impossible," said an old bear-driver. "You must let the bear quiet down. In five days' time it will be possible to surround him; but if you followed him now, you would only frighten him away, and he would not settle down."

But a young bear-driver began disputing with the old man, saying that it was quite possible to get round the bear now.

"On such snow as this," said he, "he won't go far, for he is a fat bear. He will settle down before evening; or, if not, I can overtake him on snowshoes."

The comrade I was with was against following up the bear, and advised waiting. But I said, "We need not argue. You do as you like, but I will follow up the track with Damian. If we get round the bear, all right. If not, we lose nothing. It is still early, and there is nothing else for us to do today."

So it was arranged.

The others went back to the sledges, and returned to the village. Damian and I took some bread, and remained behind in the forest.

When they had all left us, Damian and I examined our guns, and after tucking the skirts of our warm coats into our belts, we started off, following the bear's tracks.

The weather was fine, frosty and calm; but it was hard work snowshoeing. The snow was deep and soft: it had not caked together at all in the forest, and fresh snow had fallen the day before, so that our snowshoes sank six inches deep in the snow, and sometimes more.

The bear's tracks were visible from a distance. and we could see how he had been going; sometimes sinking in up to his belly and plowing up the snow as he went. At first, while under large trees, we kept in sight of his track; but when it turned into a thicket of small firs, Damian stopped.

"We must leave the trail now," said he. "He has probably settled somewhere here. You can see by the snow that he has been squatting down. Let us leave the track and go round; but we must go quietly. Don't shout or cough, or we shall frighten him away."

Leaving the track, therefore, we turned off to the left. But when we had gone about five hundred yards, there were the bear's traces again right before us. We followed them, and they brought us out on to the road. There we stopped, examining the road to see which way the bear had gone. Here and there in the snow were prints of the bear's paw, claws and all, and here and there the marks of a peasant's bark shoes. The bear had evidently gone toward the village.

As we followed the road, Damian said, "It's no use watching the road now. We shall see where he has turned off, to right or left, by the marks in the soft snow at the side. He must have turned off somewhere; for he won't have gone on to the village."

We went along the road for nearly a mile, and then saw, ahead of us, the bear's track turning off the road. We examined it. How strange! It was a bear's track right enough, only not going from the road into the forest, but from the forest on to the road! The toes were pointing toward the road.

"This must be another bear," I said.

Damian looked at it, and considered a while.

"No," said he. "It's the same one. He's been playing tricks, and walked backwards when he left the road."

We followed the track, and found it really was so! The bear had gone some ten steps backwards, and then, behind a fir tree, had turned round and gone straight ahead.

Damian stopped and said, "Now, we are sure to get round him. There is a marsh ahead of us, and he must have settled down there. Let us go round it."

We began to make our way round, through a fir thicket. I was tired out by this time, and it had become still more difficult to get along. Now I glided on to juniper bushes and caught my snowshoes in them, now a tiny fir tree appeared between my feet, or, from want of practice, my snowshoes slipped off; and now I came upon a stump or a log hidden by the snow. I was getting very tired, and was drenched with perspiration; and I took off my fur cloak. And there was Damian all the time, gliding along as if in a boat, his snowshoes moving as if of their own accord, never catching against anything, nor slipping off. He even took my fur and slung it over his shoulder, and still kept urging me on.

We went on for two more miles, and came out on the other side of the marsh. I was lagging behind. My snowshoes kept slipping off, and my feet stumbled. Suddenly Damian, who was ahead of me, stopped and waved his arm.

When I came up to him, he bent down, pointing with his hand, and whispered, "Do you see the magpie chattering above that undergrowth? It scents the bear from afar. That is where he must be."

We turned off and went on for more than another half-mile, and presently we came on to the old track again. We had, therefore, been right round the bear, who was now within the track we had left. We stopped, and I took off my cap and loosened all my clothes. I was as hot as in a steam bath, and as wet as a drowned rat. Damian, too, was flushed, and wiped his face with his sleeve.

"Well, sir," he said, "we have done our job, and now we must have a rest."

The evening glow already showed red through the forest. We took off our snowshoes and sat down on them, and got some bread and salt out of our bags. First I ate some snow, and then

some bread; and the bread tasted so good, that I thought I had
never in my life had any like it before. We sat there resting until it
began to grow dusk, and then I asked Damian if it was far to the
village.

"Yes," he said. "It must be about eight miles. We will go on
there tonight, but now we must rest. Put on your fur coat, sir, or
you'll be catching cold."

Damian flattened down the snow, and breaking off some fir
branches made a bed of them. We lay down side by side, resting
our heads on our arms. I do not remember how I fell asleep. Two
hours later I woke up, hearing something crack.

I had slept so soundly that I did not know where I was. I
looked around me. How wonderful! I was in some sort of a hall,
all glittering and white with gleaming pillars, and when I looked
up I saw, through delicate white tracery, a vault, raven black and
studded with colored lights. After a good look, I remembered
that we were in the forest, and that what I took for a hall and
pillars, were trees covered with snow and hoar frost, and the
colored lights were stars twinkling between the branches.

Hoar frost had settled in the night; all the twigs were thick
with it, Damian was covered with it, it was on my fur coat, and it
dropped down from the trees. I woke Damian; and we put on our
snowshoes and started. It was very quiet in the forest. No sound
was heard but that of our snowshoes pushing through the soft
snow; except when now and then a tree, cracked by the frost,
made the forest resound. Only once we heard the sound of a
living creature. Something rustled close to us, and then rushed
away. I felt sure it was the bear, but when we went to the spot
whence the sound had come, we found the footmarks of hares,
and saw several young aspen trees with their bark gnawed. We
had startled some hares while they were feeding.

We came out on the road, and followed it, dragging our snowshoes behind us. It was easy walking now. Our snowshoes clat-
tered as they slid behind us from side to side on the hard-trodden
road. The snow creaked under our boots, and the cold hoar frost
settled on our faces like down. Seen through the branches, the
stars seemed to be running to meet us, now twinkling, now vanishing, as if the whole sky were on the move.

I found my comrade sleeping, but woke him up, and related how we had got round the bear. After telling our peasant host to collect beaters for the morning, we had supper and lay down to sleep.

I was so tired that I could have slept on till midday, if my comrade had not roused me. I jumped up, and saw that he was already dressed, and busy doing something to his gun.

"Where is Damian?" said I.

"In the forest, long ago. He has already been over the tracks you made, and been back here, and now he has gone to look after the beaters."

I washed and dressed, and loaded my guns; and then we got into a sledge, and started.

The sharp frost still continued. It was quiet, and the sun could not be seen. There was a thick mist above us, and hoar frost still covered everything.

After driving about two miles along the road, as we came near the forest, we saw a cloud of smoke rising from a hollow, and presently reached a group of peasants, both men and women, armed with cudgels.

We got out and went up to them. The men sat roasting potatoes, and laughing and talking with the women.

Damian was there, too; and when we arrived the people got up, and Damian led them away to place them in the circle we had made the day before. They went along in single file, men and women, thirty in all. The snow was so deep that we could only see them from their waists upward. They turned into the forest, and my friend and I followed in their track.

Though they had trodden a path, walking was difficult; but, on the other hand, it was impossible to fall: it was like walking between two walls of snow.

We went on in this way for nearly half a mile, when all at once we saw Damian coming from another direction—running toward us on his snowshoes, and beckoning us to join him. We went toward him, and he showed us where to stand. I took my place, and looked around me.

To my left were tall fir trees, between the trunks of which I could see a good way, and, like a black patch just visible behind the trees, I could see a beater. In front of me was a thicket of young firs, about as high as a man, their branches weighed down and stuck together with snow. Through this copse ran a path thickly covered with snow, and leading straight up to where I stood. The thicket stretched away to the right of me, and ended in a small glade, where I could see Damian placing my comrade.

I examined both my guns, and considered where I had better stand. Three steps behind me was a tall fir.

That's where I'll stand, thought I, and then I can lean my second gun against the tree; and I moved toward the tree, sinking up to my knees in the snow at each step. I trod the snow down, and made a clearance about a yard square to stand on. One gun I kept in my hand; the other, ready cocked, I placed leaning up against the tree. Then I unsheathed and replaced my dagger, to make sure that I could draw it easily in case of need.

Just as I had finished these preparations, I heard Damian shouting in the forest, "He's up! He's up!"

And as soon as Damian shouted, the peasants round the circle all replied in their different voices.

"Up, up, up! Ou! Ou! Ou!" shouted the men.

"Ay! Ay! Ay!" screamed the women in high-pitched tones.

The bear was inside the circle, and as Damian drove him on, the people all round kept shouting. Only my friend and I stood silent and motionless, waiting for the bear to come toward us. As I stood gazing and listening, my heart beat violently. I trembled, holding my gun fast.

Now, now, I thought. He will come suddenly. I shall aim, fire, and he will drop—

Suddenly, to my left, but at a distance, I heard something falling on the snow. I looked between the tall fir trees, and, some fifty paces off, behind the trunks, saw something big and black. I took aim and waited, thinking, Won't he come any nearer?

As I waited I saw him move his ears, turn, and go back; and then I caught a glimpse of the whole of him in profile. He was an immense brute. In my excitement, I fired, and heard my bullet go "flop" against a tree. Peering through the smoke, I saw my bear scampering back into the circle, and disappearing among the trees.

Well, thought I. My chance is lost. He won't come back to me. Either my comrade will shoot him, or he will escape through the line of beaters. In any case he won't give me another chance.

I reloaded my gun, however, and again stood listening. The peasants were shouting all around, but to the right, not far from where my comrade stood, I heard a woman screaming in a frenzied voice, "Here he is! Here he is! Come here, come here! Oh! Oh! Ay! Ay!"

Evidently she could see the bear. I had given up expecting him, and was looking to the right at my comrade. All at once I saw Damian with a stick in his hand, and without his snowshoes, running along a footpath toward my friend. He crouched down beside him, pointing his stick as if aiming at something, and then I saw my friend raise his gun and aim in the same direction. Crack! He fired.

There, thought I. He has killed him.

But I saw that my comrade did not run toward the bear. Evidently he had missed him, or the shot had not taken full effect.

The bear will get away, I thought. He will go back, but he won't come a second time toward me. But what is that?

Something was coming toward me like a whirlwind, snorting as it came; and I saw the snow flying up quite near me. I glanced straight before me, and there was the bear, rushing along the path through the thicket right at me, evidently beside himself with fear. He was hardly half a dozen paces off, and I could see the whole of him—his black chest and enormous head with a reddish patch. There he was, blundering straight at me, and scattering the snow about as he came. I could see by his eyes that he did not see me, but, mad with fear, was rushing blindly along; and his path led him straight at the tree under which I was standing. I raised my gun and fired. He was almost upon me now, and I saw that I had missed. My bullet had gone past him, and he did not even hear me fire, but still came headlong toward me. I lowered my gun, and fired again, almost touching his head. Crack! I had hit, but not killed him!

He raised his head, and laying his ears back, came at me, showing his teeth.

I snatched at my other gun, but almost before I had touched it, he had flown at me and, knocking me over into the snow, had passed right over me.

Thank goodness, he has left me, thought I.

I tried to rise, but something pressed me down, and prevented my getting up. The bear's rush had carried him past me, but he had turned back, and had fallen on me with the whole weight of his body. I felt something heavy weighing me down, and something warm above my face, and I realized that he was drawing my whole face into his mouth. My nose was already in it, and I felt the heat of it, and smelled his blood. He was pressing my shoulders down with his paws so that I could not move: all I could do was to draw my head down toward my chest away from his mouth, trying to free my nose and eyes, while he tried to get his teeth into them. Then I felt that he had seized my forehead just under the hair with the teeth of his lower jaw, and the flesh below my eyes with his upper jaw, and was closing his teeth. It was as if my face were being cut with knives. I struggled to get away, while he made haste to close his jaws like a dog gnawing. I managed to twist my face away, but he began drawing it again into his mouth.

Now, thought I, my end has come!

Then I felt the weight lifted, and looking up, I saw that he was no longer there. He had jumped off me and run away.

When my comrade and Damian had seen the bear knock me down and begin worrying me, they rushed to the rescue. My comrade, in his haste, blundered, and instead of following the trodden path, ran into the deep snow and fell down. While he was struggling out of the snow, the bear was gnawing at me. But Damian just as he was, without a gun, and with only a stick in his hand, rushed along the path shouting, "He's eating the master! He's eating the master!"

And, as he ran, he called to the bear, "Oh, you idiot! What are you doing? Leave off! Leave off!"

The bear obeyed him, and leaving me ran away. When I rose, there was as much blood on the snow as if a sheep had been killed, and the flesh hung in rags above my eyes, though in my excitement I felt no pain.

My comrade had come up by this time, and the other people

collected around: they looked at my wound, and put snow on it. But I, forgetting about my wounds, only asked, "Where's the bear? Which way has he gone?"

Suddenly I heard, "Here he is! Here he is!"

And we saw the bear again running at us. We seized our guns, but before any one had time to fire, he had run past. He had grown ferocious, and wanted to gnaw me again, but seeing so many people he took fright. We saw by his track that his head was bleeding, and we wanted to follow him; but, as my wounds had become very painful, we went, instead, to the town to find a doctor.

The doctor stitched up my wounds with silk, and they soon began to heal.

A month later we went to hunt that bear again, but I did not get a chance of finishing him. He would not come out of the circle, but went round and round, growling in a terrible voice.

Damian killed him. The bear's lower jaw had been broken, and one of his teeth knocked out by my bullet.

He was a huge creature, and had splendid black fur.

I had him stuffed, and he now lies in my room. The wounds on my forehead healed up so that the scars can scarcely be seen.

THE COON DOG

SARAH ORNE JEWETT

IN THE EARLY DUSK of a warm September evening the bats were flitting to and fro, as if it were still summer, under the great elm that overshadowed Isaac Brown's house, on the Dipford road. Isaac Brown himself, and his old friend and neighbor, John York, were leaning against the fence.

"Frost keeps off late, don't it?" said John York. "I laughed when I first heard about the circus comin'; I thought 't was so unusual late in the season. Turned out well, however. Everybody I noticed was returnin' with a palm-leaf fan. Guess they found 'em useful under the tent; it was a master hot day. I saw old lady Price with her hands full o' those free advertisin' fans, as if she was layin' in a stock against next summer. Well, I expect she'll live to enjoy 'em."

"I was right here where I'm standin' now, and I see her as she was goin' by this mornin'," said Isaac Brown, laughing and settling himself comfortably against the fence as if they had chanced upon a welcome subject of conversation. "I hailed her, same's I generally do. 'Where are you bound today, ma'am?' says I.

" 'I'm goin' over as fur as Dipford Center,' says she. 'I'm goin' to see my poor dear 'Liza Jane. I want to 'suage her grief; her husband, Mr. 'Bijah Topliff, has passed away.'

" 'So much the better,' says I.

" 'No; I never l'arnt about it till yesterday,' says she; an' she looked up at me real kind of pleasant, and begun to laugh.

" 'I hear he's left property,' says she, tryin' to pull her face

251

down solemn. I give her the fifty cents she wanted to borrow to make up her carfare and other expenses, an' she stepped off like a girl down tow'ds the depot.

"This afternoon, as you know, I'd promised the boys that I'd take 'em over to see the menagerie, and nothin' wouldn't do none of us any good but we must see the circus too; an' when we'd just got posted on one o' the best high seats, Mother she nudged me, and I looked right down front two, three rows, an' if there wa'n't Mis' Price, spectacles an' all, with her head right up in the air, havin' the best time you ever see. I laughed right out. She hadn't taken no time to see 'Lizy Jane; she wa'n't 'suagin' no grief for nobody till she'd seen the circus. 'There,' says I, 'I do like to have anybody keep their young feelin's.' "

"Mis' Price come over to see our folks before breakfast," said John York. "Wife said she was inquirin' about the circus, but she wanted to know first if they couldn't oblige her with a few trinkets o'mournin', seein' as how she'd got to pay a mournin' visit. Wife thought 'twas a bosom-pin, or somethin' like that, but turned out she wanted the skirt of a dress; 'most anything would do, she said."

"I thought she looked extra well startin' off," said Isaac, with an indulgent smile. "The Lord provides very handsome for such, I do declare! She ain't had no visible means o' support these ten or fifteen years back, but she don't freeze up in winter no more than we do."

"Nor dry up in summer," interrupted his friend; "I never did see such an able hand to talk."

"She's good company, and she's obliging an' useful when the women folks have their extra work progressin'," continued Isaac Brown kindly. " 'Tain't much for a well-off neighborhood like this to support that old chirpin' cricket. My mother used to say she kind of helped the work along by 'livenin' of it. Here she comes now; must have taken the last train, after she had supper with 'Lizy Jane. You stay still; we're goin' to hear all about it."

The small, thin figure of Mrs. Price had to be hailed twice before she could be stopped.

"I wish you a good evenin', neighbors," she said. "I have been to the house of mournin'."

"Find 'Liza Jane in, after the circus?" asked Isaac Brown, with equal seriousness. "Excellent show, wasn't it, for so late in the season?"

"Oh, beautiful; it was beautiful, I declare," answered the pleased spectator readily. "Why, I didn't see you, nor Mis' Brown. Yes; I felt it best to refresh my mind an' wear a cheerful countenance. When I see 'Liza Jane I was able to divert her mind consid'able. She was glad I went. I told her I'd made an effort, knowin' 'twas so she had to lose the a'ternoon. 'Bijah left property, if he did die away from home on a foreign shore."

"You don't mean that 'Bijah Topliff's left anything!" exclaimed John York with interest, while Isaac Brown put both hands deep into his pockets, and leaned back in a still more satisfactory position against the gatepost.

"He enjoyed poor health," answered Mrs. Price, after a moment of deliberation, as if she must take time to think. " 'Bijah never was one that scattereth, nor yet increaseth. 'Liza Jane's got some memories o' the past that's a good deal better than others; but he died somewhere out in Connecticut, or so she heard, and he's left a very val'able coon dog—one he set a great deal by. 'Liza Jane said, last time he was to home, he priced that dog at fifty dollars. 'There now, 'Liza Jane,' says I, right to her, when she told me, 'if I could git fifty dollars for that dog, I certain' would. Perhaps some o' the circus folks would like to buy him; they've taken in a stream o' money this day. But 'Liza Jane ain't never inclined to listen to advice. 'Tis a dreadful poor-spirited-lookin' creatur'. I don't want no right o' dower in him, myself."

"A good coon dog's worth somethin', certain," said John York, handsomely.

"If he *is* a good coon dog," added Isaac Brown. "I wouldn't have parted with old Rover, here, for a good deal of money when he was right in his best days; but a dog like him's like one of the family. Stop an' have some supper, won't ye, Mis' Price?"—as the thin old creature was flitting off again. At that same moment this kind invitation was repeated from the door of the house; and Mrs. Price turned in, unprotesting and always sociably inclined, at the open gate.

It was a month later, and a whole autumn's length colder, when the two men were coming home from a long tramp through the woods. They had been making a solemn inspection of a wood lot that they owned together, and had now visited their landmarks and outer boundaries, and settled the great question of cutting or not cutting some large pines. When it was well decided that a few years' growth would be no disadvantage to the timber, they had eaten an excellent cold luncheon and rested from their labors.

"I don't feel a day older'n I ever did when I get out in the woods this way," announced John York, who was a prim, dusty-looking little man, a prudent person, who had been selectman of the town at least a dozen times.

"No more do I," agreed his companion, who was large and jovial and openhanded, more like a lucky sea captain than a farmer. After pounding a slender walnut tree with a heavy stone, he had succeeded in getting down a pocketful of late-hanging nuts, and was now snapping them back, one by one, to a venturesome chipmunk among some little frostbitten beeches. Isaac Brown had a wonderfully pleasant way of getting on with all sorts of animals, even men. After a while they rose and went their way, these two companions, stopping here and there to look at a possible woodchuck's hole, or to strike a few hopeful blows at a hollow tree with the light axe which Isaac had carried to blaze new marks on some of the line trees on the farther edge of their possessions. Sometimes they stopped to admire the size of an old hemlock, or to talk about thinning out the young pines. At last they were not very far from the entrance to the great tract of woodland. The yellow sunshine came slanting in much brighter against the tall tree trunks, spotting them with golden light high among the still branches.

Presently they came to a great ledge, frost-split and cracked into mysterious crevices.

"Here's where we used to get all the coons," said John York. "I haven't seen a coon this great while, spite o' your courage knocking on the trees up back here. You know that night we got the four fat ones? We started 'em somewheres near here, so the dog could get after 'em when they came out at night to go foragin'."

"Hold on, John"; and Mr. Isaac Brown got up from the log where he had just sat down to rest, and went to the ledge, and looked carefully all about. When he came back he was much excited, and beckoned his friend away, speaking in a stage whisper.

"I guess you'll see a coon before you're much older," he exclaimed. "I've thought it looked lately as if there'd been one about my place, and there's plenty o' signs here, right in their old haunts. Couple o' hen's heads an' a lot o' feathers—"

"Might be a fox," interrupted John York.

"Might be a coon," answered Mr. Isaac Brown. "I'm goin' to have him, too. I've been lookin' at every old hollow tree I passed, but I never thought o' this place. We'll come right off tomorrow night, I guess, John, an' see if we can't get him. 'Tis an extra handy place for 'em to den; in old times the folks always called it a good place; they've been so scarce o' these late years that I've thought little about 'em. Nothin' I ever liked so well as a coon hunt. Gorry! he must be a big old fellow, by his tracks! See here, in this smooth dirt; just like a baby's footmark."

"Trouble is, we lack a good dog," said John York anxiously, after he had made an eager inspection. "I don't know where in the world to get one, either. There ain't no such a dog about as your Rover, but you've let him get spoilt; these days I don't see him leave the yard. You ought to keep the womenfolks from overfeedin' of him so. He ought to have lasted a good spell longer. He's no use for huntin' now, that's certain."

Isaac accepted the rebuke meekly. John York was a calm man, but he now grew very fierce under such a provocation. Nobody likes to be hindered in a coonhunt.

"Oh, Rover's too old, anyway," explained the affectionate master regretfully. "I've been wishing all this afternoon I'd brought him; but I didn't think anything about him as we came away, I've got so used to seeing him layin' about the yard. 'Twould have been a real treat for old Rover, if he could have kept up. Used to be at my heels the whole time. He couldn't follow us, anyway, up here."

"I shouldn't wonder if he could," insisted John, with a humorous glance at his old friend, who was much too heavy and huge

of girth for quick transit over rough ground. John York himself
had grown lighter as he had grown older.

"I'll tell you one thing we could do," he hastened to suggest.
"There's that dog of 'Bijah Topliff's. Don't you know the old lady
told us, that day she went over to Dipford, how high he was
valued? Most o' 'Bijah's important business was done in the fall,
goin' out by night, gunning with fellows from the mills. He was
just the kind of a worthless do-nothing that's sure to have an
extra knowin' smart dog. I expect 'Liza Jane's got him now. Let
one o' my boys go over!"

"Why, 'Liza Jane's come, bag and baggage, to spend the winter with her mother," exclaimed Isaac Brown, springing to his
feet like a boy. "I've had it in mind to tell you, two or three times
this afternoon, and then something else has flown it out of my
head. I let my John Henry take the long-tailed wagon an' go
down to the depot this mornin' to fetch her an' her goods up. The
old lady come in early, while we were to breakfast, and to hear
her lofty talk you'd have thought 't would taken a couple o' four-
horse teams to move her. I told John Henry he might take that
wagon and fetch up what light stuff he could, and see how much
else there was, an' then I could make further arrangements. She
said 'Liza Jane'd see me well satisfied, an' rode off, pleased to
death. I see 'em returnin' about eight, after the train was in.
They'd got 'Liza Jane with 'em, smaller'n ever; and there was a
trunk tied up with a rope, and a small roll of beddin' and braided
mats, and a quilted rockin' chair. The old lady was holdin' on
tight to a birdcage with nothin' in it. Yes; an' I see the dog, too, in
behind. He appeared kind of timid. He's a yaller dog, but he ain't
stump-tailed. They hauled up out front o' the house, and Mother
and I went right out; Mis' Price always expects to have notice
taken. She was in great spirits. Said 'Liza Jane concluded to sell
off most of her stuff rather'n have the care of it. She'd told the
folks that Mis' Topliff had a beautiful sofa and a lot of nice
chairs, and two framed pictures that would fix up the house complete, and invited us all to come over and see 'em. There, she
seemed just as pleased returnin' with the birdcage. Disappoint-
ments don't appear to trouble her no more than a butterfly. I
kind of like the old creatur'; I don't mean to see her want."

"They'll let us have the dog," said John York. "I don't know but I'll give a quarter for him, and we'll let 'em have a good piece o' the coon."

"You really comin' 'way up here by night, coonhuntin'?" asked Isaac Brown, looking reproachfully at his more agile companion.

"I be," answered John York.

"I was dre'tful afraid you was only talking, and might back out," returned the cheerful heavyweight, with a chuckle. "Now we've got things all fixed, I feel more like it than ever. I tell you, there's just boy enough left inside of me. I'll clean up my old gun tomorrow mornin' and you look right after your'n. I dare say the boys have took good care of 'em for us, but they don't know what we do about huntin', and we'll bring 'em all along and show 'em a little fun."

"All right," said John York, as soberly as if they were going to look after a piece of business for the town; and they gathered up the axe and other light possessions, and started toward home.

The two friends, whether by accident or design, came out of the woods some distance from their own houses, but very near to the low-storied little gray dwelling of Mrs. Price. They crossed the pasture, and climbed over the toppling fence at the foot of her small sandy piece of land, and knocked at the door. There was a light already in the kitchen. Mrs. Price and Eliza Jane Topliff appeared at once, eagerly hospitable.

"Anybody sick?" asked Mrs. Price, with instant sympathy. "Nothin' happened, I hope?"

"Oh, no," said both the men.

"We came to talk about hiring your dog tomorrow night," explained Isaac Brown, feeling for the moment amused at his eager errand. "We got on track of a coon just now, up in the woods, and we thought we'd give our boys a little treat. You shall have fifty cents, an' welcome, and a good piece o' the coon."

"Yes, Square Brown; we can let you have the dog as well as not," interrupted Mrs. Price, delighted to grant a favor. "Poor departed 'Bijah, he set everything by him as a coon dog. He always said a dog's capital was all in his reputation."

"You'll have to be dreadful careful an' not lose him," urged

Mrs. Topliff. "Yes, sir; he's a proper coon dog as ever walked the earth, but he's terrible weak-minded about followin' 'most anybody. 'Bijah used to travel off twelve or fourteen miles after him to git him back, when he wa'n't able. Somebody'd speak to him decent, or fling a whiplash as they drove by, an' off he'd canter on three legs right after the wagon. But 'Bijah said he wouldn't trade him for no coon dog he ever was acquainted with. Trouble is, coons is awful sca'ce."

"I guess he ain't out of practice," said John York, amiably; "I guess he'll know when he strikes the coon. Come, Isaac, we must be gittin' along tow'ds home. I feel like eatin' a good supper. You tie him up tomorrow afternoon, so we shall be sure to have him," he turned to say to Mrs. Price, who stood smiling at the door.

"Land sakes, dear, he won't git away; you'll find him right there betwixt the woodbox and the stove, where he is now. Hold the light, 'Liza Jane; they can't see their way out to the road. I'll fetch him over to ye in good season," she called out, by way of farewell; " 't will save ye third of a mile extra walk. No., 'Liza Jane, you'll let me do it, if you please. I've got a mother's heart. The gentlemen will excuse us for showin' feelin'. You're all the child I've got, an' your prosperity is the same as mine."

The great night of the coon hunt was frosty and still, with only a dim light from the new moon. John York and his boys, and Isaac Brown, whose excitement was very great, set forth across the fields toward the dark woods. The men seemed younger and gayer than the boys. There was a burst of laughter when John Henry Brown and his little brother appeared with the coon dog of the late Mr. Abijah Topliff, which had promptly run away home again after Mrs. Price had coaxed him over in the afternoon. The captors had tied a string round his neck, at which they pulled vigorously from time to time to urge him forward. Perhaps he found the night too cold; at any rate, he stopped short in the frozen furrows every few minutes, lifting one foot and whining a little. Half a dozen times he came near to tripping up Mr. Isaac Brown and making him fall at full length.

"Poor Tiger! Poor Tiger!" said the good-natured sportsman, when somebody said that the dog didn't act as if he were much used to being out at night. "He'll be all right when he once gets track of the coon." But when they were fairly in the woods, Tiger's distress was perfectly genuine. The long rays of light from the old-fashioned lanterns of pierced tin went wheeling round and round, making a tall ghost of every tree, and strange shadows went darting in and out behind the pines. The woods were like an interminable pillared room where the darkness made a high ceiling. The clean frosty smell of the open fields was changed for a warmer air, damp with the heavy odor of moss and fallen leaves. There was something wild and delicious in the forest at that hour of night. The men and boys tramped on silently in single file, as if they followed the flickering light instead of carrying it. The dog fell back by instinct, as did his companions, into the easy familiarity of forest life. He ran beside them, and watched eagerly as they chose a safe place to leave a coat or two and a basket. He seemed to be an affectionate dog, now that he had made acquaintance with his masters.

"Seems to me he don't exactly know what he's about," said one of the York boys scornfully; "we must have struck that coon's track somewhere, comin' in."

"We'll get through talkin', an' heap up a little somethin' for a fire, if you'll turn to and help," said his father. "I've always noticed that nobody can give so much good advice about a piece o' work as a new hand. When you've treed as many coons as your Uncle Brown an' me, you won't feel so certain. Isaac, you be the one to take the dog up round the ledge, there. He'll scent the coon quick enough then. We'll 'tend to this part o' the business."

"You may come too, John Henry," said the indulgent father, and they set off together silently with the coon dog. He followed well enough now; his tail and ears were drooping even more than usual, but he whimpered along as bravely as he could, much excited, at John Henry's heels, like one of those great soldiers who are all unnerved until the battle is well begun.

A minute later the father and son came hurrying back, breathless, and stumbling over roots and bushes. The fire was already lighted, and sending a great glow higher and higher among the trees.

"He's off! He's struck a track! He was off like a major!" wheezed Mr. Isaac Brown.

"Which way'd he go?" asked everybody.

"Right out toward the fields. Like's not the old fellow was just starting after more of our fowls. I'm glad we come early, he can't have got far yet. We can't do nothin' but wait now, boys. I'll set right down here."

"Soon as the coon trees, you'll hear the dog sing, now I tell you!" said John York, with great enthusiasm. "That night your father an' me got those four busters we've told you about, they come right back here to the ledge. I don't know but they will now. 'Twas a dreadful cold night, I know. We didn't get home till past three o'clock in the mornin', either. You remember, don't you, Isaac?"

"I do," said Isaac. "How old Rover worked that night! Couldn't see out of his eyes nor hardly wag his clever old tail, for two days; thorns in both his fore paws, and the last coon took a piece right out of his off shoulder."

"Why didn't you let Rover come tonight, father?" asked the younger boy. "I think he knew somethin' was up. He was jumpin' 'round at a great rate when I come out of the yard."

"I didn't know but he might make trouble for the other dog," answered Isaac, after a moment's silence. He felt almost disloyal to the faithful creature, and had been missing him all the way. " 'Sh! there's a bark!" And they all stopped to listen.

The fire was leaping higher; they all sat near it, listening and talking by turns. There is apt to be a good deal of waiting in a coon hunt.

"If Rover was young as he used to be, I'd resk him to tree any coon that ever run," said the regretful master. "This smart creature o' Topliff's can't beat him, I know. The poor old fellow's eyesight seems to be going. Two—three times he's run out at me right in broad day, an' barked when I come up the yard toward the house, and I did pity him dreadfully; he was so 'shamed when he found out what he'd done. Rover's a dog that's got an awful lot o' pride. He went right off out behind the long barn the last time, and wouldn't come in for nobody when they called him to supper till I went out myself and made it up with him. No; he can't see very well now, Rover can't."

"He's heavy, too; he's got too unwieldy to tackle a smart coon, I expect, even if he could do the tall runnin'," said John York, with sympathy. "They have to get a master grip with their teeth, through a coon's thick pelt this time o' year. No; the young folks gets all the good chances after a while;" and he looked round indulgently at the chubby faces of his boys, who fed the fire, and rejoiced in being promoted to the society of their elders on equal terms. "Ain't it time we heard from the dog?" And they all listened, while the fire snapped and the sap whistled in some green sticks.

"I hear him," said John Henry suddenly; and faint and far away there came the sound of a desperate bark. There is a bark that means attack and there is a bark that means only foolish excitement.

"They ain't far off!" said Isaac. "My gracious, he's right after him! I don't know's I expected that poor-looking dog to be so smart. You can't tell by their looks. Quick as he scented the game up here in the rocks, off he put. Perhaps it ain't any matter if they ain't stump-tailed, long 's they're yaller dogs. He didn't look heavy enough to me. I tell you, he means business. Hear that bark!"

"They all bark alike after a coon," John York was as excited as anybody. "Git the guns laid out to hand, boys; I told you we'd ought to follow," he commanded. "If it's the old fellow that belongs here, he may put in any minute." But there was again a long silence and state of suspense; the chase had turned another way. There were faint distant yaps. The fire burned low and fell together with a shower of sparks. The smaller boys began to grow chilly and sleepy, when there was a thud and rustle and snapping of twigs close at hand, then the gasp of a breathless dog. Two dim shapes rushed by; a shower of bark fell, and a dog began to sing at the foot of the great twisted pine not fifty feet away.

"Hooray for Tiger!" yelled the boys; but the dog's voice filled all the woods. It might have echoed to the mountain tops. There was the old coon; they could all see him halfway up the tree, flat to the great limb. They heaped the fire with dry branches till it flared high. Now they lost him in a shadow as he twisted about the tree. John York fired, and Isaac Brown fired, while John Henry started to climb a neighboring oak; but at last it was Isaac who brought the coon to ground with a lucky shot, and the dog stopped his deafening bark and frantic leaping in the underbrush, and after an astonishing moment of silence, crept out, a proud victor, to his prouder master's feet.

"Goodness alive, who's this? Good for you, old handsome! Why, I'll be hanged if it ain't old Rover, boys; *it's old Rover!*" But Isaac could not speak another word. They all crowded round the wistful, clumsy old dog, whose eyes shone bright, though his breath was all gone. Each man patted him, and praised him, and said they ought to have mistrusted all the time that it could be nobody but he. It was some minutes before Isaac Brown could trust himself to do anything but pat the sleek old head that was always ready to his hand.

"He must have overheard us talkin'; I guess he'd have come if he'd dropped dead halfway," proclaimed John Henry, like a prince of the reigning house; and Rover wagged his tail as if in honest assent, as he lay at his master's side. They sat together, while the fire was brightened again to make a good light for the coon-hunt supper; and Rover had a good half of everything that found its way into his master's hand. It was toward midnight when the triumphal procession set forth toward home, with the two lanterns, across the fields.

The next morning was bright and warm after the hard frost of the night before. Old Rover was asleep on the doorstep in the sun, and his master stood in the yard, and saw neighbor Price come along the road in her best array, with a gay holiday air.

"Well, now," she said eagerly, "you wa'n't out very late last night, was you? I got up myself to let Tiger in. He come home, all beat out, about a quarter past nine. I expect you hadn't no kind of trouble gittin' the coon. The boys was tellin' me he weighed 'most thirty pounds."

"Oh, no kind o' trouble," said Isaac, keeping the great secret gallantly. "You got the things I sent over this morning?"

"Bless your heart, yes! I'd a sight rather have all that good pork an' potatoes than any o' your wild meat," said Mrs. Price, smiling with prosperity. "You see, now, 'Liza Jane she's given in. She didn't re'lly know but 't was all talk of 'Bijah 'bout that dog's bein' wuth fifty dollars. She says she can't cope with a huntin' dog same 's he could, an' she 's given me the money you an' John York sent over this mornin'; an' I didn't know but what you'd lend me another half a dollar, so I could both go to Dipford Center an' return, an' see if I couldn't make a sale o' Tiger right over there where they all know about him. It's right in the coon season; now's my time, ain't it?"

"Well, gettin' a little late," said Isaac, shaking with laughter as he took the desired sum of money out of his pocket. "He seems to be a clever dog round the house."

"I don't know 's I want to harbor him all winter," answered the excursionist frankly, striking into a good traveling gait as she started off toward the railroad station.

THE HUNT FOR
THE SHE-WOLF

WILLIAM DAVENPORT HULBERT

Grand Island, near the south shore of Lake Superior, was set aside by its owner, the Cleveland-Cliffs Iron Company, as a timber and game preserve. Stocked with deer, moose, elk, caribou, and other animals, the shores of the island, an island of 10,000 or 12,000 acres, are for the most part perpendicular, and so high that they are inaccessible to anything but birds. Particular pains were taken to fence in low places so that the island would be wolf-tight. But a wolf got in—mysteriously. Traps and poison proved useless. Finally thirty expert hunters and trappers and woodsmen from various parts of the Lake Superior shore contributed their combined skill to a great hunt for the wolf—a hunt that lasted nearly a month. This is the story of the life of that wolf.

THE HUNT for the she-wolf began one morning in August, when she was about four and a half months old, as she and her mother and brother were on their way to their favorite playground on a sandy, ridgelike knoll in the middle of the huckleberry marsh. The cubs liked that knoll because it was such a good place for romping and frolicking, rolling and tumbling and wrestling, and worrying their playthings, which consisted of two or three dry bones that had once belonged to one of the handsomest bucks in the woods. Their mother liked it partly because the sand was so warm and pleasant for her to lie in while the children amused themselves, but chiefly because it was high enough so that without rising she could turn her head and look all around over the open plain. Nothing could come near without being seen. But perhaps she forgot, for once, that a ridge which made such a good watch tower when gained might be the very means of hiding an enemy while she was approaching.

As they came up out of the cedar swamp, not very far from the knoll, she paused a moment behind a little balsam to make sure that the coast was clear. There was nobody in sight, and she sniffed the air carefully and found it guiltless of any suspicious odors. To be sure, an odor might not travel very far on a calm day like this. She liked a light breeze, especially if it was in her face, for then her nose could always tell her what she was coming to. There seemed to be no danger, and she stepped out from behind the balsam, with her two cubs close behind her, and trotted slowly up the old tote-road toward the knoll. Just then she happened to catch sight of a bear, having a good time all by himself among the huckleberries, and watching him she failed to see the man who suddenly appeared over the crest of the ridge and instantly dropped back out of sight.

The man was one who had trapped and poisoned a good many wolves in the course of his career in the woods, and had regularly drawn his bounties on them from the county clerk's office, but he hadn't expected to meet any this morning, and he was not prepared for them.

He was on his way to a certain hardwood ridge to look for ginseng roots, and he had not so much as a pistol in his pocket. So it was curiosity, rather than any hope of profit, that prompted him to lie still behind the knoll and watch to see how close they would come. They came very close indeed. They were halfway up the sandy slope, not more than two rods away, when the old wolf came to a sudden halt. Something was wrong. Perhaps a wandering breath of air had come down to meet her and give her warning, or perhaps she had seen the top of his head in one of the ruts of the road, or perhaps it was only a presentiment. At any rate she stopped short, stood still for an instant, and then turned and ran swiftly back toward the swamp.

The cubs hurried after her as fast as they could, but they had not thoroughly learned the use of their legs, and they were quickly left behind. They were nearly as tall as their mother, but they were awkward and clumsy, like overgrown puppies, and halfway to the swamp one of them fell into a hole in the rotten corduroy and couldn't get up. At least she thought she couldn't, and she lay there crying and whimpering until the man came running down the slope after her. It had suddenly occurred to him that he could perhaps trample her to death with his heavy river shoes, and that that would mean a few more dollars from the county clerk. But he was not quick enough, for before he could reach her a big brindled form shot out of the bushes, and the old wolf jumped over her prostrate daughter and faced him with a growl and a snarl, her eyes glaring, her teeth showing, and the hair on the back of her neck all a-bristle.

The man stopped. Heavy shoes wouldn't do here. Probably it would be best to content himself with ginseng for today, and to let the bounty wait until a more convenient season. For a moment he and the old wolf stood and looked each other in the eye. Then the cub struggled to her feet and started again for the swamp. As soon as she was well out of the way her mother turned and trotted deliberately after her.

The second act came the following winter, when the three of them ran with a pack of twenty or twenty-five wolves that were hunting deer from the Lake Superior shore clear across to the head waters of the rivers that empty into Lake Michigan.

As they were beating the woods one night, spread out in skirmish formation so as to cover as much ground as possible, one of them set up the hunting call—the wild, long-drawn cry which begins away up at the top of the scale and comes dropping down to a deep guttural, and which means that he who voices it is on the track of big game and wants help. Twenty throats sent up reply, and a few minutes later, in a hemlock grove near a small inland lake, they closed in on a fine buck. He cried out terribly as they sprang upon him and pulled him to the ground, but it was over almost in an instant, and in a very few minutes more there was absolutely nothing left of him but a little hair, a red stain on the snow, a few teeth scattered about, and part of one jawbone.

They had been pretty hungry, and when they had well feasted they felt like having some fun, so they all went down to the frozen lake, and there on the ice they romped about for an hour or two, running and jumping, wrestling with each other, and rolling over and over in the snow like so many good-natured dogs.

The next night they killed another deer, and again they repaired to the lake for a frolic, but this time they did not find things just as they had left them. Someone had been there during the day, for a network of snowshoe tracks lay across the smooth white field where they had played the night before. They did not like the look of it, and for a moment they hesitated. But the enemy, whoever he was, seemed to have departed, and they presently put aside their fears and struck out upon the ice. There they found something else besides the man-trail. Standing upright in the snow, here and there all over the lake, were sharpened sticks, each one about the height of the nose of a running wolf, and impaled on each was a piece of venison. And now they did a foolish thing. It is doubtful if there was one in all the pack who would have been rash enough to touch those baits if he had been alone, but in the crowd each one got it into his head that the others would eat the meat if he didn't, and that he must pitch right in if he wanted to get his share. A few of the oldest and wisest had enough commonsense and strength of character to hold off, but the younger ones went at it with a rush, and in a moment every chunk of meat was gone. The young she-wolf, whom the ginseng hunter had so nearly killed six months before, was one of the first to make up her mind, and she got two pieces —which was very fortunate for her.

The baits were hardly swallowed when the trouble began, and instinctively the stricken wolves turned to the woods, that they might at least hide themselves before they died. But it was very strong medicine. One of them fell before he reached the beach, and never rose again, and three more gave up the ghost a few rods farther on. The she-wolf was staggering blindly and falling down every two or three paces, while the trees and the stars danced round and round her in a mad whirl. She hardly knew whether she was on her feet or her head, and at last she fell flat in the snow, too weak to stir a limb. But as she lay there, helpless and at the point of death, there happened the one and only thing that could possibly have saved her. If she had swallowed only one bait she would have been a dead wolf, but two defeated their own ends. Her outraged stomach suddenly revolted, and the meat and the strychnine came up together, even faster than they had gone down. She was very sick for a day or two, and it was a week or more before she fully recovered, but in the end she got over it and was as fit as ever.

In the next few years she and the cubs that came to her were seldom if ever seen by human eyes, but men and traces of men were often seen by them. The road—the trail—the snowshoe print—the trapper's shack—the lumberman's shanty—the timber cruiser's camp—she came to know them all, and learned to steer clear of them. Of traps, also, she saw a good many, but they did her no harm. For the most part she knew enough to let them alone, and when at last she was tempted beyond what she was able to bear, some one else stepped in before her.

That was when she was four or five years old. The winter was a hard one and the pack was actually starving. Deer were scarce, and when found they were very hard to catch; for week after week the snow was light and soft, just deep enough to make a wolf wallow, yet not so deep but that longer, slenderer legs could find firm footing on the frozen ground beneath. The she-wolf had thought she knew what hunger meant, but this winter she was learning the lesson in earnest. To do without food for five or six days, she found, was quite endurable. She could stand that very well and still hunt, still travel, though it made her gaunt, and toward the end her appetite was something utterly indescribable. But a week or more nearly drove her mad.

Toward the end of January there came a heavy snowstorm and a prolonged thaw, followed by a very hard freeze, and the next night the hunting call made twenty hearts leap with excitement and hope, while one—just one—beat harder still with deadly fear. The tables were turned at last. To the wolves' broad, hairy paws the crust was as good as a floor, while to the doe's pointed hoofs it was like a sheet of glass that crashed beneath her at every jump. Her legs were torn and bleeding before she had made twenty rods, and in less than a quarter of a mile the pack was about to close in upon her. And then she burst out of the woods and saw below her the great frozen plain of Lake Superior, all white and radiant in the moonlight. There, perhaps, if she could only reach it, she might find firm footing and a chance for her life, for in spite of their gashes her legs were still good for a long, hard race if only there were something solid for her feet to rest upon. But Lake Superior could not help her now, for she stood not on the beach but on the summit of the Pictured Rocks. For an instant she hesitated; then the wolves broke out of the bushes at her very heels, and with a last leap she shot out over the brink and dropped two hundred feet sheer down.

The pack gathered on the edge of the cliff, and howled, and howled, and howled. To be so near, and then to lose after all, seemed more than wolfish hearts could bear. But presently they forgot the dead doe lying on the ice hummock below them, and between their cries they held their noses to windward and sniffed the air hungrily. There was something on the breeze—only a scent—an odor—but one that filled their famine-stricken souls with longing unendurable—the scent of deer—and not of one deer only, but of dozens, of scores, of hundreds. Where were they —these warm living creatures, who smelled so good and whose flesh and blood could stay the hunger that was fairly killing them? The wind was westerly, and in that direction there was only ice and snow for miles and miles. Far out on the horizon a large island lay black between the white lake and the spangled sky, but it was a long way off—a very long way. Surely the scent could not come from there?

For half an hour they paced nervously up and down—sniffing —sniffing—sniffing. Then the wind shifted a little, and of a sudden the air was again as pure and clean and tasteless as the icefields. Weary and disheartened, they ceased their clamor and stole silently into the woods.

Then it was that the she-wolf fell into temptation, and would have perished if some one else had not got ahead of her. She and a large male wolf had dropped a little behind the rest, and a few rods from the cliff he stopped and sniffed eagerly at one of the holes where the doe had broken through the crust. Early in the winter a man had laid a large piece of venison on the ground beside a deer runway which the wolves sometimes followed, and had placed a steel trap on it and left it for the snow to cover.

Again and again in the last two months the wolves had passed by
without offering to touch it. They knew better. But the trapper
was wise and patient, and he let it lie, knowing that there was a
possible chance, though perhaps a remote one, that a time would
come when they would be too hungry to turn away from anything that smelled of meat. And at last that time had arrived. The
wolf could smell the steel through the snow, as well as the venison, and he knew that he was acting like a fool, but nevertheless
he began to dig excitedly, while the she-wolf watched him with a
wistful look on her face. Presently there came a click, muffled yet
loud, and the thing was done.

Three days later, when the trapper made his rounds again, he
found him frozen to death, with his leg fast between the steel
jaws.

On the same night in which the doe escaped and the he-wolf
was caught, the pack struck the trail of a man who was making
his way on foot, alone, from a lumber camp to a distant railway
station. None of them had ever taken any part in an attack on a
human being, or even thought seriously of doing such a thing;
but tonight they were desperate. The man was never seen again.

But the she-wolf had nothing to do with this affair, for she had
left the pack forever. She had not stayed with her mate—there
was nothing she could do for him; but after he was caught she
had wandered off by herself and had come out again on the Pictured Rocks, not at the same place, but a little farther west,
where the cliffs were lower and more broken, and where, by
picking one's way carefully, it was quite possible to get down to
the ice. Here again she found that mysterious odor, and trembling with eagerness she hurried down a steep, narrow ravine and
struck out upon the frozen lake, keeping her nose to windward.

Mile after mile she trotted over the smooth snow, packed hard
by the winter gales, and little by little the scent grew stronger and
the distant island lifted itself higher against the sky. But in the
end there came a disappointment, for she found herself looking
up at a wall of tall gray sandstone, cliffs, like those of the Pictured Rocks themselves, so high and inaccessible that nothing
without wings could possibly have scaled them. In places they
even leaned out over her, as if to tell her that she could never,

never enter. She turned to the right and followed the shoreline northward for two or three miles, looking for some break in the frowning walls, and finding none. Then southward again, five miles or more. She had lost the scent by this time, but she could probably pick it up again if she could once get up the cliffs. And at last, just as the sun came over the edge of the world, she found a place that she thought she could climb. A few minutes more and she was up and hurrying northward, only to be stopped by another obstacle.

A very high wire fence, too high to be leaped, stood across her path, stretching from the edge of the cliff far back into the woods. Once more she set out to explore, and now fortune was with her, for within half a mile she found a place where a tree had fallen and bent down the upper wires. She was over in a twinkling and hurrying northward again, and that afternoon she had another piece of good luck, for it snowed so hard that by the time the gamekeeper came to repair the fence her tracks had disappeared completely. She had entered her Happy Hunting Grounds, and no one knew that she was there.

No one, that is, who could put her out or do her any harm. There were others who soon knew all about it, and within a week the she-wolf was getting fat.

The island was highest along the sides, she found, and sloped down in the middle, bowllike, toward a valley where there was a cedar swamp and a pretty little lake, and along the edges of this valley, between the swamp and the hardwood, where the hemlocks stood thick and there was shelter from the winter storms, with browse to feed upon when no other food was to be had, were the yards of countless deer and of herds of moose and elk and caribou. The strangest part of it was that the deer seemed less cautious and timid than those that she was accustomed to on the mainland. It was easier to approach them, and she could have one whenever she wanted it, almost at a moment's notice.

Later, as they learned that an enemy had invaded the island, and that their years of peace and security were over, they grew more wary, but they were so plentiful that in spite of their caution it seldom took long to get one. Henceforth she ate nothing but the very choicest cuts, and often she only drank the blood and left all the meat for the foxes. To the moose and the elk she never paid any attention, except, perhaps, at the very first, to give them a few glances of curiosity. She had never seen an elk before, and never but once had she laid eyes upon a moose. But they were too large and strong for her to tackle, and after she had grown somewhat accustomed to them they ceased to interest her, except as something to be left severely alone.

The white Newfoundland caribou were a little smaller, a little nearer her own size, and sometimes she watched them as they fed, and wondered whether she could kill one of them in a fair fight. If she could, their flesh would be a change from her everyday fare. But on the whole it hardly seemed worth while to try it.

Of the year that followed her arrival there is little to be told. There was a time when she was very lonely and restless, so much so that it seemed to her as if she could not live without the company of her kind, and then she ranged the woods for days together, seeking she hardly knew what, or sat perched upon the edge of a tall cliff, looking out across the ice toward the country from which she had come.

Once the breeze brought her the scent of the pack, just as it had carried that of the deer to the mainland, and it drove her almost wild. That day, if she could have exchanged riches and solitude for starvation with other wolves, she would have done it without an instant's hesitation. But she could not, for, though she looked for it repeatedly, she never again found the low place in the fence by which she had entered. The island had become her prison. Yet it was a pleasant prison, and after a time the restlessness passed away, and she settled down to a life as easy and carefree as the lives of the deer themselves before she came to kill them.

Of men she saw little or nothing, though she knew that there were a few on the island, and by rare good luck the whole year slipped by before they came upon any of the deer carcasses that she left lying about in the woods. It seems a little strange that no one ever heard her howl, but in all probability she kept silence, knowing that there were no other wolves within reach of her voice. Besides, why should she cry out when she never needed help with her kill, never was hungry, and, once that restless fit had passed, never was in any trouble? There was nothing to howl for.

Once, in summer, a visitor found an interesting track on the sandy shore of the little lake, and as soon as he got back to the mainland he went to the nearest long-distance telephone station and called up a certain business office in a city some score of miles away.

"There's a wolf on your island," he said, "inside the fence. I've seen his track."

But the office was slow to believe him. How could a wolf get up the cliffs or over the fence? Perhaps it was the lighthousekeeper's dog, or maybe a very large fox. Some thought it might be a lynx or a big bobcat. Anyhow, they had plenty of traps set, and what more could they do?

It was true that there were some sixty traps set in different parts of the island, and the she-wolf had seen some of them; but every one had a little log pen built over it to keep the precious deer from stepping into it, and if she noticed them at all it was with the deepest contempt for such a perfectly transparent device. Possibly a thick-headed rabbit or a daredevil weasel might allow himself to be caught in an arrangement like that, but a wolf?

So the months went by, and nothing happened except that she kept right on killing deer and having a good time. The winter came again—December—January—and then one day she followed a snowshoe trail a little way and met the gamekeeper face to face. Perhaps, in her seeming security, she had grown a trifle careless. She dodged behind a tree and was gone before he had time to lift his gun, but not before he had noted her dark, brindled back and sides, her lighter under parts, her reddish face, her pointed nose and rounded ears, and her straight, round, club-shaped brush. This was no dog, no big fox, no lynx or bobcat. It was nothing in the world but a wolf. The gamekeeper did not try to follow her, for he knew that that would be useless, but he did some very hard thinking on his way back to his lodge.

Meanwhile the she-wolf had made a wide detour through the swamp, and presently found herself near the northern end of the lake. Two caribou were out on the ice, a bull and a cow, strolling along near the shore, pausing now and then to browse on the bushes and trees, and having a quiet, pleasant, peaceful time together. The she-wolf had recovered from her fright, and she stopped and watched them from behind a cedar, and wondered, as she had wondered so many times before, whether if she tried she could kill one of them. By and by she crept a little nearer, keeping carefully out of sight, and soon she was only a few rods from them and they were still unconscious. There was a quick rush, and before they could make off she was snatching at the bull's hind leg, thinking to hamstring him. It was her favorite method with deer, and it almost always worked. But a caribou is not so easily disabled, and, though she got hold of him and tore a great piece of flesh from his thigh, she failed to bring him down.

Again and again she jumped at him, now from in front, now from behind; and at almost every leap her teeth met in his neck or his side or his flank, while he fought back as no deer had ever done, striking at her with his feet and doing his best to knock her down and trample on her. If she had been a little less nimble he would probably have killed her, for he was far larger and stronger than she, and his big cloven hoofs could hit like sledge hammers. But she was too quick for him, and no animal could long withstand such punishment as she was giving him. They tramped the snow down for a hundred feet before he would give up, but he fell at last, utterly exhausted. And then, after all, she did not eat much of him, for she was not very hungry. She was never very hungry nowadays.

The next morning the telephone rang again in the distant city and told the office that a wolf was really on the island, had been seen, and had killed one of the caribou. And this time the office believed, and word came back that they must get that wolf. No matter what it cost, no matter how long it took, or how many men, or how many dollars, that wolf must die.

A day or two later she came down again to the shore of the little lake and looked at the caribou's body, where it lay a few yards out upon the ice. She had meant to make another meal from it, but she didn't. Instead she sat down under an overhanging cedar, and looked—and looked—and looked. She did not know that here and there, all over it, were deep knifewounds, and that at the bottom of each wound there lay a little pellet of strychnine, but she did know, perfectly, that something was wrong. There were snowshoe tracks all around it, and she could detect something which she thought was a stale odor of humanity. She considered the situation carefully, and presently she got up and went away.

The following day she was wandering rather aimlessly through the woods when she happened to make a wide circle and come up again on her own track, to find it paralleled by the trails of two pairs of snowshoes. She followed it at a good brisk pace, though quietly and cautiously, to see what this might mean, and she had not gone far before she caught sight of the gamekeeper and another man, with their backs toward her and their guns over their shoulders, hurrying along the trail that she had made a little while before. She turned in another direction and ran as fast as she could go.

For a few hours nothing more happened, but late that afternoon she heard a suspicious sound behind her, and again she set off at a hard run, presently fetching a compass against the wind and coming back to a knoll, ten or twelve feet in height, that stood close beside her trail. Here, on its highest point, she hollowed out a sort of bed, not throwing the snow up so that it would show, but trampling it down carefully. As she settled herself to watch, with her nose and her forepaws resting lightly on the edge of the hollow, there was nothing to be seen of her but the top of her head, and even that was almost invisible against the trees and the underbrush. Soon the men came in sight, and she watched until they had gone by, not twenty feet away, and then jumped down from her knoll and ran at the top of her speed.

On the morrow the same program was repeated, and this time, as she fled from her pursuers, she came very near running into a third man, who was standing still on a deer runway and seemed to be waiting and watching for something. She saw him just in time.

That night she was decidedly hungry, but for the first time in a year her appetite went unsatisfied. She was too anxious to eat, and perhaps she knew instinctively that her senses would be keener if she fasted. And she needed to be at her very best, for as the days went on her enemies multiplied until she expected to see one behind every tree.

Never had there been such a wolf hunt before in all the Michigan woods. From daylight till dark one or two were always on her trail, while the rest posted themselves where they thought she would be most likely to pass. Then, about the end of the second week there came a slight change in the proceedings. So far her pursuers had moved as silently as possible. Now they carried a cowbell. At first the she-wolf was a good deal disturbed by its din, but she soon grew accustomed to it, and perhaps it really made things a little easier for her. So long as they traveled silently she was in constant suspense, for she never knew when they might come up behind her, and at the same time she dared not strike out at full speed for fear of running into some of the others. Now, with the big bell ding-dang-donging on her trail, she knew just where the trackers were, and most of the time she made it a practice to keep just far enough away so that they could not possibly see her. Thus she could take her time, travel leisurely, and keep good watch ahead. Yet even so there was constant danger of falling into an ambuscade, and again and again her keen nose was all that saved her.

One afternoon she sat on the edge of a hundred-foot cliff on the northeastern side of the island, looking out across the ice sheet toward the mainland where her friends and relations were living. She wished she was there. They might be starving, but at least they had each other, and they had room to put fifty miles between them and a hunter whenever the necessity arose. The she-wolf had eaten nothing for five days. She was hungry and tired and worried, and she heard the cowbell jangling not very far away. She felt not a little like that doe that had jumped from the Pictured Rocks. But she was not ready to give up—not by any means—and after a time she rose and started back into the woods.

Half a mile from shore she came upon a buck lying under a hemlock, and without even giving him time to get out of bed she sprang upon him and killed him. By the time the men came plodding along her trail she had drunk his blood and eaten a large part of one of his hams, and as she started on she felt that she was good for another long siege.

In all this time none of the men had seen her since the day she met the gamekeeper, but one morning, when the cowbell roused her and told her it was time to move, she made for the little lake, instead of keeping to the thick timber, as she had always done before. Perhaps she was getting tired of that everlasting game of hide-and-seek among the trees. Straight down its whole length she trotted, and then entered the woods again and kept on toward the south till she came to the high wire fence. She chose the lowest spot she could find and leaped, but the wires caught her and tossed her scornfully back. Again and again and again she tried, and every time she fell, until, fairly quivering with rage, she rushed at it and caught the wires in her teeth, striving with all her strength to twist them apart, and even biting at the posts as if she would like to kill this thing that mocked her so. But she had to give it up at last. The cowbell was close at hand, and she left the fence and made for the lake again, intending to cross it and go back to the cedar swamp.

It was very, very cold on the ice that day, and there was a fierce wind blowing. Even the she-wolf, accustomed though she was to the very worst that winter could do, felt it to the marrow of her bones. But, though she herself never understood it all, that bitter weather was probably the only thing that saved her life, for the men who had been stationed along the shores to watch for her in case she returned that way got cold feet, and some of them went back into the woods and started a fire.

She passed within a few rods of where they had been standing, and was halfway up the lake when the first shot rang out and a bullet went singing by, a few inches in front of her nose. The she-wolf stopped and stood still, a little confused, not quite certain what to do. Before she could make up her mind there came another shot from another direction, then a third, and then, in quick succession, four more, while the bullets cut the air on every side. But by that time she was flying like the wind for the nearest point of land. She made it unhurt, and once under cover she turned northward again, crossed the trail of another party of men who had been tramping up and down to keep warm when they ought to have been out on the lake, and reached the swamp in safety.

The she-wolf was growing thin. Every five or six days she killed a deer and ate her fill, but one or two meals a week, even though they are good square ones, are rather short rations. Yet she had never in all her life been more keenly alive than now, and never had her senses been so alert and so ready to serve her. Eyes and ears and nose were working as they had never had to work before. But in spite of all her vigilance there could be but one ending to such a struggle. There were thirty men after her, and it was only a question of time before one or another would get a shot at her at close range.

The next to the last day was a quiet, peaceful one, with nothing to disturb her. She had left the cedar swamp the night before and had gone to a big windfall in the southeastern part of the island. Then it had snowed, and though the hunters searched from dawn till dark they did not find her trail. But early the next morning she became aware that a man was stalking her. She had not seen him, she had heard only faint, distant sounds, and only once had she got a whiff of him, but she knew that he was there. A silent enemy was worse than the cowbell, and she decided to go back to the swamp. But now it appeared that the man was bent on heading her off.

Again and again a breath of tainted air or the swish and crunch of snowshoes told her that he was before her and that she must turn back and make a new start. She did not dare travel very fast for fear of running into him unawares—that was the trouble. Every little way she had to stop, and look about, and sniff the air, and that always gave him a chance to get ahead of her again. She did not know that he was trying to drive her back to the fence, and that if she had let him do it she would have found several gaps in the wires and a steel trap set in each. But she did know that she wanted to go to the swamp, and, though he kept her dodging all the morning, she finally slipped past him and went.

Toward the middle of the afternoon she was walking along at a rather leisurely gait through woods that were neither very thick nor very open, when she came to a halt and stood for a moment at attention. A few yards ahead of her a snowshoe trail lay across her path, and the wind, blowing from it to her, told her that it was fresh. She had best proceed cautiously, she thought, and in that, of course, she was quite right; but for once she spent her caution in the wrong direction. She was still eying the trail ahead of her when two rifles spoke, a few rods away to the right, and a bullet passed through her neck and buried itself in the snow.

The she-wolf fell, but in an instant she was up again and away. For a quarter of a mile she ran like the wind, with the blood spurting on both sides and staining the snow along the trail. Then she had to stop. She was dizzy and weak, and the trees were spinning round and round, just as they had done the night she swallowed the strychnine. She listened but could hear nothing, and she sank down wearily in the snow and tried to rest. Soon— all too soon—she heard the snowshoes, and dragging herself to her feet she ran a little farther, leaving two bright red spots in her white bed. Seven times within a mile she had to lie down, and seven times that terrible crunching roused her and drove her on.

But by that time her strength was coming back. The first shock had passed, and the bleeding had stopped, though this last may have been partly because there was so little blood left to flow. At all events she traveled slowly but pretty steadily for the rest of the afternoon, following a very circuitous track, but gradually working northwestward across the swamp, until shortly before dusk she reached the edge of the cedar and saw before her the slope of the hardwood and hemlock. She waited until she heard again that steady "crunch, crunch, crunch" upon her trail, and then she slipped out of the thicket and stole silently up over a ridge and down again into another little piece of swamp that she knew well, where in the last twelve months she had killed many a buck and doe. There she stood still again and listened. It was growing dark. Once more she heard the crunching, but this time it did not come very near, and presently it seemed to be withdrawing.

Later in the evening two tired men arrived at the lodge, and taking the gamekeeper aside they whispered to him, "We've wounded that wolf and tracked him to the little swamp in the north end of the island. Shall we take the headlights and go after him, or shall we wait till morning?"

The gamekeeper, too, was tired. Night after night he had been up till the small hours, taking care of his crew and preparing for the next day's hunt. He didn't want to tramp to the north end of the island. He wanted to go to bed. But he stepped out and looked at the sky. It was cloudy, and the air felt like snow.

"I guess we'd better go," he said.

It was very dark in the woods that night, but the she-wolf could see after a fashion, and she was still traveling. Perhaps she knew that if she once lay down she might never get up again. She had left the swamp and had wandered away toward the north-west till she was close to the shore. Now she circled and went south through the hardwood—a mile—two miles—three, per-haps, by the devious way she followed. She was very, very weary. The weariness of the three men who were following her was as nothing to hers, for it was nearly a week since she had eaten, and the loss of blood was telling on her terribly. Slower—slower—slower—till it seemed as if she could hardly drag one foot after another.

Once or twice she tried to run and jump in the old way, but her leaps were short and ineffectual, and when she came down her legs spread out from under her and she sprawled as she had not done since she was a cub. She made up her mind at last that she could go no farther, and scooping a little hollow in the snow she lay down in it and tried to rest. But even now she could not keep still. She was nervous, and, besides, she wanted to be where she could look back along her trail. So she got up and tried another place, and then another, until finally she came upon a little knoll five or six feet high, just such a knoll as she had always been partial to. She passed around it and came up from the farther side, and on its top she dug her last hole and lay down for the last time. It was very still. There was no wind, nor any stars, and the woods were dark and silent. It seemed as if there was no one left in all the world but she, alone in her pain and her misery. Pres-ently she fell shivering.

It was long after midnight when she heard again that faint, distant crunching. A little later she noticed a strange, dim light, away off among the trees, that grew brighter as she watched—not rapidly, but slowly—slowly—horribly slowly. By and by she could see that there were three lights instead of one, all quite close together, and as they moved from side to side they threw strange shadows this way and that, as if the trees were alive and walking in their sleep. And now, as the glare grew brighter, she could see what the men saw, and what they had been following for hours—her own trail, leading with many curves and windings to the spot where she lay and waited for her enemies. They reached at last the foot of the knoll, not a dozen feet away, and there, of a sudden, they came to a halt. They had seen her eyeballs shining like two red flames.

Without a doubt the she-wolf knew that the end of everything had come, but she did not flinch. She could not fight, and she could not run, but she could die game. Quick as a flash all three headlights turned upon her, and in the circle of white light she rose halfway up, held her head high, and faced them without the quiver of an eyelash. There was an instant's pause. Then a tube of polished metal gleamed beside one of the lamps, and there came a flash and a bang. Something crashed through the she-wolf's brain, and she sank down in the snow.

It was four weeks since the orders had come over the telephone. It had taken thirty men to kill her, and it had cost the company a thousand dollars. But it was done at last, and the hunting of the she-wolf was ended.

GETTING CHRISTMAS DINNER ON A RANCH

THEODORE ROOSEVELT

ONE DECEMBER, while I was out on my ranch, so much work had to be done that it was within a week of Christmas before we were able to take any thought for the Christmas dinner. The winter set in late that year, and there had been comparatively little cold weather, but one day the ice on the river had been sufficiently strong to enable us to haul up a wagonload of flour, with enough salt pork to last through the winter, and a very few tins of canned goods, to be used at special feasts. We had some bushels of potatoes, the heroic victors of a struggle for existence in which the rest of our garden vegetables had succumbed to drought, frost, and grasshoppers; and we also had some wild plums and dried elk venison. But we had no fresh meat, and so one day my foreman and I agreed to make a hunt on the morrow.

Accordingly one of the cowboys rode out in the frosty afternoon to fetch in the saddleband from the plateau three miles off, where they were grazing. It was after sunset when he returned. I was lounging out by the corral, my wolf-skin cap drawn down over my ears, and my hands thrust deep into the pockets of my fur coat, gazing across the wintry landscape. Cold red bars in the winter sky marked where the sun had gone down behind a row of jagged, snow-covered buttes.

Turning to go into the little bleak log house, as the dusk deepened, I saw the horses trotting homeward in a long file, their unshod hoofs making no sound in the light snow which covered the plain, turning it into a glimmering white waste wherein stood dark islands of leafless trees, with trunks and branches weirdly distorted. The cowboy, with bent head, rode behind the line of horses, sometimes urging them on by the shrill cries known to cattlemen; and as they neared the corral they broke into a gallop, ran inside, and then halted in a mass. The frost lay on their shaggy backs, and little icicles hung from their nostrils.

Choosing out two of the strongest and quietest, we speedily roped them and led them into the warm log stable, where they were given a plentiful supply of the short, nutritious buffalo-grass hay, while the rest of the herd were turned loose to shift for themselves. Then we went inside the house to warm our hands in front of the great pile of blazing logs, and to wait impatiently until the brace of prairie chickens I had shot that afternoon should be fixed for supper. Then our rifles and cartridge belts were looked to, one of the saddles which had met with an accident was overhauled, and we were ready for bed.

It was necessary to get to the hunting grounds by sunrise, and it still lacked a couple of hours of dawn when the foreman wakened me as I lay asleep beneath the buffalo robes. Dressing hurriedly and breakfasting on a cup of coffee and some mouthfuls of bread and jerked elk meat, we slipped out to the barn, threw the saddles on the horses, and were off.

The air was bitterly chill; the cold had been severe for two days, so that the river ice would again bear horses. Beneath the light covering of powdery snow we could feel the rough ground like wrinkled iron under the horses' hoofs. There was no moon, but the stars shone beautifully down through the cold, clear air, and our willing horses galloped swiftly across the long bottom on which the ranch-house stood, threading their way deftly among the clumps of sprawling sagebrush.

A mile off we crossed the river, the ice cracking with noises like pistol shots as our horses picked their way gingerly over it. On the opposite side was a dense jungle of bullberry bushes, and on breaking through this we found ourselves galloping up a long, winding valley, which led back many miles into the hills. The crannies and little side ravines were filled with brushwood and groves of stunted ash. By this time there was a faint flush of gray in the east, and as we rode silently along we could make out dimly the tracks made by the wild animals as they had passed and repassed in the snow. Several times we dismounted to examine them. A couple of coyotes, possibly frightened by our approach, had trotted and loped up the valley ahead of us, leaving a trail like that of two dogs; the sharper, more delicate footprints of a fox crossed our path; and outside one long patch of brushwood a series of round imprints in the snow betrayed where a bobcat— as plainsmen term the small lynx—had been lurking around to try to pick up a rabbit or a prairie fowl.

As the dawn reddened, and it became light enough to see objects some little way off, we began to sit erect in our saddles and to scan the hillsides sharply for sight of feeding deer. Hitherto we had seen no deer tracks save inside the bullberry bushes by the river, and we knew that the deer that lived in that impenetrable jungle were cunning whitetails which in such a place could be hunted only by aid of a hound. But just before sunrise we came on three lines of heart-shaped footmarks in the snow, which showed where as many deer had just crossed a little plain ahead of us. They were walking leisurely, and from the lay of the land we believed that we should find them over the ridge, where there was a brush coulee.

Riding to one side of the trail, we topped the little ridge just as the sun flamed up, a burning ball of crimson, beyond the snowy waste at our backs. Almost immediately afterward my companion leaped from his horse and raised his rifle, and as he pulled the trigger I saw through the twigs of a brush patch on our left the erect, startled head of a young blacktailed doe as she turned to look at us, her great mule-like ears thrown forward. The ball broke her neck, and she turned a complete somersault downhill, while a sudden smashing of underbrush told of the flight of her terrified companions.

We both laughed and called out "dinner" as we sprang down toward her, and in a few minutes she was dressed and hung up by the hind legs on a small ash tree. The entrails and viscera we threw off to one side, after carefully poisoning them from a little bottle of strychnine which I had in my pocket. Almost every cattleman carries poison and neglects no chance of leaving out wolf bait, for the wolves are sources of serious loss to the unfenced and unhoused flocks and herds. In this instance we felt particularly revengeful because it was but a few days since we had lost a fine yearling heifer. The tracks on the hillside where the carcass lay when we found it told the story plainly. The wolves, two in number, had crept up close before being discovered, and had then raced down on the astounded heifer almost before she could get fairly started. One brute had hamstrung her with a snap of his vise-like jaws, and once down, she was torn open in a twinkling.

No sooner was the sun up than a warm west wind began to blow in our faces. The weather had suddenly changed, and within an hour the snow was beginning to thaw and to leave patches of bare ground on the hillsides. We left our coats with our horses and struck off on foot for a group of high buttes cut up by the cedar canyons and gorges, in which we knew the old bucks loved to lie. It was noon before we saw anything more. We lunched at a clear spring—not needing much time, for all we had to do was to drink a draught of icy water and munch a strip of dried venison. Shortly afterward, as we were moving along a hillside with silent caution, we came to a sheer canyon of which the opposite face was broken by little ledges grown up with wind-beaten cedars. As we peeped over the edge, my companion touched my arm and pointed silently to one of the ledges, and instantly I caught the glint of a buck's horns as he lay half behind an old tree trunk. A slight shift of position gave me a fair shot slanting down between his shoulders, and though he struggled to his feet, he did not go fifty yards after receiving the bullet.

This was all we could carry. Leading the horses around, we packed the buck behind my companion's saddle, and then rode back for the doe, which I put behind mine. But we were not destined to reach home without a slight adventure. When we got to the river we rode boldly on the ice, heedless of the thaw; and about midway there was a sudden, tremendous crash, and men, horses, and deer were scrambling together in the water amid slabs of floating ice. However, it was shallow, and no worse results followed than some hard work and a chilly bath. But what cared we? We were returning triumphant with our Christmas dinner.

THE EYETEETH
OF O'HARA

TALBOT MUNDY

THERE WAS DARKNESS drenched with starlight and the comforting sound of many horses at a picket beyond the glowing campfire. There was a smell that included saddles, tobacco, woodsmoke, and the syces' supper. Some of the tents were dark already, but from others came talk and laughter; and there was one false note for the sake of contrast. It was written at the birth of time, presumably, that nothing human shall be perfect. Therefore Major Jones was singing, nasally off-key, a nasty song about the lights of London; nasty because it was immoral even to imagine London in that setting.

But Jones never did anything right, except to pay his bills and raise hell with the mess cook if the curry was not to his liking. Jones was due for retirement next month; this was his last ride with the tent club. He was probably trying to make himself enjoy the prospect of home and half pay.

But it was Larry O'Hara's first ride—not his first time out to "pig," but his first in distinguished company. He was the youngest present, and a lot too sensible not to know that his father's reputation was a deadly liability. The son of General O'Hara must be either a nonentity contented to be General O'Hara's son, or else he must cut such a swath for himself that even India would presently forget the proverb: "Great king's sons are little princes."

He had done well thus far. Indian native cavalry can, will, does find—swiftly and unmercifully—the weak spots in subalterns

fresh from their first year's training with a British regiment. He
had earned his transfer to the Guides and he had passed in lan-
guages; by grim self-discipline and study he had learned the difficult but absolutely necessary trick of being hardboiled and at the
same time sympathetic; reckless, ruthless, and good-humored;
proud, exacting; nevertheless, so friendly that the Rajput troop-
ers of his squadron spoke of him as Larry Sahib.

But he knew that it would take more than that to overcome his
handicap. By only one means may a man transcend a reputation
such as General O'Hara had built up for himself and burned into
the brazen rolls of time.

So he sat in the door of his tent considering—a handsome
fellow, built, like so many Irish gentlemen, as if he were intended
to be part and parcel with a fine horse. He had blue-gray eyes
that doubted all things except such as he himself had tested. He
himself was not yet tested, and he knew that. It amused him to
imagine how his self-contempt would feel if he should fail in one
essential. So, when shadow moved within a shadow and a slight
sound stole forth from the fifty silences that are the pulse of
India's night, and when a voice said, "Sahib, may I draw near?"
he was in as cynical a mood as he ever permitted himself. To
throw that off he welcomed interruption.

"Yes—come."

"I am Padadmaroh."

"I knew your voice. What is it?"

"It is not much. It is just a little matter. Are we alone, Sahib?"

"Yes. Drag up that horse blanket, Padadmaroh. Put it there,
where I can see your face against the firelight. Now sit down,
ancient of days, and tell me of this little matter that is not much."

Firelight changed the shadow into a gray-bearded bronze native, clad in cotton loincloth and an Englishman's old Norfolk
jacket out at elbow. Padadmaroh might have sat for Rembrandt
for a portrait of the least conventional Apostle. Bowed by experience, he was, and, beneath that worn look, fierce with passion for
essentials. Poverty was nothing to him, and his pride might not
be judged by any normal standard. Deep eyes, beneath a ragged
turban, saw through surfaces and did not announce what they
saw.

"So. Men tell me, Sahib, that you do well. I have heard that the squadron rides behind you as a wolf pack at the heels of a seasoned leader."

"Nonsense," said O'Hara. "I have not yet cut my eyeteeth."

"That is well said. Sahib, I was head *shikarri,* the native hunter to your father—whose father my father served as a scout in the wars up northward, in the days when death lay fifty paces off and not a mile away, as it does now. Then men shot each other. Now they shoot at nothing, and are shot from nowhere. Then, when the guns grew hot, men had at one another's throats and it was easy, Sahib—easy to learn who was pukka."

O'Hara paused for a moment, then said thoughtfully, "You have seen a lot of changes, Padadmaroh. Tanks, motors, airplanes—"

"Aye, and India is changing, Sahib. But there is one thing that does not change. He who has it has it. He who has it not is not worth trouble. But how shall he know that he has it?"

"No man ever can know," O'Hara answered. "No matter what's behind a man, there may be something ahead that will make him crack and act up."

"Sahib, there is also this that never changes. It is the way of the wild boar. He is the tester. He is the cutter of men's eyeteeth."

"They say the pigs are plentiful," O'Hara answered. "We are out after them at daybreak."

"Ah. He who will ride at a boar needs bowels. And within the bowels, entrails. And within the entrails, guts. But there are guts and guts, as there are boars and boars. And it is one thing to ride in company. It is another thing, Sahib, to ride alone against an old one who has slain men."

"Four of us ride tomorrow," O'Hara answered. "You know our custom."

"Sahib, listen to me. I am old. I said to General O'Hara, 'Sahib, bahadur, the test of a man is his courage. But the fruit of a man is the son of his loins.' And he nodded, as his way was when he was thoughtful, stroking his nose thus between thumb and finger. So I said to him then, 'Bahadur, shall I test your son when it is time?' "

"What did he say?" O'Hara answered curiously.

"He said, 'Why not? He must find out somehow. Will it matter who mistrusts him if he learns to trust himself? If he is rotten, let him know it, lest he get in good men's way.' So I answered, 'I will test him.' I am ready, Sahib."

"To the devil with you," said O'Hara. "Do you take me for a damned fool?"

"Nay, I know not. But I know this: he slew a tiger."

"Who did?"

"That one of whom I came to speak to you. He is the father of boars—a gray boar, and a lone one. All my days what was I? A *shikarri*. Since I was younger than you are, Sahib, there has not been one gray boar on all this countryside, but I knew where he kept himself, and guessed his weight, and knew his character. And before me my father did likewise. Not in his day nor in mine has such a boar been seen. This one is higher by my hand's breadth than that one they slew in Guzerat in '79; and that one was a wonder.

"That one slew two men and half a dozen horses in his last charge. There were eight against him, and I saw it. Hah! I say he slew two; and he slew six horses. There were three spears sticking in him when he charged the last time, and the officer who killed him lost his right eye, because one of those spears struck him as the boar rose at the horse's belly. That was a boar of boars, but not as good as this one. As a man's breath to a typhoon, so was that good boar compared to this one of which I now speak."

"Trot him out then and we'll ride him," said O'Hara.

"Nay."

"Why?"

"In the first place, who am I that I should waste a gray boar who has slain men? Never was one like him—never. Sahib, I say he slew a tiger."

"Did you see that?"

"Nay. But I saw the tiger; and I sold his torn pelt for ten rupees, that should have been worth three hundred had that boar not cut it to ribbons. And I saw the boar that same day, bloody from the tiger's claws that smote but could not conquer him."

"How long ago was that?"

"Six months and nine days, Sahib. I followed that boar to a waterhole and watched him wallow until he had plastered himself with clean mud and the blood ceased flowing. Since that day he is a lone one and not even a sow dares come within a mile of him. He is a boar of boars. There are a thousand devils in him, and his is the cunning of madness."

Larry O'Hara studied the old man's silhouette against the firelight.

"So is mine," he answered. "If I were as mad as you think, I'd be a lot too cunning to let you know it. What's the idea? Want to take me in a trap of some sort? What for?"

"I am an old man, Sahib. Ere I die I wish to see what would make it worthwhile to have lived. When I was your age each young sahib had to earn his spurs. They cut his eyeteeth for him on the edge of difficulty; as for instance, it was three days' ride to this place, that you come to nowadays in two hours, in a car that stinks, whose syce is a Sikh afraid of horses. It is all too easy."

"Saves time," said O'Hara.

"Even the horses came by motor truck. I saw it."

"Saves the horses," said O'Hara.

"Sahib, how are the horses?"

"Splendid. I've a nine-year-old—a mare that won the Punjab cup. She's savage. My second's a half Arab country-bred, a bit young and a trifle nervous, but as game as hell when he once gets going. And my third is a flea-bitten Kathiawari, about one-eighth Percheron—strong as an elephant, but clever on her feet and fairly fast."

"Sahib, ride that one."

"When? Why?"

Silence, as the fire died and the shadows deepened. Major Jones ceased singing and a snore came from a nearby tent. Then a horse in the picket line neighed and a syce rebuked him. Silence again, until marauding jackals suddenly began to chatter like ghouls and someone's tethered dog defied them at the top of his lungs. Presently a camp attendant heaped more fuel on the fire, so that Larry O'Hara's face glowed within the overshadowing tent and

Padadmaroh's silhouette grew sharp again. But the old man still said nothing.

Then came Major Jones, long legged, striding like a stork because there might be scorpions and he was wearing slippers. O'Hara's servant stepped unsummoned out of black night and produced a chair for him.

"I hate to drink alone," said Jones. "It's rotten morals. So I told my boy to bring us both a nightcap. Everybody else has turned in. Who is this man?"

"Padadmaroh. Used to know my father. Wants to introduce me to a special pig. He swears it's bigger than an elephant and that it makes a hobby of killing tigers before breakfast. I invited him to show it to us all, but he refuses; says it's my pig, says he wants to test my guts."

Jones leaned forward and began to question Padadmaroh, but the old man drew himself into a shell of silence guarded by assumed stupidity, the everlasting native Indian refuge from the white man's hectoring. Jones struck a match and showed him money.

"Padadmaroh, next month I leave India forever. I have never killed a record boar. If you can show me one whose tushes are a fraction bigger than the record for this tent club, I will pay you a hundred rupees. I will pay another hundred if he falls to my spear."

Silence. Then the servant came with strong drink in two tall glasses. Jones drank. Larry O'Hara sipped his and, watching Major Jones' face, spilled the rest of it—as Padadmaroh noticed.

"Did you hear me?" Jones asked. "Two hundred." Then in an undertone to Larry, "Dammit, I'd pay a thousand if I had to. I've had infernally bad luck. The only big pig that I ever rode and killed turned out to be a sow. One very big one that I actually touched got clear away; he jumped into a nullah that no horse could tackle. It's too bad to have to leave India without something decent to show for all my efforts. This looks like my opportunity."

O'Hara lighted a cigarette and answered in a low voice: "He suggested, sir, that it was my pig. So of course I told him it's the club's—or words to that effect. It'd be a lark if we could all ride at the biggest pig on record."

Jones made a muttered remark of some kind, but when he spoke aloud his voice was well under control, although he sat bolt upright, as he did when playing cards.

"Where is this big boar, Padadmaroh?"

"Nay, nay. I was speaking with O'Hara Sahib. When he was a little *butcha*—so big—not yet old enough to be sent oversea for his schooling, he would sit beside me and I used to tell him tales. So tonight I told him another, for the sake of my old memory— just such a tale as I used to tell him. Then I used to speak of boars as big as elephants, he being little, and all little ones enjoy big stories. But tonight I only lied about a boar a little bigger than he could be, since O'Hara Sahib is a grown man. Travelers have told me, Sahib, that the little fishes take the big bait but that whales—whatever they are, for I never saw one—swallow only small things."

Jones stared hard at him, moving to see him better against the crimson glow of the campfire.

"So you were lying, eh? It is rare for a man of your race to admit he was lying."

"Maybe, Sahib. But what of it? I am only an old man full of memories. When this O'Hara Sahib was a *butcha,* and I told him tales, he used to set his chin a certain way and in his eyes was laughter like the wind at daybreak. So I wished to see if it was still there."

"Was it?" Jones asked.

"I am old. My eyes are not so keen as formerly. And it is dark," said Padadmaroh.

Jones thought a minute.

"Damn all this evasion," he said suddenly. "See here, my time's short, so I'll raise you. Five hundred rupees—that's a fortune for you—if a record boar falls to my spear within the next three days. I've heard of you. A lot of men have told me you're a wizard at finding pig where no one else can. Go ahead then, and earn five hundred rupees."

Padadmaroh showed his few remaining stained teeth in a smile that wrinkled up toward his deepset eyes.

"That is a lot of money, Sahib. But I do not need it."

Jones looked sidewise at O'Hara.

"Youngster, I believe you've already bribed him."

O'Hara made no comment.

"Let me tell you," Jones said sternly, "that it isn't etiquette, to put it mildly, for the youngest member of the club to do this kind of thing."

"What kind of thing?" O'Hara asked him.

"Bribing an old *shikarri* to reserve a big pig for your private spear."

"I just now heard you try to do it. I am sorry, sir, that good form and the regulations forbid my telling you to go to hell," said O'Hara. "This gentleman here"—he stressed the word— "is my personal friend. As soon as it's agreeable to you I'd like to talk with him alone."

"That's cheek," said Jones. "I'll make you pay for it." He got up. "It's damned impudence. I'll not forgive you for it. Good night."

There was silence until Jones had stalked away and vanished in his own tent.

"Padadmaroh, do you get the point of that?" O'Hara asked then. "What I wish you'd do is to guide the rest of them to that big pig, and I'll keep out of it. It isn't that I care a damn about the major, but I don't want it even hinted that I haven't played fair. I'll pretend I'm sick and can't ride."

"Nay, nay, Sahib. Ride tomorrow, and the next day, and the next. If I know anything, I know this: that one is a *badmash*. Let me take his money. He will not dare not to pay me. I will bargain with him that the money shall be mine if I give him as much as a chance at such a great boar as I speak of. I will argue I know nothing of his skill, so he should pay me whether or not he is the first to prick that great boar. He will promise payment; but he will not believe me; he will watch you, thinking that you have bribed me first and therefore that I come deceiving him in order to protect your honor's honor."

"Listen, Padadmaroh. I don't give a damn what deal you drive with Major Jones. That's his lookout. I'll have nothing to do with it."

"But you will ride, Sahib? Tomorrow? And the next day—and the next?"

"I'll ride, yes. But I want your promise not to flush that boar for my spear."

"Nay, indeed. Why should I? He might kill you." Padadmaroh stood up. "He has slain so many men he now thinks lightly of them. Stay with the ride, Sahib. What does it matter to me who slays a gray boar?"

"Now you're talking rot," O'Hara answered. "Good night."

Padadmaroh bowed himself away into the darkness and O'Hara turned in, sleepless for a short time. So he saw through the open tent flap, by the candle lantern burning in Jones' tent, the shadowy form of Padadmaroh silently approaching; and he saw Jones' tent flap open to admit him.

"Who was it said that everybody has a yellow streak?" he grumbled. "Dammit, some men can't be sportsmen, even though they've got guts. Jones has 'em. Curse him, what do I care if he steals one? Let him live with himself afterward. That's his business."

He fell asleep, and when his servant called him for the hurried breakfast before daybreak in the mess tent he had almost forgotten Jones and Padadmaroh. There was too much else to think about, and too much of the mystic madness that runs riot in the early Indian morning: wine of wonder, stirring the imagination; squeals, kicks, whinnying from the horse line; mauve and golden half-light and a wilderness emerging out of shadow; then a sunrise such as Zoroaster and the Parsees understood as symbolizing Life, full-colored, golden, everlasting—splendid.

"Time, you fellows. Let's get underway before it warms up."

There were eight men. They divided into two rides, and the other rode off in a hurry to the southward where the beaters were already dinning in a maze of scrub to start a "sounder" of wild boar milling and preparing them for the stampede that should separate, at the right time, from their leader—reported to be a boar worth going after. Larry O'Hara was in Major Hickman's party, which included Jones and a man named Bingham, a civilian with a reputation: he had won the Guzerat Cup two years in succession. Bingham was the type of man who gets a little irritable when he finds himself in untried company: he rated Hickman as his equal, but he knew Jones for a second-rater; and since Larry O'Hara was an unknown quantity he was only barely civil to him.

"Why ride that mare?" he demanded. "She looks slower than a bullock. You'll be out of the running."

But O'Hara had chosen the Kathiawari with a trace of Percheron because he did not wish to thrust, that first day, too self-assertively. He knew that nothing under heaven is more irritating to an old hand than to have a youngster on a fast horse pass him and then bungle. Luck may favor any one, but laurels, in the long run, fall to him who bides his time and learns his game before he shows off. He forgot that Padadmaroh had advised him to select that mount. He did not think of Padadmaroh until Jones came cantering along behind him on a whaler and they trotted, side by side, behind the others. Jones was smiling. He kept stabbing with his spear at an imaginary mark, to get his eye in and his sinews limber.

"Just forget our talk last night, O'Hara," he said presently. "It'd spoil sport to remember it. I may have been a bit too ready to find fault."

O'Hara made his mare plunge, to gain a few seconds and get his face under control.

"As long as you don't think I accepted, or even thought of accepting Padadmaroh's offer," he answered.

Jones grew even more conciliatory.

"I don't doubt you. Fact is, you behaved damned well. I didn't. I was tempted. For a youngster like you, a trophy doesn't mean much—or it shouldn't. Your day will come. But this is my last chance. I'll never see this scene again. I'm off to live at Cheltenham and gossip with the other has-beens. They will lie like old women. I've a tiger skin. I'd like a record pair of tushes. Then I needn't listen to their lies. However, Padadmaroh's scheme was not good sportsmanship. I'm glad I dropped it."

O'Hara doubted him. It seemed he was protesting too much. He had seen Jones draw the tent flap to admit old Padadmaroh; and he knew that Padadmaroh was a man with Eastern notions as to what is fair play, and to whom five hundred rupees would be wealth.

"Look out for Padadmaroh. He may trick you if you listen to him," he suggested. "None of my affair, of course, but look out."

Jones flushed slightly. He resented advice from a junior. He glanced at O'Hara sharply as if, for a second, he suspected him of having seen Padadmaroh creep into his tent; but O'Hara was watching Hickman, captain of the ride; Hickman had drawn rein and was conning the landscape, choosing cover, waiting for the head *shikarri* to come running with information.

"Thanks, I don't think I need your advice," said Jones.

"Don't take it then," O'Hara answered. He cantered forward and drew rein by Hickman's stirrup.

The sun was well up, blazing like hot brass. Scrub, small clumps of trees, sheet rock, and dangerously broken plateau fenced and fringed with prickly pear lay etched around a dense grass thicket that was moving as if a million snakes made war within it. Men invaded it—a hundred of them, armed with sticks and tin cans—led by nearly nude enthusiasts whose ancestors, for possibly a thousand years, had earned their living at the heels of wild pig, heading them until they broke from cover. The head *shikarri,* sweating as he ran to Hickman's stirrup—bearded, ragged, filthy, with a turban like a coil of twisted lamp rags—spoke excitedly, without preliminaries: "Great big sounder, Sahib—many, many. Old boar, five, six year old—good one!"

Hickman pointed with his spear: "We'll take that cover downwind. Flush 'em just as soon as we're out of sight."

He led to a clump of thorn trees struggling for their lives in a thirsty undergrowth—a perfect screen; and before they reached it a din went up of shouts and crashing cans, set up by the beaters waist deep in the grass patch.

Hickman rammed his helmet down and edged his horse to the corner of the group of trees, to peer around it. All four horses fretted, snatching at their bits and kicking. Hickman, taking his spear in his bridle hand, made motions with his right for silence; all four horses instantly took that for orders to lay hoof to hard earth and go like the wind. There was a minute of staggering, snorting false start and an oath or two as Bingham's horse bucked wildly beneath him.

"There he goes!" said Hickman. "Here they all come! Give him time, or he'll turn."

A sounder of at least two hundred pigs broke cover, following a big boar scarred by half a hundred fights—sows grunting for their young, the young ones squealing—and the whole lot going like the shadow of a swift cloud.

"Good!" said Hickman. "He's a whopper."

Trouble again with the horses; they were savage, sweating, nervous to be off. They knew their business. So did the old gray boar. He heard them—understood. His business, as great-great-grandsire of the sounder was to lead out of danger and then turn and draw the enemy away until he could fight without risk of the sounder being trampled in the melee. Well out in front, where stout old captains should be, he saw Hickman—saw the others—grunted. That grunt was his trumpet blast. The sounder wheeled and scurried out of harm's way into dense, low jungle. But the gray boar carried on, and Hickman shouted— "Ride!"

It is a good half second when the gate goes up on Epsom Downs and half a million throats on Derby Day explode exultantly "They're off!" It probably was not so bad in Rome when gladiators marched in for the *Caesar salutamus!*" There are even moments in a modern bullfight when the ultimate of tenseness almost touches infinite reality, and life and death seem mingled in emotion. Those are nothing to the great game. There is no sport like it, and no adversary, barring gods and devils, half as great as a gray boar.

All four horses stuck their toes in and were off, O'Hara leading by a full length; it had been his luck to have the left end, nearest to the boar when Hickman shouted "Ride!" But he had no chance of holding that place. Hickman on a faster horse, then Bingham, and then Jones all passed him, racing neck-and-neck for first spear; for it does not count who slew the boar; whoever pricks him first and shows blood is the winner—owns the tushes. When a gray boar dies there is neither time nor opportunity to judge whose spear it was that sent his brave soul to the pigs'

Valhalla. First blood has to be the deciding issue, and that makes for reckless riding.

But the boar knows even better than a fox what sort of going punishes the horses. Warrior by instinct, he inevitably some day dies in battle; younger boars dispute his leadership; he holds it only until beaten, and he only yields it with his last breath. So he knows, too, under what conditions he can fight best—understands the value of surprise, of shock, of sudden change of tactics; and his strategy is equal to his courage.

Hickman and Bingham, neck-and-neck, rode furiously to force battle before the boar could gain the rocky, broken ground, a mile away, where the horses would be in difficulties and he at a huge advantage. One spear prick would bring him to bay. But the boar went like the wind—foam on his tushes, his angry little red eye glancing backward as he judged how much the enemy were gaining on him and selected rougher going to delay them.

Prickly pear made no impression on his tough hide, so he crashed it and the horses had to make a circuit. Ledges of rock that gave a horse no foothold were an easy stairway for him, so he scampered over them; the horsemen had to ride around and waste eternities of seconds looking for a path to follow. One of those rock ledges separated Hickman and Bingham, left and right. Jones pulled out to the right-hand after Bingham, and Larry O'Hara followed Jones, he hardly knew why, except that he supposed Jones would follow the easiest route, and Larry wished to save his own horse. He had time to wonder again why Padadmaroh had advised him to ride his strongest, slowest mount.

There came a moment when the boar was lost to view. The leaders checked to look for him, and Larry caught up. It was thirty seconds before Hickman saw the boar's back hurrying away beyond a low ridge. Hickman spurred off in pursuit with thirty lengths' advantage, and it looked like Hickman's pig so certainly that even Bingham granted it and slowed down, reserving his mare's strength and speed for the inevitable battle when the boar should turn at bay for the finish.

It was then, as he responded to Bingham's signal and took position, as the junior, in the worst place on the right flank, with

Jones on Bingham's left, so that somebody could charge the boar whichever way he turned, that Larry saw Padadmaroh. The old man was beyond the boar, between two big rocks. There was no time to see what he did.

The boar jinked suddenly to the right, took higher ground and vanished for a moment in a maze of low scrub. That put Larry in the lead, and Hickman out of it. So Larry's spurs went home as Jones and Bingham spread to either side and raced to overtake him. Hickman shouted, but no one could hear what he said. The boar burst suddenly from cover with his whole strength gathered under him and came at Larry, downhill—fifty feet to go, and all the fury of a redhot cannon ball.

Then man and horse were one, there being that which links them when the warhorse ancestry of one responds to exultation in the other. Neither horse nor man flinched. Larry's spear, held steady, met the boar midway. It took him full and fair between the shoulders as he rose to slash the horse's belly with his tushes. The mare reared and lashed out with her forefeet. The spear broke. The dying boar—no whit discouraged—charged the mare's hind legs, knocked them out from under her and set her reeling over backward. Larry rolled free just as Bingham's spear skewered the boar and finished him. Then Jones rode up and drew rein.

"Damn these Irishmen's luck!" he remarked.

"Three and three-quarter inch tushes is my guess. Damned good spear, O'Hara. Are you hurt at all?" asked Bingham.

Larry had caught his horse and was examining her hind legs.

"Nothing wrong with either of us. Not a scratch on the Begum. Knocked her wind out, that's all; she'll be all right in a minute."

Hickman rode up.

"Neatly done, O'Hara! Good spear!"

Hickman examined Larry's mare and gave his verdict.

"Nothing wrong with her. Is she slow, or did you take it easy? Care to sell her? I'll buy, but I wouldn't part with her if I were you. A mare that fights back that way with her forefeet is a gem as long as she can gallop. Well—we've time for another pig before the heat glare sets in."

Padadmaroh came up on an old gray donkey, grinning. Hickman recognized him.

"Did you see that, Padadmaroh?"

"Not bad, Sahib. It was not bad. But it was no test. I have seen a thousand sahibs who would not have failed then. This boar was a good one, but he had no cunning—none to speak of."

Hickman stared at Padadmaroh, then at Larry.

"Did you turn him?" he demanded.

"Nay, nay, Sahib. Who could turn a boar like that one?"

"How did you come to be here, at the finish?"

"Sahib, I know all this countryside. And I know pig. There was no other way that he *would* take, seeing how the wind blow sand the way they drove his sounder out of cover. Come more horses? I took thought to bring spears in case any should break."

"Horses and spears should be here in a minute," said Hickman. "However, that was thoughtful of you. Where are the spears? O'Hara Sahib needs one."

Padadmaroh gestured toward the two great rocks behind which Larry had seen him lurking. Larry eyed him curiously. Then he mounted.

"Let me see the spears."

So Padadmaroh climbed up on his old gray donkey and Larry followed him, walking his mare for the sake of her slowly recovering wind. Padadmaroh kept the donkey's rump beneath the mare's nose, talking over his shoulder.

"It was the spear that I dreaded, Sahib. I have brought a stout one. Those that I saw in camp last night are no good."

"Damn you, did you turn that boar?" asked Larry.

"Nay, nay, Sahib. Who could turn him? But he smelled the burning undergrowth beyond him that the sun set fire to."

"Sun isn't strong enough yet," O'Hara answered.

"It has burned since yesterday."

"You liar."

"Just a little burning; not a big one, Sahib. Had that boar been cunning—but he was not, and I knew it—he would have tried to set that fire between him and pursuit. Look yonder—I have men who beat the fire out."

There were twenty men, hard at it, shoveling dust and beating

down the fire with strips of *kaskas* matting. It was an irregular
patch of thorns and coarse grass, isolated by a quarter-mile of
sheet rock. Let alone, it would have burned itself out in an hour
or two.

"Here are the spears," said Padadmaroh. "Try their weight
and choose one. They are all sharp. They are all strong."

"Twenty men at work, and all that smoke, would turn a dozen
boars," said Larry. He was angry, but he chose a spear because
he liked the heft of it. "If I prove you set that fire—"

"Yes, Sahib—then what?"

Larry O'Hara held his tongue. He knew he would do nothing. He
suspected Jones of having made a bargain with Padadmaroh. He
suspected Padadmaroh of deliberate intention to deceive Jones
and to take his money. But to go to Hickman and accuse either of
them was out of the question. Even given proof, it would be
better to let the problem work itself out than to spoil a morning's
sport by making a scene. If Jones were guilty of bad sportsmanship, as he suspected, in attempting to reserve, by trickery, the
best boar for his own spear, let Jones carry on. Then let him clear
his conduct—if, as, and how he could. If he could not, who
cared? Jones was leaving India, to be forgotten.

"Let me alone, do you hear?" he commanded. "I don't want
your interference."

Padadmaroh grinned back.

"That the Sahib will not ride unfairly is a good sign. But the
signs are nothing when the trial comes."

"Confound you! What damned right have you to try me, as
you call it?"

Padadmaroh kept on grinning and his old eyes glittered.

"Do you see this, Sahib?" He produced a boar's tush from
within the folds of a filthy loin cloth. It was a very old one,
carved into the semblance of a local godlet such as old *shikarris*
sometimes carry for the sake of good luck. "I said to the general
bahadur I will send this to him when his son shall have cut his
eyeteeth. See—" he produced a metal box and opened it—"behold his writing."

On a stamped and folded strong brown envelop was written General O'Hara's name and his address in Ireland.

"It was two boars—two at once—that tried your father, Sahib; and my father saw it."

"See here—" Larry O'Hara's Irish temper changed to laughter suddenly, as the weather does in Ireland. "Damn your impudence, I don't mind being tested, as you call it, but I won't have other fellows' sport spoiled."

"Do they matter, Sahib?"

"Yes, dammit. Bring those other spears along. Today, tomorrow, and the next day we ride four in company. If you want to, on the fourth day, you may raise hell."

Padadmaroh nodded. "Does the Sahib think that troubles come like the ter-r-rain by signal? It is the unexpected that discovers weakness. It is only weakness that betrays a man. All other qualities are good, in one way or another."

"Wait until I'm free to go alone with you."

No answer. Larry turned his mare and trotted back to his companions. He found them fuming. There were no spare horses in sight, although runners had come to cut the tushes from the dead boar, so that evidently someone knew which way to take.

"I'd ride this horse again," said Hickman, "but he's split a hoof. It's nothing serious, but—"

Bingham nodded.

"It's against all the law and the prophets to stick a lame horse into it. This isn't a bullfight. I'll wait with you."

"Anything wrong with your horse?" Hickman answered. "Would you care to go and look for the remounts? Probably they're not far off. If you hurry them we might have time to get a second pig."

Bingham rode off. Hickman turned to Padadmaroh.

"Where are the beaters? What's the matter with them? Which cover do they draw next?"

"God knows, Sahib."

Jones spoke up then. He avoided Larry's eyes, or seemed to. And to Larry, who suspected him, it seemed he spoke for Padadmaroh's ears as much as anyone's: "It's late already. Remounts must have gone off in the wrong direction. It'll be noon before they get here. Do you care if I go on alone? My last chance, don't you know. You other fellows'll have scores of opportunities."

"Won't you be here tomorrow?" Hickman asked him.

"No, I'm leaving by the night train. Too bad, but I have to."

Hickman pulled his helmet off and wiped his forehead.

"All right. You and O'Hara go together. I'll wait here for Bingham. Padadmaroh probably can show you where some pig are. Good luck."

"Thanks, I'm staying," said O'Hara.

"Oh, all right," said Jones, and rode off. "Come on, Padadmaroh."

Padadmaroh followed on his old gray donkey, glancing backward. He was holding three spears and he looked like Don Quixote's servant.

"That's a damned strange thing," said Hickman. "Looks like prearrangement. Jones leads off—guide following—Jones in a hurry and guide apparently reluctant. Dammit, that man Jones is not notorious for sportsmanship. I've heard of men who won't play cards with him. Do you suppose he's bribed that damned old scoundrel Padadmaroh to provide him with a pig all to himself?"

"I couldn't say," O'Hara answered. "Would you care to ride my mare, sir, and go after him? I'll hold your horse and wait for Major Bingham."

"No, no. Go and bring Padadmaroh back here."

Padadmaroh made no trouble about turning back. He seemed to have expected it. He made his donkey trot behind O'Hara's mare, and when he drew rein he saluted Hickman with a soldierly sideswipe of the right hand that was almost impudent.

"See here," said Hickman, "was it you who sent our remounts in the wrong direction?"

"Sahib, what have I to do with remounts?"

"Where are you taking Major Jones?"

"He takes me—into danger, Sahib. He has ground his eyeteeth into powder on the mess cook's chicken bones. And now he looks for false ones for his old age."

"That'll do," said Hickman. He, no more than Larry, cared to inquire too deeply. "What did you look back for just now, when the major ordered you to follow?"

"Sahib, I looked back for what might be. My plans have gone wrong. I am too old; I no longer plan well."

"Tell us."

Padadmaroh for a moment watched the brown kites circling tirelessly above the carcass of the slain boar.

"Yonder, below, in the *ghat,*" he said then, "near where the ancient ruins lie in jungle that is difficult to enter, is a boar of boars. He learned of it."

"You meant that boar for us?" asked Hickman.

"Not I, Sahib. But for this one. And he would not."

Hickman stared hard at O'Hara. Padadmaroh talked on, shrewdly eyeing both men.

"Now my trouble is that he—that other one—it was he, Sahib, who sent the remounts to the wrong place—"

"Did he give the order?"

"Nay, he ordered me to give it. Now my trouble is that he will find that boar; for I have told him where to find it. I am an old man and my plans creak louder than my old bones! I would have cut this sahib's eyeteeth. But instead, I send a man who does not matter to a man's death that he never earned!"

Then Hickman laughed into O'Hara's eyes.

"Go on, O'Hara. Follow Jones," he ordered. "I'll stay here. As soon as Bingham comes we'll be hard at your heels." He laughed at Padadmaroh. "You go with O'Hara Sahib. Lead him to that boar ahead of Major Jones if you can do it."

So O'Hara rode off, slowly because the donkey had to follow. Fifteen minutes passed, and it was hotter than the hinges of the lid of Tophet when he came to the edge of the *ghat* and stared down into what appeared to be impenetrable jungle. It was a well-known *ghat,* where once a temple stood that archeologists dispute about in terms of baffled bigotry because it fits no period. Three hundred feet below, a mile wide, lay a dark green jungle, and no entrance to it save the winding narrow track on which the hoof-prints of Jones' horse showed distinctly. Padadmaroh halted his donkey at O'Hara's stirrup.

"Looks like tiger country," said O'Hara, surveying the valley.

"Yes, there was a tiger, Sahib. But the great boar slew him, as I told you. Down there in the valley bottom there is rich earth, full of roots that pigs love. There is a wallow, where the temple pool was formerly; it is fed by cold springs."

"It's a wild boar's heaven and a madman's hunting ground," O'Hara answered. "Where's the room to ride a boar, if we should see him?"

"There are many open spaces, Sahib. Some are clearings made by peasants who desired the rich earth. But they were driven away by the tiger. And then the boar came; and they say the boar is something not of this world."

O'Hara wiped the sweat off his face with his shirt sleeve and then shielded his eyes with his right arm, gazing downward. And because the spear was in his right hand it was something like a gesture of salute toward the kites, that circled slowly, waiting for death.

"I see Jones," he said then. "Come on."

Downward, on a mare as nervous as a filly; she could feel O'Hara's tenseness, and the smell of jungle filled her nostrils full of prehistoric terrors that a horse inherits and a man, for lack of understanding, labels instinct. Downward, until trees began to make a canopy that baffled sunlight, and a dim gloom, and an eery silence, tortured senses that O'Hara had hardly guessed he owned.

Then suddenly he heard Jones—then he saw him trying angrily to govern a distracted horse that grew quiet, although it trembled, when O'Hara's mare entered the clearing. Sudden sunlight blinded O'Hara for a moment; he could not see Jones' face until Jones had spoken.

"Quite impossible to ride a pig here. I was hoping to find some open country. Why did you come?"

Then O'Hara saw him—gray-gilled, mastering himself, but needing all his will, and none of it to spare.

"Hickman and Bingham are coming too," O'Hara answered.

Horse and mare rubbed noses, drawing comfort from each other. Padadmaroh on his donkey drew near. Jones snatched at a weak man's remedy and cursed him.

"Damn your eyes, you told me there was decent going down here!"

"Nay. But I said a great boar lives here and a man might ride him."

"You're a fool," Jones answered. "Let's turn back, O'Hara. What's the use of making idiots of ourselves?"

O'Hara grinned. It was the grin that signifies a number has been hoisted and it won't come down again until the winning post is passed. Then suddenly both horses reared and plunged into the jungle. There was something moving in the undergrowth that terrified them—something on the far side of the clearing. It took a minute of strenuous horsemanship to make them face it, but the donkey took no notice. Padadmaroh sat still on the donkey, staring at the thicket whence the sound of movement came.

"Pig," he said quietly when the horsemen had come close enough to hear him. "He was rooting. Now he goes back to his own place. Listen."

There were sounds of something thrusting through the jungle; no grunt—until suddenly a heavy animal went crashing away in the gloom. Padadmaroh spoke again.

"He is cunning. Here he will not show fight because he is not sure yet that a fight is necessary. But in his own place he is like a dog whose kennel is invaded."

"Where's that?" asked O'Hara.

"In the temple ruins. Follow that track, Sahib."

"Come on," said O'Hara, spurring forward.

"Damned young idiot!" said Jones.

But he could hardly turn back when a younger man went forward; neither could he hold his horse, that craved company. He followed, drenched with sweat and swearing to relieve his own nerves.

Larry O'Hara mastered his by mastering the mare. He petted her; he made her conscious of the bit; he let her feel the reassuring fact that there was someone on her back who liked and needed her, and presently would challenge forth her strength. So, though they rode in dim gloom, in a silence that was like the solid matrix of which silences are made, that mare became a unit,

once more, with her rider—no more timid, and no less, than he
was.

Then another clearing. Jones overtook O'Hara and recovered
more of his self-esteem by the timeworn process of rebuking a
junior.

"I haven't heard," he said, "of any new rule giving subalterns
the right to lead their seniors. The impudence of some of you
young officers is nothing less than piggish!"

"Lead, then," said O'Hara, and he drew rein until Jones had
passed him.

Jones, too, had mastered his horse; but he had done it by the
iron handed method that imposes untrusting obedience. The
horse went forward at the touch of Jones' spurs, but two-thirds of
the rider's attention was engaged in managing his mount and
when they plunged again into the jungle gloom it was a slow
procession. Padadmaroh, on the nerveless donkey, trotted behind
and kept up easily.

The heat was stifling. Men and horses sweated so that even the
merciless flies could hardly cling and sting; they merely irritated.
Larry O'Hara kept drying the palm of his hand on his riding
breeches, so that the spear should not slip when he gripped it.
Jones rode slowly, and more slowly as the gloom grew deeper,
following an ancient road whose stones lay pulled and twisted
out of place by roots of trees. Whenever his horse stumbled he
swore irritably. It was vastly worse to follow him than to ride
alone; he inspired no confidence, he merely drew attention to his
lack of it.

O'Hara gave him ten lengths' lead. He was at least that distance to the rear when the sunlight burst again through thinning
branches and a clearing—several acres of it—showed where the
archeologists had camped and dug. Old temple ruins lay in chaos
in the midst, beside a mud swamp.

"Kabadah!"

That was Padadmaroh's voice. The mare was on her toes before the warning reached O'Hara's ears. Jones' horse spun
around and bolted, coming straight back, headlong. There was
no room. But a gray boar—so huge he was fabulous—so swift
and sudden he was like a gray ghoul glimpsed in nightmare—

crashed Jones' horse and spilled his legs from under him. The fall pitched Jones into a thicket. The boar savaged at the horse and ripped his entrails—worried into him and slew him. Larry couched his spear and rammed his spurs in; charged, aiming at the boar's eye—missed it—struck his shoulder. But the boar jinked to defend himself. The spear slipped, sweat wet. Stung, infuriated, fighting mad—the gray boar skewered himself. He thrust against the spear; pain goaded him to reach and gore his adversary. And the spear kept slipping while the staggering mare reared and struck out with her forefeet.

Those three seconds were eternity. So scarred by tiger claws that one huge tush lay naked to the roots, his ear torn and his flanks still scabby from the half-healed battle wounds, his little red eyes burning with the boar lust that will yield to nothing less than death, the huge brute struggled forward, grunting. The mare lunged. The spear slipped. Suddenly the boar jinked for a flank attack, so that the spear was across the mare's throat.

There was nothing for it then but to escape. O'Hara let the spear go, shouted, spurred and rode wildly toward the clearing. And the boar came after him, the long spear sticking upward at an angle. He came as fast as the mare could gallop. Should she stumble on a loose rock, slip, meet something that she could not jump—death then, swift and savage on the froth foul tushes.

Nothing for it but to make a circuit of the ruins, full pelt, looking out for masonry half hidden amid creepers. Gallop around the ruins and then down the jungle path to Padadmaroh for another spear. But the boar took short cuts—gaining, gaining. And something was wrong with the mare; she had strained a tendon when a loose stone slipped from under her. The boar leaped on a pile of masonry. He stood there for a second frothing at the mouth. He shook himself to get rid of the spear. No escaping him now. He was in the center; he could cut that segment of a circle anywhere he pleased. And only one chance then: to snatch that spear and try to drive it home into his vitals—one chance in a billion!

The boar charged. Battle madness blazed up in him. Larry wheeled his mare and turned back by the way he came; that gave him ten more yards' advantage because the boar shot past his

mark, and stood and shook the spear again before he followed.
There was one more billion-to-one chance. Padadmaroh might—

He had! The damned old rogue had chanced it! He had followed. He had stuck two spears into the ground ten paces from
the track mouth. He was up a tree now, yelling, pointing. But the
mare could hardly gallop. Larry spurred her, shouted to her,
rode her as a jockey rides a Derby winner. He snatched a spear
and spun her around to face the boar again. There was a short
split-second then. He had to couch the spear like lightning; couch
it short—the boar was too close, rising at the mare's off-shoulder.

But his point struck straight between the great brute's shoulder
blades, and that spear did not slip. The butt of the other spear
struck O'Hara on the jaw bone as the mare rose on her hind legs,
frantic. That, and the shock of the boar's impact as the spear
went through his lungs and down into his vitals, sent them reeling, rider and mare together, over backward. Larry scrambled to
his feet and let the mare go. He was thinking of that other spear,
still in the ground. He was half stunned, breathless. Sweat was in
his eyes; he could not see the spear, although he could hear
Padadmaroh shouting.

Then he saw Jones walk out from the jungle path and pull the
spear out of the ground. He thought that Jones was coming to
defend him. It was only then that he got the sweat out of his eyes,
and looked, and saw the great boar lying dead.

"My first blood," Jones said calmly. "When he charged me in
the jungle I thrust out behind me and just got him with the spear
point. So I'll take those tushes."

"Can you show blood?" Larry asked him.

Jones was bending down examining the dead boar.

"Yes, yes. What a monster! He's a record—or I'll eat him!
Five-inch tushes! Yes, you'll find my spear beside the dead horse;
there's only a speck of blood on it. But look here—do you see
where my point went in?"

He was standing again, prodding at the hard earth with the
point of the spear he had pulled from the ground, entirely unaware that Padadmaroh had been watching him. The old man
had approached as silently as death's own shadow.

Suddenly the jungle echoed to the sound of hoofbeats. Someone shouted, and another answered. Nemesis came galloping into the clearing in the form of Hickman on a fresh horse.

"Damn the luck again!" he shouted. "Whose pig? God, what a whopper!" He rode nearer.

"My O'Hara Sahib's pig," said Padadmaroh.

Jones looked ugly.

"My pig."

Bingham cantered up.

"Oh, damn my rotten stars! Is that your pig, O'Hara? Good man!"

"My pig," Jones repeated. "I drew first blood."

Padadmaroh spoke then.

"But I saw the Major Sahib dip his spear point in the blood that trickled from the dead horse. And I saw him just now make a spear mark on the boar's snout. After that he wiped the blood off this spear thus—by sticking it into the earth repeatedly."

Jones flared.

"I never heard such lies! If you weren't nearly old enough to die of rot, I'd thrash you."

Hickman interrupted.

"Larry O'Hara, what do you say?"

"Pig's mine," Larry answered. "Case of nerves, I think. The major isn't quite himself. I've noticed it."

Jones flared again.

"Do you mean to say that you'll take that damned *shikarri's* word against mine?"

"It's O'Hara's pig," said Hickman.

"But the Major Sahib pays me my rupees, because the bargain was," said Padadmaroh, "that I only had to show him where the boar was."

"Damn you, you may go to hell," Jones answered.

"Are you going by tonight's train?" Hickman asked him. "You'll need time to pack your things, so don't let us detain you. Good-bye."

"I have no horse."

"You will meet the syces on your way. They'll have your spare horse with them. We will send a man back to the camp with your saddle and bridle. There's a dining room at the railway station, in case you'd prefer not to dine with the mess."

"You men are cads," Jones answered. "Cads, the lot of you." He walked off, slowly, trying to look dignified.

"And so I lose my money," Padadmaroh grumbled, but his grumble's edge was meshed into wide grin. "Who cares? I have cut O'Hara Sahib's eyeteeth! He is blooded. He has met death. Chota O'Hara Sahib, will you mail this to the general *bahadur?*"

He produced his envelop, unfolded it, inserted the old carved boar's tush, sealed it, held it to his forehead, bowed, and gave it —it was something like a god to him—to Larry.

"Sahib, give the general *bahadur* the salaams of Padadmaroh."

ADRIFT
ON THE
AMAZON

DEWEY AUSTIN COBB

IT WAS THE MONTH of May, and the Amazon River was sweeping down to the sea, six hundred miles away, in the majesty of a stream ten miles wide and ninety feet deep. For a month past, it had risen at Santarem at the rate of nearly a foot per day, and its every tributary was swollen by the melting snows of the Andes. Great cedar trees, torn from the banks by the resistless flood, floated down the stream; these, when captured and towed in to the scattered sawmills, furnished the most valuable lumber of all forest trees, for its quality of floating on water is rare among tropical woods.

At the time of this strange adventure, I was the guest of an old Brazilian friend, Manuel Valdez, at his plantation on the Amazon, near Santarem. The management of sawmill and plantation, with nearly a hundred laborers, left him little time for sport; but José Dean, his sturdy nephew of thirteen, was always looking for some new and daring enterprise. He and I were in the gunroom one morning, trying to plan some excursion for the day, when "Uncle Manuel" entered, and his first words scattered our half-formed program.

"The river hasn't been so high for years! Have you noticed how many big cedars are coming down? I must get some of them in for the mill, and that means sending a canoe six miles down the river, to get the chain for hauling them. I lent it to Señor Mendez, on condition that he would return it before high water, but he has failed to do so. Now I propose that we all take a holiday.

About two miles below here, there's a big floating meadow, which the water has been undermining for several years. There are over two acres, all overgrown with a jungle of trees and bushes, with a sod so thick and firm that you'd think you were walking on solid ground. There are always swarms of fish of one kind or another under these tracts: they feed on the grubs and insects that fall from it, I suppose. Let's take our fishing tackle and guns—for we may see some game—and when the men go down for the chain, we can stop at the meadow and fish until they come back for us and our catch. We ought to get home again about sunset. What do you think?"

I was delighted, and said so, and José supplemented his spoken approval with a hornpipe and whoops of joy. My host's gunroom was stocked with the latest models of all that a sportsman could require for shooting, fishing, or canoeing, and under his general directions we selected what was needed. We took everything, including a well-filled lunch basket, to the boat where the two paddlers were already waiting, and soon we were out of the little cove where boats were kept, and speeding down the river. At first the bank was steep and stony, rising several feet above the river, and surmounted by heavy woods. As we descended, the banks became lower, with here and there a strip of grass-grown meadow between forest and river, and at last turned to a sharp, straight edge of meadow turf, rising smoothly at a uniform height of about one foot above the surface of the unruffled water.

"This is the place," said Captain Valdez, "and there's no underbrush close to the water, so we can make ourselves comfortable along this edge." The boat was drawn up to the edge, and our guns, lines, bait, and lunch basket set ashore; then, after the canoemen had received instructions to call for us on the return trip, they went on down the river. We took our things back to a place of safety, then walked along the edge until we found a spot where the current would carry our bait under the sod, where the fish would see it, while we were out of their sight. It was soon apparent that this precaution was needless, for the sleepy, sluggish catfish herded there seemed destitute of any sense save that of hunger. As soon as a hook drifted near one, he would languidly take it in, make only a feeble resistance to being hauled out, and after a few perfunctory flops, lie still. We had caught perhaps a hundred pounds, when Señor Valdez wound up his line, remarking, "I've only eighty people to feed now, and we have at least a pound apiece for them, so let's quit. After luncheon, we'll look about us a little."

José quickly followed suit, saying disgustedly, "Not much fun in this kind of fishing; it's about as good sport as taking mackerel out of a kit!"

After spreading a tarpaulin over our catch, and refreshing ourselves from the basket, we strolled along the edge of the meadow, which, as far as we could judge, extended for a hundred yards out over the river. At the shore end, a dense jungle sloped gently upward to terra firma; and the turf was so thick and firmly woven together, that, though we tried to produce a wave by all springing upward together, the effort failed. We explored for about half an hour, then returned to our fish; and here a surprise awaited us.

José, who was a few yards ahead, suddenly stopped, and, in a voice of subdued excitement, exclaimed, "Look, Uncle Manuel! There's a big animal, eating the fish!" We hurried forward, just in time to hear some large creature slinking off into the thicket.

Señor Valdez questioned the boy eagerly. "Did you get a fair sight of him, José? Was he spotted like a leopard, or almost black, or yellowish-gray all over?"

"Oh, yes, I saw him plainly; he stood there with part of a fish in his mouth, and turned and walked off with it when he saw me. He was a kind of tawny yellow—like a panther I saw once at the zoo."

"It was a panther," his uncle answered, "only we call them pumas here. We have three kinds of big cats, all 'jaguars,' but we have different names to distinguish them. The different kinds hate each other, and fight whenever they meet. The black ones are the biggest and wickedest, and we call them 'tigers': the spotted ones are 'onças,' and the yellow ones 'pumas.' They live along the sandy banks of rivers, and fish a good deal; this fellow, I suppose, came to fish for himself, but was lucky enough to find dinner all ready for him." He looked at his watch, then turned to me. "Jim, I'd rather like to try for a shot at that puma, wouldn't you? It's three o'clock, and the boat won't be back for about three hours, so we'd have time to follow him up. Pumas aren't quite so shy as onças, so we might get a chance at him. José, would you mind staying here with the catch? You can keep the little gun, and fire it for a signal if the boat comes, or anything happens."

"That'll suit me better than crawling around in the thicket," answered José; "and, anyhow, if I went with you, I wouldn't dare shoot at a puma with this little bird gun. But I can fire it if the boat comes."

While we got our guns ready, Señor Valdez told us some new and surprising things about pumas. "Did you know," he said, "that the name the Indians in Buenos Aires have for the pumas means, in English, 'the Christian's friend'? A puma was never known to attack a man or a child, even in self-defense. They cringe and shed tears if hopelessly at bay, and a puma has been known to attack an onça that was threatening a child. I've had one trot ahead of me like a dog, when crossing a *campo,* stopping and waiting if it got far ahead, and at last turning into the bushes when I got near a house."

"And you're anxious to shoot a nice, friendly creature like that!" I exclaimed. "I confess, it takes away some of my enthusiasm."

He smiled wisely: "Ah, but they are the plague of planters, and we have to shoot them, to save our young stock, their favorite prey. They kill more colts and cattle than the onças do; so you needn't waste sympathy on them. Come along!"

Thus justified, I followed into the thicket where the puma had disappeared, and after advancing a little way, we found that there was a low, open path, made and preserved by the going and coming of animals to the river, for drinking or fishing. It was narrow and crooked, so we could not see far ahead; but we had not gone far, when we heard the movement of some creature in advance of us, and once we saw a dusky shadow rounding a turn in the path. We never once doubted that it was the same puma José had seen; it did not seem much alarmed, and if we kept the trail long enough, we were pretty sure of a shot at it, for it would dash ahead a few rods, then wait until we were quite near, then dart on again.

"He hates to leave those fish, or else his mate is prowling near here somewhere; they often hunt in pairs at this season. But his mate would hardly dare to hide in so small a cover as this, so he's probably waiting for a chance to get back and finish his dinner," Señor Valdez remarked. After advancing a hundred yards or so, we came to the point where the floating tract joined the solid land, marked by a slight depression extending on both sides as far as we could see. In this hollow were pools of water, which we had some trouble in crossing. As we scrambled over on an old log the trail had led us to, Señor Valdez explained the hollow at the joining. "The turf is cracked by repeated bending when the river rises and falls. It has been like this for two years now, but I never saw it quite so wide before. There goes our cat!" he broke off suddenly, pointing ahead to the puma, which was just disappearing again.

We pursued the creature through the woods until, at last, it took to a tree and hid among the dense foliage, to be brought down finally by a lucky shot; but that is too long a story to tell here. After the excitement of the chase was over, our thoughts reverted to José. More than an hour had slipped away since we had left the little chap, half forgetting him in the zest of the hunt; and though the boat was not yet due, we felt anxious lest we might have got beyond the sound of his gun. Leaving our trophy hung as high as possible, we started on the back trail; but after reaching the heavy timber, it became so dim and winding that, instead of following it far, we made straight for the river. On this account, we were not much surprised, or in the least alarmed, when we found neither the log where we had crossed, nor the little strip of water, but came to the broad river itself. Señor Valdez remarked that it was odd that he had missed the meadow, but that we must be above or below it. Then, after a moment's intense scrutiny, he almost shouted, "No, Jim! Here's our log, but the meadow has broken away and floated off, with the boy on it—alone!" Rapidly he ran over the situation, anxiety in his voice. "The canoe won't be here for an hour; and there isn't another within two miles of jungle—an hour of travel. Even then, it would be too late to overtake that island before night, and we could not find or follow it after dark!"

Just then we heard the distant and feeble report of a gun, followed by a faraway, treble shout. Leaning out over the water as far as we dared, we could see our island. It was slowly turning around, and now the meadow edge where we had fished was upstream and nearest us, but fully a quarter of a mile distant. We could distinguish the boy, standing close to the edge and waving his straw hat. It was doubtful whether he could see us under the trees, but we both shouted, and fired a volley from our repeating guns. The extravagant waving of his hat and the feeble pipe of his boyish voice told us that we were heard; and it gave us added hope and courage to feel that the little hero was animated by the spirit of "don't give up the ship!"

Manuel Valdez was a resourceful man, and one of action, not of many words, when driven to the wall. Staring blindly over the water, he said, "Jim, you must stay here and watch that island, until it goes out of sight or is hidden by the darkness. I will make my way as best I can up the riverbank, on the small chance of finding a boat or a fisherman—I've heard of one or two half-civilized squatters, at the lower end of my land, a mile or more above here. If I don't find one, I'll push on home, get a boat, come back for you, and then start in pursuit."

"But your men will be here with the chain before you return. Perhaps they'll see the lad, and take him off," I suggested hopefully.

"They're not likely to see him, even if they come, for his island may move out toward the middle of the stream, as they usually do, while the boat will be sure to hug the shore for the slower current. Then the island is spinning round, and José can't keep on the side where he will be seen. "No," as he turned his face upstream, "there is not one chance in fifty of their finding him." As he began his difficult task, he threw over his shoulder his parting instruction, "If the canoe comes before I get back, send it at once to find and overtake the island; but you had best stay right here, to give me the latest observation, then go with me." I heard him for a few moments, breaking through the thicket, and then the great silence of the forest by day fell on river and shore.

I watched the island until it was hidden behind a projecting point, half a mile farther down. It seemed to approach the shore, and was fairly in sight of a possible canoe coming up; but when it struck the cross current caused by the point, and before it was entirely hidden by the swift darkness, it was too distant to be seen and recognized by canoemen. Then I listened intently for the sound of the returning boat.

But the instant the sun had set, the nightly concert of the tropics began. Every bird and beast and bullfrog was wildly signaling its fellows. Several times I mistook the splash of a leaping fish for coming paddlers, but after what seemed hours of waiting, I heard the unmistakable rhythmic beat of hurrying canoemen. Then a shout, "Hello, Jim! Where are you?" and the flash of a swinging lantern told me that Señor Valdez had returned with assistance. Guided by the flame of a vesta in my hand, he came in, and I made my report, and learned in turn that he had hailed two fishermen, a mile farther upstream, and had impressed boat and paddlers into his service.

Just then his own men, returning with the chain, saw our light and hailed us, explaining that they were late because they had to wait for the borrower to return from hunting. They were not much concerned to find the meadow gone adrift, until they learned that José was on it. As we got underway, Señor Valdez announced his plan.

"If we go directly downstream, we shall probably miss the island in the night, for the boy has no light. Then again, at high water, the river is often thrown almost straight across its bed by projecting points of land; the island when last seen had already started for the middle of the river. But, after living on the river all my life, I have found out that any two objects, like boards falling in from the mill, will keep near together for a hundred miles. Now, if we start where the island did, and let our boats go with the current, they will follow the same course, and, by sunrise, we shall probably sight it. The poor boy will have to spend the night alone, but he is safe enough, and the lunch basket was not empty, so he will have some food."

The oldest paddler volunteered corroboration with, "That's right, Señor; that's the way we always find canoes that get adrift."

To wait in idleness, when the life of a human being is threatened by the forces of nature, utterly beyond our power to control or resist, is, perhaps, the severest strain ever brought upon a sympathetic temperament. In our case, every nerve was tense with a desire to put forth some supreme effort to serve the lad whose bravery and infectious cheerfulness had endeared him to all who knew him. With three in each canoe to take alternate watches, while the others tried to get snatches of much-needed sleep, the voyage was begun. Neither Señor Valdez nor I attempted to sleep, and we rarely spoke. At midnight, the wild creatures along the shore gradually lapsed into silence, and the only noises were the whispering of the sleepless river, or an occasional splash which meant play, or tragedy, among the swarming fish.

That was the longest night I ever knew. At last daylight slowly penetrated the mists which hung over the river, but it was a full hour before we could see the shore. Then, as if at the command of some resistless power, the mist rose; not in broken patches, but foot by foot, everywhere, until we could see that we were near midstream. Both shores and two or three floating islands were visible, but we rowed downstream a mile or more before sighting the wooded island of our pursuit, and it was nearly half an hour more before our strong paddlers brought us near enough to be certain that it was the one we sought. Something moving arrested our attention.

"Look there!" exclaimed Señor Valdez, with a laugh which held both relief and pride, "the plucky little rascal is still waving his hat!" Sure enough, there stood José; confident that we would come down the river after him, he had crossed the island, now turned half round, and was signaling to us from the side which had joined the mainland.

We returned his greetings joyfully, and were within fifty feet of him, when suddenly Señor Valdez stood up in the boat and seized his rifle. He was bringing it to his shoulder, when José shouted in great excitement, "Don't shoot, Uncle Manuel! Please don't shoot! He's as tame as a kitten, and he's been company for me all night!"

Señor Valdez complied, though he kept his gun in hand. Just then, a slight movement of a bush drew my attention to the snakelike head of a puma, peering at us with both fear and defiance in his yellow eyes. The animal stood still until Señor Valdez stepped from the boat, then, with a growl, it darted through the thicket and sprang into the river. We saw its head, as it swam swiftly to a small fragment which had become detached from our island, and then it hid quickly among the bushes.

We received a joyful welcome from our young voyager, and soon took him on board, together with the fish we had caught. The lunch basket was not forgotten, for it was not quite empty: six hungry men, however, soon attended to that. We made inshore to a slower current, and began our toilsome journey homeward; and, on the way, José told us of his voyage, and his strange companion, often interrupted by our eager questions.

"No, Uncle Manuel, I wasn't really scared," said he; "that is, not until the island got into deep water, and the waves rocked it so I could see the trees swaying. That made me feel—well, rather anxious, and sort of seasick, too, so I thought I'd better lie down awhile. Pretty soon I heard a whining noise near me, and when I looked around, there was Mr. Puma peering through the bushes with his shiny eyes! It was lucky I'd just heard your story about their not attacking people, for it kept me from being frightened; and, anyhow, I could see that the puma himself was scared at the motion. He looked at the trees waving, and then he came close and nosed my hand and smelled at it, and seemed to think I was all right, for he laid down close beside me, just like a nice old pussy cat. When I moved back to get away from the spray, he followed, and lay as close as he could; and it's funny, but I really went to sleep several times—though every time I looked, his eyes were wide open.

"We kept each other from being lonesome all night, and when the daylight came, the puma went clear around the island, looking for a place to get off; then he came back, and ate a fish I gave him. He heard the canoes long before I did, for the hair stood up on his back, and then he growled and ran behind the bush, where you saw him. But, don't you see, Uncle Manuel," José finished earnestly, "it wouldn't have been fair to shoot that puma!"

PAT'TIDGE DOG

JIM KJELGAARD

As soon as the train lurched to a stop at the little wayside station, Danny Pickett jumped from the express car. He turned to help Red, but almost before he had turned around the big Irish setter had leaped to the cinders beside him. Danny started at once for the beechwoods that began almost where the railroad property ended. The fuss and glamor of the dog show were behind them, Mr. Haggin had the blue ribbon and silver cup that Red had won. But Danny had the dog. And now they were home, here in the Wintapi.

Red paced sedately beside the boy. Nominally the property of Mr. Haggin, a millionaire sportsman who had built an estate in the wild Wintapi, the red dog had attached himself to Danny, son of a hillbilly trapper and farmer. Together, they had trailed and killed an outlaw bear that no hounds had dared follow. Mr. Haggin, an understanding man, had figured out for himself exactly what had happened on that bear hunt, had known that both Danny and the dog had played fair throughout. He had hired Danny to take care of Red, his first duty being to handle him at the New York show. But now that responsibility was ended and Red was Danny's, to do with as he saw fit.

Once in the woods, screened by trees from prying eyes that might see and comment on any letdown in dignity, the boy broke into a wild run. It seemed an eternity since he had seen the rough shanty where he and his father lived, smelled the good scent of streams, forests, and mountains, or had any part at all in the only

333

life he had ever loved. With the dog racing beside him Danny ran over the jutting nose of a mountain, trotted up a long valley, climbed the ridge at its head and descended the other side. He ran in almost a perfectly straight line through the beechwoods to his father's home. Ross Pickett would naturally be out scouting around the ridges on a fine day like this.

But his father's four hounds strained at the ends of their chains and bayed a vociferous welcome. Danny grinned at them and watched Red go up to sniff noses with Old Mike, leader of the hound pack. The three younger dogs sat on their haunches and awaited quizzically their boss's reaction to this dazzling, red-coated invader of their home. But the setter did not falter and Mike knew too much about other animals not to know when one was his superior. The two dogs wagged stiff tails, and Mike sat down to blink indifferently at Danny. Red was accepted.

Danny chuckled and tickled the old hound's tattered ears while the three pups begged for attention. Red sat back with his head cocked to one side and watched jealously. The boy stooped and unsnapped the chains. Wild to be free after a long day's confinement, the four hounds went in a mad race across the field. They came tearing back and were away again. Red raced with them, but wheeled and came back when Danny whistled. The boy tickled his silken ears.

"Leave 'em go," he said. "Leave 'em go, Red. They'll find an' tree somethin' an' Pappy'll get it when he comes in. But you got mo' impawtant work to do, Red. Youah a pat'tidge dog."

The setter walked beside him when Danny went into the house. Outside, everything had been warm sunshine. But inside, where only glancing sunbeams strayed through the single-paned windows that Ross Pickett had set in the walls of his shanty, a definite chill prevailed. Danny stuffed tinder into the stove, lighted it, and added wood when it was blazing. He pulled aside the burlap curtain that hung over the cupboard and took out a pot and skillet. Red trotted beside him when he went out to the springhouse for a piece of pork that Ross had left there to cool and returned to the house to lie in the center of the floor while Danny cooked the meat.

A little before sundown the setter got up and went to sit before the door. Three minutes later there was a heavy tread on the porch and Ross Pickett came in.

"Danny!" he exclaimed. "I knowed you was home on account I heer'd the haouns a 'bayin'. I whistled 'em in an' they come back wi' me. They had a little coon up, an' coons ain't prime yet."

"Hello, Pappy! It shuah is good to be home. You been scoutin' out a trap line?"

"Yup. Stoney Lonesome Ridge fo' foxes. Ought to be a nice take of pelts this yeah; they's lots of rabbits fo' pelt animals to eat off."

But the shine in Ross's eyes belied the workaday talk, and the warm glow inside Danny was far too intense ever to be put into words. He and his father had been so close for so long that they felt and acted and almost thought alike. Each was lost without the other, and now that they were together once more, they could be happy again.

Danny said with affected carelessness that could not hide the enormous pride he felt, "I fetched the Red dog home. Theah he is."

"Well, so you did!" Ross whirled about as though he had just noticed the magnificent setter. "That is a dog, Danny! I reckon you'n him must of cut some swath in Noo Yawk, huh?"

"Red did in the dog ring. He got some prizes fo' Mistah Haggin."

"How'd you like Noo Yawk, Danny?"

"Gosh, I dunno. It's nice but it's awful big. It's a right smart place for them that likes it, but I'd ruther abide in the Wintapi."

Ross Pickett was on the floor beside Red. His expert hands strayed over the dog's back, his legs, his withers, his chest. Danny waited breathlessly until his father finally rose.

"Danny," he said profoundly, "if that Red dog's got a nose, he's got evah'thin' any six dogs should have."

Danny's heart leaped. "He smelt you when you was still three minutes away."

"I should of knowed it," Ross breathed. "He run that big killah heah right into the groun'. Danny, that dog is goin' to be the best vahmint killah we evah had."

Danny turned away. All the joy of homecoming was suddenly gone, and a smothering hand came to still his singing heart. He should have known what his father would say. But until now it had never occurred to him that hunting to Ross meant hunting bears, wildcats, foxes, and raccoons. Every other kind of hunting was only to get meat. Danny gulped. Maybe he could explain but he felt before he started that his father wouldn't understand.

"I—I guess Red ain't goin' to be no vahmint dog."

"Huh! What use would you put such a dog to?"

"Well, he could hunt pat'tidges." Danny continued desperately, "Look, they's some things a man can do an' some he cain't. Makin' Red hunt vahmints would be like makin' one of Mistah Haggin's blooded hosses do a mule's work. It's right in Red's blood to be a pat'tidge dog."

"Oh! Maybe Mistah Haggin tol' you to make him hunt pat'tidges?"

"Mistah Haggin didn' say nothin'," Danny answered miserably. "I jus' know Red's a pat'tidge dog."

"How do you know it?"

Danny tried and failed to put into words some of the things he had learned on his brief visit to New York and in his association with Mr. Haggin. Always before he had accepted his father's notion that a dog was a dog, something to be bent to the will of its master. But that wasn't so. For thousands of years there had been special dogs for special functions—dachshunds for entering badger holes and subduing their occupants, greyhounds for coursing swift game, malemutes for sledge work, and only when you knew something of their blood lines could you really appreciate the fascinating story of dogdom. It was in Red's blood to hunt birds, and partridges were the only game birds in the Wintapi. Making him hunt anything else would verge on the criminal. But how to explain all this to his father?

"I jus' know it," Danny said miserably. "Red on'y hunted the beah on account he thought it was goin' to hurt me."

"Well—if that's the way you feel—" Ross's voice trailed off. He sat down stiffly and ate his supper. After eating, he helped wash the dishes and took his accustomed chair beside the stove. He ignored Red when the big setter tried to thrust his nose into his cupped hand and sensing the rebuff, Red went back to Danny. The boy sat moodily alone. Ross was deeply hurt. He wouldn't have been had his son been able to furnish a good reason why Red should be a partridge dog. But Danny himself knew of no reason save that the setter had been born to hunt partridges. And that sounded silly.

They went silently to bed.

The next morning when Danny got up Ross had already gone. He had taken one of the hounds with him.

But he hadn't asked Danny to go along.

Partridge season was not open yet, but it was legal to have dogs afield for training. Danny's heart was heavy within him while he ate a lonely breakfast. After eating he opened the door and a flood of the sparkling October sunshine came spilling in. Red rushed outside and went over to sniff noses with Mike. He came galloping back to Danny and reared to put both front paws on the boy's chest. Danny pulled his silky ears and stroked his smooth muzzle. If only his father were there to see Red as he saw him! Then the autumn and the sunshine worked their magic. It was enough to be afield with Red. Pappy would understand in time.

Crisp frost-curled leaves crackled underfoot when the pair entered the beechwoods. Red went racing among the trees as a gray squirrel stopped his busy digging for nuts and leaped to a tree trunk. But when Danny whistled he stopped, turned around and came trotting back. For a space he walked beside the boy. Then he leaped a few feet ahead and stopped in his tracks.

He stood with his body rigid and his tail stiff behind him. With a quick little rush he went a dozen feet and stopped again. Then, in a slow, steady stalk, he advanced a hundred feet and stopped on a knoll. He raised one forefoot, stiffened his body and tail.

Danny murmured very softly, "Easy. Easy theah, Red."

The dog trembled, but held his point. Danny leaned over and, as quietly as possible, brushed the leaves from a half-buried limb. He hurled it into the brush at which the setter was pointing and a lone partridge thundered up. The dog took three nervous steps forward, but halted at Danny's, "Back heah, Red."

Danny's knees were suddenly weak and he sat down. Red

came over with wagging tail and grinning tongue, and the boy
passed both arms about his neck. Starry-eyed he sat still, in his
mind living and reliving the scene he had just witnessed. It was a
thrill to hear hounds strike a trail, to listen to them baying their
quarry and their final frenzy when they cornered it. But this! The
hounds were good workmen, but the setter was an artist. And not
even Ross had suspected how keen his nose really was.

The early autumn twilight was just dimming out the day when
the pair arrived home. A light in the window told that Ross was
there before them. Danny opened the door and Red slid unobtru-
sively in to lie on the floor. Ross, who was standing over the
stove, turned and spoke briefly.

"Hi-ya."

"Hi-ya," Danny replied and busied himself setting the table.

From time to time he stole a furtive glance at Red, and once
looked with mute appeal at his father's back. But his eyes
squinted slightly and the same stubborn mouth that was his father's tightened in grim lines. Once more he looked at Ross's
back—and found the determination not to speak until his father
did melting away. He tried to make his voice casual.

"Wheah'd you go today, Pappy?"

"Out."

Danny flushed, and his face set in lines ten times more stubborn. Maybe his father thought he couldn't make a pat'tidge dog
out of Red. He'd show him! He'd prove such a dog was much
more valuable than a hound, and that setters were as practical as
hounds. Danny hesitated. Proving to Ross that a partridge dog
was worth the food he ate wasn't going to be any harder job than
moving Staver Plateau with a tin shovel!

After supper Danny sat by Red for a while, stroking his ears
and tickling his chin. But Ross ignored the dog completely. As
though he understood, the setter had nothing to do with him.

Partridge season and the first snow came together. Ross as usual
was up long before daylight and away on his trap line. When
Danny went out with his shotgun and Red he looked longingly at
the tracks in the snow. Always before he and his father had gone
trapping together. Resolutely he shouldered his gun and walked

in an opposite direction, toward the pine and hemlock thickets where the partridges would certainly be seeking a refuge from the storm.

They approached a thick growth of hemlock and Red ranged ahead. He came to a stiff point, and Danny edged up.

A partridge burst out of the hemlocks, showing itself for a split second between the branches, and Danny shot. A ruffled heap of brown feathers, the bird came down in the snow. Red hesitated, turned around to look at Danny as though asking for instructions.

The boy waved a hand forward. "Go on," he said. "Get him."

Red padded forward and stood uncertainly over the fallen partridge. He looked up, then back at the bird.

"Give it to me," Danny said gently.

The setter lowered his head to sniff the partridge and grasped it gently in his mouth. The boy took it in his hand. He threw it down in the snow and Red picked it up again.

They went on, and the setter pointed three more grouse. The last one Danny shot the dog picked up and brought back, though he went about it in an awkward fashion. His tail wagged furiously and his eyes glistened at the lavish praise that the feat called forth from his master. But four birds were the limit.

Danny arrived home first that night, and had supper ready when his father came in. Ross had no furs, as he had set his traps only that day, but he opened his hunting jacket and took out four partridges. He laid them on the table and turned silently away to remove his coat and wash his hands.

Danny's cheeks burned. His father had had no dog. And every one of the partridges had been shot through the head with the little .22 pistol he carried on his trap line.

By the last day of the season Danny knew that his hunch had been the correct one. Red was not only a partridge dog, but he was a great partridge dog, one in a million. He found the birds and pointed them so carefully that only the wildest ones flushed before the gunner could get in his shot. It had taken him only nine trips afield to learn perfectly the art of retrieving, regardless of how thick the brush or brambles in which the bird fell might

be. Red paid no attention to the rabbits that scooted before him
or the chattering squirrels that frisked through the trees. And
when he hunted, no scent save that of partridges drew the slightest interest. Now, on this last day of the season he and Danny
were going out for one last hunt.

Ross as usual had already gone, and a few flakes of snow
hovered in the air. Little wind stirred and the naked trees were
silent. But the blue-black horizon and the clouded sky foretold a
heavier storm to come. Danny went back into the shanty and
buttoned a woolen jacket over the wool hunting shirt he already
wore. He dropped half a dozen twelve-gauge shells into his
pocket.

"Goin' be weathah shuah 'nough," he murmured. "Wintah's
nigh heah, Red."

The hard little snowflakes rustled against the frozen leaves,
and it seemed to Danny that they were falling faster even before
he came to the edge of his father's field. But he forgot them then
because Red came to a point. Steady as a rock, he stopped just a
little way within the woods. Danny flushed the bird. It soared up
and out, dodging behind tree trunks and twisting about. But for
one split second it showed through the crotch of a big beech and
Danny shot. The bird dropped to the ground and Red brought
it in.

They went on deeper into the beechwoods where they had
found so many partridges before. But Red worked for an hour
before he pointed another, and that one flushed so wild that
Danny had no shot at it. It was noon before he killed a second
bird—and at the same time he awoke to the necessity of getting
back to the cabin before he had trouble finding it. The snow was
falling so fast now that the trees were only wavering shadows.
And there was a rising wind, which meant that the heavy snow
would be accompanied by a gale. Danny snapped his fingers.

"Heah, Red."

It was nearly dusk when they reached the cabin. Danny
opened the door, stamped the snow from his feet, and sank into a
chair. Red crouched full length on the floor, looking at the boy
from the corners of his eyes.

Danny cut thick slices from a ham and peeled a great potful of potatoes. His father would be hungry after bucking the storm, would want good things to eat and plenty of them. But the boy worked with deliberate slowness, trying in the accustomed routine of household chores to still the small worried voice that was rising in him. Pappy should have been home before this.

He went to a window and peered into the inky blackness outside. He fought back a rising panic; this was no time for a man to lose his head. He waited another ten minutes.

Then he made up a pack, a thermos of hot coffee, enough food for three days, a knife and ax, plenty of matches, and two woolen blankets. He put on his warmest coat, pulled a felt hat down over his eyes and took his snowshoes from their peg on the wall.

With a happy little whine and a furiously wagging tail, Red sprang up to join him. Danny looked at the setter. The dog could not be of any use. He would hunt only partridges, would pay no attention to Pappy's scent, even though they passed within ten feet of him. Danny shook his head.

"Reckon not, Red. This heah's one hunt I got to run alone. Not even the other dogs are trained for this."

Red flattened his ears and begged mutely. Danny looked away, and back again. The setter wouldn't help any, but he would be company and certainly he could do no harm.

"Aw ri'. Come on."

Red waited impatiently in the snow while Danny took a toboggan from its elevated platform, and when he started off on his snowshoes through the night the dog ran a little ahead. Danny watched him work carefully toward a briar patch and grinned wryly. The setter was still ashamed of his inability to locate more than two partridges, and he was trying to make up for it.

The snow was drifting down in great feathery flakes that dropped softly to earth. The wind had abated and it was not as cold as it had been. But if Pappy were helpless he could freeze. Danny put the thought from his mind and plodded grimly on. Lately he had scarcely spoken to his father, but he still knew where to look for him. Last night Ross had brought in two muskrats and a mink, pelts that could be trapped only along waterways. Therefore he must have run the traps in Brant Marsh and

along Elk River. Today he would cover his fox line on Stoney
Lonesome Ridge.

But even though he would search until he found his father
Danny was aware of the near hopelessness of his mission. If
Pappy were lying unconscious after having been caught in a slide
or struck down by a falling limb, the snow would cover him and
he might not be found until it melted. Danny admitted this. Nobody was too good at anything to guard against unforeseen accidents, not even a skilled woodsman like his father. It was just as
well to face possibilities as to close his eyes to them. He must be
ready for any emergency.

Red came trotting happily back and was away again. As
Danny dragged the toboggan up the long steep trail his father
took to Stoney Lonesome, he looked down at his feet. They
seemed barely to move. Yet he saw by a dead stub of a tree that
stood beside the trail and served as a landmark when they were
away from it, that in an hour he had come almost four miles.
That was fast travel in deep snow when a man had to drag a
toboggan.

It was too fast. A quarter of a mile farther on Danny stopped
to rest. He panted heavily, and perspiration streamed down his
face and back. He took the felt hat off and opened his jacket. Red
returned to stand anxiously beside him.

"If only I'd taught you to hunt men 'stead of pat'tidge,"
Danny half sobbed. "If only I had!"

He turned to go on. Pappy had to be somewhere, and he was as
likely to be near the trail as anywhere else. But if he wasn't, his
son would go to all the traps, and from them he would branch
out to scour every inch of Stoney Lonesome. Pappy just couldn't
die! Why there would be hardly anything worthwhile if it weren't
for his father. That foolish quarrel over Red. Danny should have
let him hunt varmints or anything else Pappy wanted. If only he
could talk to his father once more and tell him how sorry he was!

Danny stumbled and sprawled in the snow. He rose, annoyed
and grumbling. He had fallen over Red, who had come to a point
in the trail, headed off to the side.

"Go on!" Danny snapped.

Red took three uncertain steps forward beside the trail, then he stopped again. Danny rushed toward him, angry at the dog for the first time. He reached down to grasp his collar, but the toes of his snowshoes crossed and he stumbled sideways. His bare hands plunged deeply into the drifted snow. And they found something soft and yielding, something that gave before them. It was a man's trousered leg. Danny dug frantically and lifted Ross Pickett from his snowy bed. His hand went under his father's shirt.

His body was warm and his heart still beat.

Two days later, back at the cabin, Danny served his father two roasted partridges and a great heap of mashed potatoes. He propped him up on pillows and grinned when his patient began to wolf the food.

"Fo' a man as should of been daid, you shuah hungry," he observed. "How come you can eat so much?"

Ross grinned back. "Cain't kill an old he-bear like me." He tore off a great strip of breast meat and held it up in his fingers, saying, "Come heah an' have some vittles."

Red padded daintily across the floor, and his wagging tail thanked Ross for the offering. Danny's eyes shone, because the two things that he loved best now loved each other.

" 'Twas a mighty lot of foolishment to fight over the dog, wan't it? But even if I hadn't got ovah my mad an' like the mulehaid I am wan't waitin' fo' you to say somethin', I shuah would know what a pointin' dog is now. When the side of that ol' trail give way beneath me, I thought I was a cooked goose fo' certain. How come the dog foun' me, Son?"

Danny answered soberly. "Red foun' you on account he's got a better nose as any houn' dog."

It was the first time he had ever deceived his father—but it was more evasion than lie. Red was a partridge dog through and through. And when he had pointed there in the snow, he had pointed, not Ross, but the two partridges the trapper had shot and put in his pocket.

GOING FOR
THE DOCTOR

HAMLIN GARLAND

WISCONSIN IS ONE of the most picturesque of the Middle Western States. In the north, it is heavily timbered and full of game. Thirty years ago two-thirds of the state was a vast wilderness of pine forest, tamarack swamps and hardwood ridges undisturbed by the whistle of the engine or the steamboat.

Upward along the rivers the lumbermen were slowly pushing year by year, felling the great pines that stood near the water, and letting the sunlight into places where for ages it had not been.

One of the stories I have heard my father tell, relates the adventures of two loggers who were sent up early one fall to prepare the hay for a camp on the Chippeway River.

With an ox-team, a wagon, a sled, and a quantity of food and necessary tools, they pushed away from La Crosse up into the forest, cutting out the road where there was none, and taking advantage of all trails wherever possible.

Miller, the younger of the men, was a short, jolly man, and was called Chub, while Holland was a tall, sinewy young man, with keen gray eyes and curt of speech.

Their progress was slow; but passing at length the last camp—not yet occupied—they pushed on for a river bottom, nearly twenty-five miles beyond.

There they felled logs and made a sort of pen, into which they led the oxen. Then they gathered the branches into a great pile for a bed, and rolling up in their blankets near the fire fell asleep.

In the night, they heard a bear and her cubs eating acorns

nearby, but they did not allow such a little thing as that to disturb their rest.

In a few days they were busy at their haying. They worked hard, for it was late, and the hay was getting poorer each day, and the snow likely to come. Besides their haying, they had much to do in building a stable and preparing the camp.

The wolves began to come around the camp every night, and sniff and peer and howl among the shadows of the clearing, especially after Holland killed a deer and "slung it"—that is to say, bent down a sapling, and tying the carcass of the deer to it, let it swing back to place.

All went well, however, until the hay was cut and stacked, the barns built, and things made almost ready for the coming of the loggers.

There remained hardly a week's work when Miller fell violently ill one afternoon, with severe pains and vomiting, quite like the effects of poisoning.

It was about four o'clock in the afternoon when he was taken ill, and by nightfall he lay almost like a dead man, rousing only at intervals in paroxysms of agony.

All night long, while the wolves howled outside, Holland sat beside the bed of his friend, using every means in his power to ease the sufferer.

At last, just as the gray dawn was lighting the tops of the pines, and the wolves grew quiet, Holland rose with sudden resolution, and said to the sick man, whose eyes were on him: "Chub, old fellow, you're a sick man—you're an awful sick man. Now there's but one thing to do. I've got to lock you in here, and run down to Jinnytown. Doctor Adams, of La Crosse, is there hunting. Now, what do you say? Shall I go?"

Miller shook his head, and with a look that made his friend's heart stop beating for a moment, said, "I don't care."

Holland arose, pushed a chair near the bed, put a cup of water on it, and a plate of bread and meat. Then he went out, cut a pole just the right length, brought it back into the hut, and put one end of it against the side of the room. He took the butcher knife as a weapon, and said, "Now, good-by, old man. I've got forty-five miles to make today, but I'll do it. Don't worry about the wolves; when this stick falls into its place, all the wolves in Wisconsin can't break the shanty in. Good-by!"

Holland slipped out through the door, holding the brace with his left hand. He felt it slip down to the cleat—he withdrew his hand. It fell below the cleat. The sick man was safe from that quarter.

The sinewy young fellow settled his coat around his shoulders, put his knife into his pocket, and turned his face to call again from without, "Good-by! I'll be back soon!"

Then he plunged into the forest on his twenty-five mile run.

The dawn was gray and threatened snow, but the air was bracing and full of the odor of the pines.

In the shadows beside the trail, and stretching away under the interminable forests, a noiseless carpet of pine needles lay, brown and crisp, over which the wolf and deer ran soundless as shadows. Snow birds chattered in the air at times, and in the low places partridges flew up.

Holland ran with a peculiar gait learned from the Indians, a kind of lope that brought all the muscles into play, and was less tiresome than the regular running gait, and much faster than a walk.

Up hill and down, with unflagging pace, the young man pushed, his legs working like some machine of inexhaustible power. At the end of the first half hour he began to get his second wind, and pushed on at a swifter pace.

Two or three times he saw wolves slipping through the shadows of the wood on either hand, and heard a short, warning sentinel howl behind him answered far ahead. But Holland knew the habits of the wolves, and had no fear of being surrounded by them during the daylight.

Nevertheless, he was startled, as he rose from a spring where he had lain to drink, to find himself face to face with two great gaunt creatures squatted on their haunches and looking at him. It seemed so easy for them to spring on his back at any moment!

They snarled at the clubs he threw at them, and slipped into the thicket.

In making a sudden turn in the path, he came plump upon a

brown bear which was seated in the road, looking very much like a fire-blackened stump.

Holland gave a great shout, and charged down upon the surprised and scared animal; and it crashed into the bushes by the brook, like a huge pig. He could not help laughing at the comical look on the bear's face.

His anxiety for his friend, the twists and turns of the road, and his fatigue and painful breathing made the way seem endless. But at last signs of more travel began to appear. The wolves disappeared, and at about eleven o'clock he dashed into the clearing around the hotel, sawmill, and dozen houses that made Jinnytown.

All was silent; there was no one to be seen. In the barn some oxen were eating hay peacefully. Holland had forgotten that the day was Sunday!

He rushed up to the hotel where he had been before, and shouted, "Hello, Benson!"

The door opened as he came up, panting and dripping with sweat. A tall, grizzled, elderly man appeared.

"Where's the doctor?" Holland asked.

"Out in the woods somewhere. What's up? what's up?"

Holland explained the case. But there was not a man left in the camp except Benson, and not a horse. Mrs. Benson made coffee hastily, while the men talked.

No plan seemed worth considering. Holland made up his mind that the only thing to be done was for him to return. Benson was too old to make the trip on foot and did not know the way, and the snow was beginning to fall.

Holland leaped up. "Give me a revolver. Put up a little bundle of something to eat—a bottle of milk—not much; I can't carry much. And, Benson, the moment the boys come, you drive like lightning, and overtake me if you can. Dick Wood knows the trail. Bring the doctor, and take your rifles. There'll be a hundred wolves on top of that shanty."

It was noon when Holland started on his return run of twenty-five miles, back to the camp.

He saw that he must reach it before night. It was autumn, and night came early. With dark sky and threatening snow, it would come earlier than usual.

He could keep up his jog trot but an hour or two at the most, and the snow was likely to make the walking slow. Pushing on, not daring to think of giving out, he entered the forest, which began to roar now with the rising wind.

His chief fear was the terrible one that Miller might be dead before help reached him; that the wolves might force him, Holland, into a tree, to wait until the party came from Jinnytown—too late for succor.

A hope rose in his breast that the boys might return early because of the threatening snow. With these thoughts, and a vague comprehension of the awful presence of the wood and wind, he presently became conscious of a new terror—a pain in his chest and a numbness in his thighs.

Just after he fell into a walk, because of the unsupportable pain in his lungs, a wolf not far behind gave a peculiar note at the end of his howl. It went to the man's heart like a cold knife. The siege had begun!

Far ahead the call was answered. Another howl to the right was answered to the left. Shadowy forms crossed his trail, or stepped along in the shadows of the firs and tamaracks in the hollows.

The snow was only threatening. It had not covered the ground fairly, so that he pushed on with a dogged, swift walk, his revolver swinging in one hand, the bundle of food in the other.

This bundle troubled him. If he hung it over his shoulder, it seemed to hinder him, and in his hand it clogged him. At last he put the milk in his pocket, ate a little of the meat, and dropped the rest of the bundle in the road. He felt freer.

He reached a creek which he knew was just ten miles from his cabin. Night was beginning to fall.

The young man stopped, and hardly daring to lie down to drink, dipped a little water with his hand. Then he stood still to listen.

There was nothing—save the moaning snarl of the pines, the patter of stealthy feet in the covert of firs, and the call of a lone wild goose lost from its flock.

For the first time his heart failed him. He had made a run of forty miles over broken ground. He could run no more. The ground was getting white now, and while it helped him to see, it made the footing slippery. He walked on, his revolver in his hand. Thus far he had refrained from shouting, though the wolves showed themselves freely. Now he came on three, seated in the trail, refusing to move. He shouted at them hoarsely as he came up, but they only showed their teeth hideously.

Holland stopped, and taking good aim, fired at the largest of the group.

The animal bounded into the air without a sound, and disappeared with the rest.

Holland now remembered that in his hurry he had not asked Benson for cartridges. He wondered if the pistol had six charges left, but he did not stop to look. It was now too dark to see, and he staggered on, keeping the pistol ready. It was now snowing fast, and he wondered why the wolves did not close around him. Then the thought of the sick man came to his mind.

"They're besieging him! Well, so much the better; it will let me reach him," he reasoned.

Twice more he cleared his way with a shot from the revolver, only the pure white of the snow enabling him to see the snarling brutes that waylaid him. Once he looked behind, and saw a dim shadow creeping upon him noiselessly. He could not waste a shot, and he was forced to look behind him constantly.

A new fear tormented him now. He was so weak that he feared his ability to climb a tree if the worst came. He had but one hope, and that was to reach the cabin.

But how was he to get in? The door was barred, and would he not be too feeble and too much hurried to climb upon the roof and tear off a slab?

Suddenly, far ahead, he heard a rifle shot. The blood rushed to his heart, hot as a flame. Someone else was abroad in the forest!

It cleared his brain and warmed his whole body. The forest was not all the possession of night, the wolves, and the snow! A stalwart arm and resolute heart was behind that rifle shot.

The wild howling of the wolves and their angry, short yelps

told the practiced ear of the woodsman that the creatures had met their match somewhere.

Crack! sounded the rifle again. The wolves' turmoil ceased for a moment, but soon began again. Those dim gray forms which had followed the runner disappeared, attracted by the noise in front.

Holland kept on the trail, with set teeth and with his eyes peering into the darkness ahead. His thought was that some hunter had taken to a tree, and was firing upon his besiegers. He must reach him somehow.

Crack! went the rifle, so near at hand now that it almost seemed as if he could hear the bullet. Breaking into a feeble run, Holland tried to shout, "Keep it up! I'm coming!"

He rounded a point of bushes, and stood, stupefied with amazement, not knowing where he was.

Before him was a shanty. From chinks and crannies shone a dim light, and also from a hole in the roof. While he looked a savage, grizzled old wolf, reckless with hunger, leaped on the low roof, and with open mouth and lolling tongue glared down into the room.

Again the rifle cracked, and the brute rolled from the roof. Then a loud voice called, "Oh, come on! come on! I'm ready for you!"

It was Holland's own shanty, in which the hunter had taken refuge. With a joyous yell, he rushed down upon the camp, shouting, "I'm coming, Chub! I'm coming!"

The wolves, surprised at this new assault, retreated. As he rushed up to the door, Holland called, "Open the door! Open the door! It's me, Holland!"

He was answered by a sonorous shout within. There was a leap, and the door swung open. Holland, half-fainting, fell into the arms of a large, full-bearded man.

"Why, Doctor, is it you?" he gasped, as he sank into a seat.

"Yes, it's I," the doctor laughed, as he closed the door and braced it again.

"How's Chub?"

"He's easier. I always carry a little case of medicines with me. He'll pull through."

"How did you come here?"

"Oh, I thought I'd make you a little visit. I started this morning, and got here about dark. Now sit right down by the fire, Holland. I've got some venison broiling there—that's one thing that brought these wolves."

As he looked up at the hole in the roof, he said, "I had to rip off a slab to get in. I saw there must be something wrong, and I found Miller pretty low. But he's better now. He's dozing. But you see, I couldn't sleep myself—too many wolves on the roof!"

Chub stirred in his bunk. "That you, Hank?" he said, feebly.

"It's me, Chub—what there is left of me. How are you now?"

"Oh, I'm all right. But I was afraid the wolves'd down you, sure."

The stalwart doctor clambered out upon the roof and fixed the slab in place, while Holland stood, revolver in hand, to keep the beasts at bay. Then they went back and built up a rousing fire.

"The boys are likely to come in on us at any minute," said Holland.

It was very pleasant to smell the meat cooking, and see the doctor moving about the fire, making coffee and gruel. Sitting thus, the shriek of the wind and the gleaming eyes of the wolves, sullenly squatting in the snow at the edge of the clearing, had no terrors.

When Holland had eaten, he fell fast asleep against his bunk.

"There's a man!" said the doctor, as he rolled him into his blanket. "Fifty miles today! Talk about your heroes of chivalry! They couldn't come up to that."

About midnight the relief from Jinnytown came, shouting and shooting through the snow and darkness, making a lark of it all, while the wolves slunk away into the forest. The next day the sick man was moved down to Jinnytown.

To this day Holland's breath comes quick as he tells of that long day's run, and the terror of that stormy night.

THE
FIRE KILLER

STEVE FRAZEE

YOUNG BILL ORAHOOD, the Sky Hook owner, was waiting for Ken Baylor where the trail forked near the fall-dry bed of Little Teton Creek. Orahood was mostly arms and legs and a long neck. Without a word he swung his chunky sorrel in beside Baylor and they rode toward Crowheart.

They went a quarter of a mile before Orahood blurted out the question that everyone in the Crowheart country was asking: "What do you suppose got Paxton?"

Baylor shook his head. Maybe Doc Raven knew by now. Raven had not been in town late yesterday afternoon when a drifting rider brought Bill Paxton's body out of Big Ghost Basin.

"You saw Paxton?" Orahood asked. "After—"

"Yeah." It was something to forget, if a man could.

A mile from town they caught up with big Arn Kullhem. A wide chunk of a man, his flat jaw bristling with sandy stubble, Kullhem looked at them from deepset eyes and did not even grunt when they spoke. His Double K lay right on the break into Big Ghost. More than any rancher, he had suffered from what was happening down in the basin.

Bridle bits and saddle leather and hooves against the autumn-crisp grass made the only sounds around them until they came to the top of the last rolling hill above Crowheart. Then Kullhem said, "Doc Raven didn't give us no help on them first two."

Bill Paxton was the third man to die in Big Ghost. First, an unknown rider, and then Perry Franks, Kullhem's foreman. Both

Franks and Paxton, one of the twins of Crow Tracks, had staked out in the basin to get a line on the shadowy men who were wrecking the Crowheart ranchers. If they had died from bullets, Baylor thought, the situation would be clear enough.

"Who's going to stay down in the basin now?" Kullhem growled.

Orahood and Baylor looked at each other. Strain had been building higher on Orahood's blistered face the closer they rode to town. He and Baylor glanced over their shoulders at the hazed ridges that marked the break above the gloomy forests of Big Ghost.

Up here the grass was good, but when the creeks ran low, cattle went over the break to the timber and the swamps in the basin—and then they disappeared. Big Ghost was an Indian reservation, without an Indian on it. Fearful spirits, the ghosts of mutilated dead from an ancient battle with Teton Sioux, walked the dark forests of the basin, the Shoshones said. Even bronco Indians stayed clear of Big Ghost.

The cowmen had no rights in the basin; they had been warned repeatedly about trespassing on Indian land, but their cattle were unimpressed by governmental orders. That made the basin a wealthy raiding ground for rustlers from the west prairies, who came through the Wall in perfectly timed swoops.

For a time the Crowheart ranchers had checked the raids by leaving a man in Big Ghost as lookout. Franks, then Bill Paxton. Baylor knew there was not a man left up here who would volunteer to be the third lookout in Big Ghost—not unless Doc Raven could say what it was a man had to face down there.

They crossed Miller Creek, just west of town. A man on a long-legged blue roan was riding out to meet them. Baylor looked up the street at a small group of men in front of Raven's office, and then across the street at a larger group on the shaded porch of the Shoshone Saloon.

Kullhem spat. "You still say, Baylor, that Baldray ain't behind all this hell?"

"I do." Jim Baldray, the Englishman, owned the I.O.T. His range was fenced all along the break, with permanent camps where the wire winged out. Baldray had the money to keep his wire in place. I.O.T. stuff did not drift down into Big Ghost. There was nothing against the Englishman, Baylor thought, except a sort of jealous resentment that edged toward suspicion.

"You and your brother-in-law don't agree, then," Kullhem said harshly.

Pierce Paxton, the twin brother of the man now lying on Raven's table, was not Baylor's brother-in-law yet, but he would be in another month.

Hap Crosby met them at the lower end of the street. He was the oldest rancher in the country. Sweat was streaking down from his thick, gray sideburns. He looked at Baylor. "Baldray's here. Pierce wants to question him—if Raven don't have the answer."

All the Paxtons had been savagely impatient when anger was on them. Pierce, the last one, would ask questions, answer them himself, then go for his pistol. Baldray would be forced to kill him. Pistol work was the first custom of the country the Englishman had learned; and he had mastered it.

"All right, Hap." Baylor looked up the street again. He saw it now. He should have seen it before: the tension there on the Shoshone porch was as tangible as the feel of the hot sun.

"Did Doc—has he—" Orahood asked.

"No, not yet," Crosby said curtly. "Baldray's drinking with that drifter who brought Bill Paxton in."

"Does that mean anything?" Baylor asked evenly.

"I didn't say so, did I?" Crosby answered.

Four other ranchers were waiting with Pierce Paxton at the hitch rail in front of Raven's office. Paxton did not look around. Sharp-featured, tense, his black hat pushed back on thick, brown, curly hair, he kept staring at the doorway of the Shoshone. He was wound up, dangerous. He was fixing to get himself buried with his brother that afternoon, Baylor thought.

Slowly, sullenly, Arn Kullhem said, "By God, I think he's right."

"How far would you go to back that?" Baylor asked. "Across the street?"

Kullhem's deepset eyes did not waver. "I wonder sometimes just where you stand in this thing, Baylor."

Old Crosby's features turned fighting-bleak and his voice ran hard with authority when he said, "Shut up, the both of you! We got trouble enough."

It was the slamming of Doc Raven's back door, and then the whining of his well sheave that broke the scene and gave both Baylor and Kullhem a chance to look away from each other.

The ranchers stood there in the hot strike of the sun, listening to the doctor washing his hands. Orahood's spittle clung to his lips, and a grayness began to underlay his blisters. A few of the loafers from the Shoshone porch started across the street.

Doc Raven came around the corner of his building, wiping his hands on his shirt. He was a brisk, little, gray-haired man who had come to the country to retire from medicine and study geology.

"Well?" Kullhem rumbled, even before Raven reached the group.

Raven shook his head. His eyes were quick, sharp; his skin thinly laid and pink, as if it never required shaving. "He was smashed by at least a dozen blows, any one of which would have caused death. His clothing was literally knocked from him, not ripped off. I can't even guess what did it."

The sweat on Crosby's cheeks had coursed down through dust and was hanging in little drops on the side of his jaw. "Maybe a grizzly, Doc?"

Raven took a corncob pipe from his pocket. He nodded. "A silver bear would have the power, yes. But there isn't so much as a puncture or a claw mark on Paxton."

"No bear then," Orahood muttered.

Raven scratched a match on the hitch rail. "It's like those other two cases. I don't know what killed any of them."

With one eye on Pierce Paxton, Baylor asked, "Could it be he was thrown from a cliff first, then—"

"No," Raven said. "Those granite cliffs would have left rock particles ground into the clothes and flesh."

Pierce Paxton had turned his head to watch the doctor. Now he started across the street. Baylor caught his arm and stopped him.

"No, Pierce. You're off on the wrong foot."

Paxton's face was like a wedge. "The hell! How much of *your* stuff was in Baldray's holding corral that time?"

Baylor said, "You know his men had pushed that stuff out of the wire angle. There was a man on his way to Crow Tracks to tell you when you and Bill happened by the I.O.T."

"That's right, Pierce," Crosby said.

"Say it was, then." Paxton's lips were thin against his teeth. "I want to ask Baldray how it happens he can ride Big Ghost, camp out there whenever he pleases, and ride out again, but Franks and my brother—"

"I ride it, too," Raven said.

Paxton backed a step away from Baylor. "They know damned well, Doc, that you're just looking for rocks!"

"Who are *they?*" Kullhem asked.

"That's what I'm going to ask Baldray." Paxton knocked Baylor's hand away and started across the street. One of the loafers had already scurried inside. Baylor walked beside Paxton, talking in a low voice. The words did no good, and then Baldray was standing in the doorway, squinting.

The I.O.T. owner was a long, lean man, without much chin. He wore no hat. His squint bunched little ridges of tanned flesh around his eyes and made him appear nearsighted, almost simple. The last two to make an error about that expression had been drifting toughs, who jeered Baldray as a foreigner until they finally got a fight out of him. It had lasted two shots, both Baldray's.

Baldray blinked rapidly. "Not you also, Baylor?"

Paxton stopped, set himself. The Englishman stepped clear of the doorway.

"Baldray—" Paxton said.

Baylor's rope-scarred right hand hit Paxton under the ear. The blow landed him on his side in the dust. Crosby and Doc Raven came running.

"Give a hand here!" Raven said crisply. Two of them stepped out to help carry Paxton away.

"The hotel," Crosby said. He looked back at Baylor. "I can handle him now."

Baldray smiled uncertainly. "Come have a drink, men!"

Across the street, the little knot of ranchers stared silently. Then Kullhem swung up, and said something to the others in a low voice. Orahood was the last. Baylor went into the Shoshone.

The gloom of the big room reminded him of the silent, waiting forests of Big Ghost. He stood at the bar beside Baldray, who was half a head taller. Kreider, who had found Bill Paxton at the edge of the timber in Battleground Park, took his drink with him toward a table. A man in his middle twenties, Baylor guessed. The rough black beard made him appear older. Just a drifting rider?

Baldray poured the drinks. "Hard business, Baylor, a moment ago. I would have been forced to shoot him."

"Yeah." Baylor took his drink.

"Raven found nothing?"

"Nothing—just like the two others. What do you make of it, Baldray?"

The Englishman's horsy face was thoughtful. He smoothed the silky strands of his pale hair. "A beast. It *must* be an animal of some kind. As a young man in Africa I saw things you would not believe, Baylor; but I still contend there must have been credible explanations. . . . And yet there are strange things that are never explained, and they leave you wondering forever."

There was a hollow chord in Baldray's voice, and it left a chill on Baylor's spine when he thought of Big Ghost and of the way Bill Paxton had been smashed.

"The rustlers always did steal in and out of the basin, of course," Baldray said. "They nearly ruined me before I fenced the break and hired a big crew. You fellows made it nip-and-tuck by keeping a scout down there, but now with this thing getting your men. . . ." Baldray poured another drink.

The "thing" rammed hard at Baylor's mind.

"Isn't it sort of strange that this animal gets just our men, Baldray? After this last deal we won't be able to find a rider with guts enough to stay overnight in the basin. That means we'll be cleaned out properly."

Baldray nodded. "It does appear that this thing is working for the rustlers—or being used by them, perhaps. The solution, of course, is to have Big Ghost declared public domain."

"Fifty years from now."

"It's possible sooner, perhaps." Baldray's face took on a deeper color. "Fence. I'll lend what's needed for thirty miles. Damn it, Baylor, we're all neighbors."

He had made the offer before and Kullhem had growled it down in rancher's meeting. Fencing was not all the answer for the little owners. It was all right for I.O.T. because Baldray could afford a big crew, and because the cattle of other ranchers were drifting into the basin. Shut all the drifting over the breakoff, and then the rustlers would be cutting wire by night. The smaller ranchers could not hire men enough to stop that practice.

Baylor looked glumly at his glass. The immediate answer to the problem was to go into Big Ghost and find out what was making it impossible to keep a lookout there. He walked across to Kreider.

"Would you ride down with me to where you found Bill Paxton?"

No man could simulate the unease that stirred on Kreider's dark face. "You figure to come out before dark?"

"Why?"

"You could tell that this Paxton had been in his blankets when he got it. He shot his pistol empty before. . . ." Kreider took his drink quickly. "No, I don't guess I want to go down into the basin, even in daylight—not for a while." He looked at Baldray. "You don't run stuff down there, do you, Mr. Baldray?"

Baldray shook his head.

So the Englishman had hired this man, Baylor thought. There was nothing unusual about that, but yet it left an uneasy movement in Baylor's mind. "You're afraid to go down there, huh?" he asked.

Kreider stared into space. "Uh-huh," he said. "Right now I am." He was still looking at something in his own mind when Baylor went out.

She was young, with red-gold hair and an eye-catching fullness in the right places. She could ride like a demon and sometimes she cursed like one. Ken Baylor looked at his sister across the supper table at Hitchrack, and then he slammed his fist hard against the wood.

"Sherry!" he said, "I'll paddle your pants like Pop used to if you ever even think about riding down there again!"

"Can it. Your face might freeze like that."

Baylor leaned back in his chair, glowering. After a few moments he asked, "Where was this moccasin track?"

"By a rotted log, just south of where Bill Paxton had camped."

No Indian. Raven sometimes wore moccasins.

"There was a mound of earth where Bill's fire had been. Smoothed out."

Kreider had mentioned the mound, but not the smoothness. "At least, that puts a man into it," Baylor said.

Sherry gave him a quick, narrow look. "You felt it?"

"Felt what?"

"A feeling that something is waiting down there, that maybe those Shoshone yarns are not so silly after all." She hurried on. "Sure, I know whatever it is must be related in some way to the rustling, but just the same. . . ."

After a long silence she spoke again. "No one would go with you, huh?"

"Orahood. Just to prove that he wasn't scared."

After he left Crowheart that morning Baylor had found the ranchers meeting at Kullhem's. If it had not been for Crosby, they would not have invited him to get down; and even then, desperate, on the edge of ruin, they had been suspicious, both of Baylor and each other.

"Old Hap Crosby wasn't afraid, was he?" Sherry asked.

"No. But he wasn't sure that getting this thing would cure the rustling. He favored more pressure on the Territorial representatives to have Big Ghost thrown out as reservation land. Then we could camp down there in force."

The others had ideas of their own, but threaded through all the talk had been the green rot of distrust—and fear of Big Ghost Basin. Baylor told Sherry about it.

"Damned idiots!" she said. "In their hearts they know that

Baldray—or no other rancher up here—is mixed in with the rustlers!"

Baylor hoped it was that way. He got up to help with the dishes, stalling to the last. They heard Gary Owen, one of Hitchrack's three hands, come in from riding the break.

"Take *him,*" Sherry said. "He's not afraid of the devil himself."

Baylor nodded.

"I'm going to Crowheart," Sherry said. "If Pierce still wants trouble with Baldray, it will start in town—except that I'll see it doesn't start." She rode away a little later, calling back, "So long, Bat-Ears. Be careful down there."

Owen's brown face tightened when he heard the "down there." He was standing at the corral with Baylor. "You headed into the Ghost?" he asked.

"Tonight."

"Saw two men on the Snake Hip Trail today, a long ways off." Owen removed his dun Scotch cap, replaced it. He lit a short-stemmed pipe. "Want me to go along?" He forced it out.

Baylor tried to be casual. "One man will do better, Gary."

"Say so, and I'll go!"

Baylor shook his head. They could not smooth it out with talk.

Three times the ranchers had gone over the escarpment in daylight, ready for full-scale battle. On the second try they had found horse tracks leading away from cattle bunched for a drive through the West Wall. Crosby claimed the rustlers had a man in the basin at all times, watching the break. Baylor thought so, too. But the idea had been lost in the general distrust of each other after the third failure.

Baylor was not thinking of men as the neck of the dun sloped away from him on this night descent in the huge puddle of waiting blackness. The night and Big Ghost were working on him long before he reached the first stream in the basin.

He stopped, listening. The tiny fingers of elementary fear began to test for climbing holds along the crevices of Baylor's brain. He swung in the saddle, and when he put his pistol away he told himself that he was a fool.

Shroud moss hanging across the trail touched his face. He tore at it savagely in the instant before he gained control. He came from the trees into the first park. War Dance Creek was running on his right, sullenly, without splash or leap.

All the streams down here were like that. Imagination, Baylor argued. He had come over the break unseen. The moss proved he was the first one down the trail in some time. *The first rider, maybe. What is behind you now?* Before he could stop himself, he whirled so quickly he startled the dun.

Back there was blackness, utter quiet. He strained to see, and his imagination prodded him. There was cold sweat on his face. He cursed himself for cowardice.

Where the trail crossed the creek, he would turn into dense timber and stake out for the night. He was here, safe. There was nothing he could do tonight. In the morning. . . .

It was night when the Thing got Paxton. . . .

The dun's right forefoot made a sucking sound. The animal stumbled. There was no quick jar of the saddle under Baylor, and he knew, even as he kicked free and jumped, that the stumble had been nothing, that the horse had bent its knee to recover balance before he was clear of leather.

Baylor stood in the wet grass, shaken by the realization of how deeply wound with fear he was. The dun nosed him questioningly. He patted the trim, warm neck and mounted again. If there were anything behind him, the dun would be uneasy.

". . . *there are strange things that will never be explained, Baylor.* . . ." Baldray had said that in the Shoshone, and now Baylor was sure he had not been mocking him or trying to plant an idea.

Baylor spent the night sitting against a tree, with his blankets draped around him. The dun was tied on the other side of the tree. Baylor's carbine was close at hand, lying on the sheepskin of the saddle skirts. The carbine was too small of caliber, Baylor thought, too small for what he was looking for. What *was* he looking for?

Out of the dead silence, from the ancient, waiting forest, came another chilling question. *What is looking for you, Baylor?*

The night walked slowly, on cold feet. It passed at last. Baylor rose stiffly. He ate roast beef from his sack, and finished with a cold boiled potato. Raven was the only other man he knew who liked a cold spud. Raven had come to the Crowheart country just about the time cattle rustling began in earnest, after a long period of inactivity.

The nameless fears that had passed were now replaced with the suspicions of the conscious mind.

Early sunlight was killing dew when Baylor rode into Battleground Park. He picked up the tracks of Sherry's little mare, coming into the park from the Snake Hip Trail. Owen had seen two riders on the Snake Hip the day before, but there was no sign that they had come this far. He followed Sherry's trail straight to where Paxton had been killed.

Baylor studied the earth mound over the fire site. It was too smooth, and so was the torn ground around it; and yet, the earth scars still spoke of power and fury and compulsion. An ant hill made a bare spot in the grass not fifteen feet away. Paxton would have used that. Because of the nature of his business here he would have had it figured in advance.

Baylor picked up a tip cluster of pine needles. He stared at the spruces. Their lower branches were withered, but here was broken freshness from high above. He went slowly among the trees close to the fire site. Here and there Paxton had broken dead limbs for his fire, but there was no evidence that anything had come down from the high branches.

He tossed the tip cluster away and went south of the camp to the rich, brown mark of a rotted log. There were Sherry's tracks again, but no moccasin print.

Out in the grass the dun whirled up-trail. Baylor drew his pistol and stepped behind a tree. A little later Baldray, wearing a fringed buckskin shirt, rode into the park with Doc Raven.

"We knew your horse," Raven said. He was wearing Shoshone moccasins, Baylor observed.

Baldray's face turned bone-bleak when he saw a jumper fragment on a bush. "Oh! This is the place, eh?" He swung down easily. "Let's have a look, Raven."

The doctor moved briskly. "The devil!" he muttered. "See how the fire has been covered." His smooth, pink face was puzzled. He picked up the piece of jumper. "Good Lord!"

Baldray's heel struck the tip cluster of pine needles and punched them into the soft earth. "Did you discover anything, Baylor?"

"Nothing." Baylor shook his head. Raven's saddlebags appeared to be already filled with rocks. Gary Owen said the doctor started at the escarpment and tried to haul half the country with him every time he went out. "You fellows came down the Snake Hip?"

Raven was studying tree burls. "We started in yesterday," he said, "but I had forgotten a manual I needed, so we rode out last evening." He looked at Baldray. "You know, James, in the big burn along the cliffs I've seen jackpine seeds completely embedded in the trunks. I have a theory—"

"Rocks, this time," Baldray said. "If you want to look at that quartz on the West Wall before night you'd better forget the tree seeds." He blinked. "Tree seeds? Now isn't that odd?"

When the two men rode west, Baylor stared at their backs, not knowing just what he thought.

Baylor spent the day working the edges of the swamps along lower War Dance. Cattle were wallowing everywhere. He was nagged by not knowing what he was looking for; he had expected to find some sign where Paxton had been killed, at least the moccasin track.

At sunset he came out in the big burn. Several years before, Indians had thrown firebrands from the cliffs to start a fire to drive game from the basin. The wind had veered, and the fire, instead of crowning across the basin, had roared along the cliffs in a mile-wide swath. That cured the Indians. Evil spirits, they said, had blown a mighty breath to change the wind.

With the bare cliffs at his back, Baylor looked across the spear points of the trees. The parks were green islands, the largest being Battleground Park, where Paxton had died. The Wall was far to his right, a red granite barrier that appeared impassable; but there were breaks in it, he knew, the holes where Crowheart cattle seeped away.

About a half-mile air-line a gray horse came to the edge of one of the emerald parks. Bill Paxton had ridden a gray into Big Ghost. Kreider had brought out only the rig.

Once down in the timber, it took an hour of steady searching before Baylor found the right park. The limping gray knee-high in grass was Paxton's horse, all right. It saw Baylor when he led the dun from the timber. It snorted and broke like a wild animal for cover. There was never a chance to catch it.

Baylor recoiled his rope, listening to the gray crashing away like a frightened elk. The horse had not been here long enough to go mustang. The terror of the night the Thing had got Bill Paxton was riding on the gray.

Night was coming now. Gloom was crouched among the trees. The little golden sounds of day were dead. *You are afraid, Big Ghost said. You will be like Paxton's horse if you stay here.*

Baylor went through a neck of timber between parks. In the dying light on lower War Dance he cut his own trail of the morning. Beside the dun's tracks, in the middle of a mud bar, he saw a round imprint. He hung low in the saddle to look. A man wearing moccasins had been on his trail. Here the man had leaped halfway across the mud bar, putting down only the toes and the ball of one foot to gain purchase for another jump to where the grass left no mark. The foot had slid a trifle forward when it struck, and so there was no way to estimate how large—or small —it had been.

Baylor was relieved. He could deal with a man, even one who used Indian tricks like that. If this fellow wanted to play hide-and-seek, Baylor would take him on—and catch him in the end, and find out why the man had erased the track that Sherry had seen.

Dog-tired, he made a cold camp far enough from War Dance so that the muttering water would not cover close sounds. He freed the dun to graze, ate a cold meal, and rolled up in his blankets. A wind ran through the timber.

Baylor rolled a smoke, and then he crumpled it. The scent of tobacco smoke would drift a long way to guide a man creeping in.

No man killed Paxton or the others.

Baylor lay wide awake, straining at the darkness, for a long time, until finally he slept from sheer exhaustion.

The morning sun was a wondrous friend. Baylor slopped the icy water of the stream against his face. The dun came from the wet grass and greeted him.

He rode south, then swung toward the Wall, crossing parks he had never seen before. He took it slowly, not watching his back-trail. In the middle of the day, after crossing a park just like a dozen others, he dismounted in the timber and crept back to make a test.

For an hour he waited behind a windfall. The first sound came, the breaking of a stick on the other side of the tiny green spot. Baylor had been half dozing by then. Too easy, he thought; something was wrong. He heard hooves on the needle mat.

He had expected a man on foot. He crawled away and ran back to the dun, placing one hand on its nose, ready for the gentle pressure that would prevent a whinny. A little later he heard sounds off to his left. The man was going around, sticking to the timber. Slowly Baylor led his horse to intercept the sounds. The other man came slowly also, and then Baylor caught the movement of a sorrel, saw an outline of its rider.

He dropped the reins then and went in as quickly as he could. He made noise. The dun whinnied. The other rider hit the ground. A carbine blasted, funneling pulp from a tree ahead of Baylor. He shot toward the sound with his pistol. The sorrel reared, then bolted straight ahead.

It flashed across a relatively open spot. It was Pierce Paxton's stallion. "Oh, God!" Baylor muttered. "Pierce."

"Pierce!" he yelled.

There was silence before the answer came. "Baylor?" It was Pierce Paxton. He was unshaven, red-eyed.

He said, "Who the hell did you think you were trying to take!"

Baylor put his pistol away. "Moccasin Joe. Who were you shooting at?"

"Anybody that tried to close in on me like that!" Tenseness was still laid flat on Paxton's thin features. "Who's Moccasin Joe?"

Baylor told everything he knew about the man.

Paxton shook his head, staring around him at the trees. "It's not Raven. I've been watching him and Baldray from the time they went across Agate Park."

"Why?"

Paxton stared. "You know why." He rubbed his hand across his eyes. "I think maybe I was wrong. We lost two men down here, Baylor, but Baldray and Raven never had any trouble. Now I know why. They got a cabin hidden in the rocks near the Wall. They don't stay out in the open." Paxton saw the quick suspicion on Baylor's face.

"Uh-huh, I thought so too, at first, Ken. I thought they knew what's loose down here, that they were hooked up with the rustlers. I watched them for a day and a half. All they did was pound quartz rock and laugh like two kids. They may be crazy, Baylor, but I don't think they're hooked up with the rustlers."

Paxton rubbed his eyes again. "Made a fool of myself the other day, didn't I? What did Sherry say?"

"Nothing much. We both made fools of ourselves a minute ago, Pierce. . . . Let's catch your horse."

The stallion had stopped in the next park west. Paxton went in and towed the horse back on the run. It saw the dun and tried to break over to start trouble. Paxton sawed down brutally on the bit before he got the horse quieted. That was not like Paxton. The nights down here had worked on his nerves, too.

They went back in the timber and sprawled out. Paxton lay with his hands over his face.

"How you fixed for grub?" Baylor asked.

"Ran out yesterday." Paxton heard Baylor rustling in his gunny sack. "I'm not hungry." But he finally ate, and he kept looking sidewise at Baylor until he asked, "You've been here two nights?"

"Yeah."

"Any trouble?"

"Scared myself some," Baylor said. "Did you?"

"I didn't have to. Since the first night I spent here I've been jumping three feet every time a squirrel cut loose. I had a little fire on Hellion Creek that night, with a couple of hatfuls of wet sand, just in case."

Paxton had started with a defensive edge to his voice, but now it was gone and his bloodshot eyes were tight. "The stallion just naturally raised hell. He got snarled up on his picket rope and almost paunched himself on a snag. I got him out of that and then I doused the fire.

"From the way the horse moved and pointed, I knew something was prowling. It went all around the camp, and once I heard it brush a tree."

The hackles on Baylor's neck were up.

"You know how a lion will do that," Paxton said. He shook his head. "No lion. The next morning, in some fresh dirt where a squirrel had been digging under a tree, I saw a track"—Paxton put his hands side by side— "like that, Ken. No pads—just a big mess!" Paxton's hands were shaking.

"What was it, Baylor? The Thing that got Bill?"

The Thing. What else could a man call it? Baylor thought. He said, "There's an explanation to everything."

"Explain it then!"

"Take it easy, Pierce. We'll get it."

The thought of action always helped steady Paxton. "How?" he asked.

"First, we get this Moccasin Joe." Baylor thought of something so clear he wondered how he had missed it. "Did you stop in Battleground Park?"

"I didn't come down the Snake Hip."

"Old Moccasin Joe has trailed me once, and now I think I know why." The thought carried a chill. "Here's what we'll do, Paxton. . . ."

Later, Baylor divided the food. It would be parched corn now, and jerky, about enough for two days, if a man did not care how hungry he got. "Day after tomorrow," Baylor said.

They rode away in different directions, Baylor going back to Battleground Park. He found the tip-cluster that Baldray had stepped on, and dug it out of the earth and held it only a moment before dropping it again. Pine needles. Everything here was spruce. The fact had not registered the first time.

That tip cluster had come from a branch that Moccasin Joe had used to brush out sign. Probably he had carried the branch from across the creek. Moccasin Joe knew what the Thing was. He was covering up for it.

The dun whinnied. Baldray was riding into the lower end of the park. He veered over when he say Baylor's horse.

"You haven't moved!" Baldray grinned to show he was joking. He was clean-shaven. He appeared rested, calm. That came easier when a man slept in a cabin and ate his fill, Baylor thought.

"You look done in," Baldray said.

"I'm all right."

Baldray squinted at the fringes of his beaded shirt. His face began to redden. "It's no good sleeping out. Bumps and things, you know. I have a cabin near the Wall. Built it four years ago. Raven's there now. I wish you'd use it, Baylor. I'll tell you how to find it."

Paxton had taken care of that. "I know," Baylor said.

Baldray blinked. "Oh!" He raised pale brows. "Well, yes, I've been a little selfish. Reservation land, so-called. If the fact got around that someone had built here—"

Baylor picked up the tip cluster. "What kind of tree is that from?"

Baldray squinted. "Evergreen."

"Spruce or pine?"

The Englishman laughed. "You and Raven! I know evergreen from canoe birch, but that's about all."

Baldray was one Englishman who had not run for home after the big die-ups of the no-chinook years. He should know pine needles from spruce; but maybe he did not.

Baldray's face was stone-serious when he asked, "Any luck?"

Baylor shook his head.

"There are harsh thoughts about me." Baldray's voice was crisp. "Fifteen years here and I'm still not quite a resident, except with you and Crosby." Baldray looked around the park. "This won't be reservation always. Room for I.O.T. down here, as well as the rest—once the rustlers are dealt with, and the government sees the light."

Baldray slouched in the saddle, rolling a cigarette. "I have watched the breaks in the Wall from the rocks near my cabin. There is a sort of pattern to the way the scoundrels come and go.

I would say, Baylor—it is a guess, but I would say—the next raid might be due to go out through Windy Trail."

His smoke rolled and lit, Baldray started away. "Windy Trail. I'm going to tell Crosby, some of the others. Good name, Crosby. English, you know."

He rode away.

It was not entirely hunger that made Baylor's stomach tighten as he rode across the burn the next afternoon. Like the others, the night before had been a bad one, with his mind and the deep, still forests speaking to him. He did not know now whether or not he was being trailed, but he had played the game all the way, and if Paxton had done his part, things might come off as planned.

Paxton was there, crouched in the rocks near the east side of the burn. They exchanged clothes behind the jumble of fire-chipped stone.

"I went out," Paxton said. "Sherry wants to see you tomorrow morning in Battleground Park."

"Why didn't you talk her out of it?"

"You know better." Paxton was stuffing paper under the sweatband of Baylor's hat.

"What does she want?"

"I don't know. She told me to go to hell when I ordered her not to come down here. Then she rode over to I.O.T. to see Baldray. I left a note in the bunkhouse for Gary Owen to come here with her."

They were dressed.

"Keep in plain sight on the burn," Baylor said. "And keep going."

"All right." Paxton took the reins. "Kullhem found out that Kreider was riding with the rustlers on the west prairie two weeks ago."

"Fine. Just right. Get going."

He watched Paxton ride away, past the black snags and leaning trees. The dun had gone into the rocks and the dun had gone out a few minutes later, and the rider was dressed exactly as he had been when going in. It might work, if Moccasin Joe was still trailing with his little pine-branch broom. The dirty bastard.

The sun died behind the red Wall. A wind came down across the rocks and stirred the tiny jackpines in the burn. Murk crept into basin.

The man came from sparse timber at the east edge of the burn. Buckskins. Probably moccasins. Long yellow hair under a slouch hat. He paused and looked up where the dun had disappeared two hours before.

Baylor watched from a crack between the rocks. The man came clear, lifting his body easily over fallen trees. He walked straight at the rocks, then swung a little to the uphill side. Baylor drew his pistol and took a position behind a rock where the man would likely pass.

The steps were close, just around the rock. They stopped. With his stomach sucked in, breathing through a wide-open mouth, Baylor waited to fit the next soft scrape to the man's position. Silence pinched at nerve ends before the fellow moved again.

In two driving steps Baylor went around the rock. He was just a fraction late, almost on top of a beard-matted face, two startled eyes and that tangle of yellow hair. He swung the pistol.

Moccasin Joe went back like a cat, clutching a knife in his belt. Baylor's blow missed. The pistol rang on rock, and by then the knife was coming clear. Baylor drove in with his shoulder turned. The knife was coming down when the shoulder caught the man at the throat lacing of his shirt.

Baylor was on top when they went down. He got the knife arm then, and suddenly threw all his power into a side push. The man's hand went against the rock. Baylor began to grind it along the granite.

The rock was running red before Moccasin Joe dropped the knife. With the explosive strength of a deer, he arched his body, throwing Baylor sidewise against the rock. One of the man's knees doubled back like a trap spring, then the foot lashed out and knocked Baylor away.

Moccasin Joe leaped up. He did not run. He dived in. Baylor caught him with a heeled hand under the chin. The man's head snapped back but his weight came on. A knee struck Baylor in the groin.

Sick with the searing agony of it, Baylor grabbed the long hair with both hands. He kept swinging Moccasin Joe's head into the rock until there was no resistance but limp weight.

For several moments Baylor lay under the weight, grinding his teeth in pain; and then he pushed free, straightening up by degrees, stabbing his feet against the ground. The front sight of his pistol was smeared, the muzzle burred, and maybe the barrel was bent a little.

But he had the man who was going to tell him what was killing ranch scouts in Big Ghost Basin. Except for the knife, Moccasin Joe had carried no other weapon. Baylor cut the fellow's belt and tied his hands behind him. Blood was smeared in the tangled yellow hair.

Baylor had never seen him before.

Going down the burn, the prisoner was wobbly, but he was walking steadily enough before they reached the park, where Paxton was to come soon after dark. It was almost dark now. Just inside the timber Baylor made Joe lie down, then tied his ankles with Paxton's belt.

Firelight was a blessed relief after black, cold nights. "The first man killed here was one of yours, Joe," Baylor said. "You boys got on to something that makes it impossible for us to keep a man here. What is it?"

After a long silence Baylor removed one of his prisoner's moccasins. The man's eyes rolled as he stared at the fire. Baylor squatted by the flames, turning the knife slowly in the heat until the thin edge of the blade was showing dull red.

Where the hell was Pierce Paxton?

"Put out the fire," Moccasin Joe said.

"Talk some more." Baylor kept turning the blade. "That first man was one of yours, wasn't he?"

"Yeah." Moccasin Joe was beginning to sweat. The skin above his beard was turning dirty yellow.

Baylor lifted his knife to let him see it.

"Your Thing has got us stopped," Baylor said. "What is it?"

The firelight ran on a growing fear in the captive's eyes. He started to speak, and then he lay back.

"First, the flat of the blade against the bottom of your arch, then the point between the hock and the tendon. I'll reheat each time, of course." Even to Baylor his own words seemed to carry conviction.

"Put the fire out!"

Baylor lifted the knife again. The blade was bright red. "I saw Teton Sioux do this once," he lied calmly.

Moccasin Joe's breath was coming hard.

"You covered up something where Paxton was killed, didn't you? And then you checked back and wiped out a track of your own that you had overlooked."

"Yeah."

"Keep talking."

"I want a smoke. I won't tell you anything until I get a smoke!"

Baylor stared at the tangled face, at the terror in the man's eyes. For a customer as tough as this one had proved up in the rocks, he was softening pretty fast under a torture bluff.

Baylor laid the knife where the blade would stay hot. He rolled two smokes and lit them. He put one in Moccasin Joe's mouth.

"You got to untie my hands."

"You can smoke without that."

The cigarette stuck to the captive's lips. He tried to roll it free and it fell into his beard. He jerked his head back and the smoke fell on the ground. Baylor put it back in the man's mouth. He untied the fellow's hands.

Moccasin Joe sat up and puffed his cigarette, rolling his shoulders.

"Let's have it," Baylor said.

"The bunch that's been raiding here ain't the one from the west prairie, like you think. We been hanging out on the regular reservation. The agent is getting his cut."

It sounded like a quickly made-up lie. "Is Kreider one of the bunch?"

The captive hesitated. "Sure."

"Describe him."

Moccasin Joe did that well enough.

"What killed Paxton?"

"Which one was he?"

"The last one—in Battleground Park."

"I'll tell you." Moccasin Joe made sucking sounds, trying to get smoke from a dead cigarette.

Baylor took a twig from the fire. He leaned down. The captive's hands came up from his lap like springs. They clamped behind Baylor's neck and jerked. At the same time Moccasin Joe ducked his own head. Baylor came within an ace of getting his face smashed against hard bone.

He spread his hands between his face and the battering block just in time. Even so, he felt his nose crunch, and it seemed that every tooth in his mouth was loosened. He was in a crouch then, and Moccasin Joe's thumbs were digging at his throat. Baylor drove his right knee straight ahead.

Moccasin Joe's hands loosened. He fell back without a sound. Baylor stood there rubbing his knee. He could not stand on the leg for a while. The sensitive ligaments above the cap had struck squarely on the point of Moccasin Joe's jaw.

Once more Baylor cinched the man's arms tight behind his back. Let him die for want of a smoke. Blood dripped into the fire as Baylor put on more wood. He stared at the red hot knife, wishing for just an instant that he was callous enough to use it.

Where in hell is Paxton? he thought.

Blood began to stream down his lips. He felt his way to the creek and washed his face and dipped cold water down the back of his neck. After a while the bleeding stopped. Both sides of his nose were swollen so tight he could not breathe through them. His lips were cut.

I'm lucky, he told himself, getting out with only a busted nose after falling for an old gag like that.

You're not out of it yet, Baylor. It's night again.

Once more the old voices of Big Ghost were running in his mind. Baylor dipped Paxton's hat full of water and went back to the fire and Moccasin Joe.

"Sit up if you want a drink."

It was a struggle for Moccasin Joe but he made it. His eyes were still a little hazy, but clear enough to look at Baylor with hatred.

Baylor took the knife from the fire and stood over his captive, tapping his boot against the man's bare foot. Moccasin Joe looked at the glowing steel, and then at Baylor. His eyes showed no fear.

"You ain't got the guts."

The bluff was no good. Baylor drove the knife into the ground near the fire. "I've got guts enough to help hang you," he said. "We know you're one of the rustlers, and we know you've been doing chores for the Thing in the basin that's killed our men. Better loosen up, Joe."

"My name ain't Joe."

"That won't make any difference when you swing."

"Talk away, cowboy."

He's not afraid of me, Baylor thought, but it's up in his neck because of what he knows is out there.

It's out there, the night said.

Paxton should be coming. He should have been here an hour ago.

He went to the edge of the park, listening for the hoof sounds of the dun. There was nothing on the park but ancient night and aching quiet. Grunting sounds and the cracking of twigs sent Baylor running back to the fire. Moccasin Joe was trying to get away, pushing himself by digging his heels into the ground. He had gone almost twenty feet.

Baylor hauled him back to the fire. The man's muscles were jerking. "They'll kill me," he said, "but that'll be the best way. Put out the fire. I'll tell you!"

"You've pulled a couple of fast ones already."

"Put it out!"

Brutal fear came like a bad odor from the man. Baylor's back was crawling. He turned toward the creek to get another hatful of water.

Twigs popped. Something thudded softly out in the forest.

"It's coming! Turn me loose!" Moccasin Joe's voice rose in a hoarse, quavering scream. "O Jesus . . ." And then he was silent.

Standing at the edge of firelight, with his bent-barrelled pistol in his hand, Baylor was in a cold sweat.

Paxton's voice came from the forest. "Baylor!"

"Here!" Baylor made two efforts before he got the pistol back in leather. By the time Paxton came in, leading the dun, Baylor's fear had turned to anger.

"Did you make another trip out to visit and have a shave!"

Paxton was in no light mood, either. His face was swelling from mosquito bites. He had clawed at them and smeared mud from his hairline to his throat. "I got bogged down in a stinking swamp! Lost your carbine there, too." He looked at Moccasin Joe. "I see you got—What ails him?"

Moccasin Joe's eyes were set, unseeing. His jaw was jerking and little strings of saliva were spilling into his beard.

Mice feet tracked on Baylor's spine. "Umm!" he said in a long breath. "He thought you were the Thing!"

"The Thing! Good God!" Paxton's eyes rolled white in his mud-smeared face. His voice dropped. "Your horse raised hell back there a minute ago."

The dun was shuddering now, its ears set toward the creek. It was ready to bolt. Paxton drew his pistol.

"Put that popgun away!" Baylor cried. "Help me get him on the horse!" He grabbed the knife and slashed the belt around Joe's ankles. "Stand up!"

The man rose obediently, numbly, his jaw still working. Paxton leaped to grab the dun's reins when the horse tried to bolt toward the park.

Baylor threw Moccasin Joe across the saddle of the plunging horse.

"Lead the horse out of here!"

They crashed toward the park, with the horse fighting to get away, with Baylor fighting to keep Moccasin Joe across the saddle. The dun tried to bolt until they were in timber at the lower end of the park, and then it quieted.

"How far to the cabin where Raven is?" Baylor asked.

"Maybe four miles," Paxton answered. "I won't try no short cuts through a swamp this time." He laughed shakily.

They spoke but little as they moved through the deep night of Big Ghost Basin. Baylor walked behind now. Paxton broke off a limb and used it as a feeler overhead when they were in timber.

Each time he said, "Limb!" they heard Moccasin Joe grunt a little as he ducked against the horn.

Baylor guessed it was well after midnight when Paxton stopped in the rocks and said, "It's close to here—some place. I'll go ahead and see."

Baylor was alone. He heard Paxton's footsteps fade into the rocks. The dun was droop-headed now. Moccasin Joe was a dark lump in the saddle.

Relief ran through Baylor when he heard the mumble of voices somewhere ahead, and presently Paxton came back. "The cabin is about a hundred yards from here. Raven's there."

Paxton took care of the dun. Raven and Baylor led the captive inside. Moccasin Joe was like a robot. Light from a brass Rivers lamp showed a four-bunk layout, with a large fireplace at one end. There was a shelf of books near the fireplace, and rock specimens scattered everywhere else.

Raven's hair was rumpled. He was in his undershirt and boots. His pink face was shining and his eyes were sharp. He looked at Moccasin Joe and said, "I thought *I* brought in specimens."

Moccasin Joe was staring.

Raven took the man's right hand and looked at the grated knuckles. He stood on tiptoe to peer at the marks where Baylor had banged Moccasin Joe's head against the rock.

"I roughed him up," Baylor said.

"You didn't hurt him." Raven passed his hand before the man's face. "Oregon! Oregon!" he said.

"Huh?" the man said dully.

"You know him?" Baylor asked.

"I saw him out on the west prairie a month ago, camped with a group of men. They called him that."

"Rustlers, huh?"

"Probably. I ride where I like. Nobody bothers me. I've doctored a man or two out that way, without asking his business."

"What's wrong with this one?" Baylor asked.

"Shock. His mind, roughly, is locked on something. Did you try to scare him to death?"

"Not me. Something scared the hell out of me, and Paxton,

too. Maybe if we'd known what it was, we'd be like Mocc—
Oregon"

Paxton came in. Raven glanced at his face. "Wash it off, and
quit scratching the lumps, Paxton. Get some grease out of that
jar there by the books." Raven motioned Oregon toward a chair.
"Sit down there."

Doc Raven went to work. He cleansed and dressed Oregon's
hand, and took care of the cuts on his head, shearing into the
long hair with evident satisfaction. "Retire!" he muttered. "I've
got so I don't go to an outbuilding without taking a medical kit
along."

Raven was completely happy, Baylor thought.

"Help yourselves to the grub, boys," the doctor said.

Oregon ate mechanically, staring at Raven most of the time.
When Raven was briskly directing him into a bunk afterward,
the doctor asked casually, "Did Martin get over that dislocated
shoulder all right?"

"Yeah," Oregon said. "Yeah, he's all right," and then his eyes
slipped back to dullness once more.

Raven looked at Paxton and Baylor. "I think he'll be coming
out of it after a night's rest. Go to bed. I'll just sit here and read."

"I don't want that man to get away," Baylor said. "He's going
to tell me something in the morning."

Raven shook his head. "You won't get anything out of this
one, Baylor. I probed two bullets out of his chest once, and he
never made a peep."

Raven smiled at the suspicious stares of the two ranchers. "I'm
a doctor," he said. "Retired." He laughed. "Now go to bed, both
of you."

Raven was cooking when Baylor woke up. Paxton was still sound
asleep. Oregon was lying in his bunk awake. There was complete
awareness in his eyes when he looked at Baylor. Baylor said,
"Ready to talk?"

"To hell with you," Oregon said.

Paxton woke up while Baylor was dressing. He took his pistol
from under his blankets and walked across the room to Oregon.

"That was my brother that was killed by your pet a few days ago."

"Too bad," Oregon said.

Paxton turned toward Baylor. "Let's stake this bastard out by a fire tonight—and leave him!"

"That's enough!" Raven's voice cut sharply. "Oregon is yours, but let's have no more of that kind of talk."

"What'll we do?" Paxton asked. "I want to go with you to meet Sherry this morning, and—" He glanced at Raven.

"You stay here," Baylor said. "I'll see Sherry. What the hell does she want?"

The first hot meal in several days was like water in a desert. After breakfast Baylor brought the dun from a barred enclosure where a spring made a green spot in the rocks.

Paxton grumped about being left to watch the prisoner. Sherry would take some of that out of him soon enough, after they were married, Baylor thought.

Baylor went inside for one last word with Oregon. "I know you lied about your bunch hanging out on the reservation, Oregon. How about Kreider?"

"You find out," Oregon said.

Baylor looked at Paxton.

"Don't fret," Paxton said. "I'll watch him, all right."

Raven walked outside with him. "I know how you boys feel, Baylor. Out here you try to make things all black or all white. There's shades between the two, Baylor. I don't defend Oregon. I don't condemn him. You understand?"

"I'm trying to."

"That helps. You want my rifle?"

"Carbine." Baylor shook his head. "Thanks, no."

Sherry and Gary Owen were waiting in Battleground Park when he reached there. It was close to where Bill Paxton had been killed.

"What happened to your nose?" Sherry asked.

"Froze it in the creek. Nice place you picked to meet me."

"Yeah." Owen looked toward the little mound that covered the fire site. "She picked it."

Sherry said, "Did you see anyone last night?"

"Pierce and me met a man, not socially, though. Who do you mean?"

"Any of the ranchers, tight-mouth. They came in last night, the crews from every outfit. Crosby and Baldray got them together. They're going to filter around and trap the rustlers tomorrow or the next day near the Wall."

"Baldray's idea?" Baylor asked.

Owen nodded. "Him and Kreider."

"Kreider!"

"He's a special agent of the Indian Department," Owen said. "He was sent here to investigate a rumor that the rustlers were operating from reservation land. For a while he was in solid with them. From what we gathered, he's got a chum still with the bunch on the west prairie, and that fellow tipped Kreider off about the next raid."

The rustlers must have caught on to Kreider, Baylor thought. That was why Oregon had been so willing to identify him as one of the gang. Tomorrow or the next day. . . . Plenty of time for what Baylor had to do. He looked at a .45-90 Winchester in Owen's saddle boot.

"I'd like to borrow your rifle, Gary."

"I brought one for you," Sherry said. She walked into the grass and returned with a double-barreled weapon.

Baylor hefted the piece. "One of Baldray's."

"Elephant gun," Sherry said. "A .577, whatever that is." She gave her brother, one by one, a half-dozen cartridges. "Pierce told me he saw the track of something down here that scared him. Where is Pierce?"

His sister was quite a woman, Baylor thought. He told her and Owen about capturing Oregon. "I figure it will be easier to get a line on this Thing, now that Oregon is out of the way."

Owen stared at the timber edges of the park. "Thing," he muttered. "I'll stay with you, Ken."

"Take Sherry back to the benches—"

"I know the way," Sherry said. "You know something? Kreider says there's a bill going into the next Congress to make Big Ghost public land again."

"Owen's taking you back to the benches," Baylor said.

"You know who got action started on that bill?" Sherry asked. "Jim Baldray."

"Yeah," Owen said. "Even Kullhem admits now that he must have had the wrong idea about Baldray. I'll stay down here with you, Ken."

"The two of you work well together," Baylor said, "changing the subject, throwing me off. All right, get out of here, Sherry, and be sure you're good and out before night."

The girl got on her horse. Her face was pale under its tan. "Don't depend entirely on that elephant gun, Ken. Get up in a tree, or something."

"I figured on that," Baylor said. "So long, Red."

The two men watched until she disappeared into the timber at the upper end of Battleground Park.

"Fighting rustlers don't scare me no more than a man's got a right to be scared," Owen said abruptly. He dug out his short-stemmed pipe and lit it. "But after I saw Paxton—and them other two, I'll admit I didn't have the guts to come down here at night. Now I'm here, I'll stay."

Baylor was glad to have him—with that big-bored Winchester.

"I don't know what we're after," Baylor said. "But maybe in a couple of hours we'll know. Come on."

They went back in the timber, and stayed out of sight until they came to the park below the burn, the place where Baylor had built his fire the night before. The memory of the night began to work on Baylor.

He felt a chill when he saw that the fire he and Paxton had left burning in their quick retreat had been covered with a great heap of dirt and needles. There were long marks in the torn ground, but no sharp imprints. The story was there. The fire had kept on smoldering under the first weight of dirt and dry forest mat, and the Thing had continued to throw dirt in a savage frenzy until the smoke had ceased. Fire. That was the magnet.

Owen sucked nervously on his pipe, staring. "What done it?"

Baylor shook his head. "Let's try the soft ground by the creek." They stood on the east bank. Baylor stared at the choke of willows and trees on the other side. Last night he had dipped water from this very spot, and over there somewhere the Thing had been pacing, circling, working up to coming in. It must have been quite close when he threw Oregon at the dun and ran in terror.

Night will come again, the voices said.

Baylor and Owen stayed close together while they searched. Farther up the stream they found where the Thing had leaped the creek in one bound. Four imprints in the muddy bank.

"I'll be dipped in what!" There was a little fracture in Owen's voice. "That ain't no track of nothing I ever seen!"

The outlines were mushy. The mud was firm, but still there was no clear definition of form. The whole thing was a patch-work of bumps and ridges that would not fit any living creature Baylor had ever seen or heard of. "That's no bear," he said.

"Back in Ireland my grandmother used to scare us. . . ." Owen shook his head.

On a limb snag across the creek they found a small patch of short, brittle hair with a scab scale clinging to it.

"There ain't nothing in the world with hair like that!" Owen cried.

Here with the shroud moss motionless on gray limbs, in the ancient stillness of Big Ghost, Baylor was again prey to fear of the Unknown, and for a moment there was no civilization be-cause nothing fitted previous experience.

"The rustlers have seen it," he said. "Oregon said it got one of their men. They wouldn't have covered up for it if they hadn't been afraid we might recognize the sign." He stared at Owen. "Fire, Gary. Fire is what brings it!"

"I been here at night—with fire." Owen hunched his shoulders.

"It's a big hole. A man might be lucky here for a long time, and then one night. . . . Where are the ranchers going to meet?"

"They'll camp out in little bunches on those timbered hog-backs that point toward the West Wall. When they see Crosby's smoke signal from the Wall—"

"We've got to warn them, Gary. Orahood never spent a night

out in his life without building a fire. Get down there and pass the word—no fires!"

"That leaves you alone."

"I've been several nights alone. Take the dun with you. I don't want him hurt."

"Holy God, Ken! You don't want the dun hurt, but you—"

"Stick to the timber, Gary, so you won't mess up their trap."

Baylor took both ropes from the saddles. Ready to leave, Owen said, "Take my rifle. That elephant business only shoots twice."

"I'll do better than that, from where I'll be. Tonight you'll like the feel of that big barrel across your knees, Gary."

"Don't scare me. I already know I'm a damned coward. I *want* to leave here. I'll admit it." Owen rode away.

Baylor did not like to admit how alone he felt.

Big Ghost nights always seemed to settle as if they had special purpose in making the basin a black hole. From his platform of laced rope between two limbs of a spruce tree, Baylor peered down to where his pile of wood was ready for a match. He had pulled in other fuel close to the site, enough to keep a fairly large fire all night.

It was about time to light it. The sooner the better. The smoke would make a long trail through the forest, the flames a little bright spot in the murk, and this Thing that must kill fire might be attracted. It would be a cinch from here.

A cinch? Maybe the Thing climbs trees.

Baylor climbed down and lit the fire. He waited just long enough to know that it would burn, and then he climbed again to his rope perch.

The blackness laughed at his haste.

Smoke came up between the ropes and began to choke him. That was a point he had not thought of at all; but presently the fire took hold in earnest, light reached out to touch the gray holes of waiting trees, and a small wind began to drift the smoke at a lower level.

Baylor tried to settle comfortably against the ropes. The sling of the heavy double-barrel was over a limb above him, so the weapon could not fall. The four spare cartridges were buttoned in the breast pocket of his jumper. He felt the cold, big roundness of them when he took out the makings of a cigarette.

It was as dark as a pocket up in the tree. For a while the oddness of being where he was intrigued Baylor, and then he thought of a dozen flaws in his plan. But if it did not work tonight, he would stay with it until it did. He reached over to touch the .577. The four spare cartridges did not count. He had two shots coming. They should be enough.

Bill Paxton's forty-five was empty when Kreider found him.

The night lagged. Big Ghost gathered all its secrets to it, and the darkness whispered. Three times Baylor went down to put wood on the fire. Each time he took the heavy rifle, and each time his flesh crawled until he was back on the rope net once more.

He smoked all his tobacco. Thirst started. He listened to the creek. It was not very far.

Go get yourself a drink, Baylor.

He tried not to listen. His thirst grew out of all proportions, and he knew it was not real. He could not be thirsty; he had drunk just before dark.

Get yourself a drink. Don't be a fool.

He waited until the fire needed wood. After building it up, he stood a moment by the tree, with one hand on the rope that led to safety.

Go on, Baylor. Are you afraid to get a drink?

The water was icy cold against the sweat on his face. He drank from cupped hands, then wiped them on his jumper, staring at the blackness across the creek. Last night the Thing had been somewhere out there. It might be there now.

He took two steps toward the fire. Something splashed in the water behind him. He was cocking the gun and swinging around all the time he knew the splash had come from a muskrat.

For a few moments he stood drying his hands over the heat, a little gesture of striking back at the Unknown. But when he started up the tree he went all the way with a rush.

In the cold hours long after midnight he was on the ground tending the fire when he heard a soft sound beyond the limits of the light. He unslung the rifle and felt the thumping of his heart.

It's there. It's watching you.

He turned toward the tree. He heard the crush of dry pine needles. He cocked the gun and backed toward the tree, feeling behind him for the rope. Something moved on the edge of fire-light. An enormous, shadowy form emerged from blackness. It rocked from side to side. A hoarse roar enveloped Baylor.

He fired the right barrel, and then the left. The Thing came in, bellowing. Straight across the fire it charged, scattering embers. Baylor had another cartridge out, but he dropped it and clubbed the rifle. He was completely stripped now of all the thinking of evolved and civilized man.

The bellowing became a strangled grunt. The Thing was down, its hind legs in the flames. It tried to crawl toward Baylor, and then it was still. Baylor rammed another cartridge in and fired a third shot. The great bulk took the fearful impact without stirring.

Cordite rankness was in Baylor's nostrils as he kicked embers back toward the fire and put on fuel with shaking hands. The stench of burning hair sickened him. He pulled the flames away from the hind legs of the beast.

He had known what he was up against from the moment the animal had stood higher than a horse there on the edge of fire-light, then dropped to the ground to charge. He had killed a grizzly bear.

When the flames were high he examined it. The feet were huge, misshapen, lacking the divisions of pads. All four were tortured, scrambled flesh that had fused grotesquely after being cruelly burned. Along the back and on one side of the bear were scabby patches where the hair had come back crisp and short. Around the mouth the flesh was lumpy, hideous from scar tissue. The jaws had been seared so terribly that the fangs and front teeth had dropped out.

He lifted one of the forelegs with both hands. There were traces of claws, some ingrown, the others, brittle, undeveloped fragments.

The forest fire several years before! The bear had been a cub then, or perhaps half grown. The poor devil, caught by the flames, probably against the rocks, since only one side was scarred. He pictured it whimpering as it covered its face with its forepaws. And then, when it could no longer stand the pain and fear, it must have gone loping wildly across the burning forest mat.

Before it recovered it must have been a skinny, tortured brute. No wonder it had gone crazy afterward at the smell and sight of flames.

He found one of his bullet holes in the throat. That had to be the first shot, when the grizzly had been erect. The other must be in the shoulder that was underneath, and it would take a horse and rope to make sure. He cut into a lump on the shoulder that was up. Just a few inches below the tough hide, under the fat, he found a .45 bullet. One of Bill Paxton's, probably.

That was enough examination. The poor, damned thing.

He was asleep by a dead fire when the savage crackling of gunfire roused him shortly after dawn. He sat up quickly. The firing ran furiously, somewhere near the Wall. Then the sounds dwindled to single cracks, at intervals. A little later Big Ghost was quiet.

Baylor hoped there was truth in what Owen had said about the basin going back to range. For the first time in days he heard the wakening sounds of birds. Before, he had been listening for something else.

He was asleep in the sun out in the park when the clatter roused him. The ranchers were coming out. Kullhem, his left arm in a sling, was riding with Baldray in the lead. Farther back, a man was tarpaulin-draped across his saddle.

Owen and Paxton spurred ahead to Baylor, who pointed toward the tarpaulin.

"Orahood," Owen said. "The only man we lost."

Baylor was stabbed by the thought of Orahood's wife alone at Sky Hook, with a baby coming on.

Paxton said, "We caught 'em foul on Windy Trail! We broke their backs!"

"Oregon?" Baylor asked.

"He tried one of his little tricks."

Owen kept looking toward the forest.

"It's there," Baylor said wearily.

Men gathered around the grizzly.

"Good Lord!" Crosby kept saying. "Would you look at the size of that!"

"That must have been a spot of fun, eh, Baylor?" Baldray frowned, not satisfied with his words. "You know I mean a narrow place—a tight one."

Raven was all around the bear, like a fly. "Unusually fine condition," he mused. "How did he get food while he was recovering from those burns?"

"He healed himself in a swamp," Kullhem growled. "There's always cows and calves bogged down in the swamps."

"A remarkable specimen, nonetheless." Raven drew a sheath knife. "I'll have a look at that stomach and a few other organs." He hesitated. "Your bear, of course, Baylor. You don't mind?"

"Yeah." Baylor shook his head slowly. "Leave him be, Raven. The poor devil suffered enough when he was alive."

Raven stood up reluctantly. He put his knife away. "I guess I understand."

Baldray's bony face showed that he understood. "Fire killer," he said. "The poor damned beast."

THE
LONG NIGHT

EDMUND WARE SMITH

IN THE MORNING, some hours after the last jug had fallen, Uncle Jeff Coongate opened his one eye, sniffed, and, through the stronger fumes of rum, detected the odor of sweet grass. This reminded the old poacher of Indians weaving baskets in the sun. Next, he thought fondly of Tom Compus Mentis, who was still asleep beside him in the spare room in Zack Bourne's cabin on Mopang Lake. Finally, with a wave of grief, Uncle Jeff recalled his tragedy: Zibe, his beloved hound dog, was dead.

It was Tom Compus Mentis, the gentle and ancient Indian, who, on the day before, had brought Zibe home to Jeff. With the crippled hound lying in the bow of his canoe, old Tom had travelled the twenty-nine miles from Hedron Lake to Mopang in seven hours. It was a feat of loyalty and endurance which signalized a long and dignified friendship.

Zibe had been shot in the spine. His hindquarters were paralyzed, and as the old woodsman gathered him in his arms, he had whimpered, and pressed his fevered muzzle to Uncle Jeff's neck.

"Zibe," Jeff whispered, "Zibe—what hellbird done this to you?"

"Red Hackett," said Tom Compus Mentis. "I find tracks. And empty shell—.35 auto."

The one-eyed poacher carried Zibe into Zack Bourne's cabin, and the Indian stayed in the doorway. Zack, Jeff Coongate's lifelong comrade in enterprise against the game laws, looked once at Zibe's wound, and shook his head in sorrow.

"It's mortal," he said. "Poor ole Zibe—best hound ever run a moose to water."

Zack's wife, Sarah, began to cry. She had never truly loved Jeff's hound, fearing him as a primordial and fiercely roaming adventurer, like his master. But Sarah was so tenderhearted that she was touched by any misfortune.

Zibe moaned softly, and a shudder of pain racked the sleek and rangy body. It was plain that the hound was beyond hope, and suffering needlessly.

"Hand me my rifle, Zack," said Uncle Jeff.

Zack silently obeyed. Carrying Zibe and the rifle, the old woodsman stalked across the back clearing into the cedars. Presently, those in the cabin heard a shot—a sound both grim and merciful.

"Sarah," said Zack, tonelessly, "get out the rum."

"I was a-goin' to, by my own self," said Sarah, "jest this one, dreadful time."

When Uncle Jeff Coongate returned, the first jug was opened before him—and Tom Compus Mentis no longer stood in the doorway, but had drawn in a little toward the jug, his dark eyes having a look of sorrow and horizons.

Tactfully avoiding the Indian's gaze, Jeff and Zack both drank. Sarah, herself, turned a half ounce into a wine glass, and sipped. Touched by this breaking of precedent in homage to Zibe's passing, Uncle Jeff had bowed to Sarah. Then he nodded to Zack, and together they went out into the cedars with a shovel.

While they were gone, Sarah graciously bethought herself of the old Indian, who stood so patiently by the jug.

"Why, Mr. Mentis! You ain't had any of the rum—after that terrible trip, an' all. Here. I'll get you a glass.

"No thanks glass," said Tom. He enfolded the jug in both palms, and tipped it upwards. When the two woodsmen returned, the damage was begun—and they knew how dismally 'twould end.

"Honey," Zack hissed, in an aside to Sarah, "You lost your mind? Don't you know how ole Tom'll suffer? In the mornin' he'll see bugs a yard long, an' ravens perchin' on his wrists."

But morning was not yet. Nor had Tom Compus Mentis told

the story of the Hacketts, the great moose of Hedron Lake, and the wanton shooting of the far-wandering Zibe.

The Hacketts were three brothers, successful evaders of the draft, the income tax, and the obligations of gentlemen. They lived in Hedron, which, cross forest, was twenty-four miles from Zack's cabin on Mopang—twenty-nine by canoe. One of the Hacketts ran a restaurant and bar. The other two had a farm planted to kale, which attracted deer. During the war, and currently, they killed moose and deer, put down the meat in mason jars, and sold it for a dollar a pint. They took the loin and hindquarters of a critter, and left the rest to rot. It was this practice which filled Uncle Jeff Coongate with fury and contempt. Although he personally excoriated game laws, and the minions thereof, he despised the wasting of the fruit of the wild lands.

The one-eyed poacher and the butchering Hacketts differed in all their practices. Between Uncle Jeff and the successive game wardens who pursued him, there was a spirit of respect, as among duelists. Whenever they caught him, the old poacher went majestically down to jail in Mopang, where the first cell on the left was usually reserved for him. When he didn't get caught, he feasted royally with Zack Bourne, and if there were so much as a shank left over, it was dropped on the doorstep of some needy family.

But there was nothing of Robin Hood in the Hacketts of Hedron. To the Fish and Game Commissioner, they were known as the wantons of the wilderness, and he would rather have caught them even than Thomas Jefferson Coongate. Privily, the Commissioner himself would have agreed that the Hacketts' shooting of Zibe was most wanton of all. When the shooting occurred, Zibe had been deep in the sweet obsession of a fox track. As Tom Compus Mentis explained, nothing else could have lured him so far from home.

"But those Hacketts," muttered Tom, reaching for the jug, "they think maybe Zibe come to drive big moose away."

"Moose?" said the one-eyed poacher, keening. "Do you know where they's a big one, Tom?"

The old Indian's face wrinkled like a scorched moccasin. "Big!

I say big. Hacketts try to bribe me tell where he is. No tell. They got big order for moose meat—dollar pound."

Tom told how the Hacketts had tried to follow him to the moose's haunts, and how he had eluded them. As the rum became fire in his veins, he laughed reminiscently at their attempts to trail him. Early that very morning, before the wind had wrinkled the lake, Tom had been playing cat and mouse with the Hacketts. He had heard a rifle shot. Half an hour later, he had cut back through the dense growth, picked up the Hacketts' trail, and found the empty cartridge from Red Hacketts' .35 autoloading rifle. Nearby, from the spruce blowdown where he had crawled to die, Zibe had dragged himself on his forefeet to Tom's side.

It was night, now, and Uncle Jeff Coongate, listening to the Indian's tale, stood tall in the lamplight, as he planned revenge. The oaths slid wondrously from his lips, and his mustaches gleamed white. Zack fervently echoed the oaths, while Sarah covered her ears.

"Hacketts!" said the one-eyed poacher. "May they rot and fry, stricken in spleen and paunch, an' blowflies in every pore."

After Sarah went to bed, they began on the second jug. Presently Zack suggested that they simply go over to Hedron in the morning and shoot the Hacketts in a bevy.

"No!" cried Sarah from the bedroom. "Oh, no, no!"

For years she had listened to her husband and his crony conspiring against the lives of game wardens, but had realized it was merely a form of play, or entertainment for them. But this business of the Hacketts had a serious ring that made her blood run cold. Surprisingly, it was Jeff Coongate, who, this time, eased her mind.

"Sarah's right, Zack," said Jeff. " 'Course, I can see where it'd be pleasant to kill them Hacketts—angle shots, we could take on 'em. Clip off a little flesh to a time, till they was whittled to the bone. But I don't like to spend my whole life in jail—jest winters. Spring, I like to get out in time to spear a few salmon before fishin' season opens. *But—*"

It was not so much Jeff's voice, as his posture that underscored the word. Zack saw the light flaring in his comrade's eye. He sat back, waiting for Jeff to unfold, while Tom Compus Mentis, un-noticed, took a long, silent pull from the jug.

"What d'you aim to do to them Hacketts?" Zack asked, finally.

"I aim to kill their moose—that big one Tom tells about. I aim to kill it right in their face an' eyes."

So far, the idea was mere nebula; but, inspired by the rising fires of rum and glory, the avengers leaped lightly over hazards, and had the moose down.

"He'll dress out around six hundred," estimated Zack.

"Eight hundred, easy," corrected Jeff.

In the light of the many lamps which had seemed to multiply in the cabin kitchen, the moose finally tipped the scales at a thousand pounds, clear meat.

"It's too much," said Zack, sadly hefting the jug. "Some of it'll spoil, sure."

The one-eyed poacher gazed loftily at his less imaginative comrade.

"Too much? Spoil? Are you thinkin', like always, jest of your own self, Zack? Ain't there other folks goin' hungry, same as me an' you. Give, seth the Lord. Blessid is the poor."

Heads together, hands clasped in the emotion of selfless giving, they outlined a vast program of philanthropy, while Sarah listened in terror in her dark bedroom, and the old Indian's hand strayed more and more helplessly toward the jug.

"We shall feed the entire offsprings of Jumbo Tethergood."

"An' the pore li'l orphans of Tim Preston."

"With the Hacketts' moose, we shall pervide for the fam'lies of Mopang."

"An' Boomchain Junction, an' New York, an'—"

Further expansion was checked by the thick, uncertain voice of Tom Compus Mentis.

"Game warden," said Tom. "New game warden. Comin' Hedron—tomorrow."

At the time, a new game warden, zealous though he might be, seemed less like an obstacle than an added attraction.

"Good," said the outlaw of Mopang Forest. "Perfick. Spice things up a mite."

But in the morning, the new game warden loomed large, especially in the eyes of Sarah. She had read in the game laws that the penalty for killing a moose was five hundred dollars fine and three months in jail.

"Almost like for murder," she wept. "Don't you go, Zack. I beg you. Oh, Zack—please."

Ever since his marriage to Sarah, Zack had been emotionally torn. Subtly influenced by Jeff to maintain the old status of the devil and the demijohn, he was as subtly swayed by Sarah's prayers for his reform. Now, acutely miserable, he looked from one to the other. But this time, it was the one-eyed poacher who was moved by Sarah's pleading. Moreover, as Uncle Jeff savored the drama of the situation, he saw opportunities dear to his heart. Head bowed, he stood in the open doorway, and spoke.

"Zack—Sarah's right. You can't go. This mission is for a single man, with no dependints, no one to mourn for him."

"Dang it, Jeff! You always took me. We always done things—"

Jeff raised his hand in a gesture of sacrifice. "No. Zibe was mine."

So genuine was Jeff's grief for Zibe, that he no longer felt himself playing a role. Reality threw him off for a moment, and he gulped, and said: "Zack—you got any .45-70 ca'tridges? I—I used my last one—out in the cedars—yest'dy."

"No, but take my rifle, Jeff. You got to let me help that much."

"No," said Uncle Jeff, " 'Cause if that new game warden gets me, he'll confiscate the rifle. I couldn't bear to have that happen. Don't want to have my personal affairs hurt you, in no way whatever. No, Zack, this time it's a big thing. I can't take you with me. It's so big I got to play a lone hand."

The crestfallen Zack slumped into a chair, his elbows among the breakfast dishes. He resembled a boy plucked from the very entrance to a circus, and he was unappeased by Sarah's grateful murmurings.

By the lake shore, in the sand, Tom Compus Mentis drew a map of Hedron Lake, showing a hidden inlet, an unknown deadwater, and the great moose's range. As he noticed the wavering lines of the sand map, the one-eyed poacher's heart ached for the suffering Indian.

"Tom, your hand's a-twitchin' like a chicken's foot in the mud."

"You got a little bit rum left?" begged Tom, abjectly. "Me bad sick."

"No, Tom. We killed her all. You go straight home in your canoe. I got to go down to Mopang to buy ca'tridges. I'll be to your shack tonight. I'll bring you a dite of rum, but that's all. An' listen: don't you tech a drop in Hedron—not till I get to you. Mind that, Tom?"

The Indian slid away in his canoe, and Uncle Jeff Coongate saw despair in his wake. "Poor ole Tom," he muttered, and strode forth on the Mopang trail, already longing for Zack's companionship, his pleasure at Zack's frustration diminishing as he realized to the full that he had trapped himself into a considerable adventure, what with a moose, three murderous Hacketts, and—and—what was that other thing? Oh, yes! A new game warden!

In the afternoon, as he left Mopang and struck through the forest for Hedron Lake, it began to rain. His tireless stride brought him to Tom Compus Mentis' shack before midnight. But the Indian was not there—and his stove was cold.

"Tom," he muttered, "the demons was too much for you. I got to find you."

Drenched to the skin, the one-eyed poacher turned back toward the hamlet of Hedron, scorning the road, cross-cutting through the woods. He came out on the road two miles from the town, and as he stood for a moment, the headlights of a car approached. The car drew up to him, and stopped. The door swung open invitingly, and a pleasant voice hailed him.

"Howdy, stranger. Want a lift?"

Although bone-weary from the miles he had covered, the old woodsman replied with prideful reluctance: "I don't want to put no man out."

"Get in. It's raining."

Not till he had seated himself did the one-eyed poacher take full cognizance of his benefactor. But in the dim light from the instrument panel, the identity of the fellow was plain—the badge, the service cap, the uniform.

"Jest a moment, son," said Uncle Jeff. "Let me out. I never ride with game wardens."

The young warden smiled. His name was Steve Engle. He was a graduate of Anzio beachhead, the State Wildlife Training School, and a boyhood spent in Hedron, where a certain old Indian had taught him to love the woods, pound ash withes for baskets, and showed him where an otter family played. Tonight, on his first solo assignment as game warden in the Hedron district, Steve Engle had met and befriended that same old Indian. To meet the celebrated one-eyed poacher on the same night, within a few minutes, was to Steve like hitting the jackpot. He proposed to make the most of it.

Steve had never seen Uncle Jeff. But the old poacher's features, physique, and personality were unmistakable. The sweeping mustaches shone wet, the huge right hand held a Winchester between the peaked knees, and from the high-boned, imperious face, the one eye glowed like a blowtorch.

"Mr. Coongate," said Steve, almost reverently, "I haven't been a game warden very long. So maybe I won't contaminate you."

"In that case, maybe you ain't tainted yet. But hurry, son. Get me into Hedron fast. I don't want to set with you too long."

As they drove along, Jeff drew himself delicately away from the young warden as far as the seat would permit.

"Aren't you a long way from home?" asked the game warden. "What brings you here from Mopang?"

"I ain't accustomed to answer questions. But since you're new, I'll tell you: I come over here to see a sick friend."

Steve chuckled in his disbelief. "Did you find the friend well?"

"No. Didn't find him at all. So I come on back. He's prob'ly in Hedron."

Steve rapidly guessed at the miles the old man had covered afoot that day. It was incredible! He glanced with increasing respect at his passenger—and at the highlights on the rifle between his knees.

"Mr. Coongate," said Steve, "who is your friend—the sick friend that wasn't home?"

Although disdaining the impertinence of the warden's questioning, Uncle Jeff decided to be tolerant. The boy was young, and would grow up to have trouble enough.

"Tom Compus Mentis," said Jeff.

"Who? Did you say—? Why, Tom Compus is a friend of *mine!*"

"No. It ain't possible. No friend of mine could be the friend of a game warden. It jest wouldn't work out."

"It was when I was little," Steve hastened to explain. "Old Tom showed me the forests, and made moccasins for me. And—but—! Say, wait a minute!"

Drawing the car to the side of the road, the warden stopped, and glanced at his saturnine passenger. "Tom Compus Mentis *is* at home. I just left him in his shack, ten minutes ago! How come I didn't meet you on the road?"

These tidings had a sharp effect on the one-eyed poacher. He feared the worst. "When I left Tom's shack, I cut through the woods to the road—where you picked me up. That's why we didn't meet. How'd you happen to drive Tom home?"

"He couldn't walk too well."

"Was he drinkin'?"

Steve nodded. "Yes—Hackett's restaurant. The Hacketts had him in a booth, and they were loading his drinks."

"Let me out of here!" said the oldtimer.

Steve reached across and opened the car door, and the outlaw of Mopang Forest disappeared in the darkness toward Tom Compus Mentis' shack.

Driving on toward the warden's cabin on Hedron's outskirts, Steve Engle smiled elatedly. It seemed dead certain that his first solo assignment was going to be a success—with cream and sugar on top! He was holding a fistful of aces. Through the rain-wet window of Hackett's restaurant, he had seen the Hacketts lay a map of Hedron Lake under Tom Compus Mentis' eyes, and he had seen the sad, old Indian, dazed with drink, point to a hidden inlet in Anchor Island Cove. Now, *why?* What with moose meat selling for a dollar a pound, Steve thought he knew. He also thought he knew why the one-eyed poacher had appeared in the Hedron district. What a chance, thought Steve. Mine, all mine: to gather in the butchering Hacketts, and the legendary Jeff

Coongate—all in one swoop! What a tale to tell the Chief! The arrests would be simple, if he just remembered the advice old Tom Compus Mentis had given him, when he was a boy: look, listen, be still, and wait long in the night time.

In Tom Compus' shack, Uncle Jeff Coongate was indulging in similar, if craftier dreams. He had built a fire in Tom's stove, and made tea, and as he fed the Indian steaming spoonfuls, his heart was big with forgiveness.

"Hacketts make me tell about moose," Tom moaned. "Awful bad, Jeff. Awful sorry."

"Now, jest you rest easy, Tom. It's all right. I aim to get that moose, jest the same."

Uncle Jeff's one eye rolled beatifically, as he put together the pieces of his greatest and simplest conspiracy. In a single trick, he would wreck the Hacketts, avenge Zibe, outwit a game warden— a nice, pleasant new one—and possess a moose. Poor old Zack Bourne would shrivel and grow the green mold of envy.

"Tom," said Jeff, tenderly, " 'member what you used to tell me, when we was huntin' an' trappin' together, in the old days? 'Look, listen, be still, an' wait long in the night time.' Well, sir, Tom—that's what I aim to do."

"Look out new warden, Steve Engle. He smart."

"He did seem above average, for a warden," mused the one-eyed poacher. "Now, tell me how he come on you tonight in Red Hackett's place."

The Indian told his story. It was as Uncle Jeff had surmised. Putting two and two together, the young warden would be on the Hacketts' trail.

"An' wouldn't that boy jest love to catch me, too, Tom? Why, think what it'd mean to him! The Hacketts, an' ole Jeff Coongate, with a moose down—singlehanded."

Blissfully, the old woodsman slipped a spoonful of hot tea between the Indian's lips. Tom swallowed it unhappily.

"You bring old Tom little rum, Jeff?" he implored.

"Yes, a little, Tom. But not now." Before retiring, Jeff patted his friend's shoulder, and added philosophically: "Man cannot live by breath alone."

Beside the deadwater, beyond the hidden inlet in Anchor Island Cove, young Steve Engle waited long in the night time, and loneliness invaded his heart. Perhaps, in his zeal, he had assumed too much. Perhaps the Hacketts were suspicious, and Jeff Coongate gone his kingly way homeward to Mopang. Perhaps the moose was a myth—but there was no mistaking the great creature's track. It was, thought Steve, as long as a snowshoe and as broad as a stove lid. But when would the Hacketts make their kill? And where, oh where, was the one-eyed poacher?

Steve visited Tom Compus Mentis one day, and casually inquired. Tom shrugged.

"Jeff Coongate go," said the Indian, and blew to indicate a puff of smoke. He spoke the truth. He hadn't seen Jeff since the rainy night of his arrival.

"Guess I must have scared him off," thought Steve, with no special conviction, as he resumed his vigil.

The fifth night, or the sixth, Steve couldn't remember, began like all the others. In the dense cedar growth, in the darkness, the Big Silence weighted his spirit. He heard a mouse in the leaves, and tried to guess whether it was near or far. He heard a loon calling, then silence again, and the night wrapping itself around him. And then, unmistakably, the soft, hollow thump of a paddle against the gunwale of a canoe.

He tried to locate the sound. He couldn't be sure of the distance—but the direction was to his left. He lay waiting, his heart pounding. He remembered what the Chief had told him. "You'll be alone, Stevie. Watch it."

The first rifle shot came from down the deadwater, around a small point, about three hundred yards away. The echoes rolled back from the ridges, and died, and then Steve heard the second shot. He inched up on his hands and knees and crawled through the cedars. He got across the base of the little point to the edge of the deadwater, and lay still. He knew the Hacketts were waiting —and he steeled himself to wait longer.

Not over thirty yards away, he saw a match flare. He shivered to think how close he had figured it. Next he saw the steady glow of a lantern, and heard the sound of men moving. He squirmed toward the lantern, his service revolver in his right hand, his flashlight ready in his left, in case they heard him and kicked out the lantern. Then he stood up and walked in, his gun ahead of him.

They had the big moose down. Its head was pointed toward Steve, antlers palmed out wide. But—not a man was in sight! The young warden realized too late that they had trapped him into the light. He started to jump back. A crack on the side of his head made him see star shells and he lunged forward, hitting with his elbows.

Someone got an armlock on his throat. He saw a man's head within reach, and he whipped it with his gun barrel, and felt the barrel hit solid. The man went down. But there were two others. One had the armlock, and was bending his head back. The other stood in front, with a rifle at his hip, the muzzle on Steve's belt buckle. He wondered if they would finish the job, or knock him cold. He would never be able to identify any of them in court. Was that what they figured on?

The armlock tightened, and Steve felt himself blacking out. Then, to the right, he saw a jet of orange flame, and heard an explosion like a howitzer. He was sure he smelled black powder. His vision cleared. The man in front of him wasn't holding a rifle any more. It had disappeared, and the man was hugging his wrists to his sides, and howling with pain.

A flashlight blazed where Steve had seen the flash of the rifle, and a man of majestic height stepped calmly forth from the cedars. The flashlight he carried was the long, heavy, five-cell variety, and he flashed it in the eyes of the Hackett whose armlock had but lately loosened from the young warden's neck.

"I jest wanted to make sure," said the splendid voice, "that you was Red Hackett." With that, the one-eyed poacher brought the flashlight down solidly on Red Hackett's head, and Red settled deeply into the moss.

"Jeff Coongate!" said Steve.

"What's so strange about that?"

Steve laughed in nervous relief. The one-eyed poacher examined his flashlight, grinning at its dented barrel.

"That's one for old Zibe," he muttered, and straightway began the pleasant work of trussing up the Hacketts with the assistance of Steve, one pair of handcuffs, and the rawhide laces from his own moccasins.

Two hours later, the three Hacketts were in the Hedron jail, and Steve had telephoned his chief long distance. A few minutes after that, in the game warden's cabin, Steve was playing host to Uncle Jeff Coongate. He was strangely impressed by the old-timer's dignity, reticence, and superb manners.

"Mr. Coongate," said Steve, gratefully bringing out a bottle, "here's some rum. Don't know if you like the particular brand. It's Hernando's Fiery Dagger."

Coyly concealing the gleam in his eye, the old woodsman waved the bottle away. "I don't often tech intoxicatin' bev'ridges, son. But—" the great hand stole daintily forward—"to celebrate your triumph tonight, I'll take jest a small portion."

Steve watched, while Jeff drank to the extent of four bobs of his Adam's apple.

"Well—Uncle Jeff—" said Steve, haltingly. "I want to thank you for helping me out of a tough spot."

The one-eyed poacher scowled indignantly, and took a small chaser of Hernando's. "Me? Help a *game warden?* Let me set you straight, son. I have never shot a legal piece of game in my life— except by mistake. An' I have never helped a game warden."

"But you did tonight, Mr. Coongate."

Uncle Jeff shook his head. "No. An' I don't want you to tell it 'round that I helped you, neither. That's the way rumors get started. Why, son, what would Zack Bourne think of me, if he heard I'd helped a warden? I wasn't there to help you. I was there to get the man that shot my ole hound, Zibe. I'd intended to do battle with him, but you come along an' spoilt it for me. An' I may's well tell you I was also there to get that moose. That moose, you could almost say, was really *my* moose."

"So I almost thought," mused Steve. "And—doggonnit, Jeff, I'm glad the Hacketts killed it, instead of you. It leaves you in the clear."

"Yes," said Jeff, with mixed emotions, "I persume it does. Well, I got to be getting along."

"Wait. I'll drive you back to Mopang. It's nearly three o'clock in the morning."

"No. That's all right, son. It'll be daylight, time I get to Leadmine Cove, on Mopang. I'll have breakfast with Zack Bourne. Keep out of my way, Steve—an' you'll never have any bad trouble."

With that, the one-eyed poacher was gone. Steve sighed, and turned in for a few hours, till the Chief Warden arrived. Not long after daylight, they went down to haul the carcass of the moose away to the nearest hospital, for the delectation of the patients' diet. The moose, of course, was still there. As they stood looking down at it, Steve said to the Chief: "They don't make 'em any more like Jeff Coongate. Just imagine—footing it in the dark clear to Mopang Lake, at three in the morning."

"He's quite a man," said the Chief, somewhat guardedly, as he bent over the moose. "He's—why blast his old soul! This moose has been bled, and dressed out, and the hide folded back on!"

Dumbfounded, the two wardens lifted off the hide. The creature had been dressed by an expert hand. Choice portions of the loin had been sliced off with surgical precision.

"Looks to me," said the Chief, sardonically, "as if Jeff Coongate made a small detour on his nocturnal trip to Mopang Lake. Wonder what he and Zack Bourne are eating for breakfast? I'll bet the gravy's good!"

Steve Engle's look of consternation changed slowly into a smile. "The old master's touch!" he said.

"You called it, Stevie. Save a game warden's life, and steal a moose under his nose. That's Jeff Coongate. And say, I'll need a drink, when we get this job done. Got anything up in the cabin?"

"Why—uh, why, yes, Chief," said Steve. "There's a little bit left—Hernando's Fiery Dagger, it is."

THE LITTLE
FIGHTING
WHALES

JAMES B. CONNOLLY

WHENEVER THE PEOPLE of Tromsö heard that a stranger was about to take a cruise with their famous whale hunter, they would be almost sure to go out of their way to ask that stranger: "And so you are going off with our whale killer? Yes? Then surely you will hear of his great blue whale, the immense one he has been chasing these ten years now, and never yet caught—and never will, we think. Never a week by his fire in the long winter nights at home that he does not tell of that whale; never a cruise to the northward in the summer that, standing by his lance gun, he does not at one time or another tell it once again. Yes—but you shall hear him for yourself."

And now, somewhere to the eastward of Spitzbergen, the whaling steamer was patroling and the skipper, standing on the gun platform in the bow of the steamer, called for another cup of coffee. And while drinking his coffee, eyes aloft and all about, searching the sea above the rim of the cup, he told again the story of the fabulous one. "I am telling you—I who have been whaling in the Arctic for thirty-five years; and in that time I have seen many strange things—huge icebergs that crushed, seas that overwhelmed, terrific winds, and from out of the sea many awful things. But of huge creatures nothing in size to equal that great blue whale that for eleven years now I have been hunting. Ah, the thousands of miles I have steamed to get him! Aye, the tens of thousands in the hopes of getting him; and not yet have I got him. But some day, some day, I feel it in me—some day— Another cup of coffee, Fred.

"One time—where were we then? Oh yes, here it was—in this very spot almost. One time, I say, I crept upon him, and I got one shot at him. It is true. And struck him? Oh yes—the lance went in to the line—five feet of iron buried deep in his back—yes. I have killed my thousands—and it is not once in the thousand I miss. And I did not miss that time. But away he went—you would not believe the speed! The grenade? It did not explode. With all the power of the engines against him—and she steams ten miles this steamer of mine—and yet, even so, he towed us twenty-five miles—twenty-five and ten. Yes, it is true—thirty-five miles an hour. No more to him was this steamer than to this steamer would be the log astern—not one ounce.

"And he towed us, and towed us, and towed us, from seventy-six fifty to above the eightieth parallel—past Spitzbergen, clear to the edge of the icefields, and there— Another cup of coffee, Fred. It is good coffee."

"And then?"

"And then? Poof! Under the ice he went, and with him eight hundred fathoms of our stoutest line—most expensive line—for we cut it quickly when we saw it must be that or go under the ice too. Such a huge fellow! Nobody would believe. But I who have put a lance into him, I am telling you. It was hard to lose him so —there was rage in my heart that day—but it is in the luck of life. But something tells me—something tells me—that some time he will fall to me.

"Twice since that time I have seen him—once five years back, and once again three years ago. But he would not let me get near —not he, the wise one. But some time, I tell you, he will fall to me. And I will know him. Thousands of them I have killed, but the great one who escaped me I remember best."

It would have been called cold enough that morning in July were it anywhere else than in a polar zone. Two o'clock in the morning it was, an overcast sky, thin clouds, and gray shadows of them on the sea, except where here and there through tiny peepholes shot stray pale-yellow needles of the light of the midnight sun.

It was one of those stray needles of light that, striking the crest of a gently tumbling sea, disclosed to the lookout a great splashing to the northward. Hardly any need for the man in the cask at the foremast head to call out the news. The skipper, with eyes ever roving, had seen it too, and while yet the echo of the lookout's "Whale-O" was dying away, had with one hand motioned to the man at the wheel, and with the other rung cruising-speed ahead.

Forward she jumped, and to the northward turned all eyes—skipper's, lookout's, wheelsman's, deck-hands'. Even the cook in his apron and the fireman in his overalls—the white clothes and the grimy ones—stood together on the afterdeck and discussed the chances for the first whale of the trip.

Clipping along at eight knots went the steamer, and soon the vapory spoutings became more clearly marked against the gray. And then the spoutings gave way to plainly visible splashes and leaps into the air.

The skipper, noting that, inquires of above: "A blue whale, Peder?"

"Aye, sir, a blue one it must be."

"And a big blue one, Peder?"

"I think so—a great strong one."

"Good. And at play, Peder?"

There is no immediate answer from aloft, and the skipper glances up for explanation. Peder's body is half out of the cask, stomach across the chimes, and eyes intent on the spectacle ahead. His attitude makes it plain to all hands that there is something unusual going on, and looking more intently, they all soon see that it is the liveliest kind of a splashing to the northward.

"What is it, do you think, Peder?" asks the skipper again. "Oh, what is it, Peder? Surely a big one and at play?"

"A blue whale, yes—but listen." All voices become hushed on deck and soon they hear it. Down on the wind it comes to them, the scream of a great creature in pain.

"The blubber cutters!" exclaims the skipper. "The blubber cutters!" exclaim the crew, and, "Aye, the blubber cutters," affirms Peder from aloft—"the little fighting whales."

"So," says the skipper. "And they have attacked the big one?"

"Just so. And all swarming in on him—a school of them. Again he screams—you hear him? And leaps!—see him now again? Oh, the little devils!"

Full speed, signals the skipper. The fireman dives below, and others of the crew, looking out over the rail and watching the swirling foam slide past the steamer's sides, begin to mutter, "If she would but go faster—they will have him eaten before we can get there. Aye, yes, if she would but go faster."

"Patience—patience, she is doing her best—ten miles, no less." It is the skipper who advises, as it is he who pats the breech of his gun and waits, with eyes that never swerve from the scene of the combat ahead. The skipper's weight is two hundred and sixty odd pounds, no fat, and six meals a day with that, plenty of work and a sufficiency of salt air—he does not run to nerves.

One mile away is the steamer now, and no need to be to the masthead to fall into sympathy with Peder's excited exclamations. Clearly enough, now, can they all hear the big whale's screamings and make out his dark shadow against the gray haze and grayer sea as with every scream he leaps into the air.

"A tremendous great fellow he looks, but that may be the shadows. One cannot always tell." So the skipper talks in a voice still smooth and even, but it is a more than ordinarily careful examination that he makes of the powder charge as he rams it home, and again of the bomb-lance as that is slid in after it, and pats the breech, and makes sure that swivel and pinions are working smoothly—with a last few little drops of oil by way of no harm. And his eyes are brightening and his chest lifting beneath his jersey, and, looking at him, it occurs to all hands—the tale of the big blue whale their skipper has never given up hope of some day getting. Within this very hour has he not said it again? "Some time, I tell you, he will fall to me. And I will know him when he comes." One of the tales of whaling that, they said at the time, and not to be too seriously considered, they have known of other whale hunters in their time who told tales that were even more difficult to believe.

Less than half a mile away is the steamer now. One minute more, half a minute perhaps—and the skipper signals to slow down. They can plainly hear the bell ringing in the engine room below—it is still as that on deck.

And why so still? It is their business to kill whales. They, too, have been in at the death of thousands. But this is different—a life and death struggle such as man seldom sees. And there is the skipper. They watch him as he gazes, watch him as he gazes and gazes, and follow his eyes with their eyes as, contemplatively leaving the gun platform, he goes aloft. They watch him there and hear him when he exclaims, though half under his breath, "It is my great whale, Peder—my great whale." And, this when he is on deck again, "Now you shall see a real whale."

And they see. The blubber cutters, the little fighting whales, they with the teeth of a horse, are darting in and under, up and away, like demons bent on torture. There may be twenty, or twenty-five, or thirty of them—it is difficult to say, they dart, and dive, and cross so rapidly. As long as a man's thumb, and fully as thick, are their teeth, and these are their weapons. The whale, with only layers of bone in his jaws, cannot nip as can they. But he has his great flukes—and when he brings them down—so— the sea boils as if it were a little gale stirring.

The blubber cutters attack. One, two, three, five, ten—a whole school—in single file and in ranks, individually and in squadrons, in they shoot for their victim. And more rapid than any torpedo flotilla are they in attack. Their lines of advance may be followed by the swiftly, smoothly gliding fins on the surface—that is, the line of those who snap at whatever of the blue-black body that may be seen above the water. The advance of those that attack from under may be traced no farther than the edge of blood, gurry, and foam which mingles with the cold gray sea and hides everything directly below from sight. It is after that dive in, that roll over, as jaws open and into that great belly they bite, then it is that the big whale screams in his agony—the scream of a horse when he is mortally hit, but in volume of sound a hundredfold increased.

Over that cold gray waste that penetrating cry carries for miles, and in it is an infinity of suggestion. And as he screams he leaps—flings his tremendous bulk so high out of the sea that the little whale steamer could find room to pass beneath. The crew cannot help speaking of that; but to be beneath as he comes down!—w-r-r-h!

And in that instant of time when he seems to be suspended, the moment when he has ceased to rise and yet is not falling, those on the steamer get a fair look at the immense body, and so creeps over them an awe of the almost incredible power that can toss that huge bulk so high in the air—and to lift almost clear of the water, also, the leeches with the bulldog jaws, who can now be seen with their teeth locked in the flesh of their prey, quivering with the eagerness of their grip, seeming to be boring for a fresh hold as they are carried up. Whoever has given a bulldog something to take hold of and then has lifted him off his feet and swung him back and forth and tried to shake him off—that is how it was. And now the blubber cutters try to hang on, and do hang on until the tremendous one shakes his body and snaps them off—then they drop.

Seeing him at this close range the crew of the steamer cease to wonder—they in Tromsö might cease to wonder, too, could they but see—that for ten years now this skipper of theirs had been telling his story. How long he is! A hundred—yes, and a hundred and five—aye, a hundred and ten feet. And his flukes! Eighteen, nineteen, yes, and twenty or twenty-one feet across—and a head as long as his flukes. Glory of King Olaf! but those are flukes.

Those flukes it is that stand by him in the worst of the fight. When he comes down full length and shakes off those that are clinging to him to the very last, he would, ere he could gather for another leap, be at the mercy of the reserves waiting to dash in and overpower—would, but for the great flukes with which he thrashes and flails the water and puts the greater part of them to rout and so keeps their forces scattered. Every fall of those flukes and a squad of them take to the wide waters. Skedaddling away so after such thwarted attacks, they cut so close to the steamer that the men on her deck at last take to standing by with their long lances. "Ugh, you devils," grunt the crew, and stab—and miss.

So the fight goes on. The blubber cutters attack, the great whale repels—with head, flippers, and flukes he repels—churning the sea into foam for ten rods around—that foam which was clear white at first, but is now beginning to take on a strong crimson tinge. Now and then he catches one of the little savages a fair blow with his flukes; off goes the little one then in circles that widen, until at last he darts straight off, before the others discover it and put an end to him. He may be one of their own kind, but he is good eating, too.

An hour of this with never a moment's rest for the whale, and he begins to weaken. They will get him in the end—they always do when they are hungry—and these are hungry, fighting hungry. He screams more loudly than ever—a scream that now has more of fear and pain and less of anger in it. Like a call for help is his scream now. "A call for help?"—it is the skipper who interprets. "We will give him help," and he smiles grimly; and yet there is pity, too, in the smile. "Again he calls—again—he is calling to Heaven for mercy now. We will give him mercy. Mercy —yes—and cheat the blubber cutters—the little devils of blubber cutters. All clear with the line. Two knots speed now. Now—but closer yet; he is such a big fellow—it would not do to miss him. Not once in a thousand have I missed—but who can tell? Now—now—steady—steady."

The steamer is so close and the lifted flukes so high above that the skipper throws back his head the better to follow them. "Look, the size of them!" he is exclaiming, when down they come, almost touching the muzzle of the gun, and striking the surface of the water with a tremendous report. He goes under water—too far under for a good shot. It is not yet time. No, not yet—next time—it would not do to miss. Now—now left, right— no, left—now—now. "Wee—pee!" the skipper, up on his toes, screams as he pulls the trigger. "Wee—pee!" and then he laughs like a little boy, when he sees he has not missed.

After the flame the smoke puffs out, and through the cloud of it can be seen the line that follows the lance. The lance goes out of sight in the blue-gray back—lance and shaft are buried—a good shot, just aft of the middle of the back, where he lies highest out of water. It was like shooting at an inclined bank, so large and safe a mark it offered.

With the report scuttle the blubber cutters—the cowardly

blubber cutters. Their flying fins cut the water toward every point of the compass.

The whale screams no more. He comes to a full stop as if numbed. He does not seem to know what to make of it. Perhaps he fancies he is free, or, perhaps, to his whale's memory comes a recollection of the iron that pierced him years ago. Whatever he thinks or remembers—whatever it is that holds him for about three seconds—his first act after that dead pause is to shoot off to the right across the steamer's bow. There he halts again, this time for perhaps five seconds, and then begins to thrash the sea with the mammoth flukes, straight up and down, without moving half his length from the one spot. He stays thrashing there too long. A second lance has been made ready, the steamer creeps up, and the skipper shoots again. This is a good shot, too, and beside the first line a second line runs.

That second lance is barely in when the bomb of the first one explodes. Fifteen or twenty seconds later and the second bomb explodes. But there he is spouting his blood, and that is a pitiful thing to see. He is like nothing that men have been taught to care for, he is only a monster of the sea that all men have been taught to fear, and yet, even so, it is his life blood that is welling up, and it is a pitiful thing to see.

The skipper watches him for a moment, shakes his head, and orders his men to haul in. They run the line about the drum of the winch and begin to warp him in. The mere weight of him is something in itself, and he does not come in too rapidly. He makes one last effort before he is alongside—he is not giving up on command, but he does not get far. He who once towed the steamer twenty-five miles an hour for half a day, with the full power of the engines against him, does not now get a hundred yards away before he has to stop.

Even when he is alongside and almost passive, with only a little occasional tremor and frothy bubbles from the blowhole to prove that he is still breathing, the skipper is not satisfied. "There is no telling—he might yet wake up—lance him, Peder." And Peder stabs him with the long lance twice, and after each stab up spouts the thick, dark blood—two streams four feet high and thick around as a man's wrist almost.

"What a great fellow," says the skipper. Already he has said it twenty times at least—"a great strong fellow." And standing by the rail he looks his full. "Is he not what I said? Back in Tromsö will they believe me now? Will they? And the iron that I put in him years ago—see the scar of it! Later I shall myself cut that iron out—and keep it, yes. And to show them at home what a monster he is, I am almost tempted to tow him there—but it is too far—more than a hundred miles—four hundred English miles—it is too far, yes. Put the chains to him now—a strong fellow—and will bring seven—yes, eight or nine thousand kroner. And what will I do with nine thousand kroner? What? Ho—ho—ho—my oldest boy shall go to the university with it—shall go if he will. But will he? Who can say? He is like his father—he, too, cares more for whale hunting than for schools. And you, you little fighting whales"—he waved a big arm where the fins of the blubber cutters cut the sea—"you, you little devils, did I not cheat you fine? Did I not, hah? Oh, but I would like to put a lance in some of you. I have a mind to try it—'twould teach you a lesson—yes. And yet, you little fighting devils, but for you I would not have him now. No. But such a strong one—and eight thousand kroner. And the university for Olaf—yes—if he will but go. Ho—ho—such a day—such a day! Oh, Fred, a cup of coffee here. I begin to feel it. Forty hours on the platform—it is a long time without sleep. But today I sleep—eight thousand kroner—ho—ho!—the length of him, look! and eight thousand kroner. And not alone the greatest whale that ever I killed, that ever any Norwegian killed, but the greatest that any man ever killed. And oh, Fred, a cup of coffee all around—and let all hands eat, for we hunt no more today."

THE PRINCESS
AND THE PUMA

O. HENRY

THERE HAD TO BE a king and queen, of course. The king was a terrible old man, who wore six-shooters and spurs, and shouted in such a tremendous voice that the rattlers on the prairie would run into their holes under the prickly pear. Before there was a royal family they called this man "Whispering Ben." When he came to own 50,000 acres of land and more cattle than he could count, they called him O'Donnell, "the Cattle King."

The queen had been a Mexican girl from Laredo. She made a good, mild, Colorado-claro wife, and even succeeded in teaching Ben to modify his voice sufficiently while in the house to keep the dishes from being broken. When Ben got to be king she would still sit on the gallery of Espinosa ranch and weave rush mats. When wealth became so irresistible and oppressive that upholstered chairs and a center table were brought down from San Antone in the wagons, she bowed her smooth, dark head, and shared the fate of the Danae.

Josefa O'Donnell was the surviving daughter, the princess. From her mother she inherited warmth of nature and a dusky, semi-tropic beauty. From Ben O'Donnell the royal she acquired a store of intrepidity, common sense, and the faculty of ruling. The combination was one worth traveling many miles to see. Josefa while riding her pony at a gallop could put five out of six bullets through a tomato can swinging at the end of a string. She could play for hours with a white kitten she owned, dressing it in all manner of absurd clothes. Scorning a pencil, she could tell you out of her head what 1,545 two-year-olds would bring on the hoof, at eight dollars and fifty cents per head. Roughly speaking, the Espinosa ranch is forty miles long and thirty broad—but mostly leased land. Josefa, on her pony, had prospected over every mile of it. Every cowpuncher on the range knew her by sight and was a loyal vassal. Ripley Givens, foreman of one of the Espinosa outfits, saw her one day, and made up his mind to form a royal matrimonial alliance. Presumptuous? No. In those days in the Nueces country a man was a man. And, after all, the title of cattle king does not presuppose blood royal. Often it only signifies that its owner wears the crown in token of his magnificent qualities in the art of cattle stealing.

One day Ripley Givens rode over to the Double Elm ranch to inquire about a bunch of strayed yearlings. He was late in setting out on his return trip, and it was sundown when he struck the White Horse crossing of the Nueces. From there to his own camp it was sixteen miles. To the Espinosa ranch house it was twelve. Givens was tired. He decided to pass the night at the crossing.

There was a fine water hole in the riverbed. The banks were thickly covered with great trees, undergrown with brush. Back from the water hole fifty yards was a stretch of curly mesquite grass—supper for his horse and bed for himself. Givens staked his horse, and spread out his saddle blankets to dry. He sat down with his back against a tree, and rolled a cigarette. From somewhere in the dense timber along the river came a sudden, rageful, shivering wail. The pony danced at the end of his rope and blew a whistling snort of comprehending fear. Givens puffed at his cigarette, but he reached leisurely for his pistol belt which lay on the grass, and twirled the cylinder of his weapon tentatively. A great gar plunged with a loud splash into the water hole. A little brown rabbit skipped around a bunch of catclaw, and sat twitching his whiskers and looking humorously at Givens. The pony went on eating grass.

It is well to be reasonably watchful when a Mexican lion sings soprano along the arroyos at sundown. The burden of his song may be that young calves and fat lambs are scarce, and that he has a carnivorous desire for your acquaintance.

In the grass lay an empty fruit can, cast there by some former sojourner. Givens caught sight of it with a grunt of satisfaction. In his coat pocket tied behind his saddle was a handful or two of ground coffee. Black coffee and cigarettes! What ranchero could desire more?

In two minutes he had a little fire going clearly. He started, with his can, for the water hole. When within fifteen yards of its edge he saw, between the bushes, a side-saddled pony with down-dropped reins cropping grass a little distance to his left. Just rising from her hands and knees on the brink of the water hole was Josefa O'Donnell. She had been drinking water, and she brushed the sand from the palms of her hands. Ten yards away, to her right, half concealed by a clump of sacuista, Givens saw the crouching form of the Mexican lion. His amber eyeballs glared hungrily; six feet from them was the tip of his tail stretched straight, like a pointer's. His hind quarters rocked with the motion of the cat tribe preliminary to leaping.

Givens did what he could. His six-shooter was thirty-five yards away lying on the grass. He gave a loud yell, and dashed between the lion and the princess.

The "rucus," as Givens called it afterward, was brief and somewhat confused. When he arrived on the line of attack he saw a dim streak in the air, and heard a couple of faint cracks. Then a hundred pounds of Mexican lion plumped down upon his head and flattened him, with a heavy jar, to the ground. He remembered calling out, "Let up, now—no fair gouging!" and then he crawled from under the lion like a worm, with his mouth full of grass and dirt, and a big lump on the back of his head where it had struck the root of a water elm. The lion lay motionless. Givens, feeling aggrieved, and suspicious of fouls, shook his fist at the lion, and shouted, "I'll rastle you again for twenty—" and then he got back to himself.

Josefa was standing in her tracks, quietly reloading her silver-mounted .38. It had not been a difficult shot. The lion's head made an easier mark than a tomato can swinging at the end of a string. There was a provoking, teasing, maddening smile upon her mouth and in her dark eyes. The would-be-rescuing knight felt the fire of his fiasco burn down to his soul. Here had been his chance, the chance that he had dreamed of; and Momus, and not

Cupid, had presided over it. The satyrs in the wood were, no doubt, holding their sides in hilarious, silent laughter. There had been something like vaudeville—say Signor Givens and his funny knockabout act with the stuffed lion.

"Is that you, Mr. Givens?" said Josefa, in her deliberate, saccharine contralto. "You nearly spoiled my shot when you yelled. Did you hurt your head when you fell?"

"Oh, no," said Givens, quietly, "that didn't hurt." He stooped ignominiously and dragged his best Stetson hat from under the beast. It was crushed and wrinkled to a fine comedy effect. Then he knelt down, and softly stroked the fierce, open-jawed head of the dead lion.

"Poor old Bill!" he exclaimed, mournfully.

"What's that?" asked Josefa, sharply.

"Of course you didn't know, Miss Josefa," said Givens, with an air of one allowing magnanimity to triumph over grief. "Nobody can blame you. I tried to save him, but I couldn't let you know in time."

"Save who?"

"Why, Bill. I've been looking for him all day. You see, he's been our camp pet for two years. Poor old fellow, he wouldn't have hurt a cottontail rabbit. It'll break the boys all up when they hear about it. But you couldn't tell, of course, that Bill was just trying to play with you."

Josefa's black eyes burned steadily upon him. Ripley Givens met the test successfully. He stood rumpling the yellow-brown curls on his head pensively. In his eyes was regret, not unmingled with a gentle reproach. His smooth features were set to a pattern of indisputable sorrow. Josefa wavered.

"What was your pet doing here?" she asked, making a last stand. "There's no camp near the White Horse crossing."

"The old rascal ran away from camp yesterday," answered Givens, readily. "It's a wonder the coyotes didn't scare him to death. You see, Jim Webster, our horse wrangler, brought a little terrier pup into camp last week. The pup made life miserable for Bill—he used to chase him around and chew his hind legs for hours at a time. Every night when bedtime came Bill would sneak under one of the boy's blankets and sleep to keep the pup from finding him. I reckon he must have been worried pretty desperate or he wouldn't have run away. He was always afraid to get out of sight of camp."

Josefa looked at the body of the fierce animal. Givens gently patted one of the formidable paws that could have killed a year-ling calf with one blow. Slowly a red flush widened upon the dark olive face of the girl. Was it the signal of the shame of the true sportsman who has brought down ignoble quarry? Her eyes grew softer, and the lowered lids drove away all their bright mockery.

"I'm very sorry," she said, humbly; "but he looked so big, and jumped so high that—"

"Poor old Bill was hungry," interrupted Givens, in quick de-fense of the deceased. "We always made him jump for his supper in camp. He would lie down and roll over for a piece of meat. When he saw you he thought he was going to get something to eat from you."

Suddenly Josefa's eyes opened wide.

"I might have shot you!" she exclaimed. "You ran right in between. You risked your life to save your pet! That was fine, Mr. Givens. I like a man who is kind to animals."

Yes; there was even admiration in her gaze now. After all, there was a hero rising out of the ruins of the anticlimax. The look on Givens' face would have secured him a high position in the S.P.C.A.

"I always loved 'em," said he, "horses, dogs, Mexican lions, cows, alligators—"

"I hate alligators," instantly demurred Josefa, "crawly, muddy things!"

"Did I say alligators?" said Givens, with a laugh. "I meant antelopes, of course."

Josefa's conscience drove her to make further amends. She held out her hand penitently. There was a bright, unshed drop in each of her eyes.

"Please forgive me, Mr. Givens, won't you? I'm only a girl, you know, and I was frightened at first. I'm very, very sorry I shot Bill. You don't know how ashamed I feel. I wouldn't have done it for anything."

Givens took the offered hand. He held it for a time while he allowed the generosity of his nature to overcome his grief at the loss of Bill. At last it was clear that he had forgiven her.

"Please don't speak of it any more, Miss Josefa. 'Twas enough to frighten any young lady the way Bill looked. I'll explain it all right to the boys."

"Are you really sure you don't hate me?" Josefa came closer to him, impulsively. Her eyes were sweet—oh, sweet and pleading with gracious penitence. "I would hate anyone who would kill my kitten. And how daring and kind of you to risk being shot when you tried to save him! How very few men would have done that!" Victory wrested from defeat! Vaudeville turned into drama! Bravo, Ripley Givens!

It was now twilight. Of course Miss Josefa could not be allowed to ride on to the ranch house alone. Givens resaddled his pony in spite of that animal's reproachful glances, and rode with her. Side by side they galloped across the smooth grass, the princess and the man who was kind to animals. The prairie odors of fruitful earth and delicate bloom were thick and sweet around them. The sky, fire-spangled, fitted the rim of the world like a turquoise cover. Coyotes yelping over there on the hill! No fear. And yet—

Josefa rode closer. A little hand seemed to grope. Givens found it with his own. The ponies kept an even gait. The hands lingered together, and the owner of one explained, "I never was frightened before, but just think! How terrible it would be to meet a really wild lion! Poor Bill! I'm so glad you came with me!"

O'Donnell was sitting on the ranch gallery.

"Hallo, Rip!" he shouted—"that you?"

"He rode in with me," said Josefa. "I lost my way and was late."

"Much obliged," called the cattle king. "Stop over, Rip, and ride to camp in the morning."

But Givens would not. He would push on to camp. There was a bunch of steers to start off on the trail at daybreak. He said good night, and trotted away.

An hour later, when the lights were out, Josefa, in her night robe, came to her door and called to the king in his own room across the brick-paven hallway, "Say, Pop, you know that old

Mexican lion they call the 'Gotch-eared Devil'—the one that killed Gonzales, Mr. Martin's sheep herder, and about fifty calves on the Salado range? Well, I settled his hash this afternoon over at the White Horse crossing. Put two balls in his head with my .38 while he was on the jump. I knew him by the slice gone from his left ear that old Gonzales cut off with his machete. You couldn't have made a better shot yourself, Daddy."

"Bully for you!" thundered Whispering Ben from the darkness of the royal chamber.

THE ROAD TO
TINKHAMTOWN

COREY FORD

IT WAS A LONG WAY, but he knew where he was going. He would follow the road through the woods and over the crest of a hill and down the hill to the stream, and cross the sagging timbers of the bridge, and on the other side would be the place called Tinkhamtown. He was going back to Tinkhamtown.

He walked slowly at first, his legs dragging with each step. He had not walked for almost a year, and his flanks had shriveled and wasted away from lying in bed so long; he could fit his fingers around his thigh. Doc Towle had said he would never walk again, but that was Doc for you, always on the pessimistic side. Why, now he was walking quite easily, once he had started. The strength was coming back into his legs, and he did not have to stop for breath so often. He tried jogging a few steps, just to show he could, but he slowed again because he had a long way to go.

It was hard to make out the old road, choked with alders and covered by matted leaves, and he shut his eyes so he could see it better. He could always see it when he shut his eyes. Yes, here was the beaver dam on the right, just as he remembered it, and the flooded stretch where he had picked his way from hummock to hummock while the dog splashed unconcernedly in front of him. The water had been over his boot tops in one place, and sure enough, as he waded it now his left boot filled with water again, the same warm squdgy feeling. Everything was the way it had been that afternoon, nothing had changed in ten years. Here was the blowdown across the road that he had clambered over, and here on a knoll was the clump of thornapples where a grouse had flushed as they passed. Shad had wanted to look for it, but he had whistled him back. They were looking for Tinkhamtown.

He had come across the name on a map in the town library. He used to study the old maps and survey charts of the state; sometimes they showed where a farming community had flourished, a century ago, and around the abandoned pastures and in the orchards grown up to pine the birds would be feeding undisturbed. Some of his best grouse covers had been located that way. The map had been rolled up in a cardboard cylinder; it crackled with age as he spread it out. The date was 1857. It was the sector between Cardigan and Kearsarge Mountains, a wasteland of slash and second-growth timber without habitation today, but evidently it had supported a number of families before the Civil War. A road was marked on the map, dotted with X's for homesteads, and the names of the owners were lettered beside them: Nason, J. Tinkham, Allard, R. Tinkham. Half the names were Tinkham. In the center of the map—the paper was so yellow that he could barely make it out—was the word "Tinkhamtown."

He had drawn a rough sketch on the back of an envelope, noting where the road left the highway and ran north to a fork and then turned east and crossed a stream that was not even named; and the next morning he and Shad had set out together to find the place. They could not drive very far in the jeep, because washouts had gutted the roadbed and laid bare the ledges and boulders. He had stuffed the sketch in his hunting-coat pocket, and hung his shotgun over his forearm and started walking, the setter trotting ahead with the bell on his collar tinkling. It was an old-fashioned sleighbell, and it had a thin silvery note that echoed through the woods like peepers in the spring. He could follow the sound in the thickest cover, and when it stopped he would go to where he heard it last and Shad would be on point. After Shad's death, he had put the bell away. He'd never had another dog.

It was silent in the woods without the bell, and the way was longer than he remembered. He should have come to the big hill by now. Maybe he'd taken the wrong turn back at the fork. He thrust a hand into his hunting coat; the envelope with the sketch was still in the pocket. He sat down on a flat rock to get his bearings, and then he realized, with a surge of excitement, that he had stopped on this very rock for lunch ten years ago. Here was the waxed paper from his sandwich, tucked in a crevice, and here was the hollow in the leaves where Shad had stretched out beside him, the dog's soft muzzle flattened on his thigh. He looked up, and through the trees he could see the hill.

He rose and started walking again, carrying his shotgun. He had left the gun standing in its rack in the kitchen when he had been taken to the state hospital, but now it was hooked over his arm by the trigger guard; he could feel the solid heft of it. The woods grew more dense as he climbed, but here and there a shaft of sunlight slanted through the trees. "And there were forests ancient as the hills," he thought, "enfolding sunny spots of greenery." Funny that should come back to him now; he hadn't read it since he was a boy. Other things were coming back to him, the smell of dank leaves and sweetfern and frosted apples, the sharp contrast of sun and cool shade, the November stillness before snow. He walked faster, feeling the excitement swell within him.

He paused on the crest of the hill, straining his ears for the faint mutter of the stream below him, but he could not hear it because of the voices. He wished they would stop talking, so he could hear the stream. Someone was saying his name over and over, "Frank, Frank," and he opened his eyes reluctantly and looked up at his sister. Her face was worried, and there was nothing to worry about. He tried to tell her where he was going, but when he moved his lips the words would not form. "What did you say, Frank?" she asked, bending her head lower. "I don't understand." He couldn't make the words any clearer, and she straightened and said to Doc Towle: "It sounded like Tinkhamtown."

"Tinkhamtown?" Doc shook his head. "Never heard him mention any place by that name."

He smiled to himself. Of course he'd never mentioned it to Doc. Things like a secret grouse cover you didn't mention to anyone, not even to as close a friend as Doc was. No, he and

Shad were the only ones who knew. They had found it together, that long ago afternoon, and it was their secret.

They had come to the stream—he shut his eyes so he could see it again—and Shad had trotted across the bridge. He had followed more cautiously, avoiding the loose planks and walking along a beam with his shotgun held out to balance himself. On the other side of the stream the road mounted steeply to a clearing in the woods, and he halted before the split-stone foundations of a house, the first of the series of farms shown on the map. It must have been a long time since the building had fallen in; the cottonwoods growing in the cellar hole were twenty, maybe thirty years old. His boot overturned a rusted ax blade and the handle of a china cup in the grass; that was all. Beside the doorstep was a lilac bush, almost as tall as the cottonwoods. He thought of the wife who had set it out, a little shrub then, and the husband who had chided her for wasting time on such frivolous things with all the farm work to be done. But the work had come to nothing, and still the lilac bloomed each spring, the one thing that had survived.

Shad's bell was moving along the stone wall at the edge of the clearing, and he strolled after him, not hunting, wondering about the people who had gone away and left their walls to crumble and their buildings to collapse under the winter snows. Had they ever come back to Tinkhamtown? Were they here now, watching him unseen? His toe stubbed against a block of hewn granite hidden by briars, part of the sill of the old barn. Once it had been a tight barn, warm with cattle steaming in their stalls, rich with the blend of hay and manure and harness leather. He liked to think of it the way it was; it was more real than this bare rectangle of blocks and the emptiness inside. He'd always felt that way about the past. Doc used to argue that what's over is over, but he would insist Doc was wrong. Everything is the way it was, he'd tell Doc. The past never changes. You leave it and go on to the present, but it is still there, waiting for you to come back to it.

He had been so wrapped in his thoughts that he had not realized Shad's bell had stopped. He hurried across the clearing, holding his gun ready. In a corner of the stone wall an ancient apple tree had littered the ground with fallen fruit, and beneath it Shad was standing motionless. The white fan of his tail was lifted a little and his backline was level, the neck craned forward, one foreleg cocked. His flanks were trembling with the nearness of grouse, and a thin skein of drool hung from his jowls. The dog did not move as he approached, but the brown eyes rolled back until their whites showed, looking for him. "Steady, boy," he called. His throat was tight, the way it always got when Shad was on point, and he had to swallow hard. "Steady, I'm coming."

"I think his lips moved just now," his sister's voice said. He did not open his eyes, because he was waiting for the grouse to get up in front of Shad, but he knew Doc Towle was looking at him. "He's sleeping," Doc said after a moment. "Maybe you better get some sleep yourself, Mrs. Duncombe." He heard Doc's heavy footsteps cross the room. "Call me if there's any change," Doc said, and closed the door, and in the silence he could hear his sister's chair creaking beside him, her silk dress rustling regularly as she breathed.

What was she doing here, he wondered. Why had she come all the way from California to see him? It was the first time they had seen each other since she had married and moved out West. She was his only relative, but they had never been very close; they had nothing in common, really. He heard from her now and then, but it was always the same letter: why didn't he sell the old place, it was too big for him now that the folks had passed on, why didn't he take a small apartment in town where he wouldn't be alone? But he liked the big house and he wasn't alone, not with Shad. He had closed off all the other rooms and moved into the kitchen so everything would be handy. His sister didn't approve of his bachelor ways, but it was very comfortable with his cot by the stove and Shad curled on the floor near him at night, whinnying and scratching the linoleum with his claws as he chased a bird in a dream. He wasn't alone when he heard that.

He had never married. He had looked after the folks as long as they lived; maybe that was why. Shad was his family. They were always together—Shad was short for Shadow—and there was a closeness between them that he did not feel for anyone else, not his sister or Doc even. He and Shad used to talk without words, each knowing what the other was thinking, and they could always find one another in the woods. He still remembered the little things about him: the possessive thrust of his paw, the way he false-yawned when he was vexed, the setter stubbornness sometimes, the clownish grin when they were going hunting, and the kind eyes. That was it; Shad was the kindest person he had ever known.

They had not hunted again after Tinkhamtown. The old dog had stumbled several times, walking back to the jeep, and he had to carry him in his arms the last hundred yards. It was hard to realize he was gone. He liked to think of him the way he was; it was like the barn, it was more real than the emptiness. Sometimes at night, lying awake with the pain in his legs, he would hear the scratch of claws on the linoleum, and he would turn on the light and the hospital room would be empty. But when he turned the light off he would hear the scratching again, and he would be content and drop off to sleep, or what passed for sleep in these days and nights that ran together without dusk or dawn.

Once he asked Doc point blank if he would ever get well. Doc was giving him something for the pain, and he hesitated a moment and finished what he was doing and cleaned the needle and then looked at him and said: "I'm afraid not, Frank." They had grown up in town together, and Doc knew him too well to lie. "I'm afraid there's nothing to do." Nothing to do but lie here and wait till it was over. "Tell me, Doc," he whispered, for his voice wasn't very strong, "what happens when it's over?" And Doc fumbled with the catch of his black bag and closed it and said well he supposed you went on to someplace else called the Hereafter. But he shook his head; he always argued with Doc. "No, it isn't someplace else," he told him, "it's someplace you've been where you want to be again." Doc didn't understand, and he couldn't explain it any better. He knew what he meant, but the shot was taking effect and he was tired.

He was tired now, and his legs ached a little as he started down the hill, trying to find the stream. It was too dark under the trees to see the sketch he had drawn, and he could not tell direction by the moss on the north side of the trunks. The moss grew all around them, swelling them out of size, and huge blowdowns blocked his way. Their upended roots were black and misshapen, and now instead of excitement he felt a surge of panic. He floundered through a pile of slash, his legs throbbing with pain as the sharp points stabbed him, but he did not have the strength to get to the other side and he had to back out again and circle. He did not know where he was going. It was getting late, and he had lost the way.

There was no sound in the woods, nothing to guide him, nothing but his sister's chair creaking and her breath catching now and then in a dry sob. She wanted him to turn back, and Doc wanted him to, they all wanted him to turn back. He thought of the big house; if he left it alone it would fall in with the winter snows and cottonwoods would grow in the cellar hole. And there were all the other doubts, but most of all there was the fear. He was afraid of the darkness, and being alone, and not knowing where he was going. It would be better to turn around and go back. He knew the way back.

And then he heard it, echoing through the woods like peepers in the spring, the thin silvery tinkle of a sleighbell. He started running toward it, following the sound down the hill. His legs were strong again, and he hurdled the blowdowns, he leapt over fallen logs, he put one fingertip on a pile of slash and sailed over it like a grouse skimming. He was getting nearer and the sound filled his ears, louder than a thousand churchbells ringing, louder than all the choirs in the sky, as loud as the pounding of his heart. The fear was gone; he was not lost. He had the bell to guide him now.

He came to the stream, and paused for a moment at the bridge. He wanted to tell them he was happy, if they only knew how happy he was, but when he opened his eyes he could not see them anymore. Everything else was bright, but the room was dark.

The bell had stopped, and he looked across the stream. The other side was bathed in sunshine, and he could see the road mounting steeply, and the clearing in the woods, and the apple tree in a corner of the stone wall. Shad was standing motionless beneath it, the white fan of his tail lifted, his neck craned forward and one foreleg cocked. The whites of his eyes showed as he looked back, waiting for him.

"Steady," he called, "steady, boy." He started across the bridge. "I'm coming."

THE BIG BEAR

CHARLES MAJOR

AWAY BACK in the twenties, when Indiana was a baby state, and great forests of tall trees and tangled underbrush darkened what are now her bright plains and sunny hills, there stood upon the east bank of Big Blue River, a mile or two north of the point where that stream crosses the Michigan road, a cozy log cabin of two rooms—one front and one back.

The house faced the west, and stretching off toward the river for a distance equal to twice the width of an ordinary street, was a bluegrass lawn, upon which stood a dozen or more elm and sycamore trees, with a few honey locusts scattered here and there. Immediately at the water's edge was a steep slope of ten or twelve feet. Back of the house, mile upon mile, stretched the deep dark forest, inhabited by deer and bears, wolves and wildcats, squirrels and birds.

In the river the fish were so numerous that they seemed to entreat the boys to catch them, and to take them out of their crowded quarters. There were bass and black suckers, sunfish and catfish, to say nothing of the sweetest of all, the big-mouthed redeye.

South of the house stood a log barn, with room in it for three horses and two cows; and enclosing this barn, together with a piece of ground, five or six acres in extent, was a palisade fence, eight or ten feet high, made by driving poles into the ground close together. In this enclosure the farmer kept his stock, consisting of a few sheep and cattle, and here also the chickens,

geese, and ducks were driven at nightfall to save them from "varmints," as all prowling animals were called by the settlers.

The man who had built this log hut, and who lived in it and
owned the adjoining land at the time of which I write, bore the
name of Balser Brent. "Balser" is probably a corruption of
Baltzer, but, however that may be, Balser was his name, and
Balser was the hero of the bear stories which I am about to tell
you.

Mr. Brent and his young wife had moved to the Blue River
settlement from North Carolina, when young Balser was a little
boy five or six years of age. They had purchased the "eighty"
upon which they lived, from the United States, at a sale of public
land held in the town of Brookville on Whitewater, and had paid
for it what was then considered a good round sum—one dollar
per acre. They had received a deed for their "eighty" from no less
a person than James Monroe, then President of the United
States. This deed, which is called a patent, was written on sheepskin, signed by the President's own hand, and is still preserved by
the descendants of Mr. Brent as one of the title deeds to the land
it conveyed. The house, as I have told you, consisted of two large
rooms, or buildings, separated by a passageway six or eight feet
broad which was roofed over, but open at both ends—on the
north and south. The back room was the kitchen, and the front
room was the parlor, bedroom, sitting room, and library all in
one.

At the time when my story opens Little Balser, as he was
called to distinguish him from his father, was thirteen or fourteen
years of age, and was the happy possessor of a younger brother,
Jim, aged nine, and a little sister one year old, of whom he was
very proud indeed.

On the south side of the front room was a large fireplace. The
chimney was built of sticks, thickly covered with clay. The fireplace was almost as large as a small room in one of our cramped
modern houses, and was broad and deep enough to take in
backlogs which were so large and heavy that they could not be
lifted, but were drawn in at the door and rolled over the floor to
the fireplace.

The prudent father usually kept two extra backlogs, one on

each side of the fireplace, ready to be rolled in as the blaze died down; and on these logs the children would sit at night, with a rough slate made from a flat stone, and do their "ciphering," as the study of arithmetic was then called. The fire usually furnished all the light they had, for candles and "dips," being expensive luxuries, were used only when company was present.

The fire, however, gave sufficient light, and its flare upon a cold night extended halfway up the chimney, sending a ruddy, cozy glow to every nook and corner of the room.

The back room was the storehouse and kitchen; and from the beams along the walls hung rich hams and juicy sidemeat, jerked venison, dried apples, onions, and other provisions for the winter. There was a glorious fireplace in this room also, and a crane upon which to hang pots and cooking utensils.

The floor of the front room was made of logs split in halves with the flat, hewn side up; but the floor of the kitchen was of clay, packed hard and smooth.

The settlers had no stoves, but did their cooking in round pots called Dutch ovens. They roasted their meats on a spit or steel bar like the ramrod of a gun. The spit was kept turning before the fire, presenting first one side of the meat and then the other, until it was thoroughly cooked. Turning the spit was the children's work.

South of the palisade enclosing the barn was the clearing—a tract of twenty or thirty acres of land, from which Mr. Brent had cut and burned the trees. On this clearing the stumps stood thick as the hair on an angry dog's back; but the hard-working farmer plowed between and around them, and each year raised upon the fertile soil enough wheat and corn to supply the wants of his family and his stock, and still had a little grain left to take to Brookville, sixty miles away, where he had bought his land, there to exchange for such necessities of life as could not be grown upon the farm or found in the forests.

The daily food of the family all came from the farm, the forests, or the creek. Their sugar was obtained from the sap of the sugar trees; their meat was supplied in the greatest abundance by a few hogs, and by the inexhaustible game of which the forests were full. In the woods were found deer just for the shooting; and squirrels, rabbits, wild turkeys, pheasants, and quails, so numerous that a few hours' hunting would supply the table for days. The fish in the river, as I told you, fairly longed to be caught.

One day Mrs. Brent took down the dinner horn and blew upon it two strong blasts. This was the signal that Little Balser, who was helping his father down in the clearing, should come to the house. Balser was glad enough to drop his hoe and to run home. When he reached the house his mother said:

"Balser, go up to the drift and catch a mess of fish for dinner. Your father is tired of deer meat three times a day, and I know he would like a nice dish of fried redeyes at noon."

"All right, mother," said Balser. And he immediately took down his fishing pole and line, and got the spade to dig bait. When he had collected a small gourdful of angleworms, his mother called to him:

"You had better take a gun. You may meet a bear; your father loaded the gun this morning, and you must be careful in handling it."

Balser took the gun, which was a heavy rifle considerably longer than himself, and started up the river toward the drift, about a quarter of a mile away.

There had been rain during the night and the ground near the drift was soft.

Here, Little Balser noticed fresh bear tracks, and his breath began to come quickly. You may be sure he peered closely into every dark thicket, and looked behind all the large trees and logs, and had his eyes wide open lest perchance "Mr. Bear" should step out and surprise him with an affectionate hug, and thereby put an end to Little Balser forever.

So he walked on cautiously, and, if the truth must be told, somewhat tremblingly, until he reached the drift.

Balser was but a little fellow, yet the stern necessities of a settler's life had compelled his father to teach him the use of a gun; and, although Balser had never killed a bear, he had shot several deer, and upon one occasion had killed a wildcat, "almost as big as a cow," he said.

I have no doubt the wildcat seemed "almost as big as a cow" to Balser when he killed it, for it must have frightened him greatly, as wildcats were sometimes dangerous animals for children to encounter. Although Balser had never met a bear face to face and alone, yet he felt, and many a time had said, that there wasn't a bear in the world big enough to frighten him, if he but had his gun.

He had often imagined and minutely detailed to his parents and little brother just what he would do if he should meet a bear. He would wait calmly and quietly until his bearship should come within a few yards of him, and then he would slowly lift his gun. Bang! and Mr. Bear would be dead with a bullet in his heart.

But when he saw the fresh bear tracks, and began to realize that he would probably have an opportunity to put his theories about bear killing into practice, he began to wonder if, after all, he would become frightened and miss his aim. Then he thought of how the bear, in that case, would be calm and deliberate, and would put his theories into practice by walking very politely up to him, and making a very satisfactory dinner of a certain boy whom he could name. But as he walked on and no bear appeared, his courage grew stronger as the prospect of meeting the enemy grew less, and he again began saying to himself that no bear could frighten him, because he had his gun and he could and would kill it.

So Balser reached the drift; and having looked carefully about him, leaned his gun against a tree, unwound his fishing line from the pole, and walked out to the end of a log which extended into the river some twenty or thirty feet.

Here he threw in his line, and soon was so busily engaged drawing out sunfish and redeyes, and now and then a bass, which was hungry enough to bite at a worm, that all thought of the bear went out of his mind.

After he had caught enough fish for a sumptuous dinner he bethought him of going home, and as he turned toward the shore, imagine, if you can, his consternation when he saw upon the bank, quietly watching him, a huge black bear.

If the wildcat had seemed as large as a cow to Balser, of what size do you suppose that bear appeared? A cow! An elephant, surely, was small compared with the huge black fellow standing upon the bank.

It is true Balser had never seen an elephant, but his father had, and so had his friend Tom Fox, who lived down the river; and they all agreed that an elephant was "purt nigh as big as all outdoors."

The bear had a peculiar, determined expression about him that seemed to say:

"That boy can't get away; he's out on the log where the water is deep, and if he jumps into the river I can easily jump in after him and catch him before he can swim a dozen strokes. He'll have to come off the log in a short time, and then I'll proceed to devour him."

About the same train of thought had also been rapidly passing through Balser's mind. His gun was on the bank where he had left it, and in order to reach it he would have to pass the bear. He dared not jump into the water, for any attempt to escape on his part would bring the bear upon him instantly. He was very much frightened, but, after all, was a cool-headed little fellow for his age; so he concluded that he would not press matters, as the bear did not seem inclined to do so, but so long as the bear remained watching him on the bank would stay upon the log where he was, and allow the enemy to eye him to his heart's content.

There they stood, the boy and the bear, each eyeing the other as though they were the best of friends, and would like to eat each other, which, in fact, was literally true.

Time sped very slowly for one of them, you may be sure; and it seemed to Balser that he had been standing almost an age in the middle of Blue River on that wretched shaking log, when he heard his mother's dinner horn, reminding him that it was time to go home.

Balser quite agreed with his mother and gladly would he have gone, I need not tell you; but there stood the bear, patient, determined, and fierce; and Little Balser soon was convinced in his mind that his time had come to die.

He hoped that when his father would go home to dinner and find him still absent, he would come up the river in search of him, and frighten away the bear. Hardly had this hope sprung up in his mind, when it seemed that the same thought had also occurred to the bear, for he began to move down toward the shore end of the log upon which Balser was standing.

Slowly came the bear until he reached the end of the log, which for a moment he examined suspiciously, and then, to Balser's great alarm, cautiously stepped out upon it and began to walk toward him.

Balser thought of the folks at home, and, above all, of his baby sister; and when he felt that he should never see them again, and that they would in all probability never know of his fate, he began to grow heavy hearted and was almost paralyzed with fear.

On came the bear, putting one great paw in front of the other, and watching Balser intently with his little black eyes. His tongue hung out, and his great red mouth was open to its widest, showing the sharp, long, glittering teeth that would soon be feasting on a first-class boy dinner.

When the bear got within a few feet of Balser—so close he could almost feel the animal's hot breath as it slowly approached —the boy grew desperate with fear, and struck at the bear with the only weapon he had—his string of fish.

Now, bears love fish and blackberries above all other food; so when Balser's string of fish struck the bear in the mouth, he grabbed at them, and in doing so lost his foothold on the slippery log and fell into the water with a great splash and plunge.

This was Balser's chance for life, so he flung the fish to the bear, and ran for the bank with a speed worthy of the cause.

When he reached the bank his self-confidence returned, and he remembered all the things he had said he would do if he should meet a bear.

The bear had caught the fish, and again had climbed upon the log, where he was deliberately devouring them.

This was Little Balser's chance for death—to the bear. Quickly snatching up the gun, he rested it in the fork of a small tree nearby, took deliberate aim at the bear, which was not five yards away, and shot him through the heart. The bear dropped into the water dead, and floated downstream a little way, where he lodged at a ripple a short distance below.

Balser, after he had killed the bear, became more frightened than he had been at any time during the adventure, and ran home screaming. That afternoon his father went to the scene of battle and took the bear out of the water. It was very fat and large, and weighed, so Mr. Brent said, over six hundred pounds.

Balser was firmly of the opinion that he himself was also very fat and large, and weighed at least as much as the bear. He was certainly entitled to feel "big"; for he had got himself out of an ugly scrape in a brave, manly, cool-headed manner, and had achieved a victory of which a man might have been proud.

The news of Balser's adventure soon spread among the neighbors and he became quite a hero; for the bear he had killed was one of the largest that had ever been seen in that neighborhood, and, besides the gallons of rich bear oil it yielded, there were three or four hundred pounds of bear meat; and no other food is more strengthening for winter diet.

There was also the soft, furry skin, which Balser's mother tanned, and with it made a coverlid for Balser's bed, under which he and his little brother lay many a cold night, cozy and "snug as a bug in a rug."

TIME SAFARI

DAVID DRAKE

THE TYRANNOSAUR'S BELLOW made everyone jump except Vickers, the guide. The beast's nostrils flared, sucking in the odor of the light helicopter and the humans aboard it. It stalked forward.

"The largest land predator that ever lived," whispered one of the clients.

"A lot of people think that," said Vickers in what most of the rest thought was agreement.

There was nothing in the graceful advance of the tyrannosaur to suggest its ten-ton mass, until its tail sideswiped a flower-trunked cycad. The tree was six inches thick at the point of impact, and it sheared at that point without time to bend.

"Oh dear," the female photographer said. Her brother's grip on the chair arms was giving him leverage to push its cushion against the steel backplate.

The tyrannosaur's strides shifted the weight of its deep torso, counterbalanced by the swinging of its neck and tail. At each end of the head's arcs, the beast's eyes glared alternately at its prey. Except for the size, the watchers could have been observing a grackle on the lawn; but it was a grackle seen from a June bug's perspective.

"Goddam, he won't hold still!" snarled Salmes, the old-money client, the know-it-all. Vickers smiled. The tyrannosaur chose that moment to pause and bellow again. It was now a dozen feet from the helicopter, a single claw-tipped stride. If the blasting sound left one able, it was an ideal time to admire the beauty of the beast's four-foot head. Its teeth were irregular in length and placement, providing in sum a pair of yellowish, four-inch deep, saws. They fit together too loosely to shear; but with the power of the tyrannosaur's jaw muscles driving them, they could tear the flesh from any creature on Earth—in any age.

The beast's tongue was like a crocodile's, attached for its full length to the floor of its mouth. Deep blue with purple veins, it had a floral appearance. The tongue was without sensory purpose and existed only to help by rhythmic flexions to ram chunks of meat down the predator's throat. The beast's head-scales were the size of little fingernails, somewhat finer than those of the torso. Their coloration was consistent—a base of green nearing black, blurred by rosettes of a much lighter, yellowish, hue. Against that background, the tyrannosaur's eyes stood out like needle points dripping blood.

"They don't always give you that pause," Vickers said aloud. "Sometimes they come—"

The tyrannosaur lunged forward. Its lower jaw, half-opened during its bugling challenge, dropped to full gape. Someone shouted. The action blurred as the hologram dissolved a foot or two from the arc of clients.

Vickers thumbed up the molding lights. He walked to the front of the conference room, holding the remote control with which the hotel had provided him. The six clients viewed him with varied expressions. The brother and sister photographers, dentists named McPherson, whispered in obvious delight. They were best able to appreciate the quality of the hologram and to judge their own ability to duplicate it. Any fear they had felt during the presentation was buried in their technical enthusiasm afterward.

The two individual gunners were a general contractor named Mears and Brewer, a meat-packing magnate. Brewer was a short man whose full mustache and balding head made him a caricature of a Victorian industrialist. He loosened his collar and massaged his flushed throat with his thumb and index finger. Mears, built like an All-Pro linebacker after twenty years of retirement, was frowning. He still gripped the chair arms in a way that threatened the plastic. Those were normal reactions to one of Vickers' pre-hunt presentations. It meant the clients had learned the necessity of care in a way no words or still photos could have taught them. Conversely, that familiarity made them less likely to freeze when they faced the real thing.

The presentations unfortunately did not have any useful effect on people like the Salmeses. Or at least on Jonathan Salmes, blond and big but with the look of a movie star, not a football player. Money and leisure could not make Salmes younger, but they made him look considerably less than his real age of forty years. His face was now set in its habitual pattern of affected boredom. As not infrequently happens, the affectation created its own reality and robbed Salmes of whatever pleasure three generations of oil money might otherwise have brought him.

Adrienne Salmes was as blonde and as perfectly preserved as her husband, but she had absorbed the presentation with obvious interest. Time safaris were the property of wealth alone, and she had all the trappings of that wealth. Re-emitted light made her dress—and its wearer—the magnet of all eyes in a dim room, and her silver lamé wristlet responded to voice commands with a digital display. That sort of money could buy beauty like Adrienne Salmes'; but it could not buy the inbred assurance with which she wore that beauty. She forestalled any tendency the guide might have had to think that her personality stopped with the skin by asking, "Mr. Vickers, would you have waited to see if the tyrannosaurus would stop, or would you have shot while it was still at some distance from the helicopter?"

"Umm?" said Vickers in surprise. "Oh, wait, I suppose. If he doesn't stop, there's still time for a shot; and your guide, whether that's me or Dieter, will be backing you. That's a good question." He cleared his throat. "And that brings up an important point," he went on. "We don't shoot large carnivores on foot. Mostly, the shooting platform—the helicopter—won't be dropping as low as it was for the pictures, either. For these holos I was sitting beside the photographer, sweating blood the whole time that nothing would go wrong. If the bird had stuttered or the pilot hadn't timed it just right, I'd have had just about enough time to try for a brain shot. Anywhere else and we'd have been in that fellow's gut faster'n you could swallow a sardine." He smiled. It made him look less like a bank clerk, more like a bank robber. "Three sardines," he corrected himself.

"If you used a man-sized rifle, you'd have been a damned sight better off," offered Jonathan Salmes. He had one ankle crossed on the other knee, and his chair reclined at a forty-five degree angle.

Vickers looked at the client. They were about of an age, though the guide was several inches shorter and not as heavily built. "Yes, well," he said. "That's a thing I need to talk about. Rifles." He ran a hand through his light brown hair.

"Yeah, I couldn't figure that either," said Mears. "I mean, I read the stuff you sent, about big-bores not being important." The contractor frowned. "I don't figure that. I mean, God Almighty, as big as one of those mothers is, I wouldn't feel overgunned with a one-oh-five howitzer . . . and I sure don't think my .458 Magnum's any too big."

"Right, right," Vickers said, nodding his head. His discomfort at facing a group of humans was obvious. "A .458's fine if you can handle it—and I'm sure you can. I'm sure any of you can," he added, raising his eyes and sweeping the group again. "What I said, what I meant, was that size isn't important, penetration and bullet placement are what's important. The .458 penetrates fine— with solids—I hope to God all of you know to bring solids, not soft-nosed bullets. If you're not comfortable with that much recoil, though, you're liable to flinch. And that means you'll miss, even at the ranges we shoot dinos at. A wounded dino running around, anywhere up to a hundred tons of him, and that's when things get messy. You and everybody around is better off with you with a gun that doesn't make you flinch."

"That's all balls, you know," Salmes remarked conversationally. He glanced around at the other clients. "If you're man enough, I'll tell you what to carry." He looked at Vickers, apparently expecting an attempt to silence him. The guide eyed him with a somewhat bemused expression. "A .500 Salmes, that's what," the big client asserted loudly. "It was designed for me specially by Marquart and Wells, gun and bullets both. It uses shortened fifty-caliber machine-gun cases, loaded to give twelve thousand foot-pounds of energy. That's enough to knock a tyrannosaurus right flat on his ass. It's the only gun that you'll be safe with on a hunt like this." He nodded toward Vickers to put a period to his statement.

"Yes, well," Vickers repeated. His expression shifted, hardening. He suddenly wore the visage that an animal might have glimpsed over the sights of his rifle. "Does anybody else feel that they need a—a *gun* like that to bring down anything they'll see on this safari?"

No one nodded to the question when it was put that way. Adrienne Salmes smiled. She was a tall woman, as tall as Vickers himself was.

"Okay, then," the guide said. "I guess I can skip the lesson in basic physics. Mr. Salmes, if you can handle your rifle, that's all that matters to me. If you can't handle it, you've still got time to get something useful instead. Now—"

"Now wait a goddamned minute!" Salmes said, his foot thumping to the floor. His face had flushed under its even tan. "Just what do you mean by that crack? You're going to teach *me* physics?"

"I don't think Mr. Vickers—" began Miss McPherson.

"I want an explanation!" Salmes demanded.

"All right, no problem," said Vickers. He rubbed his forehead and winced in concentration. "What you're talking about," he said to the floor, "is kinetic energy. That's a function of the square of the velocity. Well and good, but it won't knock anything down. What knocks things down is momentum, that's weight times velocity, not velocity squared. Anything that the bullet knocks down, the butt of the rifle would knock down by recoiling—which is why I encourage clients to carry something they can handle." He raised his eyes and pinned Salmes with them. "I've never yet had a client who weighed twelve thousand pounds, Mr. Salmes. And so I'm always tempted to tell people who talk about 'knock-down power' that they're full to the eyes."

Mrs. Salmes giggled. The other clients did not, but all the faces save Salmes' own bore more-than-hinted smiles. Vickers suspected that the handsome blond man had gotten on everyone else's nerves in the bar before the guide had opened the conference suite.

Salmes purpled to the point of an explosion. The guide glanced down again and raised his hand before saying, "Look, all other things being equal, I'd sooner hit a dino—or a man—with a big bullet than a little one. But if you put the bullet in the brain or the heart, it really doesn't matter much how big it is. And especially with a dino, if you put the bullet anywhere else, it's not going to do much good at all."

"Look," said Brewer, hunching forward and spreading his hands palms down, "I don't flinch, and I got a .378 Weatherby that's got penetration up the ass. But—" he turned his hands over and over again as he looked at them—"I'm not Annie Oakley, you know. If I have to hit a brain the size of a walnut with a four-foot skull around it—well, I may as well take a camera myself instead of the gun. I'll have *something* to show people that way."

Salmes snorted—which could have gotten him one of Brewer's big, capable fists in the face, Vickers thought. "That's another good question," the guide said. "Very good. Well. Brain shots are great if you know where to put them. I attached charts of a lot of the common dinos with the material I sent out, look them over and decide if you want to try."

"Thing is," he continued, "taking the top off a dino's heart'll drop it in a couple hundred yards. They don't charge when they're heart-shot, they just run till they fall. And we shoot from up close, as close as ten yards. They don't take any notice of you, the big ones, you could touch them if you wanted. You just need enough distance to be able to pick your shot. You see—" he gestured toward Brewer with both index fingers—"you won't have any problem hitting a heart the size of a bushel basket from thirty feet away. Brains—well, skin hunters have been killing crocs with brain shots for a century. Crocodile brains are just as small as a tyrannosaur's, and the skulls are just as big. Back where we're going, there were some that were a damn sight bigger than tyrannosaurs'. But don't feel you have to. And anyway, it'd spoil your trophy if you brain-shot some of the small-headed kind."

Brewer cleared his throat. "Hey," he said, "I'd like to go back to something you said before. About using the helicopter."

"Right, the shooting platform," Vickers agreed.

"Look," said the meat-packer, "I mean . . . well, that's sort of like shooting wolves from a plane, isn't it? I mean, not, well, Christ . . . not sporting, is it?"

Vickers shrugged. "I won't argue with you," he said, "and you don't have to use the platform if you don't want to. But it's the only way you can be allowed to shoot the big carnosaurs. I'm sorry, that's just how it is." He leaned forward and spoke more intensely, popping the fingers of his left hand against his right palm. "It's as sporting as shooting tigers from elephant-back, I guess, or shooting lions over a butchered cow. The head looks just as big over your mantle. And there's no sport at all for me to tell my bosses how one of my clients was eaten. They aren't bad, the big dinos, people aren't in their scale so they'll pretty much ignore you. Wound one and it's kitty bar the door. These aren't plant eaters, primed to run if there's trouble. These are carnivores we're talking about, animals that spend most of their waking lives killing or looking for something to kill. They *will* connect the noise of a shot with the pain, and they *will* go after whoever made the noise."

The guide paused and drew back. More calmly he concluded, "So carnosaurs you'll hunt from the platform. Or not at all."

"Well, what happens if they come to us?" Salmes demanded with recovered belligerence. "Right up to the camp, say? You can't keep us from shooting then."

"I guess this is a good time to discuss arrangements for the camp," Vickers said, approaching the question indirectly. "There's four of us staff with the safari, two guides—that's me and Dieter Jost—and two pilots. One pilot, one guide, and one client—or of you—go up in the platform every day. You'll each have two chances to bag a big carnosaur. They're territorial and not too thick on the ground, but there's almost certain to be at least one tyrannosaur and a pack of gorgosaurs in practical range. The other guide takes out the rest of the clients on foot, well, on motorized wagons you could say, ponies we call them. And the pilot who isn't flying the platform doubles as camp guard. He's got a heavy machine-gun—" the guide smiled—"a Russian .51 cal. Courtesy of your hosts for the tour, the Israeli government. It'll stop dinos and light tanks without a bit of bother."

Vickers' face lost its crinkling of humor. "If there's any shooting to be done from the camp," he continued, "that's what does it. Unless Dieter or me specifically tell you otherwise. We're not going to have the intrusion vehicle trampled by a herd of dinos that somebody spooked right into it. If something happens to the intrusion vehicle, we don't go home." Vickers smiled again. "That might be okay with me, but I don't think any of the rest of you want to have to explain to the others how you stuck them in the Cretaceous."

"That would be a paradox, wouldn't it, Mr. Vickers?" Miss McPherson said. "That is, uh, human beings living in the Cretaceous? So it couldn't happen. Not that I'd want any chances taken with the vehicle, of course."

Vickers shrugged with genuine disinterest. "Ma'am, if you want to talk about paradox, you need Dr. Galil and his team. So far as I understand it, though, if there's not a change in the future, then there's no paradox; and if there *is* a change, then there's no paradox either because the change—well, the change is reality then."

Mr. McPherson leaned forward with a frown. "Well, surely two bodies—the same body—can't exist simultaneously," he insisted. If he and his sister had been bored with the discussion of firearms, then they had recovered their interest with mention of the mechanics of time transport.

"Sure they can," the guide said with the asperity of someone who had been asked the same question too often. He waved his hand back and forth as if erasing the thought from a chalk board. "They do. Every person, every gun or can of food, contains at least some atoms that were around in the Cretaceous—or the Pre-Cambrian, for that matter. It doesn't matter to the atoms whether they call themselves Henry Vickers or the third redwood from the big rock. . . ." He paused. "There's just one rule that I've heard for true from people who know," he continued at last. "If you travel into the future, you travel as energy. And you don't come back at all."

Mears paled and looked at the ceiling. People got squeamish

about the damnedest things, thought Vickers. Being converted
into energy . . . or being eaten . . . or being drowned in dark
water lighted only by the dying radiance of your mind—but he
broke away from that thought, a little sweat on his forehead with
the strain of it. He continued aloud, "There's no danger for us,
heading back into the far past. But the intrusion vehicle can't be
calibrated closer than five thousand years plus or minus so far.
The, the research side—" he had almost said "the military side,"
knowing the two were synonymous; knowing also that the Israeli
government disapproved intensely of statements to that effect—
"was trying for the recent past—" 1948, but that was another
thing you didn't admit you knew—"and they put a man into the
future instead. After Dr. Galil had worked out the math, they
moved the lab and cleared a quarter-mile section of Tel Aviv
around the old site. They figure the poor bastard will show up
some time in the next few thousand years . . . and nobody better be sharing the area when he does."

Vickers frowned at himself. "Well, that's probably more than
the, the government wants me to say about the technical side,"
he said. "And anyway, I'm not the one to ask. Let's get back to
the business itself—which I do know something about."

"You've said that this presentation and the written material are
all yours," Adrienne Salmes said with a wave of her hand. "I'd
like to know why."

Vickers blinked at the unexpected question. He looked from
Mrs. Salmes to the other clients, all of them but her husband
staring back at him with interest. The guide laughed. "I like my
job," he said. "A century ago, I'd have been hiking through Africa with a Mauser, selling ivory every year or so when I came in
from the bush." He rubbed his left cheekbone where a disk of
shiny skin remained from a boil of twenty years before. "That
sort of life was gone before I was born," he went on. "What I
have is the closest thing there is to it now."

Adrienne Salmes was nodding. Mr. McPherson put his own
puzzled frown into words and said, "I don't see what that has to
do with, well, you holding these sessions, though."

"It's like this," Vickers said, watching his fingers tent and flat-
ten against each other. "They pay me, the government does, a

very good salary that I personally don't have much use for."
Jonathan Salmes snorted, but the guide ignored him. "I use it to
make my job easier," he went on, "by sending the clients all the
data *I've* found useful in the five years I've been traveling back to
the Cretaceous . . . and elsewhere, but mostly the Cretaceous.
Because if people go back with only what they hear in the adver-
tising or from folks who need to make a buck or a name with
their stories, they'll have problems when they see the real thing.
Which means problems for me. So a month before each safari, I
rent a suite in New York or Frankfurt or wherever the hell seems
reasonable, and I offer to give a presentation to the clients. Nobody has to come, but most people do." He scanned the group.
"All of you did, for instance. It makes life easier for me."

He cleared his throat. "Well, in another way, we're here to
make life easier for you," he went on. "I've brought along holos
of the standard game animals you'll be seeing." He dimmed the
lights and stepped toward the back of the room. "First the sauropods, the big long-necks. The most impressive things you'll see in
the Cretaceous, but a disappointing trophy because of the small
heads. . . ."

"All right, ladies and gentlemen," said Dieter Jost. Vickers always left the junior guide responsible for the social chores when
both of them were present. "Please line up here along the wall
until Doctor Galil directs us onto the vehicle."

The members of Cretaceous Safari 87 backed against the hangar wall, their weapons or cameras in their hands. The guides
and the two pilots, Washman and Brady, watched the clients
rather than the crew preparing the intrusion vehicle. You could
never tell what sort of mistake a tensed-up layman would make
with a loaded weapon in his or her hands.

In case the clients were not laymen at all, there were four
guards seated in a balcony-height alcove in the opposite wall.
They wore civilian clothes, but the submachine-guns they carried
were just as military as their ID cards. The Israelis were, of all
people, alert to the chance that a commando raid would be aimed
at an intrusion vehicle and its technical staff. For that reason, the
installation was in an urban setting from which there could be no

quick escape; and its corridors and rooms, including the gaping
hangar itself, were better guarded than the Defense Ministry had
been during the most recent shooting war.

Dr. Galil and his staff were only occasionally visible to the
group on the floor of the hangar. The intrusion vehicle rested on
four braced girders twenty feet high. On its underside, a cylindri-
cal probe was repeatedly blurring and reappearing. The techni-
cians received data from the probe on instruments plugged into
various sockets on the vehicle. Eighty million years in the past,
the cylinder was sampling its surroundings on a score of wavelengths. When necessary, Dr. Galil himself changed control set-
tings. Despite that care, there was no certainty of the surface over
which the travellers would appear—or how far over or under it
they would appear. The long legs gave the intrusion vehicle a
margin that might otherwise have been achieved by a longer drop
than anything aboard would have survived.

"Well, this is it, hey?" said Jonathan Salmes, speaking to Don
Washman. To do so, Salmes had to talk through his wife, who
ignored him in turn. "A chance to hunt the most dangerous
damned creatures ever to walk the Earth!" Salmes' hands, evenly
tanned like every other inch of exposed skin on him, tightened
still further on the beautiful bolt-action rifle he carried.

Washman's smile went no further than Adrienne Salmes. The
pilot was a big man also. The 40 mm grenade launcher he held
looked like a sawed-off shotgun with him for scale. "Gee, Mr.
Salmes," he said in false surprise. "People our age all had a
chance to learn the most dangerous game on Earth popped out of
a spider hole with an AK-47 in its hands. All the *men* did, at
least."

Vickers scowled. "Don," he said. But Washman was a pilot,
not a PR man. Besides, Salmes had coming anything of the sort
he got.

Adrienne Salmes turned to Washman and laughed.

A heavy-set man climbed down from the intrusion vehicle and
strolled across the concrete floor toward the waiting group. Like
the guards, he wore an ordinary business suit. He kept his hands
in his pants pockets. "Good evening, ladies and sirs," he said in
accented English. "I am Mr. Stern; you might say, the company

manager. I trust the preparations for your tour have been satisfactory?" He eyed Dieter, then Vickers, his face wearing only a bland smile.

"All present and accounted for," said Dieter in German. At his side, Mears nodded enthusiastically.

"By God," said Jonathan Salmes with recovered vigor, "I just want this gizmo to pop out right in front of a tyrannosaurus rex. Then I'll pop *him,* and I'll double your fees for a bonus!"

Don Washman smirked, but Vickers' scowl was for better reason than that. "Ah, Mr. Salmes," the guide said, "I believe Mr. Brewer drew first shot of the insertion. Fire discipline is something we *do* have to insist on."

"Naw, that's okay," said Brewer unexpectedly. He looked sheepishly at Vickers, then looked away. "We made an agreement on that," he added. "I don't mind paying for something I want; but I don't mind selling something I don't need, either, you see?"

"In any case," said Stern, "even the genius of Dr. Galil cannot guarantee to place you in front of a suitable dinosaur. I must admit to some apprehension, in fact, that some day we will land an intrusion vehicle in mid-ocean." He gestured both elbows outward, like wings flapping. "Ah, this is a magnificent machine; but not, I fear, very precise." He smiled.

"Not precise enough to . . . put a battalion of paratroops in the courtyard of the Temple in 70 A.D., you mean?" suggested Adrienne Salmes with a trace of a smile herself.

Vickers' gut sucked in. Stern's first glance was to check the position of the guards. The slightly seedy good-fellowship he had projected was gone. "Ah, you Americans," Stern said in a voice that was itself a warning. "Always making jokes about the impossible. But you must understand that in a small and threatened country like ours, there are some jokes one does not make." His smile now had no humor. Adrienne Salmes returned it with a wintry one of her own. If anyone had believed her question was chance rather than a deliberate goad, the smile disabused them.

Atop the intrusion vehicle, an indicator began buzzing in a continuous rhythm. It was not a loud sound. The high ceiling of the hangar drank it almost completely. The staff personnel looked up sharply. Stern nodded again to Vickers and began to walk toward a ground-level exit. He was whistling under his breath. After a moment, a pudgy man stepped to the edge of the vehicle and looked down. He had a white mustache and a fringe of hair as crinkled as rock wool. "I believe we are ready, gentlemen," he said.

Dieter nodded. "We're on the way, then, Dr. Galil," he replied to the older man. Turning back to the safari group, he went on, "Stay in line, please. Hold the handrail with one hand as you mount the steps, and do be very careful to keep your weapons vertical. Accidents happen, you know." Dieter gave a brief nod of emphasis and led the way. The flight of metal steps stretched in a steep diagonal between two of the vehicle's legs. Vickers brought up the rear of the line, unhurried but feeling the tingle at the base of the neck which always preceded time travel with him. It amused Vickers to find himself trying to look past the two men directly in front of him to watch Adrienne Salmes as she mounted the stairs. The woman wore a baggy suit like the rest of them, rip-stopped Kelprin which would shed water and still breathe with 80 per cent efficiency. On her the mottled coveralls had an interest which time safari clients, male or female, could rarely bring to such garments.

The floor of the intrusion vehicle was perforated steel from which much of the antislip coating had been worn. Where the metal was bare, it had a delicate patina of rust. In the center of the twenty-foot square, the safari's gear was neatly piled. The largest single item was the 500-gallon bladder of kerosene, fuel both for the turbine of the shooting platform and the diesel engines of the ponies. There was some dehydrated food, though the bulk of the group's diet would be the meat they shot. Vickers had warned the clients that anyone who could not stomach the idea of eating dinosaur should bring his own alternative. It was the idea that caused some people problems—the meat itself was fine. Each client was allowed a half-cubic meter chest for personal possessions. Ultimately they would either be abandoned in the Cretaceous or count against the owners' volume for trophies.

The intrusion vehicle was surrounded by a waist-high railing, hinged to flop down out of the way during loading and unloading. The space between the rail and the gear in the center was the passenger area. This open walkway was a comfortable four feet wide at the moment. On return, with the vehicle packed with trophies, there would be only standing room. Ceratopsian skulls, easily the most impressive of the High Cretaceous trophies, could run eight feet long with a height and width in proportion.

On insertion, it was quite conceivable that the vehicle would indeed appear in the midst of a pack of gorgosaurs. That was not something the staff talked about; but the care they took positioning themselves and the other gunners before insertion was not mere form. "Mr. McPherson," Dieter said, "Mr. Mears, if you will kindly come around with me to Side Three—that's across from the stairs here. Do not please touch the red control panel as you pass it."

"Ah, can't Charles and I stay together?" Mary McPherson asked. Both of the dentists carried motion cameras with the lenses set at the 50 mm minimum separation. A wider spread could improve hologram quality; but it might prove impossibly awkward under the conditions obtaining just after insertion.

"For the moment," Vickers said, "I'd like you on Side One with me, Miss McPherson. That puts two guns on each side; and it's just during insertion."

Boots clanking on the metal stairs, the safari group mounted the vehicle. Four members of Dr. Galil's team had climbed down already. They stood in a row beside the steps like a guard of honor in lab smocks. Galil himself waited beside the vertical control panel at the head of the stairs. The red panel was the only portion of the vehicle which looked more in keeping with a laboratory than a mineshaft. Even so, its armored casing was a far cry from the festooned breadboards that typically marked experimental machinery.

Not that anyone suggested to the clients that the machinery was as surely experimental as a 1940 radar set.

Dr. Galil shook hands with each member of the group, staff and clients alike. Vickers shifted his modified Garand rifle into the crook of his left arm and took the scientist's hand. "Henry, I pray you Godspeed and a safe return," Galil said in English. His grip was firm.

"God's for afterwards, Shlomo," the guide said. "You'll bring us back, you and your boys. That's what I have faith in."

Dr. Galil squeezed Vickers' hand again. He walked quickly down the steps. The hangar lights dimmed as the big room emptied of everything but the intrusion vehicle and its cargo. Vickers took a deep breath and unlocked the T-handled switch in the center of the control panel. He glanced to either side. Miss McPherson was to his left, Mrs. Salmes to his right.

Adrienne Salmes smiled back. "Did you put me with you because you think you can't trust a woman's shooting?" she asked.

Vickers cleared his throat. "No," he lied. More loudly, he added, "We are about to make our insertion. Everyone please grip the rail with your free hand. Don't let your rifles or cameras project more than two feet beyond the railing, though." He threw the switch. A blue light on the hangar ceiling began to pulse slowly, one beat per second. Vickers' belly drew in again. At the tenth pulse, the light and the hangar disappeared together. There was an instant of sensory blurring. Some compared the sensation of time travel to falling, others to immersion in vacuum. To Vickers, it was always a blast of heat. Then the heat was real and the sun glared down through a haze thick enough to shift the orb far into the red. The intrusion vehicle lurched in a walloping spray. Ooze and reeds sloshed sideways to replace those scalloped out of the slough and transported to the hangar in Tel Aviv. The vehicle settled almost to the full depth of its legs.

"Christ on a crutch!" snarled Don Washman, hidden from Vickers by the piled gear. "Tell us it's a grassy clearing and drop us in a pissing swamp! Next time it'll be a kelp bed!" In a different voice he added, "Target."

All of Vickers' muscles had frozen when he thought they were about to drown. They were safe after all, though, and he turned to see the first dinosaur of the safari.

It was a duckbill—though the head looked more like that of a sheep than a duck. Jaw muscles and nasal passages filled the hollows of the snout which early restorations had left bare. The dinosaur had been dashing through the low pines fringing the slough when the crash and slap of the insertion caused it to rear up and attempt to stop. Reeds and water sprayed in a miniature echo of the commotion the vehicle itself had made.

The firm soil of the shore was only ten feet from the vehicle, roughly parallel to Side Four. The duckbill halted, almost in front of Washman and Jonathan Salmes. Scrabbling for traction in muck covered by two feet of water, the beast tried to reverse direction. The pilot leveled his grenade launcher but did not fire. Vickers stepped to the corner where he could see the target. It lacked the crests that made many similar species excellent trophies, but it was still two tons at point-blank range and the first dino the clients had seen in the flesh. "Go ahead," he said to Salmes. "It's yours."

The duckbill lunged back toward the shore, swinging the splayed toes of its right foot onto solid ground. Salmes' rifle slammed. It had an integral muzzle brake to help reduce recoil by redirecting muzzle gases sideways. The muzzle blast was redirected as well, a palpable shock in the thick air. The duckbill lurched, skidding nose-first through a tree. Its long hind legs bunched under it while the stubby forelegs braced to help the beast rise. If it could get to the well-beaten trail by which it had approached the slough, it would disappear.

"Good, good," said Vickers. His voice was tinny in his own ears because of the muzzle blast. "Now finish it with another one at the base of the tail." Fired from such short range, Salmes' bullet could be expected to range through the duckbill's body. It was certain to rip enough blood vessels to let the beast's life out quickly, and it might also break the spine.

The second shot did not come. The duckbill regained its feet. There was a rusty splotch of blood against the brown-patterned hide of its left shoulder. Vickers risked a look away from the shore to see what was the matter with Salmes. The client had a glazed expression on his face. His big rifle was raised, but its butt did not appear to be solidly resting on his shoulder. Don Washman wore a disgusted look. Beyond both gunners, Mr. McPherson knelt and shot holo tape of the beast leaping back toward the trees.

"Shoot, for Chrissake!" Vickers shouted.

Salmes' rifle boomed again. A triple jet of smoke flashed from the bore and muzzle brake. Salmes cried out as the stock hit him. The bullet missed even the fringe of ten-foot pine trees. The duckbill disappeared into them.

Vickers carefully did not look at Salmes—or Adrienne Salmes, standing immediately behind the guide with her rifle ready to shoot if directed. She had snickered after her husband's second shot. "First we'll find a dry campsite and move the gear," Vickers started to say.

The forest edge exploded as the duckbill burst back through it in the midst of a pack of dromaeosaurs.

In the first flaring confusion, there seemed to be a score of the smaller carnivores. In fact, there were only five—but that was quite enough. One had the duckbill by the throat and was wrapping forelegs around the herbivore's torso to keep from being shaken loose. The rest of the pack circled the central pair with the avidity of participants in a gang rape. Though the carnivores were bipedal, they bore a talon on each hind foot that was a sickle in size and lethality. Kicking from one leg, the hooting dromaeosaurs slashed through the duckbill's belly hide. Soft, pink coils of intestine spilled out into the water.

One of the half-ton carnivores cocked its head at the group on the intrusion vehicle. The men on Side Four were already spattered with the duckbill's blood. "Take 'em," Vickers said. He punched a steel-cored bullet through the nearest dromaeosaur's skull, just behind its eyes.

Washman and Adrienne Salmes fired while Vickers' cartridge case was still in the air. The pilot's grenade launcher chugged rather than banging, but the explosion of its projectile against the chest of a carnivore was loud even to ears numbed by the muzzle blasts of Salmes' rifle. The grenade was a caseless shaped charge which could be used point-blank without endangering the firer with fragments. Even so, the concussion from less than twenty feet rocked everyone on the near side of the vehicle. There was a red flash and a mist of pureed dinosaur. A foreleg, torn off at the shoulder, sailed straight into the air. Two of the dromaeosaurs bolted away from the blast, disappearing among the trees in flat arcs and sprays of dirt and pine straw.

Vickers' target had fallen where it stood. All four limbs jerked

like those of a pithed frog. The dromaeosaur Adrienne Salmes
had shot dropped momentarily, then sprang to its feet again. The
tall woman worked the bolt of her rifle smoothly without taking
the butt from her shoulder. The grenade explosion did not appear
to have disconcerted her. The guide, poised to finish the beast,
hesitated. Adrienne shot again and the dino's limbs splayed. Its
dark green hide showed clearly the red and white rosette between
the shoulders where the second bullet had broken its spine.

Dieter Jost leaned past Mr. McPherson and put a uranium
flechette through the brain of the duckbill, ending its pain. All
four of the downed dinosaurs continued to twitch.

"Jesus," said Don Washman quietly as he closed the breech on
a grenade cartridge.

Although he had only fired once, Henry Vickers replaced the
twenty-round magazine of his Garand with a fresh one from his
belt pouch. "Mr. McPherson," he said, "I hope you got good
pictures, because I swear that's the most excitement I've had in a
long time in this business."

Dieter had moved back to watch the slough with Steve Brady.
Most of the clients crowded to Side Four to get a better view of
the Cretaceous and its denizens. Adrienne Salmes had not moved
from where she stood beside Vickers. She thumbed a second cartridge into the magazine of her rifle and closed the breech. "Still
doubt I can shoot?" she asked with a smile.

"Heart and spine," the guide said. "No, I guess you can back
me up any day of the week. I tell you, dromaeosaurs aren't as
impressive as some of the larger carnivores, but they're just as
dangerous." He looked more carefully at her rifle, a Schultz and
Larsen with no ornamentation but the superb craftsmanship that
had gone into its production. "Say, nice," Vickers said. "In .358
Norma?"

The blonde woman smiled with pleasure. "It's the same rifle
I've used for everything from whitetails to elephant," she said.
"I'd planned to bring something bigger, but after what you said, I
had five hundred bullets cast from bronze and loaded at the fac-
tory for me. Johnnie—" she glanced at her husband, now loudly
describing how he had shot the duckbill to the other clients.
"Well," Adrienne continued quietly, "I'm the hunter in the

household, not him. I told him he was crazy to have a cannon like that built, but he listens to me as badly as he listens to everyone else."

"That may be a problem," Vickers muttered. More loudly, he said, "All right, I think it's time to start setting up camp on top of this ridge. Around now, it's asking for trouble to be any closer than a hundred yards to the water, especially with this much meat nearby. After Steve and I get the ponies assembled, we'll need everybody's help to load them. Until then, just try not to get in the way."

Sometimes working with his hands helped Vickers solve problems caused by the human side of his safaris. It did not seem to do so on this occasion. Of course, a client who was both arrogant and gun-shy was a particularly nasty problem.

But Vickers was irritated to realize that it also bothered him that Don Washman and Mrs. Salmes seemed to be getting along very well together.

The campfire that evening provided an aura of human existence more important than the light of its banked coals. The clients had gone to sleep—or at least to their tents. That the Salmes at least were not asleep was evident from the sound of an argument. The double walls of the tents cut sound penetration considerably, but there were limits. Steve Brady shoved another log on the fire and said, "Damn, but I swear that chainsaw gets heavier every time I use it. Do you suppose the Israelis designed them to be air-dropped without parachutes?"

"You want a high horsepower-to-weight ratio, you don't use a diesel," agreed Dieter Jost with a shrug. "If you want a common fuel supply for everything and need diesel efficiency for the ponies, though—well, you get a heavy chainsaw."

"Can't imagine why she ever married him," Don Washman said. "Beef like that's a dime a dozen. Why, you know he didn't even have the balls enough to chamber a third round? He's scared to death of that gun, scared almost to touch it now."

"Yeah," agreed Vickers, working a patch into the slot of his cleaning rod, "but the question's what to do about it. I don't have any good answers, God knows."

"Do?" Washman repeated. "Well, hell, leave him, of course. She's got money of her own—"

Brady broke into snorting laughter. Dieter grimaced and said, "Don, I do not think it is any business of ours how our clients live. The Salmes are adults and can no doubt solve their own problems." He pursed his lips. The fire threw the shadow of his bushy mustache misshapenly against his cheeks. "As for our problem, Henry, why don't we offer him the use of the camp gun? The .375? I think Mr. Salmes' difficulty is in precisely the same category as the more usual forms of mechanical breakdown or guns falling into the river."

"Fine with me if you can talk him into it," Vickers said dubiously, "but I wouldn't say Salmes is the sort to take a well-meant suggestion." He nodded toward the tent. The couple within seemed to be shouting simultaneously. "Or any other kind of suggestion," he added.

"Things would sure be simpler if they didn't allow booze on safaris," Brady said.

"Things would be simpler for us if our employers paid us to sleep all day and drink schnapps," said Dieter Jost. He tugged a lock of hair absently. "That does not comport well with economic realities, however. And so long as each of our clients has paid fifty thousand American dollars for the privilege of spending two weeks in the Cretaceous, it is unrealistic to assume that the staff will be treated as anything but the hired help. If drunken clients make the job more difficult, then that is simply one of the discomforts of the job. Like loading gear in the heat, or tracking down an animal that a client has wounded. It is easier for our employers, Mr. Stern and those above him, to hire new staff members than it would be to impose their underlings' views on persons of the sort who take time safaris."

"Moshe Cohn was head guide when I made my first insertion," said Vickers aloud. His cleaning rod rested on his lap beside the Garand, but he had not run it through the bore yet. "He told a client—a Texan, it was a U.S. safari that time too—that he'd be better off to slack up a little on his drinking while he was in the field. The client was generally too stiff to see a dino, much less shoot one." The guide's forefinger tapped the breech of his rifle as he recalled the scene. "He said to Moshe, 'Jew-boy, you sound just like my third wife. One more word and I'll whip you with my belt, just like I did her.' Moshe broke his hand on the Texan's jaw. When we got back, the government—the Israeli but very pragmatic government—fired Moshe and denied him compensation for his hand. Ten days in the field with broken bones, remember." Vickers paused, then went on, "That taught me the rules. So far, I've been willing to live by them."

Don Washman laughed. "Right, when you hit a client, use your gunstock," he said and opened another beer.

Technically Steve Brady had the first watch, even though all four staff members were up. The alarm panel was facing Steve when it beeped, therefore. "Jesus!" the stubby, long-haired pilot blurted when he saw the magnitude of the signal fluorescing on the display. "Down the trail—must be a herd of something!"

Don Washman upset his fresh beer as he ran to the spade grips of the heavy machine-gun. It was in the center of the camp, on ground slightly higher than its immediate surroundings but by no means high enough to give the weapon an unbroken field of fire. The staff had sawed clear a campsite along the game trail leading down to the intrusion vehicle two hundred yards away. Assuming that animals were most likely to enter the area by the trail, Dieter had sited the tents on the other side of the gun. The next day they could lash together a six-foot-high tower for the gun, but time had been too short to finish that the first night.

While the other staff members crouched over weapons, Vickers darted to the three occupied tents. The sensor loop that encircled the camp a hundred yards out could pick up very delicate impacts and relay them to the display screen. This signal, however, was already shaking the ground. Miss McPherson poked her head out of the tent she shared with her brother. "What—" the dentist began.

The file of huge ceratopsians rumbled into sight on their way to the water to drink. They were torosaurs or a species equally large. In the dim glow of the fire, they looked more like machines than anything alive. Their beaks and the tips of their triple horns had a black glint like raku ware, and they averaged twice the size of elephants.

The tent that Mears and Brewer shared shuddered as both clients tried to force their way through the opening simultaneously. Vickers lifted the muzzles of their rifles skyward as he had been waiting to do. "No shooting now," he cried over the thunder of the dinosaurs. "In the morning we'll follow them up."

Adrienne Salmes slipped out of her tent before Vickers could reach over and take her rifle. It was pointed safely upward anyway. Despite the hour-long argument she had been engaged in, the blonde woman looked calm and alert. She looked breathtakingly beautiful as well—and wore only her rifle. "If you can wait a moment for my firepower," she said to Vickers without embarrassment, "I'll throw some clothes on." The guide nodded.

The bony frills at the back of the ceratopsians' skulls extended their heads to well over the height of a man. Less for protection than for muscle attachment, the frills locked the beasts' heads firmly to their shoulders. The bulging jaw muscles that they anchored enabled the ceratopsians to literally shear hardwood the thickness of a man's thigh. The last thing a safari needed was a herd of such monsters being stampeded through the camp. A beast wounded by a shot ill-aimed in the darkness could lead to just that result.

Mears and Brewer were staring at the rapid procession in wonder. The left eye of each torosaur glinted in the firelight. "Mother o' God, what a trophy!" Brewer said.

"Best in the world," Vickers agreed. "You'll go back with one, never fear." He looked at the McPhersons to his other side. The dentists were clutching their holo cameras, which were almost useless under the light conditions. "And you'll get your fill, too," Vickers said. "The trip isn't cheap, but I've never yet guided a client who didn't think he'd gotten more than he bargained for." Though a drunken S.O.B. like Jonathan Salmes might spoil that record, he added silently.

Adrienne Salmes re-emerged from her tent, wearing her coveralls and boots. Mears and Brewer had been so focused on the herd of torosaurs that the guide doubted the men had noticed her previous display. She was carrying a sleeping bag in addition to her rifle. Vickers raised an eyebrow. Adrienne nodded back at the tent. "Screaming beauty seems to have passed out," she said, "but I'm damned if I'll stay in the tent with him. Going on about his shoulder, for God's sake, and expecting sympathy from *me*. Is it all right if I doss down in the open?"

The ceratopsians were sporting in the water, making as much noise as the Waikiki surf. Vickers smiled. "They could eat tree trunks and drink mud," he said, as if he had not heard the client's question. "And I still meet people who think mammals are better adapted for survival than dinos were." He turned to Adrienne Salmes. "It's all right, so long as you stay out of the gun's way," he said, "but you'll wash away if it rains. And we're bound to get at least one real gully-washer while we're here."

"Hell, there's an easy answer to that," said Don Washman. He had strolled over to the tents when it became clear no predators had followed the torosaurs. "One of us is on watch all night, right? So there's always a slot open in the staff tents. Let noble hunter there sleep by himself, Hank. And she shoots well enough to be a pro, so let her stay dry with us too." He gave his engaging smile.

The other clients were listening with interest. "Maybe if Mr. McPherson wants to trade—" Vickers began in a neutral voice.

Adrienne Salmes hushed him with a grimace. "I'm a big girl now, Mr. Vickers," she snapped, "and I think I'm paying enough to make my own decisions. Don, if you'll show me the tent, I'll resume getting the sleep I've been assured I'll need in the morning."

Washman beamed. "Let's see," he said, "Steve's got watch at the moment, so I suppose you're my tentmate till I go on at four in the morning. . . ."

They walked toward the tent. Dieter, standing near the fire with his rifle cradled, looked from them to Vickers. Vickers shrugged. He was thinking about Moshe Cohn again.

"Platform to Mobile One," crackled the speaker of the unit clipped to Vickers' epaulet. Vickers threw the last of the clamps that locked the two ponies into a single, articulated vehicle. "Go ahead, Dieter," he said.

"Henry, the torosaurs must have run all night after they left the water," the other guide announced through the heavy static.

"They're a good fifteen klicks west of camp. But there's a sauropod burn just three klicks south and close to the river. Do you
want me to drop a marker?"

Vickers frowned. "Yeah, go ahead," he decided. He glanced at
but did not really see the four clients, festooned with gear, who
awaited his order to board the ponies. "Any sign of carnosaurs?"

"Negative," Dieter replied, "but we're still looking. I spotted
what looked like a fresh kill when we were tracking the
torosaurs. If we don't get any action here, I'll carry Miss Mc-
Pherson back to that and see what we can stir up."

"Good hunting, Dieter," Vickers said. "We'll go take a look at
your sauropods. Mobile One out." Again his eyes touched the
clients. He appeared startled to see them intent on him. "All
right," he said, "if you'll all board the lead pony. The other's
along for trophies—sauropods this time, we'll get you the ceratopsians another day. Just pull down the jump seats."

The guide seated himself behind the tiller bar and clipped his
rifle into its brackets. His clients stepped over the pony's low
sides. The vehicle was the shape of an aluminum casket, scaled
up by a half. A small diesel engine rode over the rear axle.
Though the engine was heavily muffled, the valves sang trills
which blended with the natural sounds of the landscape.

Don Washman waved. He had strung a tarp from four trees at
the edge of the clearing. In that shade he was pinning together
the log framework of the gun tower. The alarm and his grenade
launcher sat beside him.

"Take care," Vickers called.

"You take care," the pilot responded with a broad grin.
"Maybe I can lose the yo-yo and then we're all better off." He
jerked his head toward the tent which still held Jonathan Salmes.
Dieter had tried to arouse Salmes for breakfast. Because Vickers
was sawing at the time, no one but Dieter himself heard what the
client shouted. Dieter, who had served in at least three armies
and was used to being cursed, had backed out of the tent with a
white face. Vickers had shut down the saw, but the other guide
had shaken his head. "Best to let him sleep, I think," he said.

Remembering the night before, Vickers wished that it was

Brady and not Washman who had the guard that day. Oh, well. "Hold on," he said aloud. He put the pony into gear.

Just west of the crest on which they had set up camp, the height and separation of the trees increased markedly. Small pines and cycads were replaced by conifers that shot over one hundred feet in the air. Everything east of the ridgeline was in the floodplain, where the river drowned tree roots with a regularity that limited survival to the smaller, faster-growing varieties. The thick-barked monsters through which Vickers now guided the ponies were centuries old already. Barring lightning or tornado, they would not change appreciably over further centuries. They were the food of the great sauropods.

The forest was open enough to permit the pony to run at over fifteen miles per hour, close to its top speed with the load. The saplings and pale, broad-leafed ferns which competed for the dim light were easily brushed aside. Animal life was sparse, but as the pony skirted a fallen log, a turkey-sized coelurosaur sprang up with a large beetle in its jaws. Mears' .458 boomed. There was an echo-chamber effect from the log which boosted the muzzle blast to a near equal for that of the .500 Salmes. Everyone on the pony jumped—Vickers more than the rest because he had not seen the client level his rifle. The dinosaur darted away, giving a flick of its gray-feathered tail as it disappeared around a trunk.

"Ah, don't shoot without warning," the guide said, loudly but without looking around. "It's too easy to wound something that you should have had backup for. Besides, we should be pretty close to the sauropods—and they make much better targets."

Even as Vickers spoke, the forest ahead of them brightened. The upper branches still remained, but all the limbs had been stripped below the level of sixty feet. One tree had been pushed over. It had fallen to a forty-five degree angle before being caught and supported by the branches of neighboring giants. The matted needles were strewn with fresh blankets of sauropod droppings. They had a green, faintly Christmasy scent. Vickers stopped the vehicle and turned to his clients. "We're getting very close," he said, "and there'll be plenty of shooting for everybody in just a moment. But there's also a chance of a pack of carnosaurs nearby for the same reason that we are. Keep your eyes open as we

approach—and for *God's* sake don't shoot until I've said to." His
eyes scanned the forest again and returned to Adrienne Salmes.
A momentary remembrance of her the night before, a nude Arte-
mis with rifle instead of bow, made him smile. "Mrs. Salmes," he
said, "would you watch behind us, please? Carnivores are likely
to strike up a burn as we did . . . and I can't watch behind us
myself."

Adrienne grinned. "Why Mr. Vickers, I think you've just apol-
ogized for doubting I could shoot," she said. She turned and
faced back over the towed pony, left arm through the sling of her
rifle in order to brace the weapon firmly when she shot.

Vickers eased forward the hand throttle. They were past the
marker beacon Dieter had dropped from the shooting platform.
The responder tab on the guide's wrist had pulsed from green to
red and was now lapsing back into fire orange; he cut it off absently. The sounds of the dinosaurs were audible to him now: the
rumble of their huge intestines; the slow crackle of branches being stripped of their needles, cones, and bark by the sauropods'
teeth; and occasional cooing calls which the clients, if they heard
them over the ringing of the diesel, probably mistook for those of
unseen forest birds.

The others did not see the sauropods even when Vickers cut
the motor off. They were titanosaurs or a similar species, only
middling huge for their order. Vickers pointed. Mears, Brewer,
and McPherson followed the line of the guide's arm, frowning.
"It's all right now, Mrs. Salmes," Vickers said softly. "The dinos
will warn us if predators get near." Adrienne Salmes faced
around as well.

"Oh, Jesus Christ," someone whispered as he realized what
Vickers was pointing out. It was incredible, even to the guide,
how completely a score or more of thirty-ton animals could blend
into an open forest. In part, it may have been that human minds
were not used to interpreting as animals objects which weighed
as much as loaded semis. Once recognized, the vast expanses of
russet and black hide were as obvious as inkblot pictures which
someone else has described.

Silently and without direction, McPherson stepped from the
pony and spread the lenses of his camera. Vickers nodded to the

others. "They won't pay attention to a normal voice," he said—in a quieter than normal voice. "Try to avoid sudden movements, though. They may think it's a warning signal of some kind." He cleared his throat. "I want each of you to mark a target—"

"That one!" whispered Mears urgently, a boy in the toy store, afraid his aunt will renege on her promise of a gift unless he acts at once. The big contractor was pointing at the nearest of the sauropods, a moderate-sized female only thirty feet away.

"Fine, but wait," the guide said firmly. "I'll position each of you. When I call 'fire,' go ahead—but only then. They won't attack anything our size, but they might step on one of us if they were startled at the wrong time. That big, they don't have to be hostile to be dangerous."

The nearby female, which had been browsing on limbs twenty feet high, suddenly stepped closer to a tree and reared up on her hind legs. She anchored herself to the trunk with her forefeet, each armed with a single long claw. It shredded bark as it gripped. With the grace and power of a derrick, the titanosaur's head swung to a high branch, closed, and dragged along it for several yards. It left only bare wood behind.

With his left hand, Vickers aimed a pen-sized laser pointer. A red dot sprang out on the chest of the oblivious titanosaur. "There's your aiming point," the guide said. "If she settles back down before I give the signal, just hit her at the top of the shoulder."

Mears nodded, his eyes intent on the dinosaur.

Vickers moved Brewer five yards away, with a broadside shot at a large male. McPherson stood beside him using a pan-head still camera on the six sauropods visible within a stone's throw. The dentist's hands were trembling with excitement.

Vickers took Adrienne Salmes slightly to the side, to within twenty yards of another male. He chose the location with an eye on the rest of the herd. Sauropods had a tendency to bolt straight ahead if aroused.

"Why does this one have bright red markings behind its eyes?" Adrienne asked.

"First time I ever saw it," the guide said with a shrug. "Maybe

some professor can tell you when you get back with the head."
He did not bother to gesture with the laser. "Ready?" he asked.

She nodded and aimed.

"Fire!"

The three gunners volleyed raggedly. The thick tree trunks
acted as baffles, blurring the sharpness of the reports. The gunfire
had the same feeling of muffled desecration as farts echoing in a
cathedral. The red-flashed titanosaur began striding forward.
Adrienne Salmes worked her bolt and fired again. A wounded
animal gave a warning call, so loud and low-pitched that the
humans' bowels trembled. Mrs. Salmes fired again. The titanosaur was a flickering picture in a magic lantern formed by open
patches between six-foot tree boles. The huntress began to run
after her disappearing prey.

Vickers grabbed her shoulder, halting her with an ease that
belied his slender build. She turned on him in fury. "I won't let a
wounded animal go!" she screamed.

"It won't go far," Vickers said. He released her. "We'll follow
as soon as it's safe." He gestured, taking in the bellowing, moun-
tainous forms padding in all directions among the even larger
trees. "They'll circle in a moment. Then it'll be safe for things
our size to move," he said.

Russet motion ceased, though the tidal bellowing of over a
dozen sauropods continued. Mears was still firing in the near
distance. Brewer had lowered his rifle and was rubbing his shoulder with his left hand. "Let's get everybody together," the guide
suggested, "and go finish off some trophies."

Brewer's expression was awed as they approached. "It really
did fall," he said. "It was so big, I couldn't believe. . . . But I
shot it where you said and it just ran into the tree." He waved.
"And I kept shooting and it fell."

The haunches of the titanosaur were twice the height of a man,
even with the beast belly-down in the loam. McPherson pointed
at the great scars in the earth beneath the sauropod's tail. "It
kept trying to move," he said in amazement. "Even though there
was a tree in the way. It was kicking away, trying to get a purchase, and I thought the *tree* was going to go over. But it did.
The, the dinosaur. And I have a tape of all of it!"

Mears, closest to the bellowing giants, was just as enthusiastic. "Like a shooting gallery!" he said, "but the tin ducks're the size of houses. God Almighty! I only brought one box of ammo with me. I shot off every last slug! God Almighty!"

The titanosaurs had quieted somewhat, but they were still making an odd series of sounds. The noises ranged from bird calls as before, to something like the venting of high-pressure steam. Vickers nodded and began walking toward the sounds. He had caught Adrienne Salmes' scowl of distaste at the contractor's recital. If the guide agreed, it was still not his business to say so.

The herd was larger than Vickers had estimated. Fully forty of the sauropods were circled, facing outward around a forest giant enough bigger than its neighbors to have cleared a considerable area. Several of the beasts were rearing up. They flailed the air with clawed forefeet and emitted the penetrating steam-jet hiss that seemed so incongruous from a living being. Mears raised his rifle with a confulsed look on his face before he remembered that he had no ammunition left.

McPherson was already rolling tape. "Have you reloaded?" the guide asked, looking from Salmes to Brewer. The blonde woman nodded curtly while the meat packer fumbled in the side pocket of his coveralls.

"I don't see the one I hit," Adrienne Salmes said. Her face was tight.

"Don't worry," the guide said quietly. "It's down, it couldn't have made it this far the way you hit it. It's the ones that weren't heart-shot that we're dealing with now."

"That's not my responsibility," she snapped.

"It's no duty you owe to me," Vickers agreed, "or to anything human."

Brewer snicked his bolt home. Vickers' laser touched the center of the chest of a roaring titanosaur. Orange pulmonary blood blashed its tiny head like a shroud. "On the word, Mr. Brewer," he said, "If you would."

Adriennc said, "All right." She did not look at Vickers.

Across the circle, eighty yards away, a large male was trying to lick its belly. Its long neck strained, but it was not flexible enough to reach the wound. The laser pointer touched below the left eye. "There?" the guide asked.

Adrienne nodded and braced herself, legs splayed. Her arms, sling, and upper body made a web of interlocking triangles.

The guide swung his own weapon onto the third of the wounded animals. "All right," he said.

Adrienne's Schultz and Larsen cracked. The light went out of the gut-shot sauropod's eye. Undirected, the rest of the great living machine began slowly to collapse where it stood. Brewer was firing, oblivious of his bruised shoulder in the excitement. Vickers put three rounds into the base of his own target's throat. Its head and neck were weaving too randomly to trust a shot at them.

Either the muzzle blasts or the sight of three more of their number sagging to the ground routed the herd. Their necks swung around like compass needles to iron. With near simultaneity, all the surviving titanosaurs drifted away from the guns. Their tails were held high off the ground.

Adrienne Salmes lowered her rifle. "God Almighty, let me use that?" Mears begged, reaching out for the weapon. "I'll pay you—"

"Touch me and I'll shove this up your bum, you bloody butcher!" the blonde woman snarled.

The contractor's fist balled. He caught himself, however, even before he realized that the muzzle of the .358 had tilted in line with his throat.

"The river isn't that far away," said Vickers, pointing in the direction the sauropods had run. "We'll follow in the pony—it's a sight worth seeing. And taping," he added.

The undergrowth slowed the hunters after they recrossed the ridgeline, but the titanosaurs were still clearly evident. Their heads and even hips rocked above the lower vegetation that sloped toward the river. The herd, despite its size and numbers, had done surprisingly little damage in its rush to the water. The pony repeatedly had to swing aside from three-inch saplings which had sprung back when the last of the titanosaurs had passed.

But the beasts themselves were slowed by the very mechanics

of their size. Their twelve-foot strides were ponderously slow even under the goad of panic. The tensile strength of the sauropods' thigh bones simply was not equal to the acceleration of the beasts' mass to more than what would be a fast walk in a man. The hunters reached a rocky spur over the mudflats fringing the water just as the leading titanosaurs splashed into the stream a hundred and fifty yards away. The far bank of the river was lost in haze. The sauropods continued to advance without reference to the change in medium. Where a moment before they had been belly-deep in reeds, now they were belly-deep in brown water that was calm except for the wakes of their passage. When the water grew deeper, the procession sank slowly. The beasts farthest away, in midstream over a quarter mile out, were floating necks and tails while the forefeet propelled them by kicking down into the bottom muck.

"Don't they hide underwater and snorkel through their necks?" Brewer asked. Then he yipped in surprise as his hand touched the barrel of his Weatherby. The metal was hot enough to burn from strings of rapid fire and the Cretaceous sunlight.

Vickers nodded. He had heard the question often before. "Submarines breathe through tubes because the tubes are steel and the water pressure doesn't crush them," he explained. "Sauropods don't have armored gullets, and their lungs aren't diesel engines inside a steel pressure hull. Physics again. Besides, they float— the only way they could sink would be to grab a rock."

As Vickers spoke, the last titanosaur in the line sank.

"Well, I'll be damned!" the guide blurted.

The sauropod surfaced again a moment later. It blew water from its lungs as it gave the distress cry that had followed the shooting earlier.

The mild current of the river had bent the line of titanosaurs into a slight curve. The leaders were already disappearing into the haze. None of the other beasts even bothered to look back to see the cause of the bellowing. No doubt they already knew.

The stricken titanosaur sank again. It rolled partly onto its left side as it went under the surface this time. It was still bellowing, wreathing its head in a golden spray as it disappeared.

"I think," said Adrienne Salmes dryly, "that this time the rock grabbed the dinosaur."

Vickers grunted in reply. He was focusing his binoculars on the struggle.

Instead of rising vertically, the sauropod rolled completely over sideways. Clinging to the herbivore's left foreleg as it broke surface was something black and huge and as foul as a tumor. The linked beasts submerged again in an explosion of spray. Vickers lowered the binoculars, shivering. They were not common, even less commonly seen. Great and terrible as they were, they were also widely hated. For them to sun themselves on mudbanks as their descendants did would have been to court death by the horns and claws of land animals equally large. But in their own element, in the still, murky waters, they were lords without peer.

"Christ Almighty," Mears said, "was that a whale?"

"A crocodile," the guide replied, staring at the roiling water. "Enough like what you'd find in the Nile or the Congo that you couldn't tell the difference by a picture. Except for the size." He paused, then continued, "The science staff will be glad to hear about this. They always wondered if they preyed on the big sauropods, too. It seems that they preyed on *any* goddam thing in the water."

"I'd swear it was bigger than the tyrannosaurus you showed us," Adrienne Salmes observed, lowering her own binoculars.

Vickers shrugged. "As long, at least. Probably heavier. I looked at a skull, a fossil in London . . . I don't know how I'd get one back as a trophy. . . . It was six feet long, which was impressive; and six feet wide, which was incredible, a carnivore with jaws six feet wide. Tyrannosaurs don't compare, no. Maybe whales do, Mr. Mears. But nothing else I know of."

There were no longer any titanosaurs visible. The herd had curved off downstream, past the intrusion vehicle and the hunting camp. They were lost against the haze and the distant shoreline by now. The water still stirred where the last of them had gone down, but by now the struggles must have been the thrashings of the sauropod's automatic nervous system. The teeth of the crocodile were six inches long; but they were meant only to hold, not to kill. The water killed, drowning a thirty-ton sauropod as implacably as it would any lesser creature anchored to the bottom by the crocodile's weight.

"We'd best take our trophies," Vickers said at last. No one in the world knew his fear of drowning, no one but himself. "The smell'll bring a pack of gorgosaurs soon, maybe even a tyrannosaur. I don't want that now, not with us on the ground."

The guide rubbed his forehead with the back of his left hand, setting his bush hat back in place carefully. "The ponies convert to boats," he said, patting the aluminum side. "The tread blocks can be rotated so they work like little paddle wheels." He paused as he swung the tiller bar into a tight circle. "I guess you see why we don't use them for boats in the Cretaceous," he added at last. "And why we didn't keep our camp down on the intrusion vehicle."

Vickers was even quieter than his wont for the rest of the morning.

The shooting platform had returned before the ponies did, the second of them dripping with blood from the titanosaur heads. Two heads had Mears' tags on them, though the contractor had finished none of the beasts he had wounded. The best head among those he had sprayed would have been the one the guide had directed Adrienne Salmes to kill—with a bullet through the skull that destroyed all trophy value.

There were no game laws in the Cretaceous, but the line between hunters and butchers was the same as in every other age.

The McPhersons greeted each other with mutual enthusiasm. Their conversation was technical and as unintelligible to nonphotographers as the conversation of any other specialists. Jonathan Salmes was sitting on a camp stool, surly but alert. He did not greet the returning party, but he watched the unloading of the trophies with undisguised interest. The right side of his face was puffy.

"We've found a tyrannosaur," Dieter called as he and the pilots joined Vickers. That was good news, but there was obvious tension among the other members of the staff. Brady carried a spray gun loaded with antiseptic sealer. A thorough coating would prevent decay for almost a month, ample time to get the heads to proper taxidermists.

When Dieter was sure that all the clients were out of earshot, he said in a low voice, "Don has something to tell you, Henry."

"Eh?" prompted Vickers. He set one of the sauropod heads on the spraying frame instead of looking at the pilot.

"I had to clobber Salmes," Washman said, lifting out the red-flashed trophy. "He was off his head—I'm not sure he even remembers. There was a mixed herd of duckbills came down the trail. He came haring out of his tent with that gun of his. He didn't shoot, though, he started chasing them down the trail." The pilot straightened and shrugged. Steve Brady began pumping the spray gun. The pungent mist drifted down wind beyond the gaping heads. "I grabbed him. I mean, who knows what might be following a duckbill? When he swung that rifle at me, I had to knock him out for his own good. Like a drowning man." Washman shrugged again. "His gun wasn't even loaded, you know?"

"Don, run the ponies down to the water and mop them out, will you?" Vickers said. The pilot jumped onto the leading vehicle and spun them off down the trail. The two guides walked a little to the side, their rifles slung, while Brady finished sealing the trophies. "It's going to have to be reported, you know," Vickers said. "Whether Salmes does or not."

"You or I might have done the same thing," Dieter replied.

"I'm not denying that," the senior guide snapped. "But it has to be reported."

The two men stood in silence, looking out at a forest filled with sounds that were subtly wrong. At last Dieter said, "Salmes goes up in the platform with you and Don tomorrow, doesn't he?"

Vickers agreed noncommittally.

"Maybe you ought to go with Steve instead," Dieter suggested. He looked at Vickers. "Just for the day, you know."

"Washman just flies us," Vickers said with a shake of his head. "I'm the one that's in contact with the client. And Don's as good as pilots come."

"That he is," the other guide agreed, "that he is. But he is not a piece of furniture. You are treating him as a piece of furniture."

Vickers clapped his companion on the shoulder. "Come on," he said, "Salmes'll be fine when he gets his tyrannosaur. What we ought to be worrying about is three more for the others. If Salmes goes home with a big boy and the rest have to settle for less—well, it says no guarantees in the contracts, but you know the kind of complaints the company gets. That's the kind of problem we're paid to deal with. If they wanted shrinks instead of guides, they'd have hired somebody else."

Dieter laughed half-heartedly. "Let us see what we can arrange for lunch," he said. "At the moment, I am more interested in sauropod steak than I am in the carnivores that we compete with."

"Damn, the beacon cut out again!" Washman snarled. There was no need of an intercom system; the shooting platform operated with only an intake whine which was no impediment to normal speech. The silence was both a boon to coordination and a help in not alarming the prey. It did, however, mean that the client was necessarily aware of any technical glitches. When the client was Jonathan Salmes—

"God damn, you're not going to put *me* on that way!" the big man blazed. He had his color back and with it all his previous temper. Not that the bruise over his right cheekbone would have helped. "One of the others paid you to save the big one for them, didn't they?" he demanded. "By God, I'll bet it was my wife! And I'll bet it wasn't money either, the—"

"Take us up to a thousand feet," Vickers said sharply. "We'll locate the kill visually if the marker isn't working. Eighty tons of sauropod shouldn't be hard to spot."

"Hang on, there, it's on again," said the pilot. The shooting platform veered slightly as he corrected their course. Vickers and Salmes stood clutching the rail of the suspended lower deck which served as landing gear as well. Don Washman was seated above them at the controls, with the fuel tank balancing his mass behind. The air intake and exhaust extended far beyond the turbine itself to permit the baffling required for silent running. The shooting platform was as fragile as a dragonfly; and it was, in its way, just as efficient a predator.

By good luck, the tyrannosaur had made its kill on the edge of
a large area of brush rather than high forest. The platform's
concentric-shaft rotors kept blade length short. Still, though it
was possible to maneuver beneath the forest canopy, it was a
dangerous and nerve-wracking business to do so. Washman circled the kill at two hundred feet, high enough that he did not
need to allow for trees beneath him. Though the primary airflow
from the rotors was downward, the odor of tens of tons of meat
dead in the sun still reached the men above. The guide tried to
ignore it with his usual partial success. Salmes only wrinkled his
nose and said, "Whew, what a pong." Then, "Where is it? The
tyrannosaurus?"

That the big killer was still nearby was obvious from the types
of scavengers on the sauropod. Several varieties of the smaller
coelurosaurs scrambled over the corpse like harbor rats on a
drowned man. None of the species weighed more than a few
hundred pounds. A considerable flock of pterosaurs joined and
squabbled with the coelurosaurs, wings tented and toothless
beaks stabbing out like shears. There were none of the large carnivores around the kill—and that implied that something was
keeping them away.

"Want me to go down close to wake him up?" Washman asked.

The guide licked his lips. "I guess you'll have to," he said.
There was always a chance that a pterodactyl would be sucked
into the turbine when you hovered over a kill. The thought of
dropping into a big carnosaur's lap that way kept some guides
awake at night. Vickers looked at his client and added, "Mr.
Salmes, we're just going to bring the tyrannosaur out of wherever
it's lying up in the forest. After we get it into the open, we'll
maneuver to give you the best shot. All right?"

Salmes grunted. His hands were tight on his beautifully finished rifle. He had refused Dieter's offer of the less-bruising camp
gun with a scorn that was no less grating for being what all the
staff had expected.

Washman dropped them vertically instead of falling in a less
wrenching spiral. He flared the blades with a gentle hand, however, feathering the platform's descent into a hover without jar-
ring the gunners. They were less than thirty feet in the air. Ptero-

saurs, more sensitive to moving air than the earthbound scavengers, squealed and hunched their wings. The ones on the ground could not take off because the down draft anchored them. The pilot watched carefully the few still circling above them.

"He's—" Vickers began, and with his word the tyrannosaur strode into the sunlight. Its bellow was intended to chase away the shooting platform. The machine trembled as the sound induced sympathetic vibrations in its rotor blades. Coelurosaurs scattered. The cries of the pterosaurs turned to blind panic as the downdraft continued to frustrate their attempts to rise. The huge predator took another step forward. Salmes raised his rifle. The guide cursed under his breath but did not attempt to stop him.

At that, it should have been an easy shot. The tyrannosaur was within thirty feet of the platform and less than ten feet below them. All it required was that Salmes aim past the large head as it swung to counterweight a stride and rake down through the thorax. Perhaps the angle caused him to shoot high, perhaps he flinched. Vickers, watching the carnosaur over his own sights, heard the big rifle crash. The tyrannosaur strode forward untouched, halving the distance between it and the platform.

"Take us up!" the guide shouted. If it had not been a rare trophy, he might have fired himself and announced that he had "put in a bullet to finish the beast." There were three other gunners who wanted a tyrannosaur, though; if Salmes took this one back, it would be after he had shot it or everyone else had an equal prize.

Salmes was livid. He gripped the bolt handle, but he had not extracted the empty case. "God damn you!" he screamed. "You made it wobble to throw me off! You son of a bitch, you robbed me!"

"Mr. Salmes—" Vickers said. The tyrannosaur was now astride the body of its prey, cocking its head to see the shooting platform fifty feet above it.

"By God, you want another chance?" Washman demanded in a loud voice. The platform plunged down at a steep angle. The floor grating blurred the sight of the carnosaur's mottled hide. Its upturned eye gleamed like a strobe-lit ruby.

"Jesus *Christ!*" Vickers shouted. "Take us the hell up, Washman!"

The platform steadied, pillow soft, with its floor fifteen feet from the ground and less than twenty from the tyrannosaur. Standing on the sauropod's corpse, the great predator was eye to eye with Vickers and his client. The beast bellowed again as it lunged. The impulse of its clawed left leg rolled the sauropod's torso.

Salmes screamed and threw his rifle to the grating. The guide leveled his Garand. He was no longer cursing Washman. All of his being was focused on what would be his last shot if he missed it. Before he could fire, however, the shooting platform slewed sideways. Then they were out of the path of the charging dinosaur and beginning to circle with a safe thirty feet of altitude. Below them, the tyrannosaur clawed dirt as it tried to follow.

Salmes was crying uncontrollably.

"Ah, want me to hold it here for a shot?" Washman asked nervously.

"We'll go on back to the camp, Don," the guide said. "We'll talk there, all right?"

"Whatever you say."

Halfway back, Vickers remembered he had not dropped another marker to replace the one that was malfunctioning. God knew, that was the least of his problems.

"You know," Brewer said as he forked torosaur steaks onto the platter, "it tastes more like buffalo than beef; but if we could get some breeding stock back, I'd by God find a market for it!"

Everyone seemed to be concentrating on their meat—good, if pale and lean in comparison with feed-lot steer. "Ah," Vickers said, keeping his voice nonchalant. He looked down at the table instead of the people sitting around it. "Ah, Dieter and I were talking. . . . We'll bunk outside tonight. The, ah, the rest of that pack of dromaeosaurs chased some duckbills through the camp this morning, Steve thinks. So just for safety's sake, we'll both be out of the tent. . . . So, ah, Mrs. Salmes—"

Everyone froze. Jonathan Salmes was turning red. His wife had a forkful of steak poised halfway to her mouth and her eyebrows were rising. The guide swallowed, his eyes still fixed on his plate, and plowed on. "That is, you can have your own tent. Ah, to sleep in."

"Thank you," Adrienne Salmes said coolly, "but I'm quite satisfied with the present arrangements."

Dieter had refused to become involved in this, saying that interfering in the domestic affairs of the Salmeses was useless at best. Vickers was sweating now, wishing that there was something to shoot instead of nine pairs of human eyes fixed on him. "Ah," he repeated, "Mrs. Salmes—"

"Mr. Vickers," she overrode him, "who I choose to sleep with —in any sense of the term—is none of your business. Anyone's business," she added with a sharp glance across the table at her husband.

Jonathan Salmes stood up, spilling his coffee cup. His hand closed on his fork. Each of the four staff members made unobtrusive preparations. Cursing, Salmes flung the fork down and stalked back to his tent.

The others eased. Vickers muttered, "Christ." Then, "Sorry, Dieter, I. . . ." The thing that bothered him most about the whole incident was that he was unsure whether he would have said anything at all had it been Miss McPherson in Don's bed instead of someone he himself found attractive. Christ. . . .

"Mr. Vickers?" Adrienne Salmes said in a mild voice.

"Umm?" His steak had gotten cold. With Brewer cutting and broiling the meat, the insertion group was eating better than Vickers could ever remember.

"I believe Mr. Brady is scheduled to take me up in the platform tomorrow?"

"Yeah, that's right," Vickers agreed, chewing very slowly.

"I doubt my—husband—will be going out again tomorrow," the blonde woman continued with a nod toward his tent. "Under the circumstances, I think it might be better if Mr. Brady were left behind here at the camp. Instead of Don."

"Steve?" Dieter asked.

Brady shrugged. "Sure, I don't need the flying time. But say— I'm not going to finish ditching around the tents by myself. I've got blisters from today."

"All right," said Dieter. "Henry, you and Don—" no one was looking directly at Washman, who was blushing in embarrassment he had damned well brought on himself—"will take Mrs. Salmes up after the tyrannosaur tomorrow." Vickers and Brady both nodded. "The rest of us will wait here to see if the duckbills come through again as they have become accustomed. Steve, I will help you dig. And if the duckbills have become coy, we will ride down the river margin a little later in the morning and find them. Perhaps Mr. Salmes will feel like going with us by then."

Thank God for Dieter, Vickers thought as he munched another bite of his steak. He could always be counted on to turn an impossible social situation into a smoothly functioning one. There would be no trouble tomorrow after all.

The bulging heads of three torosaurs lay between the gun tower and the fire. There the flames and the guard's presence would keep away the small mammals that foraged in the night. As Miss McPherson followed her brother to their tent, she paused and fingered one of the brow horns of the largest trophy. The tip of the horn was on a level with the dentist's eyes, even though the skull lay on the ground. "They're so huge, so . . . powerful," she said. "And for them to fall when you shoot at them, so many of them falling and running. . . . I could never understand men who, well, who shot animals. But with so many of them everywhere—it's as if you were throwing rocks at the windows of an abandoned house, isn't it? It doesn't seem to hurt anything, and it's . . . an attractive feeling."

"Mary!" objected her brother, shadowed by the great heads.

"Oh, I don't mean I'm sorry that I didn't bring a gun," continued Mary McPherson calmly, her fingers continuing to stroke the smooth black horn. "No, I'm glad I didn't. Because if I had had a gun available this morning, I'm quite sure I would have used it. And after we return, I suppose I would regret that. I suppose." She walked off toward the tent. The rhythms of her low-voiced argument with her brother could be heard until the flaps were zipped.

"Dieter tells me they bagged sixteen torosaurs today," Vickers said. "Even though the intrusion vehicle hasn't room for more than one per client." Only Washman, who had the watch, and Adrienne Salmes were still at the campfire with him.

"*I* bagged one," the woman said with an emphatic flick of her cigar. "Jack Brewer shot six; and I sincerely hope that idiot Mears hit no more than ten, because that's all Dieter and I managed to finish off for him." She had unpinned her hair as soon as she came in from the field. In the firelight it rolled across her shoulders like molten amber.

"Dieter said that too," Vickers agreed. He stood, feeling older than usual. "That's why I said 'they'." He turned and began to walk back to the tent where Dieter was already asleep. There had been no point in going through with the charade of sleeping under the stars—overcast, actually—since the dromaeosaurs were daylight predators. They were as unlikely to appear in the camp after dark as the Pope was to speak at a KKK rally.

To the guide's surprise—and to Don Washman's—Adrienne rustled to her feet and followed. "Mr. Vickers," she said, "might I speak to you for a moment, please?"

Vickers looked at her. As the staff members did, and unlike the other clients, the blonde woman carried her weapon with her at all times. "All right," he said. They walked by instinct to the shooting platform, standing thirty feet away at the end of the arc of tents. The torosaur heads were monstrous silhouettes against the fire's orange glow. "Would it bother you as much if I were a man?" she asked bluntly.

"Anything that makes my job harder bothers me," Vickers said in half-truth. "You and Don are making my job harder. That's all."

Adrienne stubbed out her small cigar on the platform's rail. She scattered the remnants of the tobacco on the rocky soil. "Balls," she said distinctly. "Mr. Vickers—Henry, for Christ's sake—my husband was going to be impossible no matter what. He's here because I was going on a time safari and he was afraid to look less of a man than his wife was. Which he is. But he was going to be terrified of his rifle, he was going to pack his trunk with Scotch, and he was going to be a complete prick because that's the way he is."

"Mrs. Salmes—"

"Adrienne, and let me finish. I didn't marry Jonathan for his money—my family has just as much as his does. I won't claim it was a love match, but we . . . we seemed to make a good pair. A matched set, if you will. He won't divorce me—" her dimly glimpsed index finger forestalled another attempt by the guide to break in—"because he correctly believes I'd tell the judge and the world that he couldn't get it up on our wedding night. Among other things. I haven't divorced him because I've never felt a need to. There are times that it's been marvelously useful to point out that 'I *do* after all have a husband, dearest. . . .'"

"This is none of my business, Mrs. Salmes—"

"Adrienne!"

"Adrienne, dammit!" Vickers burst out. "It's none of my business, but I'm going to say it anyway. You don't have anything to prove. That's fine, we all should be that way. But most of my clients have a lot to prove, to themselves and to the world. Or they wouldn't be down here in the Cretaceous. It makes them dangerous, because they're out of normal society and they may not be the men they hoped they were after all. And your husband is very goddamned dangerous, Adrienne. Take my word for it."

"Well, it's not *my* fault," the woman said.

"Fault?" the guide snapped. "Fault? Is it a pusher's fault that kids OD on skag? You're goddamn right it's your fault! It's the fault of everybody involved who doesn't make it better, and you're sure not making it better. Look, you wouldn't treat a gun that way—and your husband is a human being!"

Adrienne frowned in surprise. There was none of the anger Vickers had expected in her voice when she said, "So are you, Henry. You shouldn't try so hard to hide the fact."

Abruptly, the guide strode toward his tent. Adrienne Salmes watched him go. She took out another cigar, paused, and walked carefully back to the fire where Washman waited with the alarm panel. The pilot looked up with concern. Adrienne sat beside him and shook her hair loose. "Here you go, Don sweetest," she said, extending her cigar. "Why don't you light it for me? It's one of the things you do so well."

Washman kissed her. She returned it, tonguing his lips; but when his hand moved to the zipper of her coveralls, she forced it away. "That's enough until you go off guard duty, dearest," she said. She giggled. "Well—almost enough."

Jonathan Salmes hunched in the shadow of the nearest torosaur head. He listened, pressing his fists to his temples. After several more minutes, he moved in a half-crouch to the shooting platform. In his side pockets were a dozen pebbles, walnut-sized bits of quartz that he had worried from the ground with his fingers. Stepping carefully so that his boots did not scrunch on the metal rungs, Salmes mounted the ladder to the pilot's seat. He paused there, his khaki coveralls and strained, white face reflecting the flames. The couple near the fire did not look up. The pilot was murmuring something, but his voice was pitched too low to hear . . . and the words might have been unintelligible anyway, given the circumstances.

Jonathan Salmes shuddered also. He moved with a slick grace that belied the terror and disgust frozen on his face. One at a time he removed the quartz pebbles from his pocket. Stretching his right arm out full length while he gripped the rotor shaft left-handed, Salmes set each pebble just inside the air intake of the turbine. When he was finished, he scrambled back down the ladder. He did not look at his wife and the pilot again, but his ears could not escape Adrienne's contented giggle.

"Hank, she just isn't handling right this morning," Don Washman said. "I'm going to have to blow the fuel lines out when we get back. Must've gotten some trash in the fuel transferring from the bladder to the cans to the tank. Wish to hell we could fuel the bird directly, but I'm damned if I'm going to set down on the intrusion vehicle where it's sitting now."

Vickers glanced down at the treetops and scowled. "Do you think we ought to abort?" he asked. He had not noticed any difference in the flight to that point. Now he imagined they were moving slower and nearer the ground than was usual, and both the rush of air and the muted turbine whine took on sinister notes.

"Oh . . ." the pilot said. "Well, she's a lot more likely to clear herself than get worse—the crud sinks to the bottom of the tank and gets sucked up first. It'll be okay. I mean, she's just a little sluggish, is all."

The guide nodded. "M—" he began. After his outburst of the night before, he was as embarrassed around Adrienne Salmes as a boy at his first dance. "Ah, Adrienne, what do you think?"

The blonde woman smiled brightly, both for the question and the way it was framed. "Oh, if Don's willing to go on, there's no question," she said. "You know I'd gladly walk if it were the only way to get a tyrannosaurus, Henry—if you'd let me, I mean. We both know that when we go back in today, I've had my last chance at a big carnosaur until you've rotated through all your clients again. Including my husband."

"We'll get you a tyrannosaur," Vickers said.

Adrienne edged slightly closer to the guide. She said softly, "Henry, I want you to know that when we get back I'm going to give Johnnie a divorce."

Vickers turned away as if slapped. "That's none of my business," he said. "I—I'm sorry for what I said last night."

"Sorry?" the woman repeated in a voice that barely carried over the wind noise. "For making me see that I shouldn't make a doormat of . . . someone who used to be important to me? Don't be sorry." After a pause, she continued, "When I ran for Congress . . . God I was young! I offended it must have been everybody in the world, much less the district. But Johnnie was fantastic. I owe what votes I got to hands he shook for me."

"I had no right to talk," Vickers said. By forcing himself, he managed to look the blonde woman in the eyes.

Adrienne smiled and touched his hand where it lay on the forestock of his rifle. "Henry," she said, "I'm not perfect, and the world's not going to be perfect either. But I can stop trying to make it actively worse."

Vickers looked at the woman's hand. After a moment, he rotated his own to hold it. "You've spent your life being the best man around," he said, as calm as he would be in the instant of shooting. "I think you've got it in you to be the best person around instead. I'm not the one to talk . . . but I think I'd be more comfortable around people if more of them were the way you could be."

With a final squeeze, Vickers released Adrienne's hand. During the remainder of the fifteen-minute flight, he concentrated on the ground below. He almost forgot Washman's concern about the engine.

Dieter Jost flicked a last spadeful of gritty soil from the drainage ditch and paused. Steve Brady gave him a thumbs up signal from the gun tower where he sat. "Another six inches, peon," he called to the guide. "You need to sweat some."

"Fah," said Dieter, laughing. "If it needs to be deeper, the rain will wash it deeper—not so?" He dug the spade into the ground and began walking over to the table. They had found a cache of sauropod eggs the day before. With the aid of torosaur loin and freeze-dried spices from his kit, Brewer had turned one of them into a delicious omelet. Brewer, Mears, and the McPhersons were just finishing. Dieter, who had risen early to finish ditching the tents, had worked up quite an appetite.

"Hey!" Brady called. Then, louder, "Hey! Mr. Salmes, that's not safe! Come back here, please!"

The guide's automatic rifle leaned against the gun tower. He picked it up. Jonathan Salmes was carrying his own rifle and walking at a deliberate pace down the trail to the water. He did not look around when the guard shouted. The other clients were staring in various stages of concern. Cradling his weapon, Dieter trotted after Salmes. Brady, standing on the six-foot tower, began to rotate the heavy machine-gun. He stopped when he realized what he was doing.

The guide reached Salmes only fifty yards from the center of the camp, still in sight of the others. He put a hand on the blond man's shoulder and said, "Now, Mr. Salmes—"

Salmes spun like a mousetrap snapping. His face was white. He rang his heavy rifle off Dieter's skull with enough force to tear the stock out of his hands. The guide dropped as if brainshot. Salmes backed away from the fallen man. Then he turned and shambled out of sight among the trees.

"God damn!" Steve Brady said, blinking in surprise. Then he thought of something even more frightening. He unslung his grenade launcher and jumped to the ground without bothering to use the ladder. "If that bastard gets to the intrusion vehicle—" he said aloud, and there was no need for him to finish the statement.

Brady vaulted the guide's body without bothering to look at the injury. The best thing he could do for Dieter now was to keep him from being stranded in the Cretaceous. Brady's hobnails skidded where pine needles overlay rock, but he kept his footing. As the trail twisted around an exceptionally large tree, Brady caught sight of the client again. Salmes was not really running; or rather, he was moving like a man who had run almost to the point of death.

"Salmes, God damn you!" Brady called. He raised the grenade launcher. Two dromaeosaurs burst from opposite sides of the trail where they lay ambushed. Their attention had been on Salmes; but when the guard shouted, they converged on him.

The leftward dromaeosaur launched itself toward its prey in a flat, twenty-foot leap. Only the fact that Brady had his weapon aimed permitted him to disintegrate the beast's head with a point-blank shot. Death did nothing to prevent the beast from disemboweling Brady reflexively. The two mutilated bodies were thrashing in a tangle of blood and intestines as the remaining clients hurtled around the tree. They skidded to a halt. Mr. Mc-Pherson, who held Salmes' rifle—his sister had snatched up Dieter's FN a step ahead of him—began to vomit. Neither Salmes nor the other dromaeosaur were visible.

Jonathan Salmes had in fact squelched across the mud and up the ramp of the intrusion vehicle. He had unscrewed the safety cage from the return switch and had his hand poised on the lever. Something clanged on the ramp behind him.

Salmes turned. The dromaeosaur, panicked by the grenade blast that pulped its companion's head, was already in the air. Salmes screamed and threw the switch. The dromaeosaur flung him back against the fuel bladder. As everything around it blurred, the predator picked Salmes up with its forelegs and began methodically to kick him to pieces with its right hind foot. The dinosaur was still in the process of doing so when the sub-machine-guns of the startled guards raked it to death with equal thoroughness.

The broad ribs of the sauropod thrust up from a body cavity that had been cleared of most of its flesh. There was probably another meal on the haunches, even for a beast of the tyrannosaur's voracity. If Adrienne missed the trophy this morning, however, Vickers would have to shoot another herbivore in the vicinity in order to anchor the prize for the next client.

Not that there was much chance that the blonde woman was going to miss.

Adrienne held her rifle with both hands, slanted across her chest. Her hip was braced against the guardrail as she scanned the forest edge. If she had any concern for her balance, it was not evident.

"Okay, down to sixty," Don Washman said, barely enough height to clear the scrub oaks that humped over lower brush in the clearing. The lack of grasses gave the unforested areas of the Cretaceous an open aspect from high altitude. Lower down, the spikes and wooden fingers reached out like a hedge of spears.

The tyrannosaur strode from the pines with a hacking challenge.

"Christ, he's looking for us," the pilot said. The carnosaur slammed aside the ribs of its kill like bowling pins. Its nostrils were flared, and the sound it made was strikingly different from the familiar bellow of earlier occasions.

"Yeah, that's its territorial call," Vickers agreed. "It seems to have decided that we're another tyrannosaur. It's not just talking, it wants our blood."

"S'pose Salmes really hit it yesterday?" Washman asked.

Vickers shook his head absently. "No," he said, "but the way you put the platform in its face after it'd warned us off. . . . Only a tyrannosaur would challenge another tyrannosaur that way. They don't have much brain, but they've got lots of instinctive responses; and the response we've triggered is, well . . . a good one to give us a shot. You ready, Adrienne?"

"Tell me when," the blonde woman said curtly. Washman was swinging the platform in loose figure-eights about a hundred and fifty yards distant from the carnosaur. They could not circle at their present altitude because they were too low to clear the conifer backdrop. Adrienne aimed the Schultz and Larsen when the beast was on her side of the platform, raising the muzzle again each time the pilot swung onto the rear loop of the figure.

"Don, see if you can draw him out from the woods a little farther," the guide said, squinting past the barrel of his Garand. "I'd like us to have plenty of time to nail him before he can go to ground in the trees."

"Ah, Hank . . ." the pilot began. Then he went on, "Oh, hell, just don't blow your shots. That's all I ask." He put the controls over and wicked up. There was a noticeable lag before the turbine responded to the demand for increased power. The platform was vibrating badly.

"If you'll stand over here, Mis—Adrienne," Vickers said, stepping to the back rail of the platform. The client followed with brittle quickness. "When I say shoot," Vickers continued, "aim at the middle of the chest."

Washman had put the platform in an arc toward the tyrannosaur. The big carnivore lunged forward with a series of choppy grunts like an automatic cannon. The pilot rotated the platform on its axis, a maneuver he had carried out a thousand times before. This time the vehicle dipped. It was a sickening, falling-elevator feeling to the two gunners and a heart-stopping terror to the man at the controls who realized it was not caused by clumsiness. The platform began to stagger away from the dinosaur, following the planned hyperbola but lower and slower than intended.

"Nail him," Vickers said calmly, sighting his rifle on the green-mottled sternum for the backup shot.

Partial disintegration of the turbine preceded the shot by so little that the two seemed a single event. Both gunners were thrown back from the rail. Something whizzed through the side of the turbine and left a jagged rent in the housing. Adrienne Salmes' bullet struck the tyrannosaur in the lower belly.

"Hang on!" Don Washman shouted needlessly. "I'm going to try—"

He pulled the platform into another arc, clawing for altitude. To get back to camp they had to climb over the pine forest that lay between. No one knew better than the pilot how hopeless that chance was: Several of the turbine blades had separated from the hub. Most of the rest were brushes of boron fiber now, their casing matrices destroyed by rock and harmonics induced by the imbalance. But Washman had to try, and in any case they were curving around the wounded tyrannosaur while it was still—

The whole drive unit tore itself free of the rest of the shooting platform. Part of it spun for a moment with the rotor shafts before sailing off in a direction of its own. Had it not been for the oak tree in their path, the vehicle might have smashed into the ground from fifty feet and killed everyone aboard. On the other hand, Don Washman just might have been able to get enough lift from the auto-rotating blades to set them down on an even keel. Branches snagged the mesh floor of the platform and the vehicle nosed over into the treetop.

They were all shouting, but the din of bursting metal and branches overwhelmed mere human noise. Vickers held the railing with one hand and the collar of his client's garment with the other. Both of the rifles were gone. The platform continued to tilt until the floor would have been vertical had it not been so crumpled. Adrienne Salmes was supported entirely by the guide. "For God's sake!" she screamed. "Let go or we'll go over *with* it!"

Vickers' face was red with the impossible strain. He forced his eyes down, feeling as if even that minuscule added effort would cause his body to tear. Adrienne was right. They were better off dropping onto a lower branch—or even to the ground forty feet below—than they would be somersaulting down in the midst of jagged metal. The platform was continuing to settle as branches popped. Vickers let go of the blonde woman. Screaming at the sudden release of half the load, he loosed his other hand from the rail.

The guide's eyes were shut in a pain reflex. His chest hit a branch at an angle that saved his ribs at the cost of cloth and a plate-sized swatch of skin. He snatched convulsively at the limb. Adrienne, further out on the same branch, seized him by the collar and armpit. Both her feet were locked around the branch. She took the strain until the guide's over-stressed muscles allowed him to get a leg up. The branch swayed, but the tough oak held.

Don Washman was strapped into his seat. Now he was staring

straight down and struggling with the jammed release catch. Vickers reached for the folding knife he carried in a belt pouch. He could not reach the pilot, though. "Don, cut the strap!" he shouted.

A large branch split. The platform tumbled outward and down, striking on the top of the rotor shafts. The impact smashed the lightly-built aircraft into a tangle reeking of kerosene. Don Washman was still caught in the middle of it.

The limb on which Vickers and Adrienne Salmes balanced was swaying in harmony with the whole tree. When the thrashing stopped, the guide sat up and eyed the trunk. He held his arms crossed tightly over his chest, each hand squeezing the opposite shoulder as if to reknit muscles which felt as if they had been pulled apart. Nothing was moving in the wreckage below. Vickers crawled to the crotch. He held on firmly while he stepped to a branch three feet lower down.

"Henry," Adrienne Salmes said.

"Just wait, I've got to get him out," Vickers said. He swung down to a limb directly beneath him, trying not to wince when his shoulders fell below the level of his supporting hands.

"Henry!" the blonde woman repeated more urgently. "The tyrannosaur!"

Vickers jerked his head around. He could see nothing but patterns of light and the leaves that surrounded him. He realized that the woman had been speaking from fear, not because she actually saw anything. There was no likelihood that the carnosaur would wander away from its kill, even to pursue a rival. Adrienne, who did not understand the beast's instincts, in her fear imagined it charging toward them. The guide let himself down from the branch on which he sat, falling the last five feet to the ground.

Adrienne thought Vickers must have struck his head during the crash. From her vantage point, thirty feet in the air and well outboard on the limb that supported her, she had an excellent view of the tyrannosaur. Only low brush separated it from the tree in which they had crashed. The beast had stood for a moment at the point Washman lifted the platform in his effort to escape. Now it was ramping like a creature from heraldry, balanced on one leg with its torso high and the other hind leg kicking out at nothing. At first she did not understand; then she saw that each time the foot drew back, it caressed the wounded belly.

Suddenly the big carnivore stopped rubbing itself. It had been facing away from the tree at a thirty-degree angle. Now it turned toward the woman, awesome even at three hundred yards. It began to stalk forward. Its head swung low as usual, but after each few strides the beast paused. The back raised, the neck stretched upward, and now Adrienne could see that the nostrils were spreading. A leaf, dislodgcd whcn Vickcrs scrambled to the ground, was drifting down. The light breeze angled it toward the oncoming dinosaur.

Vickers cut through one of the lower cross-straps holding Washman five feet in the air with his seat above him. The pilot was alive but unconscious. The guide reached up for the remaining strap, his free hand and forearm braced against the pilot's chest to keep him from dropping on his face.

"Henry, for God's sake!" the woman above him shouted. "It's only a hundred yards away!"

Vickers stared at the wall of brush, his lips drawn back in a snarl. "Where are the guns? Can you see the guns?"

"I can't see them! Get back, for God's sake!"

The guide cursed and slashed through the strap. To take Washman's weight, he dropped his knife and bent. Grunting, Vickers manhandled the pilot into position for a fireman's carry.

The tyrannosaur had lowered its head again. Adrienne Salmes stared at the predator, then down at Vickers staggering under the pilot's weight. She fumbled out one of her small cigars, lit it, and dropped the gold-chased lighter back into her pocket. Then she scrambled to the bole and began to descend. The bark tore the knees and elbows out of her coveralls and the skin off the palms of both hands.

From the lowest branch, head-height for the stooping Vickers, Adrienne cried, "Here!" and tried to snatch Washman from the guide's back. The pilot was too heavy. Vickers thrust his shoulders upward. Between them, they slung Washman onto the branch. His arms and legs hung down to either side and his face was pressed cruelly into the bark.

The tyrannosaur crashed through the woody undergrowth twenty feet away. It stank of death, even against the mild breeze. The dead sauropod, of course, rotting between the four-inch teeth and smeared greasily over the killer's head and breast . . . but beyond the carrion odor was a tangible sharpness filling the mouths of guide and client as the brush parted.

Vickers had no chance of getting higher into the oak than the jaws could pick him off. Instead he turned, wishing that he had been able to keep at least his knife for this moment. Adrienne Salmes dragged on her cigar, stood, and flung the glowing cylinder into the wreckage of the platform. "Henry!" she cried, and she bent back down with her hand out to Vickers.

One stride put the tyrannosaur into the midst of the up-ended platform. As flimsy as the metal was, its edges were sharp and they clung instead of springing back the way splintered branches would. The beast's powerful legs had pistoned it through dense brush without slowing. It could still have dragged the wreckage forward through the one remaining step that would have ended the three humans. Instead, it drew back with a startled snort and tried to nuzzle its feet clear.

The kerosene bloomed into a sluggish red blaze. The tyrannosaur's distended nostrils *whuffed* in a double lungful of the soot-laden smoke that rolled from the peaks of the flames. The beast squealed and kicked in berserk fury, scattering fire-wrapped metal. Its rigid tail slashed the brush, fanning the flames toward the oak. Deeply indented leaves shriveled like hands closing. Vickers forgot about trying to climb. He rolled Don Washman off the branch again, holding him by the armpits. The pilot's feet fell as they would. "While we've got a chance!" the guide cried, knowing that the brush fire would suffocate them in the treetop even if the flames themselves did not climb so high.

Adrienne Salmes jumped down. Each of them wrapped one of the pilot's arms around their shoulders. They began to stumble through the brush, the backs of their necks prickling with the heat of the fire.

The tyrannosaur was snarling in unexampled rage. Fire was familiar to a creature which had lived a century among forests and lightning. Being caught in the midst of a blaze was something else again. The beast would not run while the platform still tangled its feet, and the powerful kicks that shredded the binding metal also scattered the flames. When at last the great killer broke free, it did so from the heart of an amoeba a hundred yards in diameter crackling in the brush. Adrienne and the guide were struggling into the forest when they heard the tyrannosaur give its challenge again. It sounded far away.

"I don't suppose there's any way we could retrieve the rifles," Adrienne said as Vickers put another stick on their fire. It was a human touch in the Cretaceous night. Besides, the guide was chilly. They had used his coveralls to improvise a stretcher for Washman, thrusting a pruned sapling up each leg and out the corresponding sleeve. They had not used the pilot's own garment for fear that being stripped would accelerate the effects of shock. Washman was breathing stertorously and had not regained consciousness since the crash.

"Well, I couldn't tell about yours," Vickers said with a wry smile, "but even with the brush popping I'm pretty sure I heard the magazine of mine go off. I'd feel happier if we had it along, that's for sure."

"I'm going to miss that Schultz and Larsen," the woman said. She took out a cigar, looked at it, and slipped it back into her pocket. "Slickest action they ever put on a rifle. Well, I suppose I can find another when we get back."

They had found the saplings growing in a sauropod burn. Fortunately, Adrienne had retained her sheath knife, a monster with a saw-backed, eight-inch blade that Vickers had thought a joke— until it became their only tool. The knife and the cigarette lighter, he reminded himself. Resiny wood cracked, pitching sparks beyond the circle they had cleared in the fallen needles. The woman immediately stood and kicked the spreading flames back in toward the center.

"You saved my life," Vickers said, looking into the fire. "With that cigar. You were thinking a lot better than I was, and that's the only reason I'm not in a carnosaur's belly."

Adrienne sat down beside the guide. After a moment, he met

her eyes. She said, "You could have left Don and gotten back safely yourself."

"I could have been a goddam politician!" Vickers snapped, "but that wasn't a way I wanted to live my life." He relaxed and shook his head. "Sorry," he said. She laughed and squeezed his bare knee above the abrasion. "Besides," Vickers went on, "I'm not sure it would have worked. The damned tyrannosaur was obviously tracking us by scent. Most of what we know about the big carnivores started a minute or two before they were killed. They . . . I don't mean dinos're smart. But their instincts are a lot more efficient than you'd think if you hadn't watched them."

Adrienne Salmes nodded. "A computer isn't smart either, but that doesn't keep it from solving problems."

"Exactly," Vickers said, "exactly. And if the problem that tyrannosaur was trying to solve was us—well, I'm just as glad the fire wiped out our scent. We've got a long hike tomorrow lugging Don."

"What bothers me," the blonde woman said carefully, "is the fact it could find us easily enough if it tried. Look, we can't be very far from the camp, not at the platform's speed. Why don't we push on now instead of waiting for daylight?"

Vickers glanced down at the responder on his wrist, tuned to the beacon in the center of the camp. "Five or six miles," he said. "Not too bad, even with Don. But I think we're better off here than stumbling into camp in the dark. The smell of the trophies is going to keep packs of the smaller predators around it. They're active in the dark, and they've got damned sharp teeth."

Adrienne chuckled, startling away some of the red eyes ringing their fire. Vickers had whittled a branch into a whippy cudgel with an eye toward bagging a mammal or two for dinner, but both he and his client were too thirsty to feel much hunger as yet. "Well," she said, "we have to find something else to do 'til daybreak, then—and I'm too keyed up to sleep." She touched Vickers' thigh again.

All the surrounding eyes vanished when a dinosaur grunted.

It could have been a smaller creature, even an herbivore; but that would not have made it harmless. In the event, it was precisely what they feared it was when the savage noise filled the forest: the tyrannosaur hunting them and very close.

The fire was of branches and four-foot lengths of sapling they had broken after notching with the knife. Vickers' face lost all expression. He grabbed the unburned end of a billet and turned toward the sound. "No!" Adrienne cried. "Spread the fire in a line—it won't follow us through a fire again!"

It was the difference between no good chance and no chance at all. Vickers scuffed a bootload of coals out into the heaped pine needles and ran into the night with his brand. The lowest branches of the pines were dead and dry, light-starved by the foliage nearer the sky. The resin-sizzling torch caught them and they flared up behind the guide. Half-burned twigs that fell to the forest floor flickered among the matted needles. Vickers already was twenty yards from their original campfire when he remembered that Don Washman still lay helpless beside it.

The dozen little fires Vickers had set, and the similar line Adrienne Salmes had ignited on the other side of the campfire, were already beginning to grow and merge. The guide turned and saw the flames nearing Washman's feet, though not—thank God—his head. That was when the tyrannosaur stepped into view. In the firelight it was hard to tell the mottled camouflage natural to its hide from the cracked and blistered areas left by the earlier blaze. Vickers cursed and hurled his torch. It spun end over end, falling short of its intended target.

The tyrannosaur had been advancing with its head hung low. It was still fifteen feet high at the hips. In the flickering light, it bulked even larger than the ten tons it objectively weighed. Adrienne looked absurd and tiny as she leaped forward to meet the creature with a pine torch. Behind her the flames were spreading, but they were unlikely to form a barrier to the beast until they formed a continuous line. That was seconds or a minute away, despite the fact that the fuel was either dry or soaking with pitch.

Adrienne slashed her brand in a figure-eight like a child with a sparkler. Confused by the glare and stench of the resinous flames, the carnosaur reared back and took only a half step forward—onto the torch Vickers had thrown.

The guide grabbed up the poles at Washman's head. He

dragged the pilot away from the fire like a pony hauling a travois. When the tyrannosaur screeched, Vickers dropped the stretcher again and turned, certain he would see the beast striding easily through the curtain of fire. Instead it was backing away, its great head slashing out to either side as if expecting to find a tangible opponent there. The blonde woman threw her torch at the dinosaur. Then, with her arms shielding her face, she leaped across the fire. She would have run into the bole of a tree had Vickers not caught her as she blundered past. "It's all right!" he shouted. "It's turned! Get the other end of the stretcher."

Spattering pitch had pocked but not fully ignited Adrienne's garments. The tears furrowing the soot on her cheeks were partly the result of irritants in the flames. "It'll be back," she said. "You know it will."

"I'll have a rifle in my hands the next time I see it," the guide said. "This is one dino that won't be a matter of business to shoot."

The alarm awakened the camp. Then muzzle flashes lit the white faces of the clients when the first dinosaur trotted down the trail. Even the grenade launcher could not divert the monsters. After a long time, the gunfire slackened. Then Miss McPherson returned with additional ammunition.

Somewhat later, the shooting stopped for good.

If he had not been moving in a stupor, the noise of the scavengers would have warned Vickers. As it was, he pushed out of the trees and into a slaughteryard teeming with vermin on a scale with the carcases they gorged on. Only when Mears cried out did the guide realize they were back in the camp. The four clients were squeezed together on top of the machine-gun tower.

Vickers was too shocked to curse. He set down his end of the stretcher abruptly. The other end was already on the ground. "Henry, do you want the knife?" Adrienne asked. He shook his head without turning around.

There were at least a dozen torosaurs sprawled on the northern quadrant of the camp, along the trail. They were more like hills than anything that had been alive, but explosive bullets from the

12.7 mm machine-gun had opened them up like chainsaws. The clients were shouting and waving rifles in the air from the low tower. Vickers, only fifty feet away, could not hear them because of the clatter of the scavengers. There were well over one hundred tons of carrion in the clearing. Literally thousands of lesser creatures had swarmed out of the skies and the forest to take advantage.

"Lesser" did not mean "little" in the Cretaceous.

Vickers swallowed. "Can you carry Don alone if I lead the way?" he asked. "We've got to get to the others to find out what happened."

"I'll manage," the woman said. Then, "You know, they must have fired off all their ammunition. That's why they're huddled there beside—"

"I know what they goddam did!" the guide snarled. "I also know that if there's one goddam round left, we've got a chance to sort things out!" Neither of them voiced the corollary. They had heard the tyrannosaur challenge the dawn an hour earlier. Just before they burst into the clearing, they had heard a second call; and it was much closer.

Adrienne knelt, locking one of the pilot's arms over her shoulders. She straightened at the knees, lifting her burden with her. Washman's muscles were slack. "That's something I owe my husband for," Adrienne gasped. "Practice moving drunks. When I was young and a fool."

Vickers held one of the stretcher poles like a quarterstaff. He knew how he must look in his underwear. That bothered him obscurely almost as much as the coming gauntlet of carrion-eaters did.

A white-furred pterosaur with folded, twenty-foot wings struck at the humans as they maneuvered between two looming carcasses. Vickers slapped away the red, chisel-like beak with his staff. Then he prodded the great carrion-eater again for good measure as Adrienne staggered around it. The guide began to laugh.

"What the hell's so funny?" she demanded.

"If there's an intrusion vehicle back there," Vickers said, "which there probably isn't or these sheep wouldn't be here now, maybe I'll send everybody home without me. That way I don't have to explain to Stern what went wrong."

"That's a hell of a joke!" Adrienne snapped.

"Who's joking?"

Because of the huge quantity of food, the scavengers were feeding without much squabbling. The three humans slipped through the mass, challenged only by the long-necked pterosaur. Fragile despite its size, the great gliding creature defended its personal space with an intensity that was its only road to survival. Met with equal force, it backed away of necessity.

Dieter Jost lay under the gun tower, slightly protected by the legs and cross-braces. He was mumbling in German and his eyes did not focus. Vickers took the pilot's weight to set him by the ladder. Mears hopped down and began shrieking at Adrienne Salmes, "God damn you, your crazy husband took the time machine back without us, you bitch!"

Vickers straightened and slapped the contractor with a blow that released all the frustrations that had been building. Mears stumbled against the tower, turned back with his fists bunched, and stopped. The blonde woman's knife was almost touching his ribs.

"Where's Steve?" the guide asked loudly. He was massaging his right palm with his left as if working a piece of clay between them.

Miss McPherson jumped to the ground. In the darkness the tower had drawn them. Since both boxes of 12.7 mm ammunition had been sluiced out into the night, it was obviously irrational to stay on a platform that would not reach a tyrannosaur's knee . . . but human reason is in short supply in a darkened forest. "One of the dinosaurs killed him," the older woman blurted. "We, we tried to keep Mr. Jost safe with us, but we ran out of bullets and, and, the last hour has been—"

Brewer had a cut above his right eyebrow. He looked shell-shocked but not on the edge of hysteria as his three companions were. "When it was light enough to search," he said, "I got your ammo out. I thought it might work in his—" he gestured toward Dieter beneath him—"rifle. Close but no cigar." The meat packer's fingers traced the line which a piece of bursting cartridge case had drawn across his scalp.

"Well, we put the fear of God into 'em," Mears asserted sullenly. "They've been afraid to come close even though we're out of ammo now. But how d'we get *out* of here, I want to know!"

"We don't," Vickers said flatly. "If the intrusion vehicle's gone, we are well and truly screwed. Because there's never yet been an insertion within a hundred years of another insertion. But we've got a closer problem than that, because—"

The tyrannosaur drowned all other sounds with its roar.

Vickers stepped into the nearer of the ponies without changing expression. The engine caught when he pushed the starter. "Adrienne," he said, "get the rest of them down to the slough—Don and Dieter in the pony. Fast. If I don't come back, you're on your own."

Adrienne jumped in front of the vehicle. "We'll both go."

"God damn it, *move!*" the guide shouted. "We don't have time!"

"We don't know which of us it's tracking!" the woman shouted back. "I've got to come along!"

Vickers nodded curtly. "Brewer," he called over his shoulder, "get everybody else out of here before a pack of carnosaurs arrives and you're in the middle of it." He engaged the pony's torque converter while the blonde woman was barely over the side. As they spun out southward from the camp, the guide shouted, "Don't leave Don and Dieter behind, or so help me—"

"How fast can it charge?" Adrienne asked as they bounced over a root to avoid a tangle of berry bushes.

"Fast," Vickers said bluntly. "I figure if we can reach the sauropods we killed the other day, we've got a chance, though."

They were jouncing too badly for Adrienne to stay in a seat. She squatted behind Vickers and hung onto the sides. "If you think the meat's going to draw it off, won't it stop in the camp?" she asked.

"Not that," said the guide, slamming over the tiller to skirt a ravine jeweled with flecks of quartz. "I'm betting there'll be gorgosaurs there by now, feeding. That's how we'd have gotten carnosaur heads for the other gunners, you see. The best chance I

can see is half a dozen gorgosaurs'll take care of even *our* problem."

"They'll take care of us too, won't they?" the woman objected.
"Got a better idea?"

The smell of the rotting corpses would have guided them the
last quarter mile even without the marker. The tyrannosaur's
own kill had been several days riper, but the sheer mass of the
five titanosaurs together more than equalled the effect. The nearest of the bodies lay with its spine toward the approaching pony
in a shaft of sunlight through the browsed-away top cover. Vickers throttled back with a curse. "If there's nothing here," he said,
"then we may as well bend over and kiss our asses goo—"

A carnosaur raised its gory head over the carrion. It had been
buried to its withers in the sauropod's chest, bolting bucket-loads
of lung tissue. Its original color would have been in doubt had
not a second killer stalked into sight. The gorgosaurs wore black
stripes over fields of dirty sand color, and their tongues were as
red as their bloody teeth. Each of the pair was as heavy as a large
automobile, and they were as viciously lethal as leopards, pound
for pound.

"All right," Vickers said quietly. He steered to the side of the
waiting pair, giving the diesel a little more fuel. Three more
gorgosaurs strode watchfully out of the forest. They were in an
arc facing the pony. The nearest of them was only thirty feet
away. Their breath rasped like leather pistons. The guide slowed
again, almost to a stop. He swung the tiller away.

One of the gorgosaurs snarled and charged. Both humans
shouted, but the killer's target was the tyrannosaur that burst out
of the forest behind the pony. Vickers rolled the throttle wide
open, sending the vehicle between two of the lesser carnivores.
Instead of snapping or bluffing, the tyrannosaur strode through
the gorgosaur that had tried to meet it. The striped carnosaur
spun to the ground with its legs flailing. Pine straw sprayed as it
hit.

"It's still coming!" Adrienne warned. Vickers hunched as if
that could coax more speed out of the little engine. The four
gorgosaurs still able to run had scattered to either side. The fifth
thrashed on the ground, its back broken by an impact the tyran-

nosaur had scarcely noted. At another time the pack might have faced down their single opponent. Now the wounded tyranno-saur was infuriated beyond questions of challenge and territory.

"Henry, the river," the woman said. Vickers did not change direction, running parallel to the unseen bank. "Henry," she said again, trying to steady herself close to his ear because she did not want to shout, not for this, "we've done everything else we could. We have to try this."

A branch lashed Vickers across the face. His tears streamed across the red brand it left on his cheek. He turned as abruptly as the pony's narrow axles allowed. They plunged to the right, over the ridgeline and into the thick-set younger trees that bordered the water. Then they were through that belt, both of them bleed-ing from the whipping branches. Reeds and mud were roostering up from all four wheels. The pony's aluminum belly began to lift. Their speed dropped as the treads started to act as paddles automatically.

"Oh dear God, he's stopping, he's stopping," Adrienne whim-pered. Vickers looked over his shoulder. There was nothing to dodge now that they were afloat, only the mile of haze and water that they would never manage to cross. The tyrannosaur had paused where the pines gave way to reeds, laterite soil to mud. It stood splay-legged, turning first one eye, then the other, to the escaping humans. The bloody sun jeweled its pupils.

"If he doesn't follow—" Vickers said.

The tyrannosaur stepped forward inexorably. The muddy wa-ter slapped as the feet slashed through it. Then the narrow keel of the breastbone cut the water as well. The tyrannosaur's back sank to a line of knobs on the surface, kinking horizontally as the hind legs thrust the beast toward its prey. The carnosaur moved much more quickly in the water than did the vehicle it pursued. The beast was fifty yards away, now, and there was no way to evade it.

They were far enough out into the stream that Vickers could see the other pony winking on the bank a half mile distant. Brewer had managed to get them out of the charnel house they had made of the camp, at least. "Give me your knife," Vickers said. Twenty feet away, the ruby eye of the carnosaur glazed and cleared as its nictitatating membrane wiped away the spray.

"Get your own damned knife!" Adrienne said. She half-rose, estimating that if she jumped straight over the stern she would not overset the pony.

Vickers saw the water beneath them darken, blacken. The pony quivered. There was no wake, but the tons of death slanting up from beneath raised a slick on the surface. They were still above the crocodile's vast haunches when its teeth closed on the tyrannosaur.

The suction of the tyrannosaur going under halted the pony as if it had struck a wall. Then the water rose and slapped them forward. Vickers' hand kept Adrienne from pitching out an instant after she had lost the need to do so. They drew away from the battle in the silt-golden water, fifty yards, one hundred. Vickers cut off the engine. "The current'll take us to the others," he explained. "And without the paddles we won't attract as much attention."

Adrienne was trying to resheathe her knife. Finally she held the leather with one hand and slipped the knife in with her fingers on the blade as if threading a needle. She looked at Vickers. "I didn't think that would work," she said. "Or it would work a minute after we were . . . gone."

The guide managed to laugh. "Might still happen," he said, nodding at the disturbed water. "Offhand, though, I'd say the 'largest land predator of all time' just met something bigger." He sobered. "God, I hope we don't meet its mate. I don't want to drown. I really don't."

Water spewed skyward near the other pony. At first Vickers thought one of the clients had managed to detonate a grenade and blow them all to hell. "My God," Adrienne whispered. "You said they couldn't. . . ."

At the distance they were from it, only the gross lines of the intrusion vehicle could be identified. A pair of machine-guns had been welded onto the frame, and there appeared to be a considerable party of uniformed men aboard. "I don't understand it either," Vickers said, "but I know where to ask." He reached for the starter.

Adrienne caught his arm. He looked back in surprise. "If it was safer to drift with the current before, it's still safer," she said. She pointed at the subsiding froth from which the tyrannosaur had never re-emerged. "We're halfway already. And besides, it gives us some time—" she put her hand on Vickers' shoulder— "for what I had in mind last night at the campfire."

"They're watching us with binoculars!" the guide sputtered, trying to break away from the kiss.

"They can all sit in a circle and play with themselves," the blonde woman said. "We've earned this."

After a moment, Vickers began to respond.

The secretary wore a uniform and a pistol. When he nodded, Vickers opened the door. Stern sat at the metal desk. Dr. Galil was to his right and the only other occupant of the room. Vickers sat gingerly on one of the two empty chairs.

"I'm not going to debrief you," Stern said. "Others have done that. Rather, I am going to tell you certain things. They are confidential. Utterly confidential. You understand that."

"Yes," Vickers said. Stern's office was not in the Ministry of Culture and Tourism; but then, Vickers had never expected that it would be.

"Dr. Galil," Stern continued, and the cherubic scientist beamed like a Christmas ornament, "located the insertion party by homing on the alpha waves of one of the members of it. You, to be precise. Frankly, we were all amazed at this breakthrough; it is not a technique we would have tested if there had been any alternative available."

Vickers licked his lips. "I thought you were going to fire me," he said flatly.

"Would it bother you if we did?" Stern riposted.

"Yes." The guide paused. The fear was greater now that he had voiced it. He had slept very little during the week since the curtailed safari had returned. "It—the job . . . suits me. Even dealing with the clients, I can do it. For having the rest."

Stern nodded. Galil whispered to him, then looked back at Vickers. "We wish to experiment with this effect," Stern continued aloud. "Future rescues—or resupplies—may depend on it. There are other reasons as well." He cleared his throat.

"There is the danger that we will not be able to consistently repeat the operation," Dr. Galil broke in. "That the person will be marooned, you see. For there must of course be a brain so that we will have a brainwave to locate. Thus we need a volunteer."

"You want a base line," Vickers said in response to what he had not been told. "You want to refine your calibration so that you can drop a man—or men—or tanks—at a precise time. And if your base line is in the Cretaceous instead of the present, you don't have the problem of closing off another block each time somebody is inserted into the future before you get the technique down pat."

Stern grew very still. "Do you volunteer?" he asked.

Vickers nodded. "Sure. Even if I thought you'd let me leave here alive if I didn't, I'd volunteer. For that. I should have thought of the—the research potential—myself. I'd have black-mailed you into sending me."

The entryway door opened unexpectedly. "I already did that, Henry," said Adrienne Salmes. "Though I wouldn't say their arms had to be twisted very hard." She stepped past Vickers and laid the small receiver on Stern's desk beside the sending unit. "I decided it was time to come in."

"You arranged this for me?" Vickers asked in amazement.

"I arranged it for us," Adrienne replied, seating herself on the empty chair. "I'm not entirely sure that I want to retire to the Cretaceous. "But—" she looked sharply at Stern—"I'm quite sure that I don't want to live in the world our friends here will shape if they do gain complete ability to manipulate the past. At least in the Cretaceous, we know what the rules are."

Vickers stood. "Shlomo," he said shaking Dr. Galil's hand, "you haven't failed before, and I don't see you failing now. We won't be marooned. Though it might be better if we were." He turned to the man behind the desk. "Mr. Stern," he said, "you've got your volunteers. I—we—we'll get you a list of the supplies we'll need."

Adrienne touched his arm. "This will work, you know," she

said. She took no notice of the others in the room. "Like the crocodile."

"Tell me in a year's time that it *has* worked," Vickers said. And she did.